A
SOUL
FOR
A
SOUL

The Silent Children
The Chosen Ones

Comedies:

Life Swap
Take a Chance on Me
What Happens in France
Suddenly Single

A
SOUL
FOR
A
SOUL

Detective Kate Young series

CAROL WYER

THOMAS & MERCER

Published by Thomas & Mercer, Seattle

www.apub.com

Amazon, the Amazon logo, and Thomas & Mercer are trademarks of Amazon.com, Inc., or its affiliates.

ISBN-13: 9781662506154
eISBN: 9781662506147

Cover design by Dominic Forbes
Cover image: ©stephen webber ©MarinaP ©Orla ©Gasper R. Photo / Shutterstock

Printed in the United States of America

In memory of Martin.
My respected and trusted friend, you may have
left Earth's runway one last time but now, free of
gravity, I see you playing as you so often loved to do,
in amongst the clouds above us.

CHAPTER ONE

JANUARY 2023

Darkness.

A voice in Kate's ear.

'One day, they'll find out that you killed me. And when they do, it will be the end of everything.'

She attempts to swat the voice away, yet her limbs refuse to move and so the whispering continues.

'You shot me. Whether or not that was by accident is immaterial. Because the bigger crime is that you then covered it up: disposed of my body, lied, allowed everyone to believe I had done a runner. You may think that by colluding with a sex-worker to point the finger at her pimp – who, incidentally, is dead and can't deny the accusations – you've got away with it. Wrong!'

She mumbles a denial. The voice of Superintendent John Dickson continues and although she can't see his face, she imagines the sneer that will accompany the words.

'That night, one of the members of our syndicate was also at the reservoir and observed everything. That person knows the truth and they are now playing cat and mouse with you. When you least expect it, they'll expose you. Mark my words. Then, DCI Kate Young, you will find out what it's like to be the most hated officer in Staffordshire.'

'No!' A gargantuan effort releases her from paralysis. She swings a punch that lands on the empty space next to her in bed. Half asleep, it takes a moment to establish Dickson is not beside her, and that the words she heard were mumbled by her.

This realisation jolts her to her senses. Speaking aloud has been happening more frequently of late.

At first, there were only imagined conversations with the man, like those she'd had with her late husband, Chris, in the aftermath of his murder.

But it's clear that the death of John Dickson, by her own hand, has altered something inside her. Lately, she's caught herself speaking out loud in his voice and responding as if he's in the room with her. So far, this has only happened when she's been alone; however, the thought that she might absent-mindedly speak aloud at work within earshot of colleagues is as terrifying as being caught for covering her tracks.

Stress combined with fear have caused this performance, night after night; Dickson's voice taunting her, on an endless loop. She knows why. Somebody else was at the reservoir the night Dickson died, and that person hasn't revealed themselves at any point during the four months since they left photographic evidence of what transpired on her desk.

She's oscillated between two possibilities: that the photographs were taken by either the one man she knew to be by the reservoir – Digger, a drifter – or one of the members of the syndicate that Dickson had been heading. Although she'd prefer it to be the former, it was unlikely that Digger – the loner who detested buildings, towns or being confined inside four walls – would have returned to the station and handed over the envelope, let alone be able to gain the access required to place it on her desk himself. She's asked about, but nobody manning reception had taken receipt of the envelope containing the pictures. The only possibility left after that was that they'd come from somebody who worked at the station and had access to her office – one of Dickson's co-conspirators.

She wipes the back of her hand over her damp forehead. She needs a shower. The digital clock shines numbers at her – 3.42 a.m. She tosses the duvet aside and gets up. This is her new normal and will continue to be until she establishes who took the pictures and what they intend doing about them.

Her feet brush against the cool floor tiles in the bathroom and she doesn't reach for the switch. There is adequate illumination from the outside streetlights. The shower screen emits a low squeal as she pulls it back and steps into the tray. Cold water gushes from the showerhead, cascading over her bowed head, and she remains motionless, wishing it could wash away the guilt that ensures she can never sleep properly again.

CHAPTER TWO

Dust motes, like hundreds of fireflies, pirouetted in the weak rays of morning light that fell across the lounge. DCI Kate Young stood stock still in the doorway, heart heavy. The room, indeed, the entire house, oozed melancholy, as if it too mourned the loss of the person who had occupied it for almost four decades.

She clung to the black iron door latch, pinned there by her own sorrow. This house contained precious memories of the man who had stepped up to become her surrogate father, mentor and best friend. DCI William Chase had been one of a kind and without him she would have floundered long ago. He had supported her throughout her father's illness and subsequent death, and coaxed her back from the brink after her journalist husband, Chris, was gunned down by a hitman. At work, William had championed her even when others had tried to stop her advancing through the ranks, even when there were those opposed to her successes. Bereft didn't even begin to describe how she currently felt.

The latch clicked as she released it and stepped forward. This room was where she had seen him last, on the floor, a gunshot to his head. The whole place had been forensically cleaned since then and a new carpet laid, yet still that moment of shock and realisation that he was dead could not be shaken off.

'It'll pass. Trust me. This is all yours now, Kate. You know what you have to do.' Her lips spoke the words but the voice she imagined

hearing was William's – kind and calm, a balm to her aching soul. The relief at hearing him brought a lump to her throat. If she could keep his voice in her mind, it might drown out Dickson's, just as Dickson's had repressed her husband's. Even though she'd tried endlessly to bring Chris to mind, each time it had been Dickson's voice that had replied. She needed to hear William, to ask for his advice, to feel he hadn't left her.

It had come as a shock to discover she was not only the executor of his estate but the sole beneficiary. She had inherited almost everything he owned, the only exceptions his beloved cats – for whom he had made provision at a luxury cat hotel where they would be pampered for the remainder of their lives – and his bees, which were bequeathed to the British Beekeepers Association along with a sizeable financial donation.

She had put off this moment for too long. There'd been so much to deal with since his death: tasks she had taken on single-handedly, given there was nobody else in William's life to shoulder the responsibility. Losing her father had been tough, losing Chris a horrendous ordeal; but William's death had left her numb, all the fight, life and emotion sucked from her. She was now truly alone in the world – that was, apart from her stepsister, Tilly, and her son, Daniel, who both lived in Australia.

It had been four months since William's murder and the person responsible – DI Harriet Khatri – charged for the crime, yet still Kate floated through each day like a ghost, unable to *feel*.

Promotion to DCI hadn't given her the boost she'd expected, partly because she knew it wasn't deserved. If her superiors had any idea that she had not only shot Dickson but had also covered up his death, she would find herself in the same position as Harriet, charged with murder and more.

She'd accepted promotion purely because she needed to. Somehow, she had to offset the heinous actions she'd conducted during her quest to bring Dickson to justice. For her that meant uncovering a group of corrupt officers, who William had also been attempting to expose. It wouldn't bring back Superintendent John Dickson, who had fronted the syndicate, nor could it justify why she had covered up his death, orchestrating a false testimony from a trafficked sex-worker to cover her tracks and allowing a murdered pimp with a grievance against Dickson to take the blame for his death. Chris's murder had been the catalyst for this quest. Like William, Chris had been investigating the rot in the force. Following his death, she had taken on his mantle. Today, empty and alone, with the two people she had cared about most in the world now gone, the mission was the only thing that drove her onwards. She had to see it through for her sanity and for their sake. A task that would be made easier if she could locate a document – evidence revealing who those members were – that William had hidden somewhere in this house.

A photograph of William together with her father caught her eye. Both were grinning, arms around each other: proper comrades and friends. William was family. All the same, there was no pang in her chest, or dull ache, or sense of loss as she looked at the picture.

She lifted the frame, unclipped it and checked between the glossy picture and the wooden surround for a piece of paper with a clue as to the whereabouts of the document. There was no clue to be found. Where would William have hidden the information? She'd already tried cupboards, drawers, cereal boxes, every plastic bag in the freezer. She'd hunted through books, flicking the pages upside down, felt for loose floorboards and in every possible hiding place imaginable.

She rummaged inside the chimney, knuckles scraping against rough brickwork before coming away sooty. She ignored the stinging, instead wiping the backs of her hands on her jeans before turning her attention to a well-worn leather armchair in front of the fireplace. She picked up and concertinaed a cherry-red scatter cushion, listening for a scrunching to indicate there was something other than feathers inside. Then, casting it aside, she manoeuvred the heavy chair upside down to examine the underneath and determine if there was any fresh stitching. Running a finger over it, she sighed. 'Where, William? Where have you put the bloody thing?'

The evening he was killed, she had visited him. After explaining he'd been working with the syndicate only so he could expose them, he'd offered to share the information he had on them with her. However, he'd been feeling ill and promised to show her the document the following morning. The fact that he hadn't pulled it out there and then suggested it hadn't been readily available and required unearthing from somewhere – a secret safe, a false-bottom drawer, from under the jumble of boxes in the garage, or even buried in a container somewhere in his vast garden. She'd searched all of these, only to draw a blank at every turn.

It's here in the house, Kate. I was old school – I preferred paper and pen to computers. Trust your instinct.

The voice sounded like William's, low and gravelly. She was becoming accustomed to hearing herself speak like him – in a ponderous, gentle manner. It provided her with a modicum of comfort when her brain felt scrambled. Trust her instinct. He would say something like that. He had believed in her wholeheartedly. Although it troubled her that she was verbalising imagined conversations, at the same time it felt natural and helped her conjure his image. She needed to keep William in mind and Dickson out. As long as she confined these episodes where she spoke out loud to when she was alone, it would be alright.

Dusty as it was, the room still felt like it belonged to William. She replaced the chair and plumped the fraying cushion, returning it to its usual spot. William had been houseproud and wouldn't have neglected the place like Kate had.

In her defence, time was in short supply, what with work, hunting for the document and tracking down the witness to her fight with Dickson at the reservoir. It had been William who had discovered that the drifter known as Digger had observed what had transpired. The man was a loner, moving from farm to farm in Staffordshire and keeping under the radar. To date she had been unable to track him down, but every night she woke up to hear Dickson's voice warning her that the photographs revealing what happened would come to light before long. She had to find him soon, even though she was convinced he hadn't snapped the pictures. As far as she knew, he didn't own a camera or phone. Her hope was that Digger might have spotted someone else at the scene.

She lifted an oil painting of a field of red flowers – presumably poppies – away from the wall. There was no safe hidden behind it. Her phone rang, interrupting her search.

'DCI Young?'

She still found the new title alien. 'Speaking.'

'This is Alfie Herricks from control. I was told you are on call today, ma'am.'

'Correct. What is this about?'

'We've information regarding a situation going on at Meadow Fields in Stafford.'

Meadow Fields was a new housing estate being built, one of many springing up in the town.

'What sort of situation?'

'I'm afraid we don't have much information. Only that it appears they've dug up a body.'

'Right, I'll send a team over.'

'Thank you, ma'am.'

Before she was promoted, she would have been straight out of the door with her team; now she was expected to instruct and direct her officers, leaving them to lead the investigations. Today, she didn't feel like sitting back. She needed a distraction. To that end, she rang Acting DI Emma Donaldson and arranged to meet her at the site. The document could wait another few days. As she turned to leave, her eyes fell again to the photograph. William's eyes seemed to admonish her.

'I'm not giving up, William,' she said. 'I'll find it.'

Dickson's voice hissed in her ear. *'No, you won't. Somebody else has already found it.'*

She spun around but only caught sight of her astonished face in the mirror. That time, he had sounded too real.

CHAPTER THREE

The recent deluge of rain – replacing a spell of icy weather – had played havoc with the building site. Wide-tracked yellow excavators and half-filled dumper trucks, wedged into positions haphazardly over the muddy terrain, reminded Kate of a giant abandoned toy set. Workmen with grim faces, gathered inside a large portaca-bin, stared out from grimy windows, watching her as she crossed towards the cordoned area where Acting DI Emma Donaldson was talking to a square-shouldered man with an impressive beard. His voice rose in Kate's direction.

'I was using the long-reach excavator, clearing out the area over there, when I spotted the body. It wasn't buried very deeply. I'd half pulled it out before Pete yelled at me to cut the engine.' He spotted Kate and gave her a nod, which she returned.

Emma made the introductions before continuing, 'And Pete is your foreman?'

'That's right. He's in the cabin with the others. The body . . . well, it shook him up. To be honest, it shook us all, but Pete lost his daughter last year to cancer, so it's hit him worse than the rest of us. At first, I thought it was some kind of joke, that maybe one of the lads had planted a shop window dummy or something just to spook me. When I climbed down and saw for myself, well, I knew then it was no prank.' He shook his head in dismay.

'It must have been distressing for you,' said Emma, her gentle tone warm and sincere.

Kate approved of her manner. Emma was one of the best officers Kate knew, with a bright future in the force.

'Yeah, I must admit, it was a bit grim,' replied the man. 'I guess the site will have to be shut down.'

'I'm afraid so.'

He shrugged. 'Can't be helped.'

Kate's attention was drawn to the arrival of a white van. As it parked up, a lithe figure descended from the passenger seat. Ervin Saunders, head of Forensics, was already suited up in white overalls and blue rubber boots, his hood covering his silver-grey hair.

'Would you excuse me?' said Kate, leaving the pair to continue their conversation. Ervin made a beeline for her, offering a cheery smile as she approached.

'As I live and breathe . . . DCI Kate Young! I thought they'd have chained you to the desk, hurling report after report at you.'

'It's not as bad as that, although I admit there are days when I need to get out. Today is one of those.'

'Sacrifices have to be made if you wish to climb the ladder of success,' he said. 'Although as I recall, William was also partial to adventure days and sneaked out whenever possible. Nice to see you are carrying on the tradition.'

The mention of William tumbled into an emotional void, but she nevertheless smiled in response.

Ervin cocked his head. 'Seriously, though, how are you coping . . . without him?'

'I miss him. How can I not when I now sit in his chair? The thing is, I'm managing way better than I expected. I suppose taking over his office makes me feel like he hasn't totally gone.' She caught the frown wrinkling his brow. 'Yes, yes, I know what you're thinking . . . that I'm in some sort of denial, but I'm not. I simply want to be reminded of him because that helps stave off the pain of loss, and I still want to make him proud of me, the team, everything really. Sound crazy?'

'Not in the least. Of all the people who could fill his boots, no one would be able to do it better than you. And I mean that.' His gaze rested on her a moment longer before he broke away. 'Right, that's me run out of sincerity and heartfelt offerings. What do we have here? Apart from a quagmire that will undoubtedly send at least one of my officers sprawling flat on their face before the day is out. It's like walking across quicksand. I hate this time of the year. It's either freezing cold or bucketing down with rain.' He accompanied Kate to the cordoned area and, after airily waving his ID at the duty officer, ducked under the tape and picked his way to the body. Kate followed him, mud sucking at her rubber soles.

A cream jacquard dress covered most of the corpse's upper torso and arms. Little was left of its features: long strands of black hair covered the ghoulish remains of a face, eye sockets empty. A sickening stench rose from the body. Even the fresh breeze couldn't disguise the smell of fruity and rotting meat that accompanied putrefaction.

'Given that the body has been underground during a very cold snap, I'd wager the temperature has helped decelerate the speed of decomposition, which will make establishing a date of death difficult,' said Ervin. He took a plastic sheet from under his arm and laid it on the ground before placing his forensic equipment suitcase on it. He peered at the mound of earth removed by the digger and heaped beside the body. 'Ah! I spy a shoe or, more accurately, an ankle boot with a metallic block heel.' Opening the case, he pulled out a tool and hooked the cream lace-up boot before examining it more closely. 'You can read the manufacturer's logo imprinted on the insole – Michael Kors. Judging by the repeat MK pattern on the sweater dress, I suggest that's the same brand. What?!' he said when

Kate looked up incredulously. 'You know how much I appreciate footwear and I like to keep abreast of *all* fashion.'

'You really are in the wrong job. You'd make a brilliant fashion designer.'

'I know, but why become a celebrated designer with a fashion house and your brand available in every top department store in the world when, alternatively, you could be standing in a muddy field, puzzling over an unfortunate person's demise?' His eyebrows lifted casually as he spoke. 'If it weren't taxed to the limit on a daily basis, my brain would shrivel.'

He placed the boot in an evidence bag. 'I'm guessing it wasn't worn more than a handful of times.'

He looked the body over and checked both hands. 'No watch, bracelet or rings.'

'Could have been mugged,' said Kate.

Ervin made a non-committal noise.

Emma emerged from the cabin and joined them. 'I don't think any of the workmen can help us further. They know nothing and most of them aren't even from around these parts. The first they heard of this site was when they were hired to work on it. We've taken contact details from them in case we need to question them further. Am I okay to send them away?' she asked Kate.

'Go ahead. We need the site cleared so Ervin's officers can get on with their job.'

'Is that her shoe?' Emma said.

Ervin looked up at her with a wicked grin. 'Hmm, to be more accurate, it's a boot rather than a shoe and it *might* belong to the victim.'

'Always the joker, Ervin.'

'*Moi!* Surely not.'

'Is there another boot?'

'Not that I've come across yet. It should come to light, unless it came loose and fell off before the body was buried.'

'Now who's jumping to conclusions,' said Emma.

'Touché! I won't be able to carry out a more thorough search until after the body has been taken away.'

'I don't suppose you've found anything yet to help identify her?'

Ervin shook his head. 'No handbag, phone, wallet, although, once again, they might be here somewhere. There are no identifying marks that I can see. If there were any tattoos, they've, well . . .' He gave a small shrug. 'There's no wedding ring and thanks to decomposition, I can't even establish if there are any indentations where one might have been worn. In fact, there's no jewellery at all. I don't know about you, but I find that odd. I'd expect a watch or a ring.'

'They might have been stolen, or maybe she simply didn't wear any. I don't usually wear any jewellery,' said Emma.

'You, my dear, are an exception, given you come to work directly from the gym where you kick and thump seven bells out of a punchbag . . . and then return there immediately after work. I would surmise trinkets of any description would represent some form of hazard in that situation,' said Ervin.

'I'll have you know that I've cut down on my gym time.'

'And we all know why,' said Ervin.

'I don't know what you mean,' she said, a shy smile creeping across her features.

'Emma, it's the worst-kept secret in HQ. You and Morgan have been living together for a month. Don't think we haven't all noticed the spring in your step, or in his for that matter. I expect you have neither the time nor energy for strenuous workouts.'

'Shut up!' she said with a laugh.

'Teasing aside, I think you make a delightful couple,' Ervin added. 'Now, bugger off and leave me to my work. I'll let you know if we find anything to shed light on the victim's identity. We'll probably need Terry to examine the body.' Terry Wiggins was a leading forensic anthropologist who worked in the same building as Ervin.

Emma turned to Kate. 'I'll have my team look into individuals who've been reported missing in the area over the last couple of months.' Emma took another glance at the body. 'I wonder how she died?'

'At this stage, your guess is as good as mine. It might even have been of natural causes, although I doubt anyone would go to the trouble of burying the body here if it was. My money is on foul play, Emma.' Ervin pulled out lengthy tweezers from his kit and prodded at something in the earth, lifting a small object.

'A button. I doubt it's from this dress. I can't see any buttons on it,' said Kate.

He gave a small shrug. 'All the same, it would be wise not to overlook it. Might belong to a garment worn by the assailant.' He dropped it into a plastic bag.

Kate turned to Emma. 'This was wasteland up until they started work on the new housing estate three weeks ago,' she said. 'I'm surprised the murderer buried her here, especially as this land has been earmarked for development for ages. They must have known the body would be unearthed.'

'That suggests they weren't bothered if it was found or they're out-of-towners who had no idea about the site and dumped the body before work began,' Emma said. 'Would you lean on Terry for me, please? The sooner we can get an idea of the victim's identity and work out exactly when she went missing, the sooner we can make some headway. Until then, it'll be slow going.'

Emma's eyes sparkled as she spoke. Kate understood how she must be feeling, her first big case as Acting DI. She ignored the small stab of envy that came from nowhere.

'I'll press him. Let me know if you need anything else. Now, I'd better get back to the station.'

Kate left the scene, wishing she could sink her teeth into the investigation more directly. Not only did she miss being involved in such cases as she used to be, but it would be the perfect distraction from her troubles.

She changed her filthy boots for smart, clean ones and climbed back into her Audi. Now she was in the vicinity, she should take the opportunity to drive a little further and try asking at some of the farms around Uttoxeter where Digger had hung out. Surely somebody had an idea of where he was!

She pulled away, eyes flicking back to Emma, who was now greeting Harvey Fuller, the pathologist. Being a DCI gave Kate kudos, but not the same buzz as being a DI had. Maybe it had been a mistake to accept the promotion after all.

'You'll grow into the role,' said William's voice.

'I'm not sure I still have the same appetite for it,' she replied, in her normal voice.

Emma listened intently to Harvey Fuller, who sighed gently as he peeled back clothing to examine the cadaver's torso. She was determined not to screw up in any way, and to take every little detail into account.

When Kate had phoned and asked her to attend this scene, she had almost fist-bumped the officer nearest her. This was her first major investigation since her promotion to acting DI and a chance to prove her mettle. She and Morgan had been told back in September that with two Detective Inspector positions available, they were both being given the opportunity to take them up, although permanent roles depended on a twelve-month probationary period and success in the inspectors' exam to be held in October.

Morgan was working with DI Ali Rind on Operation Moonbeam, but Emma had been given Kate's old boxroom office and four officers. That Kate had chosen her to take charge of this investigation proved she had faith in Emma's ability and Emma had no intention of letting her down.

'We have partly decomposed remains of an adult female. There appears to be no dental attrition, so she could be any age from seventeen to mid-thirties. Judging by the signs of decomposition, I'd hazard death occurred anything from ten days to a month ago. The low temperatures will have played their part. The body is in early stages of putrefaction,' Harvey said, pointing to the dark flesh. He replaced the dress with care. 'She's not wearing any tights, and her underwear appears to be undisturbed.'

'No idea of cause of death?'

'Sorry, Emma. I can't help you there other than to say the hyoid bone appears to be intact, so she wasn't strangled. There's no visible damage to the skull or bones, although Terry might be able to shed further light for you. I'm afraid my expertise ends here.'

He got to his feet.

'Thanks for coming out,' said Emma.

'Not a problem. You never know what you're going to come across when you get the call to a scene. I hope you can find out what happened to this victim.'

'Me too. I've a lot riding on it.'

'Yes, I heard congratulations were in order. How are you finding life as a DI?'

'It's like life as a DS, only people get to call you ma'am instead of sarge and they don't race you to get the last bar of chocolate from the vending machine.'

He gave a soft chuckle. 'Must be odd not working with Morgan and Jamie though?'

'Yeah, I miss working with the big guy. Still, I get to see more of him than I ever did when we were simply teammates. And as for Jamie . . . well, he always needs somebody to control his abundant enthusiasm, so I'm glad Morgan got that pleasure and not me. I don't think Jamie's simmered down at all. Every time I mention his name to Morgan, he rolls his eyes and groans.'

'Ha! I can imagine. Right, I'll wish you the best of luck. See you again, Emma.'

She watched him depart, mentally ensuring she'd covered everything she ought to at this stage. She waved at Ervin as she headed back to the building site.

The body would now be transported to the Forensic department at the university. If she wanted a speedy result, time was of the essence. She couldn't wait to tell Morgan about this. He'd be thrilled for her.

She paused, mid-step. *Wouldn't he?*

Operation Moonbeam had been operational for several months and still hadn't yielded any results. The last couple of weeks, Morgan had seemed far more tense than usual, and grumpy. She'd put his odd behaviour down to frustration at the lack of progress. Maybe she shouldn't be so quick to tell him about this investigation. It would be awful if they became competitive or spent all their free time discussing work.

She was still finding her way around being one half of a couple, never mind a couple who were both in the same line of work. She'd never expected that at this point in her life she'd be in a serious relationship while simultaneously stepping into the role of DI. She hoped one wouldn't jeopardise the other because if push came to shove, she couldn't be sure she would choose her relationship over her career, or indeed if she could say the same for him.

◆ ◆ ◆

Kate knocked on the farmhouse door, setting off loud barking followed by a gruff, 'Pack it in!'

The door creaked open. 'Bloody thing needs oiling,' said the man, ignoring her for an instant while he examined the hinges. 'Nah, they're slipping. Need tightening, that's all. Sorry, what do you want?'

Given she was dressed in a dark-navy belted coat and dark trousers, she understood why she hadn't been taken immediately for a police officer, which suited her for the time being.

'I'm looking for somebody who I understand works for you from time to time – name of Digger.'

'What do you want with him?' he replied, beetle eyebrows lowering to almost obscure his upper eyelids.

'It's personal business. I really need to find him urgently,' she replied.

He studied her for a minute, then gave a crooked smile. 'You look like a lawyer. Has he come into some money?'

Even though she bristled internally at being mistaken for a lawyer, Kate decided to roll with his supposition. It might yield better results than if she revealed that she was a detective. 'I'm not at liberty to discuss such matters.'

'He has, hasn't he?' He wagged his finger as he spoke. 'An inheritance most likely, eh? Ha! You know, I never really bought the whole wandering hobo without-a-penny-to-his-name act. Nice enough fellow, though. Hard-working.'

'Have you any idea where I might find him?'

'I haven't seen him for a couple of months. Then again, I haven't had a great deal of need for any extra labour, what with the weather being so poor. Have you tried Gorse Farm at Kingstone?

They were looking for extra hands to help wean calves and with the lambing.'

'Calves? I thought they were born in springtime.'

He guffawed. 'City folk. You know nothing about country life. Calving and lambing can take place any time between November and May, although the peak is during spring.'

'Oh, right. I had no idea. I haven't tried Gorse Farm.'

'Have a word with Malcolm Hardcastle then. He runs the farm with his dad. And if you find Digger, tell him he owes Geoff Unwin – that's me – a pint for sending you in the right direction.'

She thanked him and returned to the car, where she discovered a voicemail had been left on her phone.

She started when she recognised the voice. It was ex-DI Harriet Khatri, the woman currently being held in custody for killing William Chase.

'Kate, I know you have every reason to say no, but I desperately need your help. You're the only person I feel I can turn to. Please come and visit me. I have real grounds to believe I've been set up.'

She stared at a group of plump white sheep grazing on the slopes. She owed Harriet nothing. The woman was part of a corrupt syndicate and had even almost had Kate killed.

'You know she's been adamantly denying all knowledge of the syndicate, Kate.' William's voice seemed to fill her mind and the car. *'You found no evidence at her house to link her to it, nor did she appear to have a clue what happened to you in the warehouse.'*

'For fuck's sake, William! Her alibi for that afternoon was that she had parked up outside the warehouse where I was held prisoner to visit her snitch, Tommy Clayton, in the nearby housing estate. Since then, Tommy has conveniently vanished into thin air. I maintain she led me into a trap.'

'What happened to the Kate who used to check all the facts? I taught you to follow every avenue and not to be prejudiced by your own assumptions.'

'They're not assumptions. They're facts. Her car was outside the warehouse. When I went inside to look for her, I was jumped. Somebody was lying in wait for me. And there's no doubt as to her guilt. The footage on your pet camera app shows her shooting you.'

'It could have been falsified.'

'It was examined by a cyber-crime and forensic laboratory! The people who work there don't make mistakes.'

'Listen to me. There is a chance she was set up, most likely by the syndicate, which would mean the real culprit or culprits are still at large and they're laughing at you and Harriet. Consider that option. Hear her out. What have you got to lose?'

'My fucking sanity!'

'I think we can both agree that's been in the balance for some time, although you know you're not crazy. This behaviour is simply your way of coping with all the horrendous crap that's happened since Chris was murdered. Be reasonable. Harriet wouldn't have contacted you if she didn't have something important to share with you. She knows you don't take any bullshit. Listen to what she has to say. If I were in your shoes, I would.'

A sheep lifted its head, jaw moving continually as it chewed, eyes fixed on Kate. She looked away, and started the engine with an exasperated, 'Oh, what the hell. Okay, I'll visit her.' The animal turned away, as though it thought she was doing the right thing.

CHAPTER FOUR

Pranit Khatri – Harriet's husband, and a highly regarded solicitor – had argued that Harriet's life would be in danger if she was imprisoned during the waiting period before she faced trial. Having assured the judge that there was no significant risk that, if released on bail, Harriet would commit an offence that would be likely to cause physical or mental injury to another person, the court had offered stringent bail terms ensuring Harriet would remain housebound and under the watchful eyes of her family until her court appearance.

Situated in an Area of Outstanding Natural Beauty and described as the 'Gateway to Cannock Chase', where herds of deer could often be spotted from several of the properties, Brocton was one of Staffordshire's most sought-after villages. As Kate drove past houses that dripped affluence and charm in equal measure, she understood why somebody like Harriet would have chosen to settle here, away from the hustle and bustle of town life, in a place that could provide anonymity and peace.

Towards the top of a climbing road, Kate came across the property, which was, for the most part, hidden behind a high hedge. Metal gates across a wide drive were shut, so, pulling into the entrance, Kate exited her car and pressed the intercom button. The gates opened almost immediately. As she manoeuvred the Audi next to Harriet's Volvo, she spotted the woman standing in the porchway, arms wrapped around her slim frame. Dressed in an oversized sweater, faux-leather leggings and UGG boots, she looked nothing like her usual formidable self. Her hair, normally scraped back from her face, fell against sunken cheeks. At first glance, she resembled a frightened teenager.

She greeted Kate with thanks and led her down a well-lit corridor filled with professional photos of Harriet, Pranit and their son – smiling, happy pictures that oozed love – past an upright piano and into a modern kitchen. Kate's eyes were immediately drawn to the far end of the room, where a feature wall of red, white and black striped wallpaper framed French windows and a wood stove burned brightly in the corner. Harriet directed her to the curved white sofa, complete with bright-red cushions and a black-and-white throw, that stood in the middle of the room, facing a television set where a daytime drama was playing.

'I know . . . I should be doing something more productive, but I can't. I'm . . . in a vacuum. Alexa, turn off the television.'

The set went blank.

'Can I get you something to drink?'

'I'm fine, thanks,' said Kate. 'Are you alone?'

Harriet shook her head. 'My father-in-law is here. He went upstairs to give us some privacy. I'm not supposed to be left alone. Although I'm unlikely to go wandering off, am I?'

She pointed to her right ankle. Kate couldn't see the electronic monitoring device, hidden as it was under her boot, but she knew it was there. It had been one of the conditions of Harriet's bail.

Harriet pulled out a bright-red stool from under a glass-topped island and turning it, so she could look Kate in the eye, perched on it.

'Cards on the table, I'm at my wits' end,' she said. 'I don't know how to convince you, or anyone else for that matter, that I did not kill William.'

'The footage from the pet camera quite clearly shows you in William's lounge and your face is visible only seconds after he was shot.'

'That's where I have issue. I fully admitted during my interviews that I was in William's house. I made no secret of the fact I was there. When I left, he was still alive! I didn't shoot him. Somebody, somehow, has altered that footage – spliced it, Photoshopped it, or whatever – to make it appear as if I held the gun to his head and shot him in cold blood before escaping through the French windows. I didn't do any of that. He was still alive when I left. Through the front door. The same way I entered.'

Kate held her tongue. The team who had examined the footage had declared it to be genuine, and Kate had no reason to question their findings. There was – according to the evidence – no room for doubt. Yet something about the intensity in Harriet's eyes and demeanour was troubling. Known at the station as the Ice Queen for her uncompromising and frosty manner, Harriet had never seemed this vulnerable and Kate had certainly never heard her ask for help before. From anyone.

'Why did you visit William at his home?' she asked.

Harriet looked away for a second. 'It was for private reasons.'

'That doesn't wash with me. You spoke to him earlier that day at the office. What was so important you felt you had to drive to his home to discuss the matter in person?'

Harriet shook her head. 'Okay, this is awkward. I was fired up about you.'

'Me?'

'Yes. You'd begun treading on the toes of my investigation and kept information about people traffickers from me. On top of that, I didn't think you were handling Superintendent Dickson's disappearance professionally. If you must know, I thought you were overwhelmed by everything. I tried to bring the subject up with

William earlier in the day. He refused to listen to me. After that, I became more . . . het up about the situation. I wanted William to remove you from the investigation into the super's disappearance because I was convinced you were becoming side-tracked about a trafficked girl. You see, I'm not somebody who can accept incompetence and I believed you weren't doing your job properly. After work that night, I went straight to the gym, but the workout didn't calm me down. In fact, I got even more agitated, so on my way home I stopped off at William's house to talk to him about it again. This was around eight o'clock, yet the footage shows me arriving much later than that. I was in and out in ten minutes. William gave me short shrift and told me to go away and cool off. He had a headache and wasn't prepared to discuss anything further with me until the following morning. He saw me out and I went for a drive and then came home. That's it. I swear.'

Kate wasn't convinced. There had been ample time for Harriet to concoct a convincing story. 'To an empty house?'

Harriet sighed. 'Yes. Pranit was away on business and my son was on a sleepover.'

Kate said nothing.

'I understand how you must feel. You probably hate me,' Harriet continued, 'but I want you to know that this wasn't a vendetta because I actually think highly of you, and I was wrong to go behind your back. The thing is that I demand high standards from my team, from myself, and anyone in the job. It may be a failing but it's simply who I am. I want to be the best version of myself and for good or bad, I expect the same of everyone I work with. In the past, my husband has criticised my lofty standards. He reckons I place too much pressure on people, including our son. He's right, yet how does somebody change who they are or what they believe, or accept second best from people when they've always striven to be the best in everything they do?'

Harriet's intense blue gaze drilled into her. 'For what it is worth, if the tables were turned, I would help you.'

Kate bit back a laugh. 'I find that difficult to believe.'

'Why? Because I haven't been over-friendly to you, or anyone else, for that matter?'

'That's one reason.'

'I'm not good at all that sort of stuff and, face it, neither are you. We're similar in many ways: we both want results, success, and demand justice for our victims. We're both driven individuals. You and I are loners. We don't form friendships easily.'

Harriet's words hit home, causing Kate a flash of self-doubt. For an instant, she thought Harriet might be telling the truth. The moment passed. 'So far, you've not told me anything to convince me you are innocent. I've heard only protestations and wild accusations concerning falsification of evidence,' said Kate.

'Then help prove me right. Imagine how it would feel to expose those individuals who are hell-bent on framing me. I've had a lot of time to consider who might be responsible and I keep coming back to the same thought – it was somebody who had a grudge against William or needed him silencing. You knew him better than anyone and I'm sure you can't think of anyone who would want him dead for the former, so it must be the latter. What did William know that got him killed? I've been over and over this and I can only imagine it is somebody within the force.'

Harriet crossed to the fridge, where she took out a bottle of orange juice. 'Want some?'

'No, thanks.'

Harriet unscrewed the cap, all the while talking. 'I was repeatedly questioned about a syndicate. A group of officers involved in some clandestine group. I hadn't a clue about this organisation – not one inkling it even existed. But imagine if William had known? What if he'd uncovered the people involved, and they were the ones who had him killed? My turning up at his house when I did provided them with a scapegoat and if they were able to manipulate the footage, which I know they did, hey presto! They got away with murder.'

The juice sloshed into the glass and Harriet set the bottle aside.

Kate digested the other woman's words. Certainly, they had been unable to uncover any evidence to indicate that Harriet was involved in the syndicate or had motive to murder William. The only proof that she was responsible was the pet camera footage.

Harriet spoke softly. 'I had absolutely no reason to kill William. Think about it, Kate. Why would I shoot him in cold blood?'

Kate wasn't giving in easily. She knew what she had seen on the footage – the assailant, same size and shape as Harriet, dressed in the same clothing as she had been wearing; Harriet's face as she turned to leave William for dead.

'All I know is what I saw – you, behaving in a suspicious manner. You visited a senior officer out of hours at his home. You even wore a hoodie pulled over your head, like you didn't want anybody who might have spotted you to identify you,' she said.

'I grant that looked suspicious, but my hair was still damp from the shower, and I don't like people to see me looking unkempt, especially my boss.'

Her response was quick, her eyes locked on Kate's.

Kate shook her head. 'I can't buy your story, Harriet. Not after what happened that afternoon when I was jumped at the warehouse—'

'Please, Kate. Give me a break. I told you what happened. My informant, Tommy Clayton, sent me a text to arrange a meeting. I parked, as I always do, in front of the warehouse. He didn't show, so after about fifteen minutes of waiting near the flats, I returned to my car and headed back to the station. I had no idea you were following me, and I certainly knew nothing about you being held prisoner in the warehouse. I swear on my son's life.' She glanced in the direction of a photograph where a boy in school uniform beamed a wide smile.

Kate hesitated. It was clear from all the family pictures around the place that her son meant the world to Harriet.

Harriet continued, 'You know that Tommy has disappeared into thin air, don't you? Which means nobody has been able to contact him to confirm he sent that message. Well . . .' She took another sip of the juice. 'Do you want to hear my theory?'

'Go on.'

'Somebody who knew Tommy was my confidential informant used his phone to contact me, knowing I would park by the warehouse. I suspect they wanted to lure me inside and ended up with you instead. Now, I have no idea why that might have been the case, but it could have something to do with the investigation I was heading. Operation Moonbeam was after some very big players. That's the only explanation I can come up with for what happened to you and why they released you unharmed. Unless you have a better theory.'

William's voice murmured in Kate's head, *'Harriet could be on to something here.'*

She swallowed hard to ensure she didn't speak out loud in any voice other than her own. Torn between divulging what she knew about the syndicate, and explaining her reasons as to why she, not Harriet, had been the intended target, or keeping silent.

Sharing information might mean she'd also have to admit that she'd been after the syndicate ever since her husband's murder, and that he'd left her a list of names of police officers he believed to be involved in corruption, Dickson's name among them.

'That's a great idea. Spill the beans. Harriet will then work out that you were after me and were somehow involved in my death.'

That wasn't William's voice. She could almost feel Dickson's breath on her earlobe as he taunted her.

However, instead of goading her into a confession, Dickson's words brought her to her senses. To tell Harriet anything could lead to Kate's downfall.

It was best for Kate to go along with Harriet's supposition as though she knew nothing.

She shook her head. 'No. I can't come up with anything.'

'Give her theory some credence, Kate,' said William quietly, forcing his way back to the front of her mind and taking Dickson's place. *'After all, you could be wrong in thinking that you were the intended victim. Harriet might also have sailed too close to the wind, resulting in the syndicate wanting her out of the way. And in turn, that means they could have somehow set her up for my death.'*

Harriet swigged the juice, replacing the glass on the island before returning to the stool, where she sat with her hands on her knees. Her voice had taken on an excited timbre. 'It's plausible, isn't it? And if there is a syndicate that is embroiled in people trafficking, it makes sense for me to be taken out of the picture, which means . . . somebody on my team or higher up the chain of command is involved.'

Kate's pulse quickened. Harriet was awfully close to the truth. There was a chance she knew more than she was letting on and was playing a cat-and-mouse game with Kate. Could she be watching Kate to see how she reacted?

'Of course she is,' hissed Dickson.

She attempted to throw Harriet off the scent by behaving like somebody who knew nothing about any syndicate. 'I don't know, Harriet. That sounds fantastical—'

'No! It doesn't. And you might think you can fool me with that poker face, but your body language tells me that you know

I'm on to something. Superintendent Dickson was discovered to be corrupt. There are other unethical officers yet to be exposed.'

'I could be one of them.'

'Don't make me laugh. You're as straight as they come. Everyone at HQ knows if you were cut you would bleed morality, which is why I asked you here.'

Kate couldn't say the same about Harriet, and there was no way she was going to divulge what she knew about those who had supported Dickson and been part of his circle.

'What have you got to lose? If I'm right, we might be able to expose these people. You'd want that as much as me, wouldn't you?'

Kate had heard enough. There was only one way she was ever going to believe what Harriet had to say and that was by determining if the footage from William's pet camera had been falsified. 'Alright. I'll play along. I don't see how I can get my hands on the footage though.'

'Leave that to my lawyer. He's already challenged its validity and demanded it is re-examined. For the record, Pranit is no longer representing me. He felt it wasn't . . . appropriate. And I'd stand a chance with a more qualified lawyer. Howard Lonsdale has taken over my case.'

Kate had encountered Lonsdale – rated one of the top criminal lawyers in Staffordshire – on a number of occasions in court, and wondered who was paying for his notoriously expensive services.

'If Howard Lonsdale can get hold of it, I'll talk to Felicity, because I don't know anyone better qualified than her.'

Felicity Jolly was head of Technology and one of the few people Kate could count as a friend.

'I'm not sure about using her expertise,' Harriet said. 'She probably won't see me in a favourable light. She might even detest me, given what I am being accused of. She's too close to the investigation.'

'You asked for my help, and I trust Felicity to remain unbiased and behave in no other way than completely professional. If she feels she can't do this, or hasn't the skills required, she'll hopefully point me in the direction of somebody else who can. This is non-negotiable. Either I run this past Felicity, or you are on your own.'

Harriet nodded several times, quickly. 'Okay. Absolutely. Go ahead. And thank you.'

'I haven't done anything yet.'

'You've listened, and you've not pooh-poohed my theory.'

For a fleeting moment, Kate had an urge to unburden herself, tell Harriet what she already knew about the syndicate and maybe even openly discuss Harriet's theory.

'Go on,' urged Dickson, inside Kate's head.

His words – when would he ever have thought of what was best for Kate? – made her maintain the invisible barrier that existed between her and Harriet. There was no way she could allow Harriet to begin to suspect Kate of chasing after the syndicate. 'Don't get your hopes up too high. I'm not leaning one way or the other until there's some solid proof to support your claim.'

Kate detected a soft sigh. Not from Harriet, but from William, who whispered, *'Shame. You had an opportunity there to gain an ally.'* A sudden concern that she might have accidentally spoken out loud forced her to look directly at Harriet.

Harriet showed no sign of having heard her speak to herself and got up. 'I understand.'

She accompanied Kate outside, where a breeze whipped Harriet's hair across her face. She ignored it, instead wrapping her arms around her body. As Kate pulled off the driveway, the gates began to close, and she glimpsed the forlorn figure watching her depart.

Information sheets lay scattered in front of Emma. Next to her, DS Scott Hart – a forty-two-year-old giant of a man – rested his palms on the desk and spoke quietly. His Yorkshire accent, along with his demeanour, exuded an impression of perpetual calm.

'All these women are aged between seventeen and thirty, match the victim's description and all of them have disappeared within the last month. They are recorded as living at addresses in Staffordshire,' he said. 'Of course, our victim could be from outside the region, which will mean widening our net, but for now we should focus on these five women.'

Emma nodded. Although thousands of people went missing each year, many returned unharmed. The photos were of women Missing Persons had been unable to locate. Scott pointed at the first. 'This is twenty-two-year-old Ellie Roper, who left home to visit friends on the evening of Friday December thirtieth. She lives with her father, who didn't report her missing until the following Monday. Apparently, she has a history of storming off for a few days following some drama or other, usually with her on-off boyfriend, but this time her dad became worried when her friends rang him to ask where she might be.'

'The thirtieth was just over a month ago. I suppose if the cold weather really slowed down decomposition, or she'd been held captive before being killed, the body could be Ellie.'

'My thoughts exactly,' said Scott. He pulled two pictures forward. 'These two disappeared three weeks ago, one on the third of January, the other was last seen on Friday the sixth.'

'Have Missing Persons got any intel on them?'

'Only one of them. The second one. Leah Fairbrother. Her credit card was used during the first few days she went missing. She bought a ladies' Cartier watch, a mobile phone and a laptop.'

'How could someone be allowed to make three expensive purchases on a credit card and not have them red-flagged by the bank?'

'It appears this wasn't unusual expenditure for Leah. She maxed out on her card almost every month. There was a healthy limit set at eight thousand pounds, but she settled the full payment on every due date. Thanks to her spending habits, these slipped under the radar.'

Emma pulled a face. Her credit card limit was a fraction of Leah's. She couldn't imagine spending almost eight grand a month. 'I still don't get why she'd purchase those items,' she said.

'MisPers suspected Leah was starting afresh. Friends suggested all was not well in her marriage and she'd been behaving differently for over a month – more secretive. A couple of them even suspected there was a new man on the scene.'

'A watch wouldn't be my first choice if I'd walked away from a relationship and was striding out alone or even with a new partner. Cartiers are pricey too.'

'Some are mega expensive. The one she bought was at the cheaper end of the scale, a steel Panthère, costing £3,950.'

Emma let out a low whistle. 'What I could do with four grand! Seems a frivolous waste of money.'

'Maybe she simply fancied treating herself or it was some sort of final, rebellious act of defiance: a two-fingered salute to her husband.'

'I suppose that's possible. People never fail to astound me with their actions. If it's Leah, then that watch is now missing. She wasn't wearing any jewellery, not even a wedding ring.'

Scott pointed to the final two photographs. 'These are the most recent. Charlotte Wainwright and Aimee Ruskin. They've both been missing for ten days. There's no connection that MisPers are aware of. Charlotte's a thirty-two-year-old driving instructor and mother to three kids. Aimee's a nineteen-year-old university student. To date, MisPers have nothing on where they might be.'

'Can we get dental records for all these women sent across to the pathology lab?'

'I've already arranged that.'

'Great. That might speed things up and help us ID the victim.'

'One thing struck me,' said Scott. 'The cadaver wasn't wearing tights or stockings. I'd have thought it was a bit bloody cold to be parading around the streets in bare legs. My wife's been wearing leggings under her jeans the last two weeks.'

'Well, some women are quite hardy when it comes to dressing up for an evening out and if she was meeting somebody in a warm place, she might not have worn them.'

'Or she took them off. Or, had them taken off,' said Scott, eyebrows lifting to make a point. 'She might have been raped. The fact that one of her boots was missing makes that theory sound more plausible.'

'There wasn't any bruising associated with an attack. Let's get an ID first and find out what Ervin has uncovered before we go too far down that route.'

She tapped the photographs into a pile and handed them to Scott. Her phone chirped with a message from Morgan. She didn't read it until Scott was out of the room.

Another crappy day with nothing to show for it

In dire need of curry and beer

Fancy a takeaway tonight?

I'll collect it on my way home

M X

34

She replied with a capital YES and added an emoji heart that she then deleted. There was no need to become super soft; besides, if his investigation wasn't going well, he would be in a grouchy mood again. Operation Moonbeam seemed to be affecting his usual positive mood as well as their relationship. They no longer shared the same easy camaraderie they'd enjoyed in the past.

Once again, she wondered if the pressure of promotion was to blame for the changes, then questioned if it was maybe her who was at fault and that she was becoming more nit-picky and demanding. Serious relationships had never been her thing and now, with the chance at last to advance her career, she'd become heavily involved with somebody – worse still, a work colleague.

With a sigh, she shoved all thoughts to one side, added an emoji of two beers glasses clinking cheers and sent the message.

CHAPTER FIVE

As Kate drove back to HQ, her thoughts were on the footage that had been streamed to William's mobile via the pet camera application. To her knowledge, the camera was activated whenever there was movement or noise in the room and a notification sent to alert the pet owner. The device could also be switched on or off and if the owner was at home, it could be disabled. That William had left it running seemed strange, yet maybe he always left it on overnight in case his cats got up to something they shouldn't. Also, he hadn't been feeling well. It could simply have been an oversight on his part.

She didn't understand enough about how either the app or device worked to fathom if it would have been possible to corrupt the video. Given the victim in question was a DCI, and the suspect was one of his detectives, the entire case had been handled by a specialist team and the footage sent to an external laboratory. This was a highly sensitive investigation and there would have been no room for errors. All the same, something in Harriet's earnest regard had triggered a concern. Had the cyber-crime team overlooked something?

There was something else nagging in the back of her mind; DC Jamie Webster, who she had believed to be one of Dickson's minions, had downloaded the footage from William's phone on to his computer. Might he have been able to corrupt it or replace it in some way? With increasingly wild theories racing through her head, she backed into her designated space in the car park and made for the building next to HQ.

Felicity Jolly lifted a full mug from her desk. 'Fancy a brew? There's some tea left in the pot.'

'No, thanks. I'm not staying long.'

'I suppose you have mountains of reports and officers to juggle – not literally. Although that might make for an entertaining video game. I should maybe run the idea past Bev. I'm sure she could come up with some very interesting avatars for it.'

Kate smiled at the comment. Felicity's partner, Bev, was a games designer.

Felicity's light-grey eyebrows lifted playfully as she sipped her tea and then, placing the mug on the desk, said, 'Well, come on. Spit it out. Why are you here? You have a face as long as a wet weekend.'

'It's . . . tricky.'

'I love tricky. The trickier the better. I enjoy a challenge.'

'You might not enjoy this one. It's to do with Harriet Khatri.'

Felicity's top lip curled. 'Oh.'

'I understand how you feel about her. I share your opinions, but I've just come from her house.'

'Her house! Okay, okay. Sorry. You caught me by surprise.'

'No, I get it. I don't know whether it was the fact she asked me to help her or curiosity or just simply because I wanted to see her and have another go at her myself, but I went along and I was . . . surprised by her attitude.'

Felicity nodded.

'She wasn't her usual bolshy self. She desperately wants to prove her innocence and believes the footage from William's camera has been falsified. Would you – if we can get it to you – examine it?'

'Me? That footage went through a digital forensic and cyber-crime accredited laboratory. They won't have made any mistakes.'

'Nevertheless, would you look at it?'

'I suppose so. I'm not one to throw spanners into works, but how do you propose making this happen? It's evidence to be used against her.'

'She's confident her lawyer will be able to arrange for it to be re-examined.'

'She's clutching at straws.'

'That might be the case.'

Felicity was not persuaded. 'Why are you helping her? She shot William!'

Kate shrugged. 'A hunch. A feeling that I ought to explore the possibility. It could be something to do with the corruption surrounding Dickson.'

'But that's all out in the open and has been plastered across the press for weeks on end. Everything he did was to cover up his involvement in the murder at the Maddox Club.'

'There's something more to it. I think other officers were and are still involved in something big. That's why I asked you to keep an eye on those burner phone numbers, on the off-chance they go live.'

A hunt through William's office had turned up Dickson's burner containing several code names and numbers in his contact list. Each number had been assigned a Greek letter of the alphabet, with Dickson being Alpha. It was William who explained the names had been assigned alphabetically and he was Beta purely because his surname had come first alphabetically. Kate knew somebody with the code name Gamma had contacted William and had believed that person to be Harriet; however, not only had Harriet vigorously denied it, but no burner had been located during searches at Harriet's house and office. Although William knew the names of most of the syndicate members and had written them down and hidden them somewhere in his house, he claimed to have been unable to identify two members – Gamma and Iota.

Felicity gave her a small smile. 'No, it's over, Kate. Superintendent John Dickson is dead. The past has been buried with him. And those phones have undoubtedly been disposed of. That group has been disbanded. Harriet shot William. We don't know why, but we have evidence to prove she did it. Why rattle any more cages?'

'Because until I'm completely satisfied that footage is genuine, I can't allow someone to take the blame for something they might not have done. What if she really is innocent and has been set up?'

'By whom?'

'Somebody linked to the people-trafficking operation. Maybe a fellow officer.'

Felicity gave a half-hearted nod.

'This has got me thinking . . . even questioning whether she might have been framed. She's turned to the one person who has more reason to hate her than anyone here – me. Why would she do that when she knows how much William meant to me, unless she really is innocent? And after listening to her story, I need to be satisfied that there's no way the pet camera footage could have been doctored. I must find out if Harriet is simply messing with me . . . or whether somebody managed to make it appear as if she killed William. There can't be any room for doubt.'

Felicity held up her palms in resignation. 'I'll look at it. However, it's going to be quite a feat to prove one of those fancy cyber-crime labs got it wrong.'

'Thank you.'

Kate suppressed a sigh. Felicity was right on both counts. The pay-as-you-go mobiles that the syndicate members used to contact Dickson and each other would have been destroyed by now. She had hoped beyond hope that at least one of them would fire up and lead them to another of the syndicate members. 'Will you continue to monitor those burners?'

'For certain.'

'I appreciate that.'

She left the tech department for HQ. Today, her heart felt as heavy as the door she had to shove to open. Knowing William's killer had been caught had helped heal the gaping wound his death had left. Should it transpire they'd got it wrong, and Harriet was blameless, they'd be back at square one, only this time there'd be no way of finding out who had shot him. It was, in many ways, easier to stick to the facts and evidence they already had, yet here she was, making waves for a woman that up until now she'd had little time for. Why?

William's voice in her head attempted to untangle her thoughts. *'Because you think Harriet was set up by the syndicate and more than anything, you want everyone associated with it banged to rights.'*

She acknowledged the statement with a slight nod that was mistaken for a greeting by an officer, who replied with a polite 'Ma'am'. Damn! Another slip-up. She needed to watch how she was behaving in public. The last thing she needed was a psych evaluation.

The floorboards creaked as Kate marched along the landing to her office where, without removing her coat, she threw herself into the chair and, ignoring various messages left on the desk for her attention, rang Terry Wiggins, the forensic anthropologist who was working on the body found earlier that day.

The chirpy Canadian was, much like Ervin, usually upbeat. His fast talking reminded Kate of the actor Jim Carrey, while his large frame and bearded face had earned him the nickname Hagrid.

'Jeez, give a guy a break, will you? The second Ervin told me that Emma was taking the lead on this one, I knew you'd be on my back. In fact, Ervin and I had bets on how soon it would be before you rang to hassle me.'

'Who's won the bet?' she asked.

'Ervin, of course. I had you down as calling around noon, but he said you'd go easy on me and give me until teatime. I guess four thirty qualifies as time for tea and now I owe him a vodka martini. I just hope he doesn't turn up at the pub for it wearing his 007 outfit.'

Kate felt her lips twist into a smile. She knew the one he meant: a stylish kilt and waistcoat ensemble that he believed made him look like Sean Connery.

'So, I expect you're ringing to ask me to speed things up for Emma, aren't you?'

'You know me too well.'

'I think we all do over here. And, because I do, I've already had a good look at the cadaver and will send over a preliminary report within the next half an hour. I'm waiting on some dental records for some missing women. Might even be able to give this Jane Doe an identity by end of play today.'

'What have you turned up so far?'

'Vic is around thirty. Can't be clear on cause of death yet. I need to do further tissue analysis. One thing though, she was pregnant. The foetus was around twelve weeks. The paired blocks of tissues called somites have disappeared to form vertebrae. This occurs around eight weeks into pregnancy. The arms are almost fully formed, but the legs are still bud-like. They don't generally fully form until around fourteen weeks.'

'Oh!' The idea a tiny life had also been snuffed out caused a pang in her chest.

Terry grunted. He had five children ranging from five to eighteen and was proud of all of them. 'That's all I can tell you for the moment.'

41

'I'm grateful to you for prioritising the case.'

'All of my *guests* are important here, but I figured Emma needed to get going with this one. Besides, she helped Sammy when he went through that awful phase of being bullied at school by giving him some private training in taekwondo. She wouldn't take a penny for her time and no amount would have been too great to see him regain his confidence like he did, so this is a sort of payback.'

This news didn't surprise Kate. Emma was big-hearted. Having suffered a tough upbringing herself, she would have gone out of her way to help another youngster who was going through a difficult patch.

Mission accomplished, Kate thanked Terry and let him get back to work.

She stared at the blank computer screen in front of her for what felt like an eternity. Switching it on would mean becoming embroiled in work, whereas she really ought to be tracking down either Digger or the information secreted in William's house. Getting involved in assisting Harriet was only going to put even more pressure on her limited free time. As it was, she had little to no life. Dragging backwards and forwards from HQ to William's house, and from her own home to the environs of Uttoxeter in search of Digger, even her regular Skype calls to her stepsister in Australia had recently fallen by the wayside.

Even with everything going on in her life, she wished she could trade places with Emma and bury herself in the Jane Doe investigation. That would at least distract her from thinking about the photographs, hunting for other corrupt members of the syndicate, and the worrying chorus of voices in her head that now accompanied her on a daily basis.

She spun her chair around and faced the bookcase, still containing some of William's possessions: an old police whistle, a Victorian police helmet and a 1950s' electric hand lamp stood on the top shelf, while a glass award presented to Kate during her time as a DS was on a lower shelf, along with a framed certificate and a photograph of William and her father, both in uniform. At times, she could still imagine this was William's office and she was merely sitting in it waiting for him to return. Today, however, the memorabilia only served to remind her that he'd never walk through the door again.

Lost in thoughts about William, it was a good quarter of an hour before she picked up the phone to update Harriet. Whatever the outcome, she was committed now and if it happened that Harriet had been falsely accused, then they would have to deal with the fallout. Once she'd done that, she'd check her emails, deal with any urgent business, then visit Gorse Farm in Kingstone. She flicked open her notebook, where she read the name of the farmer, Malcolm Hardcastle. She hadn't met him before and hoped he'd be more accommodating than some of the others she'd already spoken to.

The knock on the door stopped her in her tracks. Emma's cheeks were flushed. 'Terry's rung. The dental records we sent across to him are a match. We have a name – Leah Fairbrother.'

'That was quick!'

'The info just came through in the last few minutes. Turns out one of Leah's front incisors was an implant so she was easy to identify. I'm headed over to notify her husband now.'

'Want me to come?'

'Thanks, but I'll take Scott. I can handle this.'

Kate gave her a small smile. 'Okay then, keep me in the loop.'

'Goes without saying. I don't want to mess up, Kate. I'm going to do this completely by the book.'

She was gone in an instant, her footsteps like rapid gunfire, ricocheting down the corridor. Kate turned on the computer and typed in the dead woman's name, convincing herself as she pulled up the Missing Person's file on Leah that she wouldn't interfere, merely acquaint herself with the relevant details to ensure a smooth running of the investigation. It wasn't only Emma's reputation at stake but her own, because if the investigation stalled or didn't go to plan, Kate would have to answer to the newly appointed superintendent, Bree O'Sullivan, who was determined to erase the tarnished image of the force. There was no room for errors or heel-dragging and if that meant Kate assisting from the sidelines, then she would do so.

As she studied the young woman's unblemished face in the photograph, she forgot all about Harriet and Digger and almost felt like her old self again.

CHAPTER SIX

Scott manoeuvred the silver Astra into a tight space behind a Honda Jazz bearing a yellow and black diamond sticker that read *Grandchildren on Board.*

'Number thirty-four should be three houses along. Sorry I couldn't get any closer,' he said.

'It's lucky we found a parking spot at all. Could have ended up a few streets away.' Emma eased the door open so as not to knock it against the lamppost next to the car and caught the sound of distant chimes as she wriggled her way out. Although it was only just gone six o'clock, the sky was pitch-dark, and the semi-detached houses were half hidden in the darkness.

The car indicators flashed as it locked and Emma matched Scott's strides, her head held high. Breaking bad news to a loved one was always tough. She hoped there'd be no children in the house. It was even harder when there were. Curtains or blinds were drawn at every window. Only a pale, honey-coloured glow from streetlights illuminated the pavement.

They reached a plain brown door, where Scott rang the bell. The curtains in the front window were edged open and dropped quickly. Within moments, the occupant – a lean-faced man – was standing in front of them, his brow creased. 'Have you got news about Leah?'

'Mr Fairbrother?'

'That's me. Have you found her? Is she okay?'

Emma held up her ID card. 'I'm Acting DI Emma Donaldson. Would you mind if we came inside for a moment, please?'

His features froze for a second then he spoke, his voice catching as words fell over themselves.

'Oh, God. Something terrible has happened to her, hasn't it? She's dead. They wouldn't send somebody so high-ranking if she was alive. Or is she injured? Tell me she's injured. Not dead. Please, Lord. Not dead!'

Emma was immediately suspicious as to why he might jump to this conclusion so quickly. Had she used the wrong tone, causing him to think the worst? Or was he already aware of why they would be knocking at his door, and her rank confirmed it?

People reacted in different ways to this sort of dreadful news. One distraught wife had thrown herself into Emma's arms for comfort, while a victim's girlfriend, unable to fully digest the news, had sat in a fugue-like state. Others had raged at the officers bringing the news, one mother screaming for them to get out of her home when she'd learned of the death of her son. Emma remembered every one of the visits she'd had to make. She recalled the looks on their faces and understood the pain they were experiencing. She'd found her own mother dead in her bedroom – a sex game that had gone wrong – a memory that she could never shake off. She maintained what she hoped was a professional yet kind tone.

'Mr Fairbrother, let's go inside?'

He led them into a room where he crumpled on to a grey settee pushed against an equally dark grey wall on which hung modern artwork in subdued colours. The remaining walls were pale grey and set off a black cast-iron art nouveau fireplace surround, containing painted tile inserts of green and orange flowers. Coffee-table books perched on an intricate stand added further splashes of the same colours and a hexagonal mirror placed strategically over the mantelpiece added depth to the room. Emma felt it was the sort of room an upwardly mobile couple would inhabit, quite unlike the place she shared with Morgan.

There was no easy way to break the news. 'I'm sorry to inform you that we found a body today that we've identified as your wife, Leah,' said Emma.

The groan seemed to come from the pit of his stomach. He dropped his head into his hands and remained motionless.

'Is there anybody we can contact for you?'

The man didn't respond. Emma looked at Scott, who crouched down beside the man.

'Mr Fairbrother, can we ring somebody to be with you?'

The reply was a soft, 'No.'

'What about friends or family?'

'No. Nobody.'

'Mr Fairbrother, can I call you Russell?'

The man nodded.

'Russell, I understand how difficult this is for you, but you shouldn't be alone. We'll arrange for a Family Liaison officer to come as soon as possible, but for the time being, maybe there's a neighbour—'

'I said, no.'

'Then can I make you a drink, a cup of tea—?'

Russell ignored the question, voice thickening as he spoke. 'I fully expected her to come home in her own good time. I was sure she'd walk through that door as if nothing had happened. I told myself she just needed some time out. That was what I thought . . . what I *believed*. I don't want to be with anybody. I want to be with *her!*'

Scott gave Emma a quick look before getting to his feet. She suspected he was either finding Russell slightly over-dramatic or was concerned that the man would break down further.

'Russell, do you think you could manage to answer a few questions about Leah?' she asked.

'What sort of questions?'

'Regarding the last time you saw her.'

'I told officers everything I knew three weeks ago, when I reported her missing.'

'We can obtain that information from them, but it will help us hugely if you'd talk to us now.'

He sniffed and wiped his nose on the back of his hand. 'She went out about seven thirty that evening to meet her best friend, Dee, and some other girlfriends in town.'

'This was on Friday the sixth of January?'

Russell nodded. 'They were going out for something to eat in Stafford, then clubbing afterwards, so I expected her home late. I went to bed around eleven. When I woke up the following morning, she hadn't returned. Her mobile was switched off. I left it for a while, thinking she might have crashed out at Dee's. By mid-afternoon, when I hadn't heard from her, I rang Dee, who hadn't seen her for a few days. She knew nothing about any meeting in town. Dee spoke to some other friends, but nobody knew where Leah was. She hadn't posted anything on social media to give us a clue. I tried her mum, who lives in Bristol, and she hadn't heard from her either. Then I panicked and rang the police.'

'How did Leah seem when she left that evening?'

He dropped his eyes and began fiddling with the fringe of an orange and green cushion. 'Fine.'

'That's it? Just fine?' said Scott.

'She might have still been miffed with me. We'd had a bit of a set-to.'

'An argument?'

He nodded. 'Not a big one.'

She wondered if, having realised what he'd admitted, that they had rowed, he was now playing that situation down. 'What was it about?' asked Emma.

'Her going out. I was pissed at her. I thought we'd be spending a night in, chilling. She said she didn't have to run everything past me. I . . . We had cross words and she flounced off anyway.'

She noted his use of 'cross words' and 'flounced', again wondering if he was now downplaying what had really happened.

'I told the other officers about this. They thought she might have been teaching me a lesson and staying away for a few days, especially after they found out she'd been spending on her credit card.' His Adam's apple bobbed up and down and he began to stammer. 'I . . . I wish . . . I hadn't been such a dick.'

'What did you do?' urged Emma.

'I didn't do anything. It was more what I said. I told her she looked like a tart. She didn't. She looked lovely, but I was angry.'

'Angry because she was going out with her friends?' said Scott.

'Yes. I know how that sounds to you, but it was supposed to be our date night . . . a film, bottle of wine . . . her and me. We'd got stuff to discuss about the new business we were setting up. It was . . . so stupid!'

He snuffled noisily and excused himself to look for a tissue.

Emma whispered to Scott, 'What do you think?'

Scott shrugged. 'He seems genuine enough to me.'

'I'm not so sure. Then again, I'm a cynic.'

She waited until Russell returned, his eyes and nose now red.

He folded on to the settee again and ran a hand over his dark bristles. 'You haven't told me how she died.'

'I'll be honest with you,' said Emma. 'We are treating her death as suspicious. Workmen digging on the new housing estate at Meadow Fields uncovered her body.'

He swallowed again. 'Buried. Somebody buried her?'

'It would appear so. We're going to need all the help we can get from you and Leah's friends to help piece together what happened the night she disappeared. Did your wife go out regularly with her girlfriends?' said Emma.

'Yes. Once a month. Sometimes twice.'

'And do you have lads' nights out?'

'I'm a marketing director for a multifaceted group, providing specialist services that meet client needs. Which in essence means that by the end of the day, I've had enough of people. I enjoy home comforts, along with peace and quiet.'

'And what did Leah do?'

'She worked in hospitality. We met when my company used hers for a client event.'

'And would you say you had a happy marriage?'

'Without doubt.'

'How long were you married?'

'Three years this March.'

'You hadn't experienced any . . . difficulties during that time?'

'No more than anyone else.'

'How would you describe your wife?'

'Popular. Positive. Career-minded. We were in the throes of setting up a joint venture in hospitality. With her personality and my marketing skills, it would have been amazing and successful. We shared a dream to create a successful business and go global, move abroad, live the high life.' He wiped his eyes again. 'Fuck! We had so much going for us. And now—' He blew his nose once more and turned glassy eyes on to Emma. 'I don't know who would want to hurt her.'

'Did she air any concerns about anyone? Maybe somebody at work? A neighbour? Someone online?'

'Not to me. Her biggest worry was working out how to tell Jackson that she was quitting.'

'Jackson?'

'Jackson Collins. He runs Harlequin Events.'

'Did she get along with him?'

'Absolutely! They're good friends. That's why she couldn't bring herself to tell him about her plans. She felt like she was shafting him.'

'Did anybody else know about this new venture of yours?'

'No. We were planning to quit our jobs at the end of this month, work our notice and then aim to launch at the beginning of April.'

It was clear from the *objets d'art* strategically placed around the room – vintage metal hearts displayed in a sculpture under a glass cloche, an art-deco-inspired sleek black panther ornament and a gold and black vase – that the couple already had decent salaries and expensive tastes. It didn't surprise Emma to learn they were ambitious and wanted more from life. What did astonish her was that Leah was apparently going ahead with a new, demanding venture while expecting a child. It was also strange that Russell hadn't mentioned the fact his wife was pregnant.

A sixth sense, however, prevented her from bringing up the subject. Instead, she focused on what little they already knew about the disappearance.

'Your wife apparently made some purchases soon after she went missing,' she said.

'Yes, I was told she had.'

'Did that surprise you?'

'Too true, it did. Especially the watch. There's a Dior Diamond and an Apple watch upstairs. As for why she'd buy a mobile and laptop—' His shoulders slumped. 'It made no sense to me.'

'Can you remember what jewellery she was wearing that night?' asked Emma.

'She had on a long cream sweater dress, with a sort of roll-neck . . . so I don't think she was wearing anything other than her usual rings and earrings.'

'How many rings?'

'Her wedding and engagement rings, and a sort of squiggle curved ring in gold and aqua on her middle finger. On her other hand, she wore a large black onyx in a gold-plated brass setting that her dad bought for her twenty-first birthday. He passed away soon afterwards, so she was very fond of that ring. Never took it off.'

'And earrings?'

'Hoops. Large gold hoops. Are you asking for identification purposes? I thought you'd already established it was Leah who was found. Is there a chance it isn't her?'

'No, sorry. We are certain it's her. Your description matches the clothing she was wearing. Can you recall what shoes she had on?'

'Cream ankle boots. They were her favourites. Michael Kors.'

Ervin had also mentioned the brand, but where he was a fashion aficionado, Emma wasn't convinced that somebody would know the make or brand of their partner's clothing. Morgan, for one, certainly wouldn't have a clue as to what Emma was wearing or had worn the day before.

Russell continued, unaware of Emma's suspicions. 'She bought them in a sale last summer. They're tie-ups with a zip down one side and a gold heel. Like I said, she looked lovely – stunning, really.'

'Is that Leah?' asked Emma, spotting a photograph of Russell with a dark-haired woman sitting by a beach bar, glasses raised in a toast.

'Yeah. Our . . . honeymoon,' he replied. His eyes became damp as he spoke. 'Would you . . . Would you ring her mother for me? I can't—' His voice cracked, and tears spilled.

'An officer from the Bristol force will break the news. Are you sure we can't get hold of anyone for you?' said Emma.

'No. I'd rather . . . be alone . . . for now.'

After a few more questions, and sure that Russell would be alright on his own, they took their leave. It was almost seven and it was only as they pulled away that Emma remembered Morgan's message and that he would be expecting her. She typed a quick text to say she'd got held up and, sighing, she sent it.

'Everything okay?' asked Scott.

'Just letting Morgan know I'll be late home.'

'My wife's not expecting to see much of me over the coming days and weeks. I rang her as soon as I knew we were assigned the investigation. Bloody job. It eats into your personal life, doesn't it? Still, at least Morgan will understand.'

Although she made noises like she agreed with him, internally she had her doubts. She and Morgan had always been in similar situations career-wise and had worked on numerous investigations together, so hadn't been tested before. Now separated at work and with his own operation going nowhere, there was a chance Morgan would become green-eyed about her own sudden advancement. She mentally crossed her fingers and hoped her concerns were unfounded.

Kate pulled up in front of a five-bar gate, then rested against the supportive head restraint with her eyes closed. Her neck muscles had bunched up so badly that she had the beginnings of a tension headache – something that was happening with increasing frequency these days.

A few months ago, she'd have looked forward to a glass of wine to help her relax, but she'd given up alcohol for good and increased her already punishing exercise routine to ensure she stayed on top of her game and her mind razor sharp, although what with being unable to track down Digger or William's hidden document, and the wretched voices that had her talking to herself aloud, she was beginning to worry that she'd lost some of her edge.

She hoped this wasn't going to be yet another fruitless visit. Digger was proving to be extremely elusive. The drifter had no mobile phone or any permanent address, moving from farm to farm to assist those who required him, or simply to doss for a few nights. She tried relaxing her shoulders but gave up. It would have to be pain relief, a warm shower and a session with the massage roller again when she got back home if she didn't want this to become a head-banger.

The beam from her headlights fell across a rustic sign for Gorse Farm, attached to the wooden gate. Beyond it was a rutted track. She dragged herself from her car into the darkness and brisk wind. The gate squealed a solo to the backdrop of branches deforming and striking each other like a percussion section in an orchestra. She heaved it to one side, hoping it wouldn't swing back against her car. Once through, she stopped again to shut it, mindful that animals might be in the fields, before bumping along the track to a yard where she parked behind a Land Rover.

A man in overalls, padded jacket and a dark beanie hat emerged from an open barn as she got out.

'Can I help you?' he called.

'I'm looking for Malcolm Hardcastle.'

As the man approached, she realised he was elderly, grizzly-faced with thick white eyebrows. His rheumy eyes narrowed as he took in the stranger standing in front of him.

'Who's asking?' he said.

'Geoff Unwin sent me,' she replied, deflecting the question. The mention of another farmer only seemed to appease him momentarily.

'And who are you?'

'My name is Kate Young.'

'What do you want with Malcolm?'

'I just wanted to ask him about somebody.'

'Well, I'm his father, and I run this farm. So if you have anything to ask him, you can ask me.'

There was no point insisting she speak to Malcolm, although she was reluctant to speak to this gnarly old gent who looked like he might take issue if she explained she was a police officer. The last farmer had been easier to talk to. She decided to be slightly more open in this conversation, thinking he'd appreciate the honesty. 'It's about Digger. I wondered if Malcolm or you had seen him recently.'

'No. Is that it?'

'When did you last see him?'

'A few months ago.'

'Mr Unwin seemed to think he might be here.'

'Well, he isn't, so Geoff is mistaken. Shut the gate on your way out.'

He turned on his heel and marched back to the barn. Kate climbed back into the Audi and waited for a moment. The man had been very quick to say no. What was it with these countryfolk and their unwillingness to divulge the whereabouts of a drifter? She was about to start up the engine when she spied the door opening to the main house. Another man emerged, wrapped up against the weather. She got out again and called out, 'Mr Hardcastle?'

'Yes.'

'I'm Kate Young. Sorry to bother you but Geoff Unwin said I might find Digger here.'

'Ye—'

A loud voice shouted, 'I told her to sling her hook!'

'Mr Hardcastle?' she said quietly. 'Is Digger here?'

'Who are you really?'

William's voice spoke calmly. *'There's no point in hiding anything. Gain this man's trust or he'll clam.'*

She weighed up his words. So far she'd had no success in rooting out Digger and given the way the man was staring at her, she had little to lose by admitting who she was. He already looked like he was going to shut her out.

'I'm a police officer – DCI Kate Young. Sir, I need to speak to Digger urgently about an incident he witnessed a few months ago. It's unofficial business. He's not under any suspicion.'

Malcolm was about to speak again when his father arrived. 'I told you Digger hasn't been here for months. There's no need to pester my son. Now, if you wouldn't mind, we're busy.'

'She's a police officer, Dad,' said Malcolm.

'I don't care if she's the bloody prime minister, we've got livestock to sort out and no time to waste talking about somebody we haven't seen in a while. Good evening to you, officer.'

He hustled his son in the direction of the barn, leaving Kate sure that Digger was somewhere nearby. If they were delivering lambs, they'd need his assistance, and no farmer would want to lose an extra pair of hands at such an important time. She got back into her car and started it up. If they thought they'd got rid of her, they were wrong. Digger was here. She could feel it in her bones.

◆ ◆ ◆

Emma's team had departed for the evening, leaving only her and Scott in the office.

'Well, that's another of Leah's friends who couldn't help me, other than to say Leah had seemed out of sorts and more subdued than usual, prior to her disappearance,' said Scott.

'That seems to be the consensus among her friends. The Missing Persons' report confirms it too. Most of her friends suspected she was unhappy in her marriage, although she played her cards close to her chest and wouldn't discuss the matter when pressed on it. Russell painted a different picture to the one we're hearing from everyone else. Any joy with her best friend, Dee?'

'She was at work and couldn't talk on the phone, so she's coming in first thing tomorrow.'

'Good. Also, according to the report, a neighbour spotted Leah climbing into a white car close to her house.'

'No one else saw it. The neighbour in question was unable to identify the make or model and wasn't even sure it was Leah that they saw, so MisPers couldn't really follow it up.'

'Do we know which direction it headed in?'

Scott shook his head. 'Would it be okay if we call it a day and I shoot off?'

'Sure.' Emma, still buzzing from the adrenaline of working her first big case and still unsure of how Morgan would react to her late return, was reluctant to leave.

She stared at her screen, where Leah's address was circled in red on a map, and wondered if it was worthwhile asking the tech team to drag up CCTV footage from around the time Leah walked out of the house to catch a lift with 'a friend'.

'See you tomorrow,' said Scott. He crammed his Spider-Man plastic lunchbox, a present from one of his kids, into his backpack.

'See you, and thanks for all your help today. We're making progress.'

He paused by the door. 'I hope you don't mind me speaking my mind, but if I were you, I'd head home too. This could be a long, tedious investigation and if or when it begins to stall, you'll need your energy reserves. Just saying. I don't want you to burn out too soon. First major investigation and all.'

She threw him a smile. 'Good advice. I remember telling Kate something similar.'

'And, no disrespect intended, but look how haggard she is these days. Promotion is all very well, but it can take its toll. Go home to Morgan and have some downtime. It's how I get through the tough days.'

His words stayed with her long after he'd left, and she reluctantly switched off the computer. He had a point. It was day one and she was excited, but if she got wound up too quickly, she could soon make errors or simply run out of steam.

She grabbed her coat. Hopefully, Morgan wouldn't have scoffed all the curry by the time she got home.

Kate picked her way back down the uneven track. Without car headlights to guide her, she had to rely on her phone torch and hope nobody spotted its beam as she hugged the hedgerow towards the farm buildings. What she was doing was tantamount to trespassing; however, the need to determine if Digger was at Gorse Farm was greater than the fear of breaking any laws.

Her heels sank into the damp earth, slowing her progress. Plaintive distant calls, like ghosts moaning, reached her ears, carried by the driving wind that slapped and numbed her cheeks. The farm seemed much further away on foot than when she had driven it. Nevertheless, she forged ahead, head bowed against intense gusts that at times halted her in her tracks. Her tenacity eventually paid off and, crossing the yard once more, she spotted movement in the largest lit barn, and a figure huddled over a stall. Moving towards the open door, she spied three men assisting a bleating sheep. All attention was on the birthing animal, allowing Kate to move close enough to identify the trio. The old farmer, back to her, was watching his son and another man pull out a breeched lamb. She immediately recognised the third person, who she'd last seen in an interview room at the station.

It was the elusive Digger.

◆ ◆ ◆

Emma bustled into the sitting room, smile on her face. 'Hey!'

Morgan barely glanced up. 'Curry needs warming up. There's still some wine left.'

His glum demeanour immediately doused her cheerful mood. She didn't know why she felt the need to apologise, yet all the same the words tumbled from her lips. 'I'm sorry I'm late and messed up plans.'

'It's okay. I got your message. Shit happens,' he said, eyes still on the television.

Emma made for the kitchen, where a bottle of red stood open next to a stack of foil containers. Her hunger evaporated and instead of reaching for the bottle, she turned on the kettle. By the time it had boiled, and she'd made a cup of tea, she was seething. Morgan hadn't asked her at all about her day and was sulking like a bloody teenager. What had happened to him? The last couple of weeks, he'd become increasingly morose, and it was troubling. Morgan never let an investigation get to him. Not only was she not used to this side of his personality, but she also didn't like it.

She took her mug into the sitting room and dropped down on to a chair instead of taking up her usual position beside him on the settee.

'Come on then,' she said. 'Spit it out. Who's pissed on your chips today?'

He finally looked up. 'Pretty much everybody. DI Ali Rind for one. He was brought in to head Operation Moonbeam, and yet we're no further forward than we were in September last year. I'm sick of playing second fiddle to somebody who bulldozes his way about and doesn't listen to me. And worst of all, that fucking Jamie Webster is so far up Rind's arse, he's making me want to puke up my own liver.'

'Bit graphic, but I get the idea!' she replied. 'So, basically, you're behaving like a dick to me because things aren't going your way. I have news for you. Things don't always run smoothly. I'm sure DI Rind feels as frustrated, if not more so, as you do. As for Jamie, he's Jamie. He's over-enthusiastic and irritating at times, but he means well. He used to be Kate's "yes man", now he's DI Rind's. Get over yourself, big man, or this will suck the life out of you and us.'

'Ouch. Say what you mean, Emma.' He gave her a hurt look that made her wonder if she'd been too harsh in her choice of words. That hadn't been her intention. He surely knew by now that she often spoke directly. After all, she always had been that way with him. She considered apologising then decided not to, because not only should he not have taken offence but part of her was irritated he'd launched into his 'poor me' monologue and hadn't even asked her about her day. All the same, she aimed for a more light-hearted tone and tried again.

'Forget the puppy-dog eyes. I don't have the energy to pamper to your ego.'

Morgan's lips twisted into a crooked smile. 'I'm being a fucking bore, aren't I?'

'Let's just say you're in danger of giving me the ick.'

He sat up straight. 'The ick? That's serious.'

The sudden return to his playful self was welcome. Lately, this side of his nature – a part of him she especially loved – had been absent, overtaken by snappy outbursts or periods of moody silence. Emma had begun to wonder if these swings were because of her. 'Exactly, so snap out of it. Why don't you ask Kate if you can be moved to another investigation?'

'For one, it would affect my promotional prospects. Secondly, if we could just crack this case, I'd get a massive pat on the back and huge kudos for my part in it. Lastly, I'd probably end up on another dead-end investigation or worse still, transferred.'

'Then you know your options. Right, I'm done dispensing advice and I'm going for a bath.'

'Thanks.'

'What for?'

'Putting me straight.'

'Somebody has to. You've got to stick on the right path if you want that promotion.'

'Yeah. Seems like it's a long way off though. Anyway, what's all this I hear about you being assigned an investigation?'

'It's a suspicious death.'

'What? Really? Wow!'

'A body was unearthed this morning. Turns out it was a woman who went missing three weeks ago.'

'That's a biggie. Congratulations.'

She got to her feet. 'Bit soon for congratulations. We're a long way off finding out what happened or indeed who buried her.'

She left the room before the conversation went any further. Despite his effusive reaction, she had detected a flatness to his voice that suggested while he was pleased for her, he was also disappointed that the investigation had gone to her. If things didn't pick up on Operation Moonbeam, there would be more tense conversations like this one, a prospect Emma didn't relish.

◆ ◆ ◆

Kate had spent the last hour in her car, parked in a lay-by on the road leading to the farm, hoping to catch Digger alone when he left, as he would have to at some point.

Dickson chuckled in the darkness. *'Digger is likely to be there all night and maybe even tomorrow, for that matter. You really aren't on the ball, are you? You're getting sloppy, making poor decisions and, quite frankly, losing your grip. Why didn't you march into the barn and demand to speak to him?'*

She gritted her teeth. The truth of his words was even more biting than the seeping cold that was travelling through her veins. But he was right. She should have confronted Digger the moment she spotted him.

And she would have, if he had been alone. But the men with him would have thrown her off the land.

The decision to lie in wait to confront him had seemed the only option. Yet now it was clear it was foolish, another example of how bad her decision-making had become recently.

She hated hearing Dickson's voice. William's was at least more welcome, but Chris's was the only one she really wanted in her head, the way it had been in the time after his death.

She whispered her husband's name, and then William's, but nobody answered, and so, with neither one's advice to follow, she decided to face up to all the men at the farm and drag Digger from the barn if she had to. If she didn't do this now, she might not find Digger again; so, rubbing some life into her frozen hands, she prepared to start up the engine, only to spot headlights weaving along the track. She ducked down, hidden from view in the dark cockpit, and watched the vehicle approach.

An old Land Rover rattled past her. Even though she couldn't see their faces, she knew who the two occupants were – the driver was Malcolm Hardcastle and, beside him, the passenger was the man she was searching for: Digger.

CHAPTER SEVEN

Kate had lost the Land Rover down a country lane and, after a futile search, decided to go home. She was furious with herself for not grabbing Digger when she had the opportunity.

Little by little, as her frustration subsided, reason was restored. She would speak to the Hardcastles once more. Maybe Malcolm could be persuaded to divulge where Digger had gone.

She was fifteen minutes away from home when the phone call interrupted her thoughts of a cup of tea and a hot shower. She cursed when she saw the name of the person ringing her. She'd forgotten all about keeping Harriet Khatri updated. Tempting as it was to ignore the call and ring the woman in the morning, she accepted it, deciding to jump in before Harriet could speak first.

'Sorry I haven't got back to you sooner, but something came up and I had to deal with it. Felicity has agreed to check the footage.'

Harriet caught a sob then blurted, 'Thank goodness. I've been tearing my hair out, wondering if you'd managed to convince her. Thank you, Kate. You don't know how much this means to me.'

There was a pause, during which Harriet blew her nose before speaking again. 'I'll inform Howard Lonsdale immediately and have him courier the footage to her. She won't tell anyone, will she?' Her voice rose as she spoke, each word becoming more urgent. 'I know this will sound paranoid, but if whoever framed me is capable of corrupting that video, then I'm sure they'll stop at nothing to prevent Felicity from proving it. You have warned her, haven't you?'

'Harriet, you need to calm down.'

Harriet took a deep breath. 'I know. I know. It's just this is . . . it's all too much. What is happening . . . is . . . inconceivable. I would never have imagined that I'd be in this position . . . Me! I can't begin to comprehend how it's come about, or even why, and trying to find an explanation that doesn't sound fantastical is driving me crazy. Worse still, nobody truly believes me. My lawyer makes placatory noises, but I can see in his eyes that he thinks I'm lying through my teeth, and even those people who are close to me are exhibiting doubts. That footage condemns me. How can I fight that?'

Kate interrupted the verbal flagellation. 'Felicity is on board. And I know it's easier said than done, but try not to get over-wrought about the situation. It's out of your hands for the time being. Wait for the result.'

'I'm struggling to keep my emotions in check. It doesn't help that I've become a prisoner in my own house. Friends and relatives shun me. If Felicity can't find evidence to prove it's a fake, then everyone will believe I am the monster who killed William, regardless of my plea or the fact I have no motive. I don't know how I'll cope.' Her voice cracked. If Harriet was acting, she was putting on a star performance. 'This has been the worst time of my life. You've given me a spark of hope. You've listened when others haven't. Up until today, I felt utterly abandoned. I had nobody to talk to.'

'What about your husband?'

'He's . . . he's gone away. Our son was being bullied, receiving . . . horrible messages, even threats from his schoolfriends, so Pranit took him out of school. They're both staying with his brother in Surrey. It's probably for the best. I miss them both though. So much.'

The tremors in her voice were impossible to ignore. Kate struggled with her own feelings towards her rival, who had the moniker 'the Ice Queen' for a good reason, yet needed some kindness. The fact that Harriet's husband had abandoned her in her hour of need, taking their ten-year-old son with him and leaving Harriet to deal with the fallout, suggested all was not well with their marriage.

Before Kate could ask any questions, she heard a soft, 'Anyway, thanks again. I'd better go. I really must speak to Howard and move this along.' And the call ended.

'I wish you could tell me what happened that night,' she said aloud; then, when William's voice didn't respond, she realised she didn't need his answer. Her decision on whether Harriet was guilty would hinge purely on evidence and nothing else. All the same, the idea the syndicate had framed Harriet nagged at her. Before work tomorrow, she would return to William's house and hunt again for the evidence hidden there. If she found that, she might be in a better position to believe or discredit Harriet.

Emma spooned against Morgan in bed. The spat, such as it was, had been forgotten. She thought back to earlier when, in the bath, there'd been a tap on the door and Morgan had brought her a glass of wine. He'd sat on the side of the bath and asked about her investigation and seemed genuinely interested in what she was doing . . .

'I miss us working together,' said Morgan. 'That's probably why I'm finding Operation Moonbeam so hard. Let's face it, I'd rather work with you than Jamie any day. Anyhow, I'm not moaning again. I'm over it and tomorrow I'll hit the floor running.'

'Not everything gets solved in a few days or even weeks. You're dealing with some very clever people who seem able to stay under the radar.'

'Yeah, that's the thing. We've had a couple of strong leads recently and yet when we checked them out, there was nothing. It was like that time when the team raided the motel to catch the trafficked girls and Trevor Wray thought we'd warned the traffickers off. I think somebody might be in league with the main traffickers and is keeping them informed of our movements.'

'A leak in your team?' she said.

'Uh-huh.'

'Have you told DI Rind of your suspicions?'

'Do you think I should?'

'Of course you should! If it had been Kate running the show, you wouldn't have hesitated to voice your concerns.'

'DI Rind isn't as approachable as Kate. Besides, I don't want to stuff up any chances of making DI.'

'If anything, I'd say asking the question would enhance your chances. You'd be showing Rind that you aren't afraid of confrontation and want what's best for the team. Bloody well tell him. Or, if you want to test out your theory first, speak to Kate and ask her what she thinks.'

'Yes. I might do that. I like chatting stuff through with you. You make things seem more clear cut. You're good for me.'

'I know.' She'd blobbed bath foam on to his nose, making him laugh.

'Would you like your back scrubbing?'

She'd returned his smile. 'Yeah, why not?'

These thoughts started to drift as tiredness weighed down her limbs. The steady rise and fall of Morgan's chest lulled her into a dark void, the gap where reality and dreams merge and sleep paralysis sets in. A woman's ruined face floated before her. Gradually, the flesh reappeared to form Leah Fairbrother's oval face with eyes the colour of a tiger-eye gemstone. Her lips parted, but Emma didn't hear what she had to say as darkness swept her away for the night.

◆ ◆ ◆

The wind has eased. He thrusts his icy cold hands deeper into his pockets. Ordinarily, he'd pretend to be studying his phone because nobody gives a person scrolling through their phone a second look. At this time of night, that somebody was probably booking an Uber or sending a message to one of their mates telling them what a good night they'd had or a drunken message to an ex saying how much they missed them.

Friday nights are the best nights for hunting. Everybody wants to party on a Friday night, especially when it's close to the end of the month and they've been paid. People last got paid before Christmas and so, with money back in their accounts, they are once again frittering it away.

He's never understood people's desire to head to a busy bar, club or pub to spend the night getting wasted; however, that they do is advantageous to him. A person's senses are usually affected by alcohol and their reactions slow.

His eye is drawn to the doorway that he's had under observation. A woman wearing a red miniskirt suit and thigh-length boots stumbles out. On unsteady legs, she peers into her clutch bag and pulls out a vape pen. As she does so, the bag tumbles to the ground, allowing its contents to scatter on to the pavement. She curses and, swaying slightly, crouches down to pick them up.

Nobody else is in sight. This is the perfect opportunity. He checks for witnesses one more time and, deciding the street is empty apart from his victim, he begins to cross towards the woman now scooping a lip gloss and a small purse into the bag. She looks up, her eyes unfocused, one hand still clasping her vape stick. One of her scarlet hair slides has come loose and a tendril of black hair has escaped from it to curl across her cheek. She swats at it as if it is a fly. This is going to be so easy. But before he's had a chance to render the woman powerless, the door opens with a clatter, and a man appears.

He stops in his tracks, but the man doesn't seem to notice him, his eyes on the woman now on all fours on the ground.

'For fuck's sake, Livvy! What are you doing down there?' he says.

The woman giggles. 'Dropped my bag. My shit's gone everywhere. Give us a hand, will you?'

'You're a liability, you know,' he says with a laugh as he bends down to help retrieve the items.

He turns on his heel and marches away before either person notices him. A minute or two later and this man would have caught him in the act. He'll take it as a warning not to proceed tonight.

Still, as they say, when you've killed once, the second time is always easier.

CHAPTER EIGHT

The strip light in William's garage flickered above Kate's head as she sorted through the paraphernalia that her mentor had accrued over the years.

While his house was tidy, and his garden had been maintained to perfection, both the garage and the attic were crammed with junk. She'd just finished hunting through a large freezer chest, checking every wrapped package, box and resealable zipper storage bag to ensure nothing other than food had been secreted inside them. She rubbed her hands together rapidly to regain some feeling in them, then clamped them under her armpits while she walked around what little floor space there was, considering where to look next.

She'd checked the metal cabinet containing screws, tools and handyman odds and ends, taking each drawer out in turn and turning them over in case William had taped the evidence to the underside. She'd been through four boxes of old paperbacks, flicking through the pages of every book. And there were still another twenty or so boxes to search through.

William would have hidden the incriminating document in a place that a member of the syndicate would not consider. However, if Harriet was right, and he'd been murdered by someone linked to the syndicate, they might already have found the information and all this searching was pointless. Another, darker thought crossed her mind: that William had been lying to her and hadn't infiltrated the group to expose them but was very much part of it.

She flexed her fingers and grabbed a box marked 'Christmas'. Buried under piles of green and gold tinsel were boxes of baubles. She was in the process of checking the third one when her phone rang.

Morgan sounded subdued. 'Morning, Kate. Sorry to bother you, but could I have a word with you – face to face – before my shift starts?'

'Sure. How about in half an hour?'

'Thanks. That would be great.'

The call was a good reason to stop her fruitless and frustrating efforts. She put away tree ornaments and, after repacking it, kicked the box.

'Where the hell have you hidden it, William?'

Once again, there was no reply.

She snapped off the light and stomped back through the house. The place needed cleaning, but she didn't want to employ a cleaner until she'd turned it upside down and, at present, she had no time to do any housework herself. It would have to wait. She shut the door and turned the key. She'd known William a very long time; surely she could fathom how his mind worked. It was only after she'd joined the traffic on the main road that it struck her. William's hobby – apiculture. Nobody would think to search his hives. The problem was that she'd donated the bees to the British Beekeepers Association, who had since rehomed them. The hives might even have been destroyed.

She balled her fist and thumped the side of the car. Shit! She was getting sloppy.

Emma was coming out of the coffee shop when she collided with another customer entering the place. She managed to hang on to the cup but not the sandwich, which the young man picked up with apologies.

'Oh, hi, Andy.' Andy Sullivan was a regular at her brother's gym. He worked out as frequently and as hard as she had before she'd started dating Morgan. She was drawn to like-minded individuals who understood her own drive and need to push herself to her limits because they felt the same way. She'd connected with Andy from the off, even partnering him during weight sessions.

He held out the sandwich with a surprised expression. 'Hi, Emma. Haven't seen you in ages. I've missed you at the gym. You been sick or something?'

'No. Just really busy at work. Hence breakfast on the go,' she added, taking the sandwich from him. 'How are you getting on?'

'Yeah, good, thanks. Greg's been making noises about me turning professional.'

'Wow! You must have impressed him.'

He gave a shy smile. 'Thanks. I've been putting in the effort, so it's a result. Fergus has been pushing me to my limits.'

'Only because he sees more potential in you. You know he used to train me?'

'Yeah, he told me. We should have a bout next time you're at the gym.'

'I'd floor you in an instant,' she said.

Andy laughed, teeth on display, eyes crinkled. 'I'd like to see you try.'

The way he held her gaze as he spoke was undeniably sexy and she enjoyed the moment of flirtation. Even though she'd had a bit of a crush on Andy from the off, she hadn't told him or done anything about it. Then soon after his arrival at the gym, she and Morgan had hooked up. While she still found Andy attractive, she

71

would never lead him on, especially not now she was in a couple with Morgan.

'If I ever get time off, I might take you up on your challenge. For now, I must get to work.'

'Nice bumping into you,' he said.

'Literally,' she said, earning another smile.

She headed off, reminding herself that she was living with somebody she really cared for. While it had been flattering to think other men might be interested in her, one man was more than enough to handle, especially when that man was Morgan Meredith.

Emma had only been back at her desk a few minutes when a tap at the door made her look up. Morgan was standing in the doorway.

'Thought you might like to know that I'm seeing Kate in half an hour.'

'That's good. You'll feel better once you've spoken to her.'

'I hope so. Anyway, thanks again for the advice. What are you up to?'

'Prepping for an interview.'

'Hope it goes well.'

'Me too. I could do with some leverage on this case. Ervin hasn't turned up anything suspicious and Terry's report doesn't help us determine cause of death, so I'm currently feeling my way.'

'You'll crack it.'

'I hope so. Oh, morning, Scott,' she said as a figure loomed behind Morgan. Morgan stepped out of the way, greeting the man with a nod and a smile.

'Morning, both,' said Scott. 'Thought I'd make a start. Early bird and worm and all that.'

Morgan lifted a hand. 'Catch you later, Emma.'

'I didn't disturb anything, did I?' Scott said as he unpacked his lunchbox and flask.

'Nothing whatsoever.'

He reached into the bottom of the bag and pulled out a clementine. Turning it towards Emma, she saw a smiley face had been drawn on it. 'My youngest,' he explained. 'She leaves surprises in my backpack.'

'Cute.'

'She is that.' He balanced the fruit on top of the box then cleared his throat. 'I was thinking about Leah's husband last night. He never once mentioned her being pregnant, so I was wondering if he knew about the baby. That's an important piece of news to share and my wife told me as soon as she knew – even before, when she suspected she was pregnant. I might understand it if Leah had only been a few weeks gone, but twelve – that's tough to hide. My wife suffered badly from morning sickness with all of our children, round about the six-week stage. I can't believe Russell didn't have an inkling that she was expecting.'

Emma agreed. 'We should discuss this with Dee before we broach the subject with him.'

'Good idea. For what it's worth, I think Leah kept it secret on purpose. Russell seemed to be full-on about the new business venture. Maybe she was scared to bring it up. Or dare I say it, she was considering having a termination. If she was as career-minded as him, she might have been considering that option, rather than have their plans interrupted by having children.'

'Talk to her doctor.'

'Will do.'

'I was trying to get some info about those purchases on Leah's credit card. MisPers discovered that they were delivered to a PO Box address in Stoke-on-Trent, registered to Hasty Holdings. I've looked for a company of that name and come up with nothing.

Would you get somebody to dig deeper? And would you please set up a meeting for us with Jackson Collins, Leah's boss?'

'Will do. I also thought we'd send a couple of the team out to knock on doors along Leah's road. We need a better description of the car that picked her up that night.'

Emma nodded. According to MisPers, none of Leah's girl-friends drove a white car. 'Have everyone check for surveillance equipment on the other properties while they are there. We might get lucky. I'll visit the tech unit now and see if I can persuade the techies to assist with CCTV. Give me a call when Dee comes in.'

As she made for the technology laboratory, she thought back to the conversation with Russell. His reason for the argument had sounded plausible, yet what if he'd discovered Leah was pregnant? That might have sparked the quarrel, resulting in Leah intentionally staying away from home.

When Kate arrived, she found Morgan waiting outside her office. She ushered him in and urged him to sit down while she removed her coat.

'Sorry, I won't take up much of your time,' he began.

'Stop that immediately,' she said.

'I don't follow.'

'Apologising before you've even begun to explain why you are here. You wouldn't have rung if it hadn't been important, so relax, sit down and tell me what the problem is.'

He lowered himself on to the chair opposite hers and clasped his hands together like a candidate hoping to get their dream job.

'It's about Operation Moonbeam,' he began. 'I'm not sure how to put this without sounding like I'm complaining.'

'Just spit it out.'

'I'm concerned that we're not making the progress we should by now. There've been two recent instances when we were given hot tips detailing the whereabouts of those people masterminding the trafficking in the region. On both occasions, when we got there the premises were empty.'

'Yes, DI Rind informed me of this.'

'Did he suggest that we might have a leak within the team?'

'No. I asked him that very question and he assured me that the information passed over to the team had been inaccurate and not as reliable as you'd been given to believe.'

Morgan cleared his throat and caught her gaze. 'One of those tips came from a trustworthy and accurate source, one of mine. When I questioned my informant about it afterwards, they swore it was one hundred per cent reliable and suggested somebody on the inside had alerted the traffickers. As you'd expect, I passed this on to DI Rind, who refused to pursue it, saying sources like mine weren't always to be trusted, no matter what I thought.' He looked away for a moment before meeting her eye again. 'You know how I operate. It's taken me years to cultivate relationships with my informants, and this particular one has never let us down before. I'm convinced that we have a leak. I also think DI Rind is out of his depth with this investigation. He may have a formidable reputation back in Manchester, but this isn't his patch and he's turned many of our informers against us with his ham-fisted handling of the investigation. He has intimidated rather than cajoled and, in my experience, that never works.' He pressed his lips together.

Kate gave a nod of encouragement. She had always liked Morgan, not only because he was an excellent officer with good instincts, but because he was straight-talking. They had an easy relationship, bordering on friendship, and she knew him to be trustworthy. If he had concerns, they deserved her attention.

Morgan went on to mention the incident during their last major investigation as a team, when he and Emma were observing DI Harriet Khatri leading her team to uncover human traffickers who were hiding out in a motel. On that occasion also, the traffickers had escaped.

'If you remember, DS Trevor Wray alerted our team – via Jamie – to the whole operation and we piggybacked it. Trevor and his team even had the audacity to suggest we had leaked the information.'

At the time, Kate had believed Harriet had warned off the traffickers. However, if Harriet truly had nothing to do with the syndicate and once again traffickers were pre-empting raids, then it was possible a member of the syndicate was still at large. Moreover, that person was somebody on DI Ali Rind's team. Her then DC, Jamie Webster, was now a DS, and part of that same team. Could he be the culprit? She chewed her bottom lip, wondering if she might have missed something that pointed to his guilt.

Morgan was looking earnestly at her.

She was tempted to share her thoughts about Jamie but decided against it. Until she had some proof to substantiate them, she ought to keep her suspicions to herself. 'Leave it with me. I'll have a word with DI Rind.'

Morgan got to his feet and smoothed the creases in his trousers. 'Thank you.'

'Could you convince your informant to come in to HQ to talk to us?'

'I doubt it.'

'If not, set up a meeting elsewhere. I'd like to meet this person.'

'I'll see what I can do, but you know how they can be.'

The door shut. Kate chewed over the conversation. Ever since she discovered Jamie had been part of Dickson's undercover operation to track down underage sex-workers, she had harboured doubts about her officer. Dickson had used Operation Agouti as a front to hunt down two girls in particular – Stanka and Rosa – who had information that would expose him as corrupt. Kate remained uncertain as to whether Jamie had known the real reason behind the investigation or if he'd merely acted out of orders. Moreover, she'd been convinced Dickson had placed Jamie on her team to spy on her. Those reservations had existed right up until the evening he confessed his part in Operation Agouti but assured Kate his loyalty lay firmly with her. He was a team player. He'd proved himself by single-handedly bringing down a dangerous killer. He was always super enthusiastic and got stuck in. She scratched her head. While it was true that Jamie had obtained information regarding Harriet's team locating traffickers at the motel from his friend DS Trevor Wray and had passed it on, she doubted he would have done so if he'd intended warning off the traffickers. She shouldn't still harbour suspicions about him.

'*That's right. If you can't trust those loyal officers who are on your own team, then who can you trust?*' said William.

Kate would have agreed with him had she not heard a deep chuckle and Dickson's voice. '*Well, she couldn't trust you, could she?*'

She suppressed both voices. She needed to trust her instinct on this matter and although Jamie had given her reason to doubt him in the past, there had been explanations for his behaviour. He had proved himself a team player and hard worker. He hadn't been part of Operation Moonbeam until recently, so it was unlikely he had anything to do with the failings of that investigation. Despite the reasoning, the nagging feeling remained. If only she could be completely sure about him.

◆ ◆ ◆

He shakes rain from his coat and hangs it over the banister. The house smells of burned cheese and, wrinkling his nose, he makes

77

for the kitchen, where he is sure he will find his mother. She looks up when he enters and manages a lopsided smile.

'Ah, here he is. Dropping in to see his mother.' The speech is slurred but not because of alcohol, not any more.

'How are you doing, Mum?'

She gives the standard response. 'So-so.'

She extends her right arm, picks up a small blue and yellow cardboard piece and slots it into the puzzle on the kitchen table, softly tapping it into place with a balled fist. 'What about you?'

'Same old,' he replies, taking in the mess by the sink. The bloody help is late again. If he could be arsed, he'd phone the council and give them a bollocking, but he isn't a saint or even a good son. She'll have to get by until somebody turns up.

His mother eases back in her wheelchair. 'Couldn't get your old mum a cup of tea, could you? I'm parched.'

He hates the way her mouth twists when she speaks and is revolted by the dribble that slides from the corner of her lips. She picks up the handkerchief that permanently resides in her lap and dabs at it. He has no intention of making her a drink. He'll have to use the baby beaker and hold it against her lips while she sips. The home help can do that. That's what they're paid for.

This powerless woman who can barely look after herself, with her drooping face and left eye that looks as if it will pop out of its socket any moment, is a far cry from the woman who brought him up. That woman had been tough, unwavering and at times cruel. Life had dealt her a bad hand: his father's fists had split her lip and broken her bones on more than one occasion, only serving to make her angry with everyone in the world, including her son, the spitting image of his father. That man was now out of the picture for good. Although he'd been in and out of prison most of his son's life, his latest stint in Wakefield prison would be for life.

His mother looks at him with something akin to helplessness, making his skin crawl with a million invisible insects. He isn't here to look after the bitch. This is business.

'I'll stick the kettle on later. Just going upstairs for a bit.'

She stares at him, and he looks away before the sight of her turns his stomach further. She must have a good idea of the real reason he is here. Before her stroke, he never visited. Now that she's defenceless, he has returned because she can no longer hurt him. He turns without speaking or going near the kettle. She knows better than to argue the toss.

Upstairs, he removes a box that's been secreted under floorboards in his old bedroom. He created this hidey-hole when he was twelve to hide stolen cigarettes, money, sweets, mobiles, anything he could filch, often using menace to get what he wanted. He felt no guilt, not even after he knocked ten-year-old Barry Cross unconscious while wrestling for the kid's phone. The boy's head had slammed against a paving slab and resulted in him being carted off to hospital, where he lay in a coma for three months until they switched off his life support.

Accidents happen, right? Besides, apples never fall far from the tree, right? Like father, like son and all that shit. With a father as warped and violent as his, he was always going to turn out bad.

He shrugs at the thought. He has no strong feelings about what happened, although he'll always remember Barry Cross, the dumb-arse kid who tried to stand up to him. What a fool!

He opens the box and pulls out the Cartier watch. His contact has found somebody who'll give him a good price for it, no questions asked. He's confident that no one will ever trace it back to him. He's adept at this now. As soon as he gets his hands on his targets' credit cards, he heads to an internet café where he purchases saleable goods that get delivered to a post box in the name of Hasty Holdings. This is where he keeps his victims' personal possessions. His eyes fall on to a black onyx ring set in gold-plated brass. It's quite showy, although not as flash as the diamond engagement ring Leah also wore, which he'll easily sell. Not round these parts, of course. He'll head to London to dispose of these pieces, drop them off at some posh pawnbroker's where all the toffs go to raise cash against their valuables, spin the usual story about inheriting the stuff and take whatever he can get for them. He'll bide his time though. It pays to be cautious. The new purchases were a different story. He's already sold both the laptop and the phone. It's always best to get shot of those items quickly, before the police get involved.

There'll be no way the cops will trace anything back to him. He pockets the item and heads downstairs. His mother is hunched over the table, another piece of puzzle in her trembling hand. He doesn't say goodbye. The front door closes quietly behind him.

Dee Lockwood removed her olive-green cross-body bag and fumbled at the zip of a stone-coloured hooded coat, which eventually swung open to reveal a simple cream turtleneck sweater teamed with jeans. She sank on to the wooden seat, eyes fixed on Emma, who gave her a smile to ease her tension.

Emma noted the cream lettering across the wide strap of the bag spelling the brand, Loewe, which also matched the name written on the wide leather patch on the coat. 'We really appreciate you coming in,' she said. 'I'm so sorry for your loss. I understand you and Leah were close friends.'

Dee opened her mouth to speak but shut it again, eyes immediately filling with tears. She rested the bag on her knees, fingers curled around the strap.

'Would you like a tea or coffee, or maybe a glass of water?' Emma said.

This time the woman spoke, her voice squeaky with emotion. 'No, thanks.'

Scott took up his position next to Emma, a notepad open in front of him.

'Was it really her?' Dee asked.

'There's no doubt,' Emma replied.

Dee nodded slowly.

'It would help us if you could tell us a little about Leah.' Emma threw the woman another smile.

'She . . . was . . . lovely. We first met at an evening aerobics class back in 2019 and hit it off straight away. We became friends, used to go for coffees after class.'

'Did you still see her regularly?'

'Not so much after she started seeing Russell. Then of course they got married, and we tried to have a girls' night out at least once a month, or catch up whenever we found time in our work schedules. Being in hospitality, Leah would sometimes manage to swing free passes at one of the spa retreats nearby for us and we'd go on a pamper day or a weekend. She was very generous. She gave me this bag and coat. She had a big heart.' Her voice faltered.

'Russell said she was due to meet you the night she disappeared but that wasn't the case, was it?'

'No. We hadn't made any arrangements to meet. In fact, she pulled out from all the last four evenings we'd planned . . . at the last minute.'

'Did she give any reason why?' Emma asked.

'Too tired. Not feeling well.'

'Was that strange?'

'Thinking about it now, yes, I suppose it was. She was usually always up for it, even if she had a lot on at work. In fact, the busier she was, the more she wanted to let off steam. Although, at the time, what with Christmas coming up, and more functions than usual to plan for, I wasn't over-surprised that she was run down.'

'When did you last speak to her?'

'The day before she went missing. I'd been away in Scotland, celebrating Hogmanay with my family. I rang her when I got back. I'd found a yoga retreat with availability at the end of the month and wanted to know if she fancied going.'

'And when you spoke to her, did you get any impression that something might be bothering her?'

'Not in the slightest. She was excited about the idea. Said it would be perfect because she really needed some downtime, a chance to think things over. She didn't sound wound up . . . If anything, she sounded weary.'

'Did she divulge exactly what things she needed to think over?'

'No, but I expect it was about going into business with Russell. She'd spoken about it when I last saw her.'

Scott, who had been making notes, looked up from his pad. 'Can you remember when that was?'

'It was the twenty-eighth of December. I remember because I was heading to Scotland the following day.'

'How did she seem then?' he asked.

'Quieter than normal. We met for lunch. Leah was in a rush to get back to work though, so we didn't have much time to chat. She hardly touched her food.'

Emma spoke next. 'And at that lunch, she mentioned the new business venture?'

Dee gave a soft sigh. 'Yes. She made me promise not to tell a soul. She was worried that Jackson, her boss, would find out about the venture, even though she'd got cold feet and no longer wanted to go through with it. She was concerned that working together with Russell would change the dynamics of their relationship. The trouble was, Russell was mega keen on the idea and having been enthusiastic herself to start with, she was anxious about telling him she had misgivings. I advised her to follow her heart. If she was happier working at Harlequin, then she should tell Russell or at the very least discuss her concerns with him.'

'Why do you think she was so worried about discussing the matter with him?'

'I don't know Russell very well, but he can be . . . determined. He likes things his way and when that doesn't happen, he can make life difficult.'

'Was he abusive?'

'No. At least . . . I don't think so. Leah never said he was. But there are various forms of abuse, aren't there? I think sometimes Leah was scared of upsetting him.'

'Can you elaborate?' asked Scott.

'It's difficult to pin down anything in particular. In truth, I envied them . . . what they had, I mean. Russell was always so . . . attentive. He was always touching her: holding her hand, putting an arm around her. One time, we were out in a group, and he never left her side. Not like my partner at the time, who hung out with the other lads by the bar and ignored me. He was . . . proud of her and happy to be with her. But then there was another occasion when Leah and I went out for the night. She got text after text from him, asking what time she was coming home.'

Emma pricked up her ears. This sounded like Russell might be possessive.

'At first, she laughed them off, but her phone kept pinging and she became increasingly edgy. In the end, she apologised and said she had to leave, even though it was only eight thirty.'

'Were there any other occasions like that?'

'I can't think of any.'

'Did she complain about Russell? I know my wife moans to her girlfriends about me and my bad habits,' Scott said, with a helpless smile.

'Not really. She hated it when they argued, though.'

'Did they argue a lot?'

'A fair bit.' Dee's eyes widened. 'You don't think Russell killed her, do you?'

'We're just gathering information to get a picture of what might have happened the night Leah went missing,' Emma replied smoothly.

Dee fiddled with the bag strap, her fingers caressing the material as she spoke. 'When it came to talking about Russell, Leah never gave much away.'

She dropped her gaze, focused instead on the bag on her lap. 'To be honest, before Leah met Russell, she was more fun, more easy-going. I'm not saying he was wrong for her, but I believe he suppressed her. Still, I don't see how that helps you. And I want to help. I . . . I want whoever hurt her to be punished.' Her eyes became glassy again. This time, tears trickled down her cheeks. She flipped the bag open and searched for a tissue.

'Are you okay to continue?' asked Emma.

Dee sniffed back more tears and wiped her face. 'Ever since the day she went missing, I've been waiting for her to call me. Up until yesterday, I still clung to the hope that she was alive, that she'd just taken off because things got too much for her. Now . . . there's no hope.'

'Did Leah ever talk about having a family?'

'Yes. Russell didn't want kids though. He wanted to build up an empire instead.'

'How did she feel about that?'

A light frown wrinkled Dee's forehead. 'She wanted children. When the time was right. She hoped that by then he'd have changed his mind. Why are you asking me about this?'

Emma wondered why Leah hadn't confided her pregnancy to her best friend. She decided to come clean. 'Leah was pregnant.'

Dee gasped. 'I had no idea.'

'We believe she kept it secret. We're not even sure Russell was aware that she was expecting a baby.'

'Why didn't she tell me? I wouldn't have said a word to anyone else!' Dee now worked the tissue, rubbing it between her fingers.

'For the time being, I'd like you to keep this information to yourself,' said Emma.

Dee nodded. 'Poor Leah. She must have been worried sick about telling Russell. A baby would have changed everything! Do you think he found out about it?'

'We'll be discussing the matter with him. We never speculate in these matters.'

'Oh, I've thought of something else. The day we had lunch, Leah was antsy. Instead of leaving her mobile on the table as usual, it was on her lap and she kept glancing at it, like she was expecting a text.'

'Did she receive one?'

'I don't think so. She was definitely a bit nervy though.'

Emma cocked her head. 'Dee, did Leah ever cheat on Russell?'

'She would never do the dirty on Russell. No matter what they were going through, she wouldn't.'

While Dee might believe that her friend wouldn't stray, Emma knew affairs happened, and most of them were never planned. Maybe identifying the baby's father would help clarify that issue.

'She wouldn't do that to Russell.'

'You seem sure about that,' said Scott.

'I am.'

'Even though they were having difficulties and Russell was, as you implied, "pushy"?' His eyebrows lifted as he spoke, his voice gentle and coaxing.

Dee shrugged. 'Relationships aren't always plain sailing, are they?'

She kept her head lowered while she spoke. Emma wondered why she wasn't being more direct. Scott obviously felt the same way.

'Did you get any impression that Leah was unhappy in her marriage?' he asked.

Dee wetted her lips and hesitated before answering. 'They had ups and downs like any married couple, but they were good together. Leah was one of the kindest-hearted people I've ever met. She wouldn't do anything to upset Russell. She wasn't that sort of person.'

Emma thought a close friend should have known far more than Dee seemed to, and would have been able to give them greater insight into Leah's relationship or state of mind. The woman clearly upset about her friend's death, yet she had little other than a few basic facts to give them. Had Leah deliberately kept Dee in the dark? Or was Dee hiding something? It was an avenue she might have to explore further.

◆ ◆ ◆

'You can't ignore the likelihood that Harriet Khatri was not leaking information to traffickers. After all, she's been unable to contact any-one while she has been housebound and Morgan told you about recent instances, times when Harriet couldn't be responsible.'

Kate digested William's words. The last half an hour, his voice and Dickson's had been arguing about who was responsible for the leaks.

'As part of the syndicate, Harriet has access to a great deal of out-side support. You would be surprised at what can be achieved, even if somebody is being watched closely.'

Kate was sick of this. She needed clarity, but Dickson was only muddying the waters further. She ached to hear her husband's voice instead.

'Chris, I need you. You'd be able to help me fathom this out,' she said.

'You can do it without him,' said William. *'Just be logical. Consider the possibility that Harriet is completely innocent in all of this, that she isn't the syndicate member known as Gamma. Think about who else might be. That could be the way forward and would lead to your mole.'*

William's gravelly voice had the desired calming effect. If Gamma was somebody else working on Operation Moonbeam, they could be responsible for the leaks. However, if Harriet wasn't this member of the syndicate, then who the bloody hell was?

Studying the list of officers involved in Operation Moonbeam, she gave a heavy sigh. She'd worked with all these dedicated individuals. Not one of them struck her as capable of subterfuge. At this rate, she'd never be able to weed out the culprit, any more than she could guess the identity of any of the syndicate members.

'Who, though, William? You told me you'd uncovered the real names of everyone associated with the syndicate apart from the two members known as Gamma and Iota. Even if I can find the list of names that you've hidden, I'll still not know the identity of these two.'

'I can't help you, Kate. You'll have to work it out.'

'Whoever Gamma and Iota are, their surnames come after yours alphabetically, which means I can only exclude two officers from the list of those working on Operation Moonbeam: Anderson and Bell. That leaves twenty more to consider, including Jamie Webster.'

'Remember that Jamie hasn't always been part of that investigation.'

'I know, but I can't discount him. He's friends with Trevor Wray. They might have discussed it out of hours. After all, Trevor passed on the info about the raid on the motel.'

Having put in a call earlier to the British Beekeepers Association, she was relieved when an expert rang back on her mobile, interrupting the internal debate.

'Firstly, I wanted to let you know that the colonies have adjusted well to being rehomed.'

'That's very good to hear,' said Kate. 'Could you tell me where they've gone?'

'Yes, they're with one of our members, Ann Gore, who lives in Hyde Lea. We were able to transport the hives without losing too many bees.'

'Hyde Lea is only a couple of miles away from Stafford. I expected them to be miles away.'

'Well, they are classed as northern bees and as such could be rehoused elsewhere, but that would have meant removing them from their hives altogether, which is far more disruptive for them. More to the point, if they are transported more than three miles away from their original base, most of the worker bees will die and then the nurse bees would lose their pheromones.'

'Would it be possible to visit Ann?'

'I imagine so, although can I ask why?'

'I need to examine the hives.'

'Examine them?'

'I believe the original owner might have hidden something, a document, inside one of the hives. I understand this is highly irregular, but it is extremely important.'

'I can give you Ann's phone number and you can discuss it with her, although I suspect she will be loath to let you get up close to the hives. Maybe she could search on your behalf, DCI Young.'

She took down the details. Luck was on her side. The hives hadn't been destroyed during the relocation. Maybe, just maybe, she would find what she was looking for.

CHAPTER NINE

Emma's stomach rumbled, reminding her she'd missed lunch. Glancing at her watch, she realised it was close to three o'clock. The day had sped past so quickly she'd barely had time to catch her breath. She was currently in the same room where they'd interviewed Dee earlier, her notes spread across the table. She was wording her questions for Russell when a soft knock on the open door broke her concentration.

'Emma, we've got a lead.' Scott rested a hand against the door frame as he spoke. 'Leah was spotted walking by the river on the evening of the sixth of January with a man.'

'Why didn't this come to light during the investigation into her disappearance?'

He shrugged a response. 'We got lucky. MisPers didn't. The appeal boards we erected around town got a result and Frankie just got a call from the owner of a barber's shop in town. She emailed him a photo of Leah and he confirmed it was her.'

DC Francesca Porter was a twenty-two-year-old singleton who lived with her twin sister. Frankie, as she preferred to be known, was the opposite of Scott: a ball of enthusiasm with a big personality and loud, infectious laughter. She was brash but very keen and dogmatic. Truth be told, Emma felt she and Scott complemented each other. When Scott couldn't coax information out of people,

Frankie seemed to be able to shake it from them through a series of stern looks.

'This happened three weeks ago. How can he be so sure it was Leah who he saw?'

'He was returning to his car with a takeaway from the Balti on Mill Bank when he spotted a couple crossing the bridge opposite. He noticed Leah because there seemed to be some sort of altercation going on. He heard Leah shout "fuck off" before running off. The man caught up with her and seized her wrist. Thinking she might be in trouble, the witness hung around in case she needed assistance. However, he decided all was okay when after a moment or two they then hugged, and when they walked away they were hand in hand.'

'What time was this?'

'Around eight o'clock. He'd been working late. He locked up at seven thirty, walked down the street to collect his car, then drove to the Balti, where he waited a good ten minutes for his order.'

'Yet he didn't come forward when MisPers were hunting for Leah?'

'He had no idea she was missing.'

'Could he describe the man she was with?'

'He was wearing a jacket with jeans and a shirt. Tall, about six foot, athletic build. Dark, trimmed facial hair.'

'Okay, have you spoken to the tech—'

'I've asked them to hunt through any CCTV footage in that vicinity for that evening.'

'Good job. Let me know if they find anything.'

'Goes without saying.'

'Where's Frankie now?'

'In town. She's checking out all the bars and restaurants along Mill Bank for further sightings.'

Emma nodded. 'Great.'

'Tech team is still trying to find out more about Hasty Holdings, who used the post box address, but it's appearing increasingly likely that it's a fictitious company. Oh, and Jackson Collins is now available for interview but would prefer it if we'd visit him at his business premises. I've got the address.'

'You free now?'

'Yes.'

'Then let's do it.'

◆ ◆ ◆

'I'm dreadfully sorry, DCI Young, but there is absolutely nothing hidden in any of the hives,' said Ann Gore. 'I've searched thoroughly. Twice.'

Kate's stomach sank. She'd been convinced William would have chosen to hide something this important somewhere only he would be able to access. She was torn between thanking the woman for her trouble and looking for herself. The problem was that she couldn't do so without protective gear or the bees' new owner. Ann didn't want her colony disturbed. Kate had little choice other than to accept the woman's word, which sent her back to the drawing board as far as the documentation was concerned. She thanked her then leant back in the chair, gloomily staring into space. She felt alone and thwarted again. What the fuck was wrong with her? Had killing Dickson and covering up his death changed her so much she'd lost her detective skills?

She needed to talk to somebody. Maybe she should ring her stepsister. Even though Tilly lived far away, she could at least call, vent, and ask for advice.

She had never felt so utterly isolated.

It was a good shout, William's voice said, as though coming to her aid in this moment of doubt. *But I wouldn't have left it somewhere inaccessible to you.*

'But you were keeping it safe from the syndicate, not me. Which meant that the hives would have been the perfect hiding place. Especially as you were the only person who could have retrieved it. When we last spoke, you said you would show it to me in the morning. Where the hell did you hide it?'

William's voice fell silent, leaving her brooding some more. If the document hadn't been hidden in what she considered to be the safest of safe places, where was it?

'It doesn't exist,' said Dickson. *'I've told you before, you place too much faith in William. He duped you good and proper. If there had been a document, he wouldn't have put you off until the morning to see it. You may hate me, but you know I speak sense.'*

'Dickson never says anything helpful. He only puts doubts in your mind. Ignore him. I wouldn't have lied to your face. We had a pact. I promised to tell you the truth if you promised to tell me the truth about Dickson – that you didn't kill him.'

'Well, there you have it,' said Dickson. *'You lied to him, Kate. What makes you think he didn't do the same to you?'*

She covered her ears with her hands. This 'good angel, bad angel' routine was doing her head in.

Concentrating on something other than William and the sodding document, she pulled up Harriet's number, wondering whether to ring her. She missed William. She'd always gone to him for advice or to run ideas past him. Her fight against Dickson and the syndicate had been a lone quest. If only William hadn't been killed, they could have worked together, brought down every single one of the corrupt bastards.

She replaced the phone on her desk with a heavy sigh and stared hard at a photo of her father and William. How would they have handled this crazy shit that was happening?

She heard the beginnings of Dickson's voice again, threatening to erupt from her mouth, a wisecrack about William being as corrupt as those she was chasing after. She clamped her lips shut. She was not setting that voice free to wreak havoc again. She would only talk to and listen to William's voice and Chris's if he chose to speak, although he'd hardly said anything in the last few weeks.

William deserved justice and she wanted to do right by him so badly, she almost didn't want to believe Harriet. It was easier to believe Harriet was guilty of murder. The evidence against her was strong and the most damning piece of all was the camera footage. She shut her eyes, replayed the scene . . .

William enters the sitting room first, followed by his assailant. The person has their back to the camera but from William's expression it's clear they are arguing. He waves his hand, then his face changes. A look of horror replaces the anger. He lifts his palms, lips moving. His eyes grow large. The person steps forward and fires into the side of his head. He falls backwards. His assailant crouches down and places the gun in William's hand. They are wearing black gloves. The killer stands back up and turns to face the camera.

Then Harriet Khatri pulls her hood over her head and departs via the French doors.

A lip-reader brought in to examine the footage had confirmed that William's last words were, 'Killing me won't keep you safe.'

Harriet had been the person he was speaking to. She had to be. They'd found identical black gloves in her bag. She'd admitted to being in the house. All the same, Kate doubted herself. Could that footage have been tampered with? And if Harriet wasn't Gamma, then she might have been made a scapegoat. The remaining syndicate members would protect themselves at all costs. Superintendent John Dickson had ensured that anyone who could have brought him down had been dealt with, so why wouldn't other members commit atrocities to ensure they remained safe?

'William, what would you do?' It was comforting to pretend he was in the room with her. William's presence was similar to that of her husband's, Chris. He helped her order her thoughts, provided a balanced view.

The fact that you have doubts about her guilt is not a bad thing. Like any good officer, you are now considering other possibilities, not being blinkered. You might get a clearer picture if you could track down the person she was supposedly meeting when you followed her to the warehouse.'

She fiddled with a pen, spun her chair so she was facing the window and spoke again. 'I have a history of struggling to find people who wish to remain hidden. Besides, Tommy Clayton might even be dead.'

Dickson barked a laugh. *'He's definitely dead. You know the syndicate always covers its tracks. If he hadn't been silenced, Tommy would have been able to support Harriet's version of events. We're not amateurs, Kate.'*

'No. My money is on him having been paid off and gone to ground. Speak to Harriet about his habits, where he likes to hang out, friends and so on. He might have family nearby. Harriet is virtually under house arrest and hasn't been able to look for him, but she might be able to give you some leads as to his whereabouts.'

William's logic made sense.

But Dickson's voice had to have its say. *'William is an optimist. Even if Tommy was alive, you'd never get close to locating him. Besides, you're a one-person band and no match for the syndicate. It's way bigger than you'd ever imagine. Tommy's dead. Forget this wild goose chase and get on with hunting for Digger before the syndicate finds him too.'*

His words zapped her energy and drive. The task of finding Tommy was too great. He would be impossible to locate.

'Impossible? Since when did you become defeatist, Kate?'

The comment, along with an image of William's craggy, earnest face, rekindled her resolve. It was worth a try. She lifted the mobile again and tapped the call button.

◆ ◆ ◆

'If being in the hospitality industry has paid for this place, I'm definitely in the wrong job,' said Scott, his eyes fixed on the huge black and white manor house that loomed in front of them. The sign at the end of the driveway had read 'Harlequin Events' and another similar sign was at the entrance to a small car parking area in front of a group of converted single-storey outbuildings.

'I doubt Jackson owns all of this. These must be let out to various businesses,' Emma replied. 'Come on.'

She strode to the first building, read the three nameplates beside the intercom and pressed the top buzzer. 'See. There are different names on them.'

A voice responded with, 'Hello, can I help?'

'Acting DI Emma Donaldson and DS Scott Hart to see Jackson Collins,' she replied.

The door opened automatically with a quiet click, and they found themselves in an empty hallway, glass doors to the left, right and centre. A figure appeared at the door to the right and greeted them, waving them through. 'Good afternoon. Thank you for coming here. I'm sorry I couldn't make it to the station but I've an important Teams meeting in twenty minutes.'

The man was in his early to mid-forties, of medium height and build, with a strong jaw and unruly thick wavy dark hair that curled over the collar of his cream polo-neck jumper.

He led them into a cramped space, predominantly white, including the round rug and circular table. The far wall, which appeared to be constructed of square white tiles, made Emma squint for a moment.

'Please, have a seat,' said Jackson, pulling out one of the three chairs fashioned from wood and chrome. He lifted his trouser legs slightly so they wouldn't crease, revealing bare feet in leather loafers. Dropping on to a maroon cushion pad, he crossed his legs. 'I had hoped you'd rung with some good news about Leah. I still haven't quite digested what's happened. I've known and worked with her for a long time. I can't imagine Harlequin without her.'

'I'm very sorry for your loss, sir,' said Emma.

'A huge loss.' His eyes filled, and he wiped them immediately. 'Tears won't bring her back, eh?'

'We wondered if you could tell us a little about Leah,' said Scott.

'Where to start? She was brilliant at her job. We plan, organise and run promotional, social and business events for anyone: from an independent company to larger corporations. Leah was imperative to the smooth running of this place.'

'How many people do you employ, Jackson?'

'We're only a small team of five. Leah was my right-hand person. My go-to when a problem required fixing. She would always sort it out in a jiffy, no matter what it was.'

'I take it you all get along here?' asked Scott.

'Very well. It's a happy place to work. At least, that's what I like to believe.'

'How long has Leah been at Harlequin?'

'Four years.'

'Before she married Russell, then,' said Scott.

'Yes.'

'And the others?'

'They came on board more recently. Zac joined us two years ago, then Pieter last year, and Adam two months ago.'

'Were you and Leah close?' Emma asked.

A furrow appeared between his eyebrows. 'Close? Work colleagues only,' he said with a slight shrug.

'She didn't talk about her home life at work, then?'

He cleared his throat. 'Er, no.'

'And you didn't socialise?'

'Again, no.'

'I suppose you attended some functions together?'

'Yes, but those were work-related.'

'Was she close to anyone at work?'

'Listen, detectives, I'll spare you your valuable time. Leah was purely work-driven. Like everyone here, she left her private life outside of the office. She will be seriously missed by us all, but conversations are only ever confined to what we are doing. We don't bring baggage to work. We don't chit-chat about families or partners. When we're at work, we focus on the job in hand. That's why we're so good at what we do.'

'No socialising outside? No Christmas drinks?'

He sighed. 'Harlequin is in the business of organising events. We work long hours and by the end of it, we really don't feel up to arranging anything for ourselves. If Leah met up with any of the others, it was without my knowledge.'

'I understand,' said Emma. 'May I ask if Leah gave the impression she was concerned about anything prior to her disappearance? Or if you noticed a change in her?'

A cloud flittered across his features so quickly Emma almost thought she'd imagined it. 'No,' he replied. 'I didn't pick up on anything strange. We were ridiculously busy pre-Christmas. Leah was holed up a lot of the time in her office.'

'Did Leah work on any projects alone?'

'Everything here is a team effort, coordinated by Leah. Except for the clients. Those I handle myself. That way, they feel they're receiving a tailor-made experience. Leah wouldn't have worked on anything without my involvement.'

'I take it that you haven't received any negative feedback from your clients?'

'None whatsoever. We pride ourselves on our reputation. In fact, many of the companies we have worked with have gone on to recommend us to others. We were featured in *Staffordshire Life* magazine two months ago. We were described as the best event organiser in the county.'

'Could we take a look at her office?'

'I'll show you it on the way out, although there's very little for you to look at. She kept all details of projects on her laptop, which I assume is still either with the police who investigated her disappearance or at home.'

'How did you coordinate your events if she kept that information on her laptop?'

'We have SharePoint hub. Everyone is in the loop at any given time.'

'Is there anything else you could tell us that might help with our inquiries?'

'Sorry. No. At the time of her disappearance, I couldn't fathom why she would simply up and leave. I suppose I always suspected something dreadful had happened. She wouldn't have taken off mid-project, not without letting us know.'

'If you can think of anything at all, would you please give me a call?' said Emma, standing to pass over a business card. 'Oh, and one last thing, did she ever talk to you about leaving Harlequin?'

His hand stopped mid-motion. 'Leave? Whatever makes you think she'd want to go?' He took the card from Emma and held her gaze.

Emma gave him a small smile. 'Simply checking some details.'

'Well, whoever told you that is wrong. In fact, the week before she vanished, I floated the idea of a partnership. I wanted Harlequin Events to become a joint venture. It was something I'd been thinking about for a long time. I planned to grow the business, leave her to run this place while I set up another branch in Manchester. Together, we could have really turned Harlequin into something huge.'

'How did she respond?'

He faltered for an instant, eyes blinking away emotion. 'She said she'd love to.'

He reached for a sheet of A4 that had been on the white table. 'These are the contact details for everyone who works here. We are all shocked and appalled by what's happened. I'm sure none of them would mind speaking to you. I really hope you find out what happened to her.'

'Her office?' said Emma.

'Oh, yes.' He glanced at his watch before opening the door.

Emma guessed his mind was on the impending online meeting, but she wasn't going to be hustled out of the place. They followed Jackson to the end of the corridor and into a functional room, dominated by a wide brown table, under which were four coloured stools, their chrome legs reflected on the shiny floor surface. The only nod to personalisation appeared to be a tall plant in a white container, which Emma felt sure was artificial. There was nothing that indicated Leah used this office day after day. There was no disarray, no clutter, unlike her own desk. Even the whiteboard that covered the far wall was spotlessly clean.

'Do you mind?' asked Emma, pointing at the row of white drawers to the left of the table.

'Go ahead. You'll only find files with details of all the people and places we use.'

Sure enough, as she drew out the top drawer, Emma spotted a fat folder marked *Catering*. She checked each drawer, to satisfy her curiosity, then turned to Jackson.

'We'll be in touch again. Thank you for your time, Mr Collins.'

He accompanied them to the entrance. As soon as the door had shut behind them, Scott said, 'I didn't like him.'

'Why not?'

'He lacked empathy. He was more upset that Leah wasn't going to be able to help him grow his sodding business than by what has happened to her.'

'We're not here to judge people.'

'Doesn't change how I feel. And how can you work with somebody for four years and know nothing about their personal life? Her friends spotted a shift in her mood in the weeks before she went missing, yet the man who valued her so much he wanted to make her a partner didn't notice a thing. He ought to have sensed something was up with her, unless he truly is wrapped up in his own business or up his own arse.'

Emma felt her eyebrows lift high. 'Wow! You really didn't like him.'

'There was something off about him. Don't tell me you didn't think the same thing?'

'Okay, I'll admit, I felt the same way. I don't know what it was about him or his answers to our questions, but I felt fobbed off.'

Scott nodded. 'We should find out a bit more about him. Maybe he was hiding something like the fact he knew Leah more intimately—'

'Stop right there, Scott. We don't make assumptions. Facts only.'

'Yeah, yeah. I don't normally jump to conclusions. It was the way he acted.'

Emma unlocked the car and got in. Scott never got riled like this. Ordinarily, he had a balanced perspective. Maybe his gut instinct was in overdrive. That said, her internal radar had picked up on something too; however, she couldn't put her finger on what it was about Jackson Collins that bothered her. When they reached the main road, it struck her. He hadn't asked for any details about Leah: where she was found, what they thought had happened to her. He hadn't wanted to know anything about her.

'I'd like to talk to those people on that list,' she said. 'You okay for time?'

'Yeah. Rae's taken the kids to their grandparents in Wales for the weekend. There's nothing spoiling at home apart from a freezer meal, a couple of cans and a night of box-set bingeing.'

'Then we'll start with the first name – Pieter Anders.'

Harriet answered Kate's call with a quiet, 'Well?'

'I'm not saying I believe you, but I am willing to investigate your claims.'

There was silence and then, 'Thank you. Thank you so much.' Harriet's voice cracked. Kate was sure she could hear a sigh of relief.

'While we're waiting for Felicity's verdict on the camera footage, I want to find your CI, Tommy Clayton. Tell me everything you can about him.' The confidential informant was the only person who could support Harriet's claims.

'I don't know much about him. I have no idea where he lives. We always met in the same place: in front of the flats, by the bin area.'

'What does he drive?'

'I don't know.'

'Was he always on foot when you met up?'

'Yes.'

'And he didn't want you to drive right up to the flats in case somebody spotted your car?'

'That's right.'

'Then maybe he lives in one of those flats.'

'I suppose so.'

'When did you first come across him?'

'It was during a drugs investigation about three years ago. You know how it works, Kate. He saw my offer to be my informant as an opportunity to stay out of prison.'

'You must have uncovered some facts about him during the time he was working for you.'

'He's a mess. He already had form before we got hold of him. Spent five years in jail for dealing when he was in his twenties. During that time, his wife ran off with one of his mates, and his mum passed away. After he came out, he tried to go straight, couldn't find employment, lost his way, and ended up getting mixed up with a gang. That's when we came in. He handed over the names and we kept him out of prison on the proviso he went to a clinic and got clean.'

'Do you believe he's stayed clean?'

'Yes, I do. He got a job with a local delivery company – Daily Drop. He's been there for about eighteen months. As far as I know, he lives alone. He's still hung up on his ex-wife, although I don't have a clue as to where she might be living.'

'Where does he get the information that he passed on to you?'

'The usual haunts. There are a few other ex-cons working for Daily Drop and he's good at listening to the chatter.'

'Have you tried speaking to his boss?'

'It's impossible to get hold of anyone when you aren't allowed to leave your house. Like many logistic companies, you go online to arrange a drop-off or pick-up. I couldn't exactly leave a message for him, not with other ex-cons working there. If word got back to those people he snitched on, well, I don't need to tell you of the consequences.'

'Okay, I'll start there.'

'Hey, hang on a minute. Didn't you hear what I just said? If anyone puts two and two together and works out he's an informant, he'll be dead meat. You can't march in and wave your warrant card about.'

'If your theory holds water, he's already dead. Don't worry, I'll treat it as a missing persons investigation. I'll say a girlfriend is worried about him.'

Harriet fell quiet again for a moment. Kate imagined her clenching her jaw, as she often did when she wasn't happy about something. 'Okay,' came the reply. 'For the record, his ex is called Casey. Just in case you need her name.'

'I'll catch up with you again when I have something to report.'

A sigh. 'Thank you. It's been so . . . damn lonely. I truly appreciate having somebody on my side.'

'I'm only checking up on facts, Harriet. Don't think I'll be going easy on you until I'm sure what you've told me is proven. And if you've been playing me, I'll make sure you regret it for the rest of your life and beyond.'

She hung up. The office felt claustrophobic. Getting to her feet, Kate opened the door and stood in the corridor, listening to the sounds of the building. It was after five and there was noise associated with the general exodus as some shifts ended and new ones began.

She loved this place, where her father had worked before her. What would he have made of all of this? The answer was simple. He would have done everything in his power to ensure William's murderer was caught. She owed him that much. And William too. She owed Harriet Khatri nothing; nevertheless, as a fair, unbiased police officer, she would afford Harriet the courtesy of chasing up on her supposed alibi for the afternoon that Kate was imprisoned in the warehouse in Fenton.

The front door banged shut, and for a moment there were no sounds of voices and footsteps. She spun on her heel and returned to her desk. She wanted Daily Drop's opening hours. She needed to get her teeth into this, if only to prove Harriet was no more than a convincing liar.

'Stay focused,' said William's voice as she threw herself into his old leather chair. *'More haste and less speed.'*

She was about to agree with him when she was sure she could hear Dickson's mocking laugh and a whispered, *'You old fool!'*

The bastard of a fence has stitched him up. The Cartier watch is worth far more than the five hundred pounds he's begrudgingly handed over, rather than the promised one thousand, and they both know it. However, it won't pay to argue the toss about it. He'll need the shitbag's help again soon enough to move more stuff on, and it's best if he comes across as subservient and grateful. It's taken every ounce of self-control to stop himself from booting the guy in the throat and then smashing his fists into the little prick's face over and over until he hands him what the watch is really worth, but there's the bigger picture to consider. This time, he has reined in the anger. He doesn't always manage to.

He sips his fruit juice and looks around the café. Most of his victims have been selected in places like this one. Sitting quietly, with his head bent over his phone, nobody could suspect that he is observing every person who comes through the door. He wears the cloak of invisibility he adopted from an early age. Invisible people can do anything they want without getting caught.

He had selected his next target while he was in this café, at the same table where he is now sitting. She had dark-brown hair and expressive eyes, and he watched her while she chatted animatedly to a friend. It wasn't her looks that drew him to her but the leather designer handbag on the floor beside her and the large sparkling ring on her wedding finger.

He checks the time. It's twenty past five. In another ten minutes, she'll be locking the front door to Property Plus, the sales and letting agency where she works as the manager, and where she is always the last to leave. He glances outside to the dark street. The cold weather has sent most of the usual Saturday shoppers home, and the pub-goers have not yet come out. It's a perfect night to do it.

He finishes his drink, clears away his tray, ensuring all the rubbish is dropped into the bin, and leaves without attracting any attention.

He slips out into the chilly night. Digging his hands deep into his coat pockets, he feels for the Ziploc. The bag contains the magic powder that will make this mission a success. Known as Devil's Breath, it's a powerful hypnotic drug that instantly reduces its victims to a zombified state: conscious but helpless.

He first learned about the compound – scopolamine, a plant-based psychoactive alkaloid – a few years ago in a pub when he overheard a couple of Australian backpackers regaling two young women with tales of their recent travels. He had been irritated by their loud voices and was about to leave when one of them mentioned fellow backpackers who'd become victims of robbers and rapists, their drinks having been spiked with the drug. These hapless souls became highly suggestible to whatever others told them and handed over their money, valuables and even the PINs of their credit cards. Moreover, later, they had no memory of what had befallen them.

It sounded far-fetched, so he googled it, discovering news reports of people being robbed blind thanks to the effects of this odourless and tasteless yet potent drug: marched to cash machines where they drew out large sums of money, which they willingly handed to their attacker. A plan began to take shape in his mind. This was way better than breaking into people's houses to steal goods to sell. It was far less risky.

He found Devil's Breath for sale on the dark web. After several risky attempts to spike drinks, he changed tack. This powder was so powerful he could gently blow it into a victim's face, and it would have the same, immediate effect.

In the next half an hour, the estate agent will become his obedient slave.

CHAPTER TEN

Leah's co-workers Pieter and Adam both had cast-iron alibis for the night she disappeared. They seemed to know very little about their colleague, offering no more insight than Emma and Scott had already gleaned from their boss, Jackson. Emma was hoping that the third person on the list would prove more helpful.

Zac Kendal wrapped sinewy arms around his slim frame, clamping his hands under his armpits as he shifted on the dining-room chair. Emma had allowed Scott to take the lead on this interview, preferring to observe the man's body language rather than ask questions. Given that Zac matched the description that the barber had given of Leah's companion, she was on the alert for any giveaway or tell that might indicate he knew more than he was willing to share.

He'd seemed nervous from the off, when he'd invited her and Scott inside, instantly tightening one hand around his other upper arm before leading the way into the lounge that doubled as a dining room. Steam rose from the mug of tea in front of him and she watched it spiral until he was ready to answer Scott, who had asked him how well he had got on with Leah.

Zac drew a breath and began to speak. 'We got on well. She was kind to me after my partner of seven years walked out on me. She was the only person at work to notice how upset I was and ask if I was okay. She invited me out after work for a drink. She just . . . listened while I opened up about everything: my girlfriend's cheating, the lies, how I was right royally mugged off. She was very understanding and sympathetic. Afterwards, she checked in on me almost daily. We went straight from work to the pub at least once a week for a couple of months before she said we had to stop because she didn't want Russell to find out and get the wrong idea.'

Emma wondered if that was true or if Leah had been trying to fob him off with an excuse. Zac struck her as the clingy sort.

'I was in a bad place after my partner left me. Leah helped me through the worst of it. I didn't have any friends who I could talk to. All the people I knew and socialised with are Michaela's friends too. They sided with her and ghosted me.'

'When did Leah tell you she could no longer see you after work?'

'A month ago.'

Emma calculated that Leah was pregnant by then and wondered if Zac might be the father. She didn't interrupt, allowing Scott to take things at his own pace.

'But you remained friends?'

'We had the odd chat at work, but it was mega busy in the lead-up to Christmas and the New Year, so we didn't get many opportunities to have a proper heart-to-heart.'

'Did Leah talk to you about her home life?'

'Yes. She was having difficulties too, which was why she was able to relate to what I was going through. She felt a bit trapped at times. Russell was . . . controlling.'

'In what way?' asked Scott.

'Russell wanted her all to himself, hated it when she went out with friends, and was putting pressure on her to leave Harlequin to go into business with him. She couldn't find the courage to tell him that she didn't want to.'

Scott cocked his head. 'Did she explain why she felt that way?'

'No. I don't understand why she didn't just tell him from the start that she didn't want to go ahead. Reading between the lines, I think she was afraid of him. I told her to have it out with him. I remember she just chewed her lip and then mumbled she would try to. After that, she wouldn't discuss the matter with me, and the subject didn't crop up again until two days before she went missing. We were going over some planning together and she suddenly mentioned she'd let the situation drag on far too long, that Russell was heaping on the pressure for her to hand in her notice. He even wanted her to poach several of our clients to get their venture started, which didn't sit well at all. To cap it all, Jackson had invited her to become his business partner, so she was going to have it out with Russell over the weekend. I never saw her again.'

He hung his head and sniffed.

'I'm going to be frank, sir. I hope you don't mind me asking, but did you and Leah have consensual sex with each other?'

Zac shook his head immediately but didn't look up.

'Not even a one-night stand?'

'No.'

'And again, my apologies, but I have to ask you where you were the evening of the sixth of January?'

'At home. Alone. And before you ask, there's nobody who can confirm that. I was watching catch-up television.'

'Can you remember what you were watching?'

'Not really. I drank a fair amount and was a bit out of it.' He looked up at last. His eyes weren't damp, but his voice cracked when he asked, 'Is that everything?'

'Almost done, sir. Do you happen to know if Leah was seeing somebody else?'

'Not that I know of. Besides, Russell checked up on her activities. That was why she ended our friendly after-work sessions.'

He rubbed a hand over his chin as he spoke, a sure sign to Emma that he was still nervous.

'Mr Kendal,' she said, ensuring she had his attention. 'When did your partner leave you?'

'Last October. October the thirteenth. Friday the thirteenth.'

'And you struck up a friendship with Leah the following week?'

'Yes.'

'Prior to that, how would you describe your relationship with Leah?'

'Workmates. Colleagues . . . nothing more.'

'Thank you, sir. That's all I needed to ask.'

Zac looked from Emma to Scott. 'Is that everything?'

'Yes, thank you for your time.'

'You will find whoever killed her, won't you?'

'We will do our utmost, sir,' said Scott, getting to his feet and placing a business card on the table in front of Zac. 'Don't get up. We'll see ourselves out. If you think of anything else that might help us, please ring us. Our number is on the card.'

Scott waited until they were back in the squad car before asking Emma why she had asked the questions she had.

'To observe his reaction. He was nervous as hell throughout that interview. When you asked him about having sex with Leah, he kept his head down, but his throat flushed. The same thing happened when I quizzed him. He might be lying about his relationship with Leah. There's a photo of Zac on Harlequin's website. Take a screen grab and ask that barber to look at it. See if he recognises him.'

'Will do.'

She fell silent, letting her mind digest the information she'd gleaned this evening. The car drew up in front of traffic lights where a moped repeatedly revved its engine, a large blue delivery bag slung over the driver's shoulders. She paid it scant attention, her mind elsewhere. The information didn't add up. According to Russell, Leah was excited about their new venture. If Jackson was to be believed, she had wanted to accept the offered promotion. Zac had confirmed Jackson's version of events, adding that Leah had intended telling Russell about her decision over the weekend. Why would Leah accept a promotion to become Jackson's business partner yet allow her husband to believe they were going to set up a new venture together, especially as she was expecting a child? Moreover, Leah didn't seem to have told either man about the pregnancy. The lights changed and the moped whined off at speed.

'I'd like us to talk to Russell again first thing tomorrow,' said Emma. 'I want to get his take on this mysterious man that Leah was with. But I also think we need to get a better feel for their relationship.'

'Given most femicides are committed by partners or ex-partners, I agree,' said Scott. 'I'd like to dig into Jackson Collins's background too.'

'Good thinking. And we really need to chase up Leah's doctor. It would help to know if she'd discussed options with the doctor and if she'd been considering an abortion.'

'I'll get on to that first—'

He was interrupted by a phone call. Frankie's voice was loud through the speaker.

'I'm ringing just to report that, so far, I've not spoken to anyone else who might have spotted Leah with the tall athletic man. Some of the staff who were on shift the night she went missing aren't working tonight. I thought I'd try again tomorrow.'

'No problem. It's time we all called it a day anyway.'

'I'll see you in the morning, then.'

'Night, Frankie.' Emma turned towards Scott. 'The same goes for us. We're done for today. Would you mind dropping me off at home?'

He answered with a nod and as they drove towards Morgan's house she mentally went through her plan of action for the following day. She started when the phone rang again. This time, it was Rachid, one of the tech assistants.

'We've found some CCTV footage from Weston Road that might be of interest to you. Shall I email it to you?'

'Please.'

She heard typing, then, 'There . . . done.'

'Cheers, Rachid. I'll speak to you later.'

'Could you make that tomorrow, Emma? I was supposed to go off duty at five. My wife sent a text ten minutes ago to say if I don't get home soon, my dinner will be in the dog.'

Emma couldn't help but smile. 'Get home before the pooch scoffs it. I'll talk to you in the morning.'

'Will do. Night.'

Scott kept his eyes on the road while she downloaded the video clip. 'Is it Leah?' he asked.

'It's her. She's with somebody. Looks a bit worse for wear – drunk, I'd imagine. She's staggering.' She studied the video again.

'Is she with the same athletic-looking man?'

'No, she isn't. She's with some hooded figure. I can't make out their face at all. That's strange. What time did the barber see the couple cross the bridge?'

'Eight-ish.'

Emma made an uh-uhm sound before speaking again. 'This footage was taken an hour and a half later. Nine thirty-five, to be exact.'

'She was with a different man?'

'Can't be sure who she is with. It could be the same person, except he's wearing a hooded top instead of a jacket. I'll ask Rachid if the images can be enhanced. Like everything else, it will all have to wait until morning.'

She stared out at the empty streets. She could really do with puzzling over this investigation in peace, in her own space, not be returning home to Morgan. Yet again she wished they were working on this case together. As it was, she would have to set it aside, be the dutiful girlfriend and ensure they talked about anything unconnected to work. Morgan wouldn't want to hear about her day or her theories. Not for the first time, she wondered if their relationship could survive this career step up both of them were taking.

'Penny for them?' asked Scott.

'How do you manage to push work aside when you go home?'

'Easy. I have noisy, demanding children who all want "Daddy time" as soon as I walk through the front door. There's no chance of thinking about anything else when there's bath times to sort out and stories to be read.'

The idea of finding herself in a similar domestic situation horrified Emma. She simply wasn't the maternal sort. Her own upbringing had made sure of that – a house full of brawling, testosterone-fuelled brothers and a mother who had scant interest in her only daughter. Given she wasn't a great cook or, indeed, a homemaker, Emma was beginning to wonder if she was relationship material at all. She wasn't even especially tidy, which was the opposite of Morgan, who appeared to be extremely fussy when it came to his home.

She searched her heart, acknowledging that tonight she didn't want to sit down in front of the television with Morgan, hastily prepared food on trays on their laps. Nor did she want to listen to him bleat on about DI Rind. In truth, she didn't want to even go home. She would rather return to the office and go through everything she had learned so far in this investigation. She wanted to prove her worth, establish what had happened to Leah and bring her killer to justice. For a moment, she considered telling Scott she had changed her mind and to drop her back at the station instead, before deciding she had to face facts – she'd chosen to move in with Morgan and if she wanted their relationship to succeed, she would have to work at it, not shove it on the back burner.

The decision made, she once again looked out of the window and wondered why, as they got closer to Morgan's home – no, *their* home – the sinking feeling in her stomach was becoming stronger.

CHAPTER ELEVEN

Emma chugged the bottle of water purchased from the vending machine at work. Although there had been no arguments the evening before, Morgan had been quiet rather than sulky, spending the evening engrossed in *Avengers: Endgame* – a film that lasted a little over three hours – during which time he barely spoke to her. She'd wondered if he'd deliberately streamed it so he wouldn't have to talk to her, and had even asked at one point if everything was alright, only to see confusion in his eyes at why she would even ask the question. He'd replied that of course everything was okay and smiled, but the distraction remained, and so she in turn had given up making any attempt to converse, turning her thoughts to the investigation.

This morning, his enthusiasm appeared to have been reignited. She'd woken very early and while staring into the dark, alone with her thoughts, heard him shift then get up . . .

'You're an early bird,' says Emma.

'Oh hey! Sorry, I was trying not to disturb you.'

'You didn't. I was already awake.'

The bed sinks with his weight as he drops down on to it, leans over and kisses her briefly.

'Somebody's in a good mood,' she says, after he breaks away.

'Got a call overnight. There's to be a morning briefing and a dawn raid. Looks like we have another strong lead. We need this, Emma. We've been grinding along, getting nowhere for too long. The whole team is flagging and demoralised, not just me. This could potentially be the pick-me-up we all need. So, as much as I'd like to climb back under the duvet with you, I'd better go.'

He rolls away, turns on the bedside light and she watches him while he chooses a fresh shirt from those hanging in his wardrobe. When he turns back, he spies her watching him. 'You look very sexy first thing in the morning. Too sexy, in fact. Now I'll have to have a cold shower.'

'Want me to join you?'

He groans and then smiles. 'No, and now it'll have to be a very cold and short shower.'

'My car's at work. Can I go in with you?'

'You do know it's only just after five, don't you? If I were you, I'd go back to sleep.'

She's thrown by the change in his tone that suggests he isn't happy about this request. All the same, she continues, 'I have stuff to do. I'd rather work in peace in the office than hang around here and catch an Uber in a couple of hours.'

'I have to be off in fifteen minutes, so get a move on.'

That same tone – slightly exasperated. Doubts as to why he's irritated creep in.

She calls out, 'I'll be ready.'

The shower bursts into life, the sound of water splashing against the cubicle walls drowning out any reply.

Surely these mood swings are down to work stress, and not anything to do with her? With that in mind, she throws back the duvet and scurries to get ready. She's reading too much into the situation and shouldn't be wasting time worrying about it. Morgan is immersed in Operation Moonbeam and focusing on the raid, while she has her own important case to handle. Nevertheless, as the water is turned off and *the cubicle door is shut with such force it clatters, she can't shake the feeling something is awry.*

Emma unwrapped an energy bar and took a large bite while reading through her list of suspects. She had considered the possibility that the killer used Leah's credit card after her death purely to give the impression that she was still alive, yet the items purchased were an anomaly: a laptop, a watch and a mobile phone. Moreover, that person had maxed out on the card. It would have been more plausible if they'd made smaller purchases, items that would have suggested Leah had left home and was setting up a new life.

'Morning, Emma.'

Kate's arrival took Emma by surprise. She pushed the fruit and nut bar to one side.

'Morning. You're in early.'

'I could say the same of you,' Kate replied. 'Any updates for me?'

'Nothing significant yet, although I need to talk to a couple of people again. There are some things that feel . . . off.'

Kate threw her a smile. 'Trust your instinct.'

Emma nodded. 'I'm going to speak to Leah's husband this morning. I don't think their relationship was as rosy as he led us to believe.'

'You need anything?'

'Only a break so we can nail the fucker that killed her.'

Kate put a hand on her colleague's shoulder. 'Stick at it and that'll happen. I'm going into the briefing room. There's been a development in Operation Moonbeam, although I'm sure you already know about it.' She gave Emma a gentle pat and left.

Emma read through her notes again to ensure she wasn't missing anything. She had a lot to prove, and she couldn't afford to stuff this up.

♦ ♦ ♦

Kate strode up the corridor towards the briefing room. DI Ali Rind had rung her in the early hours to inform her that he'd received an anonymous tip-off. It came as no surprise that this amazing breakthrough had occurred only hours after Morgan had voiced concerns about a mole on the team. She'd put nothing past the syndicate and was sure this had been arranged so Kate wouldn't follow up Morgan's allegations.

Ali's team was assembled, all with determined looks on their faces. Ali himself was in front of a wide screen on which was a map of an area of Stoke-on-Trent known as Pitts Hill, Tunstall. Ali acknowledged her with a nod and continued, while she stood with her back against the door.

'Our informant says that they believe a group of men who are trafficking individuals are currently residing in this house on Sparrow Street.' A pointer indicated the property. 'Once they are apprehended and taken into custody, the informant is willing to testify against them.'

'How can we trust this person, sir?' The question came from DS Trevor Wray. Kate eyed him cautiously. She wasn't sure about Trevor's own trustworthiness, especially as he had willingly passed sensitive information regarding a sting operation to one of her own team: DS Jamie Webster. Having leaked the information, Trevor had been the first person to get uppity when the operation failed. He was a fine one to talk about trust. She noted that Trevor was sitting next to Jamie, who nodded enthusiastically at this question.

'I've every reason to believe they are being upfront. This source admits to being an illegal who, in exchange for this information, hopes to attain legal status in this country,' said Ali.

Trevor leant closer to Jamie and held a brief whispered conversation with him, after which Jamie spoke up. 'But, sir, we can't promise the source that, can we?'

'I haven't discussed the matter yet with the authorities, but as I said, they *hope* to attain legal status. No promises or assurances have been made,' said Ali.

Kate maintained a poker face even though she was sorely tempted to dress down Ali. How dare he go ahead without discussing the matter with her first. This could blow up in their faces if the informant didn't get what they wanted. Not to mention the fact that it was placing her in a very awkward position. She spotted Morgan at the back of the room, leaning against the wall. Judging by his set expression, this wasn't washing with him either.

She glanced back at Jamie and Trevor, both in whispered conversation again. They broke off the moment Ali spoke. He set out the plan of action, with four teams approaching the house from every direction, ensuring there could be no escape route.

'Team Alpha, you will wait in front of the fish and chip shop on the corner of Sparrow Street.'

The mention of the Greek alphabet letter set Kate thinking again about the syndicate, and who in this room might be the mole. Given he had been loose-lipped in the past, Trevor was an obvious suspect. The other person she still had doubts about was Jamie. The fact the pair were so chummy rang alarm bells. Could they be in league? A quiet voice in her head whispered, *'Still can't work it out, can you? And you never will.'*

Dickson was back. Damn him. She silenced his words by dragging her attention back to Ali, who'd almost finished the briefing.

'Once in position, you will await the command *Go, go, go!* then proceed to the property. Everybody clear?'

There was a chorus of 'Yes, sir'.

'Okay, get kitted up and we'll convene in the car park.'

Jamie and Trevor were the first to get to their feet. Passing her, Jamie acknowledged her with a nod and a courteous 'Morning, boss'. She responded with a greeting and, dodging a trio of exiting officers, made her way to Ali.

'A word, DI Rind,' she said.

She waited until the room had cleared before speaking. 'You should have run everything past me.'

'It was the middle of the night and I had to make a decision there and then. There was no choice other than to give my informant an assurance, or he wouldn't have talked.'

'All the same, you should have brought it up before this meeting. There's no guarantee we can arrange a visa.'

'It's been done before,' he said, holding her gaze. 'What about the prostitute who was willing to testify against Superintendent Dickson?'

She held her tongue. William Chase had pulled a huge number of strings to prevent the young sex-worker, Stanka, from being deported. The girl had helped them to find a small group of human traffickers and to bring down Dickson.

Kate had never asked William how he'd managed it, but Stanka was now no longer on the streets and was living a normal life in Staffordshire.

Dickson's quiet voice made the hairs on her neck stand up. *She did more than that, didn't she, Kate? She lied about who had killed me. She saved your neck.*

She didn't flinch and kept her eyes on Ali. 'As I said, there are no guarantees.'

'I have to go,' he said.

Kate stepped aside without a word. The battle lines had been drawn. If DI Ali Rind had a problem with her, she didn't care. She had her concerns about his handling of the investigation that she would discuss with him later.

◆ ◆ ◆

Emma sorted through the photographs, pulling out one of Russell and setting it next to a screen grab of the hooded figure who'd been captured on CCTV alongside Leah. Russell was about the same height and build as that person but so was Leah's co-worker, Zac.

Then, for the umpteenth time, she turned her attention to the goods purchased using Leah's card. Not only did the choice of items continue to puzzle her, it also seemed unlikely that they would still be in the killer's possession. They'd have been dumped or sold as soon as an opportunity presented itself. None of this was making sense. If the credit card hadn't been used to lend weight to the theory that Leah was still alive, then maybe the woman had been a victim of a robbery with violence after all. Then again, if that were the case, where did the man arguing with her, and the hooded person who had helped her along the street, come into the equation?

Exasperated by her own thoughts and lack of clarity, she rang the tech department. Felicity Jolly picked up, her voice loud and cheerful as she greeted Emma.

Once the initial exchanges were over, Emma asked, 'I'm trying to make sense of something. Did MisPers request footage from ATM machines during their investigation into Leah's disappearance?'

'They did and, as I recall, we obtained a clear shot of her face. At the time, she made a withdrawal of three hundred pounds.'

'That's the maximum amount somebody can take out in one day, isn't it?'

'To my knowledge. I generally don't carry cash.'

'Me neither. Who does any more?' Felicity's words had set her thinking again. 'Thanks, Felicity, I'll badger them for the photo.'

'You haven't got the case files?'

'They're dragging their heels, although, to be fair, this is only day two of the investigation.'

'Hopefully they'll send them over today. Anything else I can do?'

'No, you've been helpful enough. Is Rachid in yet?'

'Bit too early for him. Want me to tell him you're after him?'

'No, I'll catch up with him later. I wanted to ask him if he could enhance the video that he emailed me yesterday.'

'I'll ask him for you.'

Placing the phone back on her desk, she mused over what was rapidly becoming a muddied picture. Leah might have withdrawn cash so that she left no credit or debit card trace.

Another possibility was that she'd taken it out to pay off somebody – the hooded figure or even the athletic man. Or there was a third possibility. That somebody seeing her withdraw the money robbed her of it, along with her valuables. The Missing Person's file would show the exact time of Leah's cash withdrawal, which in turn would help provide them with a timeline. She rushed off an email to the Missing Persons department, requesting it be sent immediately.

She pressed 'Send' and sat back, hoping somebody in the department would get a wriggle on. If not, she'd ask Kate to kick their arses. At that moment, Scott came in.

'I stopped off at the barber's on my way here. He didn't recognise her co-worker, Zac, as Leah's companion that night. I showed him a photo of Russell too, but it was a no-go,' he said.

'I'm still not going to eliminate Russell from our inquiries. We've yet to establish the identity of the person in the hooded top, and it could be him as much as anyone else. I've been wondering why Leah withdrew three hundred pounds in cash. It might have been for one of the men she was spotted with.'

'Blackmail?'

'Anything's possible at this stage.'

She'd hardly finished speaking when Frankie turned up, pink-cheeked and out of breath.

'Traffic was dreadful. I thought I was going to be late.'

Scott looked up at the clock. 'Bang on time, Frankie. As usual.'

Frankie released the bicycle clips from the bottom of her trousers with a flourish before plonking them, along with a pink helmet, on top of the filing cabinet near her desk. She shrugged off a matching backpack and placed it beside her chair. 'I've got some contact numbers for staff who were on duty the night Leah disappeared. I thought I'd ring them rather than wait until this evening to speak to them.'

Emma was pleased the girl had used her initiative. It would speed things up.

'Oh, and Emma, would you like me to talk to Leah's doctor? She'd already left when I rang the health centre yesterday. I spoke to Nola, one of the practice nurses, instead. She told me Leah had an appointment only a few days before she disappeared, on . . . hang on . . .' She took a notepad from her backpack and flicked through the pages. 'January the third. After the appointment, she spotted Leah crying in the corridor. Before Nola could talk to her, Leah hightailed it out of the place.'

Kate got the best results from people through encouragement and praise. Emma could do worse than abide by that example. 'Good work. I'll let you follow that up,' she said. Frankie gave her a bright smile.

The other members of her team turned up soon afterwards. DC Harry Ling was technologically minded enough to have been an asset to Felicity's tech unit, while DC George Younger – fresh-faced and keen – was so quiet she often forgot he was in the same room.

Emma greeted them and then – like Kate used to do – stood quietly to ensure she had everyone's attention before she began the briefing. Once all eyes were on her, she pulled out sheets of A4, passing one to each of her colleagues. 'Okay then, this is our plan of action for today. I've put initials beside the tasks in hand. I think everything is self-explanatory.'

She gave them all a moment to check the lists.

'Any questions?'

George and Harry shook their heads.

'All clear,' said Frankie.

'As a bell,' added Scott.

'Great! Then let's make some good progress today. We've got this, people.'

Rousing speech over, Emma grabbed her bag and keys. She was going to take Kate's advice and trust her gut over this. Russell was hiding something, and she was determined to shake it out of him.

He walks into the petrol station, stopping in his tracks as soon as he spots the front-page headline on a copy of the *Gazette*: 'Woman Found Buried on Building Site.' He picks up a copy of the paper from the stand, shoves it under his arm and joins the queue to pay.

He blinks away images of the night he buried Leah hastily in what he believed was wasteland. He lines up behind a wide man in overalls who requests several scratch cards along with his fuel bill; all the while, the pictures continue to flicker. He hadn't intended killing the woman. Then again, he never does. He usually blows what he considers to be sufficient Devil's Breath into his subject's face to make them lose control. After a visit to a cashpoint machine where they willingly withdraw money for him, and give up their PINs, he takes them elsewhere, where he abandons them, woozy and confused, unable to recall what's happened. Sometimes it goes wrong. That particular night had gone according to plan right up until he decided to rape Leah.

'Thirty-eight pounds, please!'

He looks up. The cashier throws him an exasperated look.

'Sorry, mate. I was miles away.' He hands over the cash and pushes the newspaper over the counter. He leaves with his head lowered, annoyed that he's drawn attention to himself – something he usually avoids at all costs.

Back in his car, he scans the article and swears. He should have left Leah's body somewhere else altogether. If only he hadn't tried to fuck her.

He pulls off the forecourt, his mind whirring. Yes, he's made a mistake, but it'll be okay. After all, there have been other *mistakes*, but so far none that have caused the police to beat a path to his door. He controls his breathing, reminding himself he's a pro. This setback isn't important.

So what if the police have uncovered a body. Big deal. Their hunt for him will be akin to searching for a polar bear in a snowstorm. Plus, they'll never prove he was guilty of Leah's death.

He's done his research. Scopolamine is only detectable in bodily fluids for a short period, hours not days, so it won't be identified, especially in a corpse that's been buried for three weeks. No problems. Except for the fact they'll soon discover another one of his mistakes. Will they link the two deaths? Nah! He'll be safe. There's nothing to connect the two women to each other or to him.

The tension in his shoulders begins to melt away. It doesn't even matter if the cops unearth all his victims. He's invisible. He also has the upper hand. He knows exactly who is looking for him. The newspaper article came with a photo of the very officers in charge of the investigation: DCI Kate Young and DI Emma Donaldson.

He knows Emma. Very well. He smiles at the thought.

He's sorely tempted to spin this situation around.

It might be fun for the hunted to become the hunter.

CHAPTER TWELVE

A wild-eyed Russell opened the door to Emma and Scott. He looked from one officer to the other before stuttering, 'Have you . . . have you found whoever killed her?'

'Could we come inside for a few minutes?' said Emma.

He shuffled aside to let them in. Emma detected the unique musky scent of cannabis, the distinctive smell produced within the plant by compounds known as terpenes.

'You know the way,' he said, indicating they should head for the lounge. Emma caught a movement as he reached for another door handle, quickly pulling it to – but not before she spied unwashed crockery and discarded cardboard takeaway boxes strewn over kitchen work surfaces.

Russell bent to remove an empty vodka bottle perched on top of the coffee-table books, before falling backwards on to the settee with a sigh. 'Had a heavy night. You can understand why. So, have you? Found the bastard that killed my wife?'

'I'm afraid it's still early days,' said Emma.

'Course it is. Too fucking soon. He's probably fucked off miles away by now anyway.' He waved his hand as if dismissing them both. It didn't take a genius to work out that he was under the influence of drink and probably drugs. All the same, Emma intended quizzing him.

'We have some more questions for you.'

He straightened up, still holding the bottle in his hand. 'Fire away.'

'You might want to put that down,' said Emma, indicating the bottle.

'Oh yes.' He cast about before placing it on the carpet, then looked up at Emma. 'I'm ready.'

'Did Leah mention that Jackson had offered to make her his business partner?'

'No.' He gave a tight smile. 'Next question.'

'Did she voice any concerns to you about going into business with you?'

'What are you talking about?'

'We understand she was getting cold feet about starting up a new venture.'

He shook his head slowly. 'Nope. That's crazy. She was excited. We both were. We'd begun planning. The website is under construction.'

'Russell, we've heard from her work colleagues and friends, who have all told us that she wasn't keen. She'd accepted a promotion at Harlequin.'

He shook his head again but said nothing.

Scott took over from Emma, his voice smooth and calming.

'We've been hearing the same story over and over. She didn't want to leave Harlequin.'

'Okay, she maybe had a few concerns, but we talked them through. And she was willing to take a chance on us.'

'When did you have this heart-to-heart?'

He blinked several times before saying, 'The day she disappeared.'

Emma stepped in. 'Last time we spoke, you said the argument was about her going out. Are you now saying it was about the business venture?'

'We'd been discussing the whole business venture thing when she stormed off and said she was going out.'

'Russell, were you discussing this venture or arguing about it?' asked Emma.

He sighed again. 'A bit of both. She kept putting up negatives. But she *was* coming back around to the idea. Before she buggered off out.'

'Then, given you were arguing about it, I'll ask you again: did she mention becoming a partner at Harlequin?'

'She floated the idea.' He dropped his gaze.

'Did she tell you?'

'Yes . . . No . . . Not as such. She mentioned she'd be tempted to stay if she was offered a partnership. She didn't say that Jackson had already spoken to her about it.' He rubbed the back of his neck and sighed. 'Look, what does it matter what we were rowing about? The fact is, she went out and never came back. Since then, I've hardly slept and now . . . Now I wish we'd sorted it out and she'd stayed at home that evening.'

'I realise this is difficult for you,' said Emma, 'but we need to ask you, what did you do after she left that evening?'

'I got drunk. I stayed in and got hammered.' His eyes filled. 'The drink doesn't help. Nothing helps.'

'We believe Leah was in the company of another man the evening she went missing. Someone described as athletic, about six foot, with facial hair. Does that description ring any bells?'

'A man?' Russell's jaw slackened.

'Do you recognise that description?'

'That could be anyone. Christ, even I fit that bill!'

'Did you have any reason to suspect Leah might have been seeing somebody?' asked Emma.

'A lover? You think Leah might have been having an affair?'

'We don't know anything about her—'

He pointed his finger at Emma and raised his voice. 'No . . . you don't! You know nothing. She wouldn't cheat on me. Not Leah.'

'Sir, please remain calm,' said Scott. 'We're only doing our job. Leah was spotted having an altercation with a man in Mill Bank.'

'Then is he the person who attacked her?'

'We don't know. We're trying to identify him.'

He shifted to the front of the cushion, felt for a tissue in his jeans pocket and blew his nose. 'If he's the one, I want him caught and banged up for life.'

Emma decided to go for the big one. 'I realise this is sensitive, but had you and Leah been trying for a baby?'

His eyes opened wide. 'Are you joking? We had a business to build up. There was no room for children in our lives. Besides, Leah didn't want kids any more than me.'

'Did you practise safe sex?'

He leant forward. 'Really? You're asking very personal questions. Why?'

'I'm sorry to inform you that your wife was approximately twelve weeks pregnant.'

Russell's mouth dropped open. His face turned a shade of pale grey and he shot to his feet, hand over his mouth. He was out of the room and down the hallway before they could say any more. The sound of retching reached them.

'I guess he didn't know,' said Scott.

'Don't bet on it. He could be playing us. We'll try him again when he hasn't been puffing weed and downing vodka.'

◆ ◆ ◆

The noisy conversation and boisterous shouts indicated that Ali's team was back. Kate didn't have to wait long before Ali himself appeared at her open doorway. 'We got two of the fuckers!'

'That's excellent.'

'We're processing them downstairs and then it'll be a waiting game until their lawyers show up. You still want to speak to me?'

His manner was slightly too cocky for her liking. However, she put it down to the fact he was undoubtedly pleased with the outcome of the raid. After several months of dead ends and far too many man hours to count, they'd got a result. There was every chance one or both suspects could give them further information, even disclose the identity of the officer who'd been protecting them. It was important to give the man and his team the back-slapping glory they deserved, yet the fact remained that it had been a tip-off that had steered them in the right direction, and one given in exchange for a promise that couldn't be fulfilled. She prepared to pass on the news that would come as a disappointment to him.

'First off, congratulations on your result.' She allowed him a moment to digest the praise before continuing with, 'Unfortunately, I've spoken to the chief constable and I'm sorry to report that he isn't in favour of rewarding your source with a visa.'

'Oh, come on, Kate! Thanks to the informant, we've caught two fucking traffickers who are high up the chain of command. It's not a lot to ask. You can arrange one poxy visa. They're not asking for a king's ransom or something that would be impossible to supply. Surely you can swing it?'

'It wasn't my decision to make. If you want to take it up with anybody, take it up with Chief Constable Atwell.'

Ali's nostrils flared. 'Yeah, right. I can imagine how hard you pleaded on my behalf. This is personal, isn't it? You were pissed at me for not talking to you about this visa before the meeting and now . . .'

'That'll do, DI Rind,' she said sharply. 'I suggest you stop before you say something you might regret.'

'No. I'll have my say. You had it in for me because I didn't run this past you first. It's nothing more than sour grapes.'

'I said, that will do! If you want to put forward your request yourself, then do so. It is out of my hands.'

He glared fiercely at her and hissed, 'I bet DCI Chase pulled out all the stops for you, his blue-eyed protégée, when you asked for something similar for your witness. That girl. What was her name? Stanka?'

'Out, Ali. Now!'

He thumped the doorway and stormed off, leaving Kate rattled. It wasn't that she feared the man or was even bothered by the fact he'd go to the chief constable. She'd been perfectly honest when she'd told Ali that she had pleaded his case. Chief Constable Atwell had refused point-blank to entertain the idea. What perturbed her was what Ali might uncover should he probe into the whole business with Stanka. Stanka had not only given damning evidence against Superintendent John Dickson, but she had also provided a solid statement claiming that her pimp, Farai, had killed Dickson. She had stuck to her story many times during interviews. Stanka had lied to protect Kate and now it was best if the girl's name did not come up again or her right to remain in the UK become challenged.

'It's going to unravel,' said Dickson's voice.

Her hands began to tremble. If Ali caused ructions, somebody might start asking questions about the girl, which in turn could lead back to what really happened to Dickson.

'Take a breath. Ali's annoyed. That's all. He'll soon be wrapped up in interviews and up to his neck in paperwork. He'll simmer down.' William's gentle tone was welcome, and keeping him in her mind helped prevent Dickson's voice from taking over. *'The chief constable won't entertain him if he goes off on one in front of him or listen to him if he starts shouting about visas.'*

She took comfort from William's words. Ali was unlikely to broach the subject with anyone senior.

'We'll have to see about that, won't we?' whispered Dickson.

Emma rubbed her temples. Progress was too slow for her liking. Even using the latest software, Rachid had been unable to clean up the video footage of Leah and the hooded figure. Doctor Schmidt had been called away on an emergency and hadn't returned to the health centre, and the file still hadn't arrived from Missing Persons.

Emma's desire to get results had been amplified, thanks to Operation Moonbeam's recent success. If Kate was leading this investigation, she'd set aside her mental fatigue and disappointments. She'd be considering new angles, hunting for fresh leads or going back over what they'd already uncovered. Emma wondered if she should consider retracing old steps.

'Wish those noisy fuckers would calm down,' muttered Frankie as feet clattered up the stairs and somebody shouted congratulations.

'We'll be the same when we crack this case,' said Scott.

'I hardly think so. We're far more restrained,' she replied. 'Can't imagine George and Harry yelling like that.' She grinned at Harry, who gave her the finger without turning around. 'Although I'll defo let my hair down at the celebratory after-work drinks party.'

'As long as you promise not to perform karaoke like you did at the Christmas bash,' said Scott, earning a snigger from George in the far corner of the room.

Frankie thrust out her bottom lip. 'Oh, come on, who doesn't love Cher?'

'But "Bang Bang My Baby Shot Me Down"? Complete with actions and a plastic gun!'

'Admit it, sarge. You loved it. I saw you singing along. Next time you and I should duet.'

Emma couldn't help but smile. Frankie had been hugely entertaining on the night in question. She considered herself very fortunate to be surrounded by work colleagues she valued and whose company she enjoyed. Their working relationships and environment were a far cry from Leah's. She wouldn't trade her team or the cluttered chaos of their office for one of the trendy huddle rooms at Harlequin Events.

She turned her attention back to her computer screen, looking up only when somebody knocked at the door.

'Ma'am, this has arrived and is marked for your attention,' said the officer. He held out a cardboard box.

'Great, I've been expecting that. Thank you.'

She took it from him and opened it on the nearest desk, removing a manila file marked *Leah Fairbrother*. She flicked through it, searching for the photograph taken at the ATM.

When she found it, she held it up to the light. The time stamp showed it had been taken at nine forty-five, only ten minutes after Leah had been spotted on CCTV.

'Okay, we've got a timeline,' said Emma. 'Harry, I need a map of Stafford, please.'

Harry responded and after a few keyboard clicks, a map appeared on his screen. Emma pointed out the bridge that crossed into Mill Bank.

'The barber saw her here around eight o'clock. At nine thirty-five she was on camera entering Greengate Street. Ten minutes later, she was captured by the Lloyds ATM further along the street. After that, she disappeared,' she said.

'She might have hung around the bars and restaurant area near Mill Bank. It isn't far from Greengate Street,' said Scott.

Frankie nodded. 'That's the area I have been concentrating on. George has been further afield at the other end of the pedestrian precinct.'

'Both of you should stick at it. You've still got a few people to interview, haven't you?'

'Uh-huh. They won't be at work yet. I'll head out again later to talk to them.'

'So, where do we think Leah might have been between eight and nine thirty?' asked Harry.

Frankie shrugged. 'Anywhere. She could even have got a lift to the athletic guy's house then come back into town.'

'Pity we haven't found them together on CCTV,' said Scott.

'That would have made this too easy,' said Emma. She studied the photograph. Leah was leaning in close, her eyes on the keypad. There was nobody behind her, nothing to give away the identity of the person she'd been seen with. Although she reasoned that Greengate Street was a pedestrian area and even at that time of night there would surely have been people around who might have seen Leah, she knew she was clutching at straws. It was too soon after the Christmas and New Year holiday for people to be out and about.

'Right then, we're not getting anywhere with this so let's go through the files. If we dig hard enough, we'll find something.'

A seed of doubt crept in, making her words feel hollow. She shook it off by telling herself this would be Kate's approach. It was the right way.

◆ ◆ ◆

Kate stared out of the office window across the car park and watched Trevor and Jamie pull up in Trevor's car, where they sat in conversation for a few minutes before getting out. On their way to the main entrance, they were stopped by another couple of officers, one of whom slapped Jamie on the back. The raid had given DI Rind's team the boost they needed, and news of its success had spread quickly. Chief Constable Atwell was already preparing for a news conference where he and Superintendent Bree O'Sullivan would be able to give the positive news.

Although she was pleased that they'd had a productive outcome, it was only the start as far as she was concerned.

The trafficking operation was huge, and she knew that officers from this very station were involved. Those people would do everything they could to protect themselves.

She also couldn't shake off the feeling that this result – catching two traffickers who were supposedly high up in the chain – had been almost too easy.

Adding to her concerns was the fact that Ali Rind had now requested a meeting with the chief constable to discuss overturning his decision to not grant Ali's informant a visa. Unable to shake the unease that was causing her stomach to knot itself, she decided to go to William's house and search again for the elusive document.

'That's if it really exists. You haven't considered the possibility that William was bullshitting you. He didn't want you to know that he was one of us from the outset. You were too afraid to believe bad of him and gobbled up his story about pretending to infiltrate the group.' Dickson's voice was cold and harsh. Fuck! Why was she torturing herself like this?

'Because, Kate, you have doubts. Genuine, gut-wrenching doubts. How well did you know him? He played his cards close to his chest. He kept secrets from you.'

'Give it a rest, Dickson. You know nothing,' said William.

'I know all about deception and if you think she believes that you were trying to amass information on the syndicate, then you are the old fool that I had you pinned for.'

Kate shouted, 'Stop it!' Then, dropping her voice, said, 'I kept things from William. It didn't mean he couldn't trust me. The same applies to him. He might have kept me in the dark at times, but he would never have lied to me.'

'Why not? You lied to his face. You swore to him that you didn't kill me.'

Kate balled her fists. Dickson's voice was jarring her nerves. She knew why she'd welcomed both Chris and William's voices: they helped her work out her problems and offered advice and made her feel secure. But why Dickson's?

'It's quite simple. My voice is the result of the all-consuming guilt you carry every moment of every day. I'm your constant reminder that you have gone against your moral code and are no better than the criminals you hunt down.'

She jumped at the sound of her phone ringing and cursed her nervousness.

'We received a call from a member of the public ten minutes ago, at 1.22 p.m., reporting the body of a woman in the alleyway behind the Mini Market on Salter Street.'

'Anyone in attendance?'

'Paramedics have been dispatched.'

'Any other details?'

'None so far.'

'Okay, I'll send a team immediately.'

She weighed up the options. With no spare officers to send, there was only one person who might be able to handle this on top of their own workload – Emma.

◆ ◆ ◆

He strolls down Salter Street, aware of the blue flashing lights ahead. He never behaves this boldly. Or this stupidly, depending on how you look at it. This time is different because if he's right, DI Emma Donaldson will be sent to investigate. He wants to observe her in her professional capacity. Maybe that will even give him some sort of thrill.

He's watched enough true crime documentaries to know killers who attend their own crime scenes get caught. The cops always check out crowds of onlookers, sometimes even videoing those people to later examine faces in more detail.

A small group has gathered near the scene; voyeurs who take delight in others' pain and misery. He smiles to himself. Human nature is bizarre. These same people, who are so eager to discover what has befallen some unfortunate individual, will relish the moment then shout out about it on social media or rush off to tell their friends and neighbours, accompanying it with sad faces and commenting on how terrible the world has become. The simple truth is that people love to be shocked.

He maintains a healthy distance from the bystanders, taking up a position in an open doorway, all the while keeping an eye on proceedings. He ensures his hood is pulled well over his head, confident he won't be spotted. Nobody wants to notice homeless people.

Squad cars block the road at both ends. An ambulance is in front of a mini supermarket, blue light still flashing, and at its rear stands a couple of paramedics deep in conversation with an officer. His gaze travels to the crime scene tape flapping gently in the wind and the serious-faced person in a white forensic suit who ducks under it before disappearing into the back alley.

He closes his eyes, imagining the scene as the police officer will see it: the pretty woman lying in the middle of all-pervading squalor and decay. She's positioned to make it look like she simply collapsed, which is pretty much what happened: one minute she was stumbling alongside him, the next, grabbing her head with her free hand and groaning loudly before slipping from his grip. It was only after he lifted her from the pavement that he detected the smell of alcohol, which, combined with the administered drug, had caused her to die. He ought to feel remorse, guilt or at least some sense of regret, yet there is nothing. He lacks such emotions. Back when he had therapy, he was told that he suffered from emotional blindness – alexithymia – a state where somebody can't name or classify emotions. That isn't completely accurate. While he doesn't comprehend many feelings, he experiences some: lust for one, although it has to be said, that doesn't happen very often.

A squad car approaches, drawing to a halt by the ambulance. The driver exits the vehicle in one swift movement and bends down to drag on some plastic covers over their shoes. When they stand up, it is clear who it is – Acting DI Emma Donaldson.

Perfect.

It's time for the games to begin.

Having pulled on the plastic overshoes, Emma braced herself for what she was about to uncover. As instructed, Scott and Frankie had secured the scene and extra officers were present to assist with roadblocks and canvassing. That Kate had charged her team with this while simultaneously investigating another case filled Emma with pride. She searched the faces of the bystanders, scanning for journalists yet seeing none. Word must be out by now. They would soon arrive.

She strode towards the cordon, warrant card held high, affording the officer only a glimpse of it before ducking under the tape where she caught up with Frankie, who had a notebook open in her hand.

'I've spoken to the paramedics. She was dead by the time they arrived. They can't second-guess what happened but say it appears she collapsed and died on the spot. Could be any number of reasons why that might be the case. They mentioned alcohol.'

'Okay, well, that's a start.' Emma gestured towards the people gawping on the far side of the road.

'Check if any of that lot saw anything and if they didn't, move them on. We can do without an audience.'

Frankie was off like a shot, her voice commanding as she addressed the crowd.

Spindly weeds poked from a cracked brick post that marked the entrance to the access area, which could only be described as dingy. In Emma's eyes, the tarmac resembled a modern piece of artwork, a canvas of oil and tyre marks, while the backdrop consisted of industrial units in faded greens and blues. Industrial bins and piles of cardboard boxes haphazardly strewn in front of shuttered rear doors added to the sense of decay and neglect, and the accompanying sour smell caused Emma to hold her breath. Scott was in front of a shabby door.

She called out, 'You done?'

'Yes. All recorded. You can come forward.'

Emma moved towards the figure on the ground, meeting Scott beside the body. He let out a sigh. 'She's not very old. Thirties, maybe,' he said.

Emma's gaze fell upon the shoulder-length dark-brown hair that cushioned an expertly made-up face, eyebrows on point, combed and gelled into place, eyelids sparkling with gold shadow and lashes so long Emma thought they might be false. The victim's full lips glistened with a light coral gloss. At first sight, she could be mistaken for being asleep.

'I couldn't see any clear evidence of an attack,' said Scott. 'Clothes appear intact, make-up undisturbed.'

Emma took in the smart woollen coat, buttoned to the victim's neck, the patterned black tights and the thigh-length boots. There were no signs of a struggle, no rips, no bruising. Then an itching began in her scalp as she realised the woman wasn't wearing any rings or a watch. Maybe it was a coincidence but here was another well-dressed victim who wasn't wearing any jewellery.

'No rings. No watch,' she said.

'And there's no phone, handbag, wallet or ID.'

His words hit home, intensifying the prickling sensation. Could the cases be related? 'It's odd that only a day ago we found another well-dressed victim, also without ID or jewellery.'

'Coincidence? This vic hasn't been buried,' said Scott.

Emma crouched down, leant over the woman and sniffed. There was a faint alcoholic aroma. She got to her feet again and said, 'She'd been drinking but her lip gloss isn't smudged.'

'She could have reapplied it after she'd finished drink—' Scott made an 'ah' sound. 'But to do that she'd have had to have her lipstick on her person, and it isn't here.'

'Exactly. Somebody has stolen her belongings.'

'Or she was so drunk she left them somewhere,' Scott reasoned. 'Or somebody did her make-up for her after she was dead.' He paused. 'Actually, that last one sounds a bit ghoulish and far-fetched.'

Reflecting on how Kate would handle this, Emma said, 'No, we ought to consider all possibilities. A blood alcohol test will throw some light on how drunk she was. Who found her?'

'Nicholas Taylor, who lives in the flat above his music shop in town. He was walking his girlfriend's dog when it slipped its lead and raced off. He followed it here, where he came across the victim. Nicholas thinks he recognises her. He's sure he bought the shop from the sales and letting agency where she works – Property Plus.'

'Does he know her name?'

'No, and the agency will be shut today because it's Sunday, so I'll have to do some digging. I've already instructed the extra officers to start canvassing the area.'

'Good. I'll get the ball rolling on CCTV, although I could do with an approximate time of death.'

'I'm no expert, but given the state of rigor, I'd guesstimate she died late evening.'

Emma was no fan of assumptions, but it gave them a sensible starting point. 'Okay, I'll run with that. We'll know more once the pathologist has completed their findings. I'm going to report back to DCI Young. First and foremost, we need her name. I'll leave that with you.'

'No problems. What about Leah, though? Are we going to handle the case separately or as being potentially connected?'

'I need to talk to the DCI first. There's no obvious evidence to suggest this person was a victim of an aggressive attack. Which could only mean she wasn't assaulted, or she gave up her belongings without kicking up a fuss. If the latter, it has echoes of what happened to Leah.'

'True. There are similarities, but this woman might not have been wearing any jewellery. More to the point, she was found here, not buried on an estate. That's a big difference,' he said.

'If the killer had wanted Leah to remain undiscovered, there are plenty of other places he could have dumped her body other than a site due for development. There were even boards up with dates of due completion. Part of me thinks whoever left Leah there wasn't bothered about her being found. DCI Young can decide how best to play it. For the time being, we'll follow procedure and gather as much knowledge and evidence as we can.'

She walked away, heart beating a wild rhythm. If the deaths were connected, then this investigation could turn out to be way bigger than she'd expected and far more demanding. Get it wrong or let it drag on for too long and she ran the risk of it blowing up in her face, with all hopes of impressing her seniors being dashed. Back at her car, she was pleased that Frankie had successfully moved the crowd on and was now talking to a middle-aged couple, making notes as they spoke. Emma was lucky to have her team. They might be a small unit but when Kate had been dragged back to work from sick leave, she had only been given Morgan and Emma to work with, yet together they'd cracked a huge murder case. She could do the same, couldn't she?

She jumped back into her car and sped off in the direction of the station. As she drove away, she caught sight of a man loitering by the tape. She guessed he worked for the local paper, the *Gazette*.

Bugger!

The vultures were already circling.

Kate was torn between hanging around the station where she might find out what DI Ali Rind had said to the chief constable, heading out to the latest crime scene to join Emma, or going to William's house. She'd wasted the last twenty minutes pacing back and forth in her office, trying to keep William and Dickson's voices out of her head.

'You can't trust William. The fact that you haven't found the document he claimed to have secreted proves there is none.'

'Kate, don't listen. You are only doubting yourself. Keep searching. I know you'll find it.'

With it proving impossible to keep them silent while she was alone, she decided to get out of the office. She was halfway to the door when the phone rang. She answered the call, only to discover Chief Constable Atwell wanted to speak to her.

'Ali will have put across his concerns and Stanka's name will have been mentioned. You're in for a grilling.' Dickson sounded smug.

William was quick to reply. 'That's not what is going on. Ali doesn't know any of the details or even who authorised Stanka's requests. Moreover, he hasn't had enough time since speaking to you, Kate, to establish what happened. Only a few people know what was agreed and by whom.'

Satisfied with this reasoning, she headed upstairs.

On a table in the corner of Chief Constable Atwell's office, a coffee machine gurgled and spluttered. The capsule ejected with a clatter, and he removed the cup and saucer before facing her.

'We have a problem.'

For a split second, Kate didn't know where to look. She settled on brazening it out with him. If Ali had protested about Stanka, then she could always say that it had been William's decision alone to go ahead with arranging a visa for the girl and play dumb as to why it had been important.

'That won't wash.' Dickson's sinister whisper made her blood run cold.

'Sir?' she said.

'Operation Moonbeam.' He took a sip of his drink, then settled down at his desk, placing the cup and saucer in front of him. 'I had rather hoped today would turn out differently. Superintendent O'Sullivan and I are due to hold a press conference in an hour, during which I was going to congratulate and praise the entire team on their excellent result. Now, it appears, I shall have to rewrite some of my speech.'

Kate waited for the punchline, that moment when he began bawling her out. Her heart hammered in her ears, threatening to drown out his words.

'DI Rind is no longer heading Operation Moonbeam. It was decided that it would be better if he returned to Manchester with immediate effect, which in turn means the operation requires a new lead officer. Morgan Meredith would be ideal for the role, and I'd like to speak to him about it ahead of the conference, unless you have any objections.'

He picked up his cup again and took another sip. She struggled to quell the wave of relief that almost unbalanced her. The news shocked and delighted her. With Ali gone, there was no need to worry about him or anyone else probing the business regarding Stanka. The thought was immediately consumed by another. Had Ali walked off the job or been ordered to leave? She brushed it aside. She didn't want him to think she was deliberating over the question.

'No objections whatsoever. Morgan will do an excellent job.'

'Good. I'll call him in then. I wanted to run it past you first.'

'Thank you. I can certainly vouch for him.'

He pushed the cup to one side. 'As for DI Rind, well, it might come better from you if you explain that he missed his old unit and had been heading Operation Moonbeam far longer than anticipated. Following the success of today's sting, he felt it was an opportune moment to pass on the baton and return home. Wait until I've spoken to Morgan first.'

'I'll do that. Er, sir?'

'Yes.'

'Why the sudden departure? Could he not have stayed a little longer?'

'A serious complaint was lodged against him. And that is all you need to know.'

'Yes, sir.'

She took her leave, wondering who had pulled the strings to have Ali removed, and what allegation might have been serious enough to send him packing, yet not warrant an internal investigation. She suspected it was down to the interference of the syndicate.

For some reason, they had wanted Ali out. On this occasion, however, the syndicate's actions had worked in her favour. She bounded downstairs, delighted for Morgan.

Dickson's voice stopped her in her tracks. *'Tut-tut, Kate. You've allowed your sudden exuberance to dull your senses and missed something important. Chief Constable Atwell is one of us. He trumped up accusations purely to get Ali out of the picture. Ali was aware that there was a mole and was trying to snare them. We, the syndicate, pounced first.'*

'Ignore Dickson, Kate,' said William.

This time, she couldn't take William's advice. Her mind was spinning again.

'Kate, for goodness' sake. If Atwell was part of the syndicate, he would have had the code name Beta, not me. The first letter of his surname is ahead of mine alphabetically,' urged William.

She released the breath she had suddenly been holding. William spoke sense. She reached her landing and made for the office. No sooner had the door shut than she heard Dickson's voice clearly.

'Who's to say all the members of the syndicate were in my phone's contact list? I had a lot of information professionally deleted from it. Names of those highest up in the syndicate were removed.'

Kate leant against the door. This was all too much for her. Never had finding William's document seemed so important. She had to find out who she could trust and who needed bringing down before they wreaked any more havoc.

◆ ◆ ◆

Emma was on her way back to the station when DC Harry Ling's voice came over the Airwave.

'The sarge emailed me a picture of the vic and asked me to check out Property Plus where she worked, then let you know what

I found out. I've been on their website and I'm certain I've found a photo of her. Or if it's not, it's her doppelgänger.'

'What's her name?'

'Victoria Hannover. She's the manager at Property Plus. I'm sending the photo to your mobile now.'

Her phone blipped.

'Hang on. There's a lay-by ahead. I'm going to pull over.'

Once there, she stared at the picture. There was little doubt. This was their victim.

'Looks exactly like her. I'll find out who her next of kin are and see if she's been reported missing. Good job, Harry.'

'I can't take the credit. Sarge said the person who found her recognised her. We struck lucky.'

She started up the car again, keen to reach Kate. Rarely did things fall into place so quickly. She took it as a good sign. She was going to crack these cases, and soon. She could feel it in her gut.

◆ ◆ ◆

Kate didn't have to wait long before Morgan was knocking at her door, a mile-wide smile across his face.

'The chief constable asked me to let you know that you can make the announcement now,' he said.

Kate got to her feet. 'Happy to. Congratulations, Morgan. I expect more results from the team and for the operation to progress more swiftly.'

'You can count on it.'

'Have you any suspicions as to who might be leaking information?'

Morgan took a deep breath before saying, 'Nobody really jumps out in terms of their behaviour or potential motivation. I even wondered if it might have been DI Rind all along. It would go some way to explaining why he wouldn't take my complaints seriously and fobbed me off.'

'I can see why you might think that he was responsible, but, Morgan, he wasn't leading the investigation or even working at this station when the team raided the motel last September. DI Khatri was in charge then.'

A frown replaced the smile. 'He might have been in contact with somebody else on the team. Harriet Khatri?'

She shook her head. 'Unlikely.'

'Then . . . we still have a mole.'

Kate chewed on her bottom lip. It would be convenient to believe Ali Rind had been responsible for leaking information, yet wouldn't that be exactly what the syndicate would want everyone to think? If they were able to pin a murder on Harriet, they'd be capable of framing Rind, or at least put him in the situation so she and Morgan might suspect him.

'Did you tell anyone else that you had complained to DI Rind about the lack of progress?'

He shrugged. 'I mentioned it to Jamie.' Before she could respond, he added, 'But he wasn't on the team either when they raided the motel.'

'Morgan, Trevor gave him the heads-up about that raid. He knew details about it and didn't pass those on to me until the morning it happened.'

'True, but Jamie! Really. He's so bloody enthusiastic about everything. You should have seen him earlier. He was euphoric when we brought in those traffickers. I can't believe it would be him. You know what he's like – a proper team player.'

She could see Morgan wasn't going to be swayed. He needed hard evidence, and she didn't want him to think she was gunning for Jamie. 'Then we need to set a trap to catch this person, whoever they are. I'll give it some thought, and we'll discuss it again. Tread carefully though.'

He nodded. 'The success of this investigation is crucial. I'm not going to see it screwed up.'

She hoped that would be the case. Morgan had two traffickers in custody and the chance to further the investigation, even crack it. She nodded at him. He was the right person to lead it. 'I'd better give your team the good news. Can you gather them in the main briefing room? I'll be down in five minutes.'

'Sure. And Kate? Thanks.'

'What for?'

'I'm sure you backed me and told the chief constable I was up to this challenge.'

'You earned it. Your record speaks for itself.'

'Possibly. If DI Rind hadn't decided to return to Manchester mid-investigation, I wouldn't be in this position. Bit of a surprise though. Him leaving so abruptly. Do you think he was pissed off about his snitch not getting any favours and walked off the job?'

As tempted as she was to share her concerns, now wasn't the time. Morgan was pumped, ready to grab the reins. 'I think it's best not to speculate. Whatever his reasons, they've allowed you to step up. Those are the breaks. Grab them when they are offered. Morgan, if you can make more headway on this and bring in the big guns responsible for the trafficking, you will get serious kudos. You know that, right?'

He nodded. 'And I intend to do just that.'

Kate smoothed down her jacket. She was sure Ali wasn't responsible for leaking information. If the mole persisted in sabotaging Operation Moonbeam, Morgan would struggle and, in the worst-case scenario, also find himself removed from his new position. She couldn't allow that to happen. She felt strongly about her protégés. Both Morgan and Emma deserved to succeed. To that end, it was imperative that both she and Morgan plug the leak and unmask this individual. Morgan had told Jamie that he was going to challenge Ali. To that end, she couldn't fully trust Jamie. There had to be a way to trip him up.

Her mobile buzzed and she answered without checking the caller identity. Felicity Jolly spoke in a hushed voice.

'Kate, we need to talk. Are you free in about twenty minutes?'

'Yes.'

'Could you meet me in the Costa in town?'

'Will do.'

The phone went dead, leaving Kate puzzled. Why wouldn't Felicity meet her in the lab? It had to be to do with the app footage. She thrust aside all speculation and headed downstairs. She still had one job to do before she could leave the building.

CHAPTER THIRTEEN

Emma pulled up outside the station in time to see Kate walking to her car. She wound down her window and called out. Kate stopped and waved before she came over.

'Have you got a minute?' asked Emma.

'I need to be somewhere, but if we keep it brief—'

'I believe the woman who was found dead today is Victoria Hannover, the manager of Property Plus in Stafford. There's a possibility that the same person who killed Leah Fairbrother might also have murdered this woman.'

'Killed? Emma, it's way too soon to jump to such conclusions. We don't even know how Victoria died. Or Leah, for that matter. You aren't even one hundred per cent sure that this person is Victoria Hannover.'

Emma ploughed on, even though she was beginning to lose confidence in her argument. 'I'm sure it is. The man who discovered her body also identified her. Her photograph is on the Property Plus website. She isn't wearing any jewellery and there's no ID, no phone, no bag, nothing. Just like Leah.'

'Somebody might have found her body and stolen those items. We'd need more than that to link the deaths. Sorry, Emma. I'm not buying it.'

It was a punch to the stomach. Emma had been so convinced these deaths were related, she hadn't considered providing Kate with stronger evidence at this stage. She'd been hoping that Kate would allow her to run with her theory. Kate had always followed her instinct.

She tried again. 'Kate, if you felt there was a connection, you'd want to pursue this angle. You always told me to trust my gut. Well, that's exactly what I'm doing.'

Kate glanced at her watch. Emma stood her ground. It struck her that she was desperate for Kate's approval and for a moment she regretted having dashed back to speak to her. What had she expected? A pat on the back? She was about to speak, agree that she was being hasty and that she would stick to her original case and, after gathering information on Victoria, pass this one to another team, when Kate nodded.

'Okay, go ahead. A word of warning though, Emma: don't force these pieces together. If the cases are unconnected, let me know so we can deal with both appropriately.'

'I will do. Thank you.'

'Now, I must go. Keep me posted.'

With that, Kate headed to her car. Emma made for the entrance. She had a pile of work to do if she was going to prove her worth, and more importantly, discover what had really happened to the two dead women.

◆ ◆ ◆

Unable to find a parking space, Kate was running late by the time she entered the café. She spotted Felicity, who was sitting in the far corner, reading a newspaper. She made straight for the table.

'Sorry. Emma caught me just as I was leaving.'

Felicity perched orange-framed glasses on top of her steely grey hair and tapped the newspaper, open at the crossword puzzle page. 'Not a problem. I managed to work out three down: eight letters,

Jack-of-all-trades. The answer is factotum – a person with diverse abilities or responsibilities. A bit like your good self at present.'

'Ha! You've got that right,' said Kate.

'I took the liberty of getting you a maple hazel hot chocolate with a light dairy swirl,' said Felicity, pointing to the frothy filled glass mug. 'They are to die for and if you don't like it, I'll happily take it off your hands.'

'It looks delicious.' She sat down and lifted the glass to her lips; the cream was soft, the drink warm and sweet, perfect for a cold day. She made appropriate appreciative noises as she sipped.

'I'm addicted to them. As you can tell.' Felicity patted her stomach. 'I'm supposed to be on a diet after overindulging at Christmas, but you only live once.'

Kate took another sip, then set down the drink. 'So? On to business?'

'I thought it best to discuss this outside the workplace. I've been through the video multiple times and at first it seemed completely legit, then I picked up on the tiniest discrepancy. A micro-blip.'

'What sort of micro-blip?'

'It's tricky to describe. It's not obvious, like a badly spliced film. I even started to wonder if I was imagining it because I'd looked at the damn thing so much, but there's a microsecond where it seems off. There may be an outside chance that it has been tampered with. I don't have the correct equipment or wherewithal to find out exactly what is wrong. I'm sending it to a very old friend, who flies under the radar, so to speak. He works for the military in cyber security and if anyone can get to the bottom of it, it'll be him.'

'Then Harriet might be telling the truth!'

'Don't get too excited. I wanted to let you know that there *could* be something in what she's been saying. And if the app footage has been corrupted, then you're looking for somebody who's extremely talented in this field.'

'Would a hacker be able to alter the footage?'

'Hacker, cyber expert, computer whiz-kid, expert or someone who works with computer-generated imagery or deepfakes. I really couldn't say who. They'll be far cleverer than me.'

'But you think it could be done?'

'We're getting ahead of ourselves. First let me send the footage to my friend and establish if I'm right. Then go from there.'

'Shit! If Harriet didn't kill William, who the fuck did?'

Felicity shrugged. 'That's one puzzle I can't help you with.'

◆ ◆ ◆

Emma was alone in the office, her mind on the latest victim, Victoria Hannover. Late Saturday night, Victoria's husband, Craig, rang emergency services, concerned that his wife had not returned from work and wasn't answering her phone. He'd tried ringing friends, family and hospitals without success. Finally, having driven to her place of work, and spotting her car in its usual spot, he'd contacted the police.

She wasn't aware of Morgan's presence until he cleared his throat.

She glanced towards the door where he stood, a big grin on his face 'Oh, hi. Sorry, I didn't hear you knock.'

'I didn't. The door was ajar. I have news. Big news. Although you might already have heard about it.'

'I know about the raid. Well done. You deserved that break.'

His grin widened. 'Not that. Something even better.'

'Go on, then.'

'Well, I had rather hoped to tell you about it over a quiet meal for two and a bottle of fizz. My treat.'

'I'm really sorry, but I can't tonight. We've taken on another case and we're working flat out.'

The grin vanished. 'A second case? You're already working on a murder inquiry.'

'It's another suspicious death. Kate's given me the go-ahead to see if the two are linked. So, come on, what is this great news?'

'DI Rind has returned to Manchester. I've replaced him as lead on Operation Moonbeam.'

A small squeal escaped her lips, and she leapt up to hug him. 'That is awesome! You are going to be mega!' He returned the hug with equal enthusiasm before letting her go.

'Okay, forget the meal. How about a glass or two of champagne and an early night instead?' he asked.

Even though this would mess up her plans to work late into the night, his earnest face won her over. 'That would be ace.'

'Good. I'll buy the proper stuff too, not a cheap bottle of prosecco.'

He rushed off, leaving Emma in a quandary. She was, she reasoned, genuinely happy for him. After all, he'd been given a real chance to show his potential, just as she had. All the same, she resented having to leave work sooner than she'd banked on. She wanted to give these investigations her undivided attention. She shook her head to dispel the negativity. She loved Morgan and this was his special moment. She should share it with him.

Throwing off thoughts that threatened to drag her down, she collected her car keys and set off to visit Craig Hannover. She could still pack a fair bit into the day before spending much-needed quality time with Morgan later.

◆　◆　◆

Kate was still reeling from her conversation with Felicity. The idea that Harriet really had been set up proved that the syndicate was even more powerful and sinister than she could possibly have imagined and, moreover, a huge threat. They had the ability to shatter people's lives and careers, and all for what? Money was a possibility, but there had to be more to it than that. After all, they'd wrecked lives and crossed all sorts of lines to achieve their ends.

Because of this, instead of heading once again to William's house to spend some time hunting for the elusive document, she'd decided to check out Harriet's alibi for being at the warehouse the day Kate was taken prisoner. The manager at Daily Drop, where Tommy Clayton worked, had informed her that Tommy had resigned from the job at the beginning of October. This left her with no option other than to track down Tommy's ex-wife, Casey.

It had taken several phone calls to establish that Casey's last known local address had been in Hanley. Employment records showed she'd worked at the betting shop in Piccadilly in the centre of town until July 2021.

Kate had drawn a blank at the property and was trying her luck at Casey's workplace. Though she'd rarely set foot inside a bookmaker's, she imagined it was typical of many: grey carpet tiles, television screens along the wall, some showing horse races, some football matches, and others displaying adverts. Bingo machines and slot machines flashed bright coloured lights and played loud tinny music as she passed empty tables and chairs that reminded her of school classrooms, towards the counter where a woman was dealing with the only customer in the place. She waited until he wandered off then presented her ID.

'I'm looking for somebody who used to work here. Maybe you know her – Casey Clayton?'

The oversized hooped earrings that dangled from the assistant's earlobes swung as she nodded. 'I know her. She left a long time ago.'

'I don't suppose you know where she went, do you?'

'Nah, sorry. She didn't say.'

'Is there anyone else here who I could speak to who might know? I really need to find her.'

'She in trouble?'

'No. I need her help.'

'Oh, right. Um, have you tried her daughter?'

Kate was unaware that Casey or Tommy had any children and was therefore slightly taken aback. 'I didn't know she had a daughter.'

'Avril's her stepdaughter from a previous marriage. I went to an Ann Summers party at Avril's place. It's a two-minute walk away, off Percy Street. The big red-brick building next to a sports shop. I can't remember the flat number, but it's on the third floor.'

'I don't suppose you ever met Tommy, did you?'

'Nah, but Casey had plenty to say about him. He sounded a complete twat. She was glad to see the back of him.'

'Was she seeing anybody else that you know of?'

'She dated one of the regulars here for a few weeks, but no, there wasn't anybody serious.'

Another customer appeared. Thanking the woman for her time, Kate swapped the warm, bright interior for the cold, silent street.

To her left, a door opened, releasing the excited voice of a football commentator, followed by background cheers. The man who had exited the bar walked briskly up the street ahead of her, peeling off to the right at the top of the road.

She questioned her sanity. She ought to be in front of the television with her feet up, not pounding the streets of Hanley. The problem was that home no longer felt like the sanctuary it had once been. Ever since she had lost touch with Chris's voice, the place had felt emptier, and she couldn't relax there for long.

If she was honest with herself, it wasn't simply the fact she could no longer talk to Chris that made her feel adrift; the appearance of

Dickson and now William's voice played their part in causing her to be continually restless. As if that wasn't enough, a growing disquiet gnawed at her. Somebody out there had evidence that she was the one who had killed Dickson. Why hadn't they come forward with it though? Were they just playing with her?

'I understand why you won't speak to me, Chris. You're angry that I crossed a moral line and covered up Dickson's death, but if you'd been alive, I know you'd have forgiven me, understood my reasons. You believed in me. You *knew* me. I need you. So why have you left me with Dickson and William?'

She knew he wouldn't respond. After his death, she'd heard his voice all the time. He'd been her support through the anguish of losing him and fathoming who had been behind his murder. Then, after she killed Dickson, Chris's voice began to fade, usurped by Dickson's complaining tirades – constant reminders of the guilt she carried. All the same, she tried hard to hear even the slightest whisper from Chris and when nothing was forthcoming, she went back to her musings.

Not only was she dealing with the conflicting voices of William and Dickson and the frustration at being unable to locate William's document, it now seemed she'd also have to prove that Harriet was innocent then ascertain who had really killed William. All the while, she was aware of the syndicate's ever-tightening net. They must surely be waiting to trip her up. If they possessed the incriminating photos, then she was sitting on a time bomb that, when it went off, would destroy not only her but everyone she cared about. Given Chris wouldn't respond, she had no choice but to turn to the only other voice she could trust.

'Fuck, I don't think I can handle all of this, William,' she mumbled as she walked.

I always believed in you. You've got this. One step at a time,' said William.

'I haven't the energy to do this alone.'

'You're not alone. I'm here. You can always count on me.'

She nodded to herself. William had been a friend and mentor but, unlike Chris, he hadn't been her rock or her love, and that was what she needed now. She needed Chris more than ever.

Or . . . maybe there was somebody else other than William who she could talk to? Somebody still alive. Like . . . her stepsister? She hadn't visited Tilly as promised. The shock of losing William and adjusting to her new position had put that plan on hold. Even though Tilly hadn't admonished her about it, Kate was still aware she'd let her stepsister down. Moreover, she hadn't been staying in touch with Tilly as often as she ought to.

The idea helped lift her mood. The first chance she got, she would ring Tilly and confide in her.

She arrived at the building where Avril lived – a classical-style construction with Romanesque Doric doorways, built, she guessed, during the 1830s. Had her father still been alive, he would undoubtedly have been able to fill her in on all the historical details of not only this property but the surrounding area. History had always been his forte and passion, and a lump began to form in her throat as she recalled days out with him.

Dispersing the memories with a shake of her head, she turned her attention to the names written beside a series of intercom buttons. Logic dictated she choose the one marked Miss A. Broadway. A cautious voice answered almost immediately, and Kate introduced herself. She was buzzed inside and climbed the stairs, hoping Avril was going to prove to be as helpful as the woman in the betting shop. If she could track down Casey, she might find Tommy, who could corroborate Harriet's story.

'Forget Harriet. She was collateral damage,' Dickson's voice chimed in. *'As was Tommy Clayton . . . who has of course been silenced. And no amount of searching will turn him up. You will never*

beat the might of the syndicate. You may as well give up now. You're wasting valuable time, time you should spend working out what you will do once the syndicate finally exposes you as my killer!'

Her pulse accelerated at Dickson's words, her palms turning sweaty. She clung to the mantra 'One step at a time'. Her hunt for Digger would have to remain on hold until she'd sorted this out.

'You don't have enough time left to put it on hold. It's crazy to be looking out for others rather than yourself. Still . . . you know best. Well, I say that, but I don't think you do any more. I think you're so confused that—'

A door opened, and Kate's lips clamped shut, although, judging by the music volume coming from the flat, it seemed unlikely that Avril would have heard Kate remonstrating with herself.

The sullen-faced young woman didn't invite Kate inside but instead drew the door to and kept her waiting on the landing. 'You wanted to ask me some questions about Casey?'

'I need her help in finding her ex-husband, Tommy. I don't suppose you have a contact number for her, do you?'

'Yeah.' She pulled out her mobile from her back pocket and read out the number to Kate before sliding it back into her jeans. 'I don't think she'll know or care where Tommy is though. She gave up on him ages ago. He's a total loser.'

'You don't have an address too, do you? In case I can't get hold of her on the phone,' Kate said.

'No. She moves around a lot. She was hoping to rent a room in Guildford Street. I don't know if she did or not. I haven't seen or spoken to her since Christmas. We're not *that* close.'

'Okay. I'll try her phone.'

The girl gave a curt nod and slipped back into the flat. Kate waited until she was sitting in her car before she tried the number and heaved a sigh when it went directly to voicemail.

'She's not out. She's gone. Forever,' said Dickson.

'Fuck you. She's not. I know what you're trying to do – put me off my stride. It isn't going to work.'

Leaving a brief message, asking Casey to ring back as soon as she got it, Kate drove in the direction of Gorse Farm in Kingstone, still hoping to locate Digger, who was proving to be as elusive as Casey's ex-husband.

◆ ◆ ◆

Emma had difficulty in getting away from Craig Hannover's house. The man was in bits about his wife, and she'd waited until a Family Liaison officer arrived before she dared leave him. He'd described the outfit Victoria had been wearing the day before and confirmed that she had been wearing her engagement and wedding rings and a Rolex watch. Emma was now even more convinced the cases were connected.

Given it was after seven, and with her mind awash with thoughts concerning the investigation, she opted for returning to HQ. Time alone at the station might help her sort them out. Morgan could surely wait another hour.

The call from Terry Wiggins, the forensic anthropologist, came out of the blue.

'Hi, Emma. Sorry to bother you so late. I hope I'm not disturbing you.'

'Not at all. I haven't clocked off yet. I'm too pumped for a cosy night in front of the telly.'

He let out a low laugh. 'I know that feeling. Hence the call so late in the day. It's regarding Leah Fairbrother. I haven't been able to determine an exact cause of death; however, there is something suspicious that requires further investigation. There's evidence of significant cerebral oedema.'

'What is that? Brain swelling?'

160

'Yes. It's a life-threatening condition that causes fluid to develop in the brain. In turn, this fluid increases the pressure inside the skull. We in the profession usually refer to it as intracranial pressure.'

'Is that what killed her?'

'It's a possible cause of death, although I haven't yet ascertained the reason behind it. I've sent toxicology samples off. They might indicate if she had been taking any drugs or medicines. Otherwise, there are no clear signs of substance abuse: no needle marks, no damage to mucus membranes, nothing to indicate she was using. I thought you should know. Maybe her doctor can give you more information.'

His suggestion reminded her that Frankie had not yet come back to her about Doctor Schmidt.

'Thanks, Terry. I'll get on to it first thing.'

'I've put a rush request on the samples.'

'I appreciate that.'

'Night then. Hope you grab a few hours' sleep.'

'You too.'

No sooner had he hung up than she rang Frankie, who answered with a cheery, 'You caught me slacking, boss. I'm sitting on the wall in Sheridan Centre car park with a takeaway pizza box on my lap. It smells . . . mmm!'

'I won't keep you. I was wondering if Doctor Schmidt got back to you.'

'Damn! She didn't and I forgot to chase her up. Sorry. I was busy checking out the whole area near the Property Plus agency, which turned out to be productive because I found out that Victoria had a late lunch in the Market Vaults with a gentleman described as tall with dark hair. Unfortunately, the bartender couldn't tell me any more than that and CCTV there doesn't cover the whole pub.

It did, however, pick up Victoria paying for the meal and drinks at 3.10 p.m.'

'That's interesting. Another tall, dark-haired man. Could be the same person who was with Leah.'

'I've walked the route from the pub to the agency a few times and can't spot any surveillance cameras. If Victoria headed straight back to work afterwards, we'll be unlikely to get anything on CCTV.'

'Her lunch date might explain why there was a smell of alcohol on her. Any idea how much she drank?'

'They shared a bottle of Cabernet Sauvignon and finished off with liqueur coffees. I spoke to the person who served them, but she didn't recall any details about them. Oh, one other thing, when Victoria paid the bill, the video shows her placing a large bag on the counter and her withdrawing a purse. I got a screen grab of it. Looks classy.'

'I spoke to her husband. He told me she had a thing for hand-bags. She got that one for Christmas. It's a Prada tote bag.'

'Prada? Mine came from ASOS,' said Frankie. Emma could hear the smile in her voice.

'Thanks for all your hard work today. You are headed home with that pizza, aren't you?'

'I wasn't planning on it. I want to check out something.'

'What?'

'What if whoever attacked Victoria found her car keys in the bag they stole? They might decide to nick her car too. It's a BMW. So, I've come to check the car park for surveillance equipment and thought I might even hang here for a while in case somebody turns up for it.'

In the face of such cheerful dedication, Emma felt guilty that she'd even considered going home. All the same, she couldn't allow Frankie to spend all night at a car park.

'I'll send an officer over to Mr Hannover's house to collect the spare key, and have it driven to his house.'

'But what if the perp turns up?'

'If they knew where the vehicle was parked, they would have taken it by now. Getting rid of a handbag and some jewellery is a lot easier than ditching a pricey motor. I appreciate you going the extra mile; however, you've already put in another long shift. Go home. Get some sleep and we'll tackle it all again tomorrow.'

'Okay, but first I'm going drop by those restaurants and clubs that are still on my list. There's only a bottle of cider waiting for me, and a grumpy guinea pig who ignores me unless I have food for him.'

Emma left it at that. Frankie was a permanently fizzing ball of energy, a free agent who could spend all night working if she wanted to, without any constraints. Up until a few months ago, Emma had been the same. Now she found herself thinking of abandoning work in favour of a drink with her boyfriend.

She'd sensed his irritation when she first declined his offer, even though her explanation for taking a rain check should have been enough for him. She wasn't sure why she'd agreed to an evening in and a celebratory drink, especially as it kept her from her work, yet at the time it had seemed more important to keep him happy. Maybe Morgan's recent mood swings were down to her. Maybe she had changed too – becoming more driven, more like Kate – and, for some reason, Morgan wasn't happy about it.

Her ruminations only served to make her more downbeat. She loved Morgan and any other time she'd have relished celebrating with him. Just not when she was struggling with a major investigation. And, she reasoned, Morgan should feel the same way. Rather than clinking glasses in front of the television with her, he should be interviewing the traffickers who'd been arrested that morning.

She gritted her teeth and, flooring the accelerator, made for the station. There was still work to do before she could call it a day. She had to make progress, to find a connection between the two cases and make Kate pleased and also proud of her. And if Morgan didn't like that, then tough shit.

◆ ◆ ◆

Maybe it's because it's almost ten o'clock, or because her mind is on the investigation, but Emma Donaldson doesn't appear to be as much on the ball as he expects her to be.

He has tailed her from the station to the house she shares with Morgan Meredith. Admittedly, it is easier to pursue somebody in the dark and the headlights of oncoming traffic periodically blind them. Emma certainly didn't seem to notice his car keeping a sensible distance behind her own. Ordinarily, he prefers to follow his prey on foot. In streets he can blend in with crowds, but he feels conspicuous in a vehicle, even one like this, that draws little attention to itself.

On this occasion, he's broken with tradition. He isn't targeting Emma for the usual reasons – to steal money and jewellery. This time it is different. His plan affords him what he assumes must be the feeling of pleasure – a slight frisson that causes the hairs on his arms to stand to attention. The moment is fleeting, quickly replaced by ambivalence. He sneers as she fumbles in her bag for the door key.

It's his birthday soon, and Acting DI Emma Donaldson is going to be an early present to himself.

She's attractive, agile and fierce. He noticed those qualities the first time that they met, when she openly flirted with him. He should have asked her out when he had the chance, but he thought she was so career-minded she'd reject him, and he wasn't somebody who would take rejection. Now she's living with that beefcake, and the opportunity to have her to himself has passed. Nevertheless, Emma is the sort of woman who requires stimulation; a career woman who relishes a challenge, and he, not Morgan Meredith, represents that in spades.

Emma disappears into Morgan's house, shutting the front door behind her.

He waits a further five minutes before he drives off.

Emma slipped off her shoes, leaving them on the purpose-built shelf below a row of coat hooks. She had quickly discovered that Morgan was surprisingly fastidious about his home, and everything in it had a place. He was quite unlike most of her brothers, who thought nothing of dropping wet towels on bathroom floors after they'd used them or left their clothes in an untidy heap in the hope somebody – usually her mother – would sort them out for them. Morgan's upbringing was a taboo subject, although she knew it had been even tougher than hers. It had, however, resulted in him taking great care of his belongings, which meant all dirty clothes were put into a wash-basket in one corner of the bathroom; his work clothes were checked to ensure they were still clean and hung back up on hangers in his wardrobe for the following day. He was no stranger to a vacuum cleaner or an ironing board, and Emma felt she didn't live up to his standards when it came to housekeeping, especially when she was tired or her mind was elsewhere.

The door to the sitting room was ajar. The sound of singing enticed her to check it out. The sight made her heart sink: rose petals laid out on the dining-room table, places set for two, candles, a large wine cooler and, sticking out from it, the base of a champagne bottle.

Morgan was slumped on the settee, eyes shut. She wasn't sure if he was sulking and feigning sleep or had dozed off after glugging the contents of the bottle. She edged into the room.

'Morgan?'

He opened his eyes. 'Oh!' was all he said. He got to his feet, steadying himself as he rose. On the television, drunken celebs were duetting a karaoke number, voices screeching, making Emma wince.

She held up her hands. 'I'm so sorry. I got held up at work.'

'A text would have been nice.'

'I didn't think.' Even as she spoke, she knew the words sounded hollow. She had put Morgan to the back of her mind. She would have hated it if he'd done the same to her.

'No. You didn't.' He walked past her, brushing slightly against her as he left the room.

'Don't walk away. I really want to apologise.'

'Save it. I'm going to bed. I've got an early start. The rabble we brought in have finally decided they want to talk. You can sleep in the spare room so that I don't disturb you when I get up.'

'Morgan!'

He faced her, eyes narrowed. 'I haven't got the energy or inclination to argue with you. I need rest. I don't want to be kept awake having a stupid conversation about this. I get it. You were busy. I understand, okay?' With that, he turned his back and made for the staircase.

She balled her fists, annoyed not only with herself for having caused this rift, but by Morgan's attitude. There was no need for them to sleep apart. He was punishing her and that rankled. It hadn't been so long ago he would have put work before their relationship. When they were together on Kate's team, and even before then, they'd always both been very work-driven. The old Morgan wouldn't have thrown his dummy out of the pram because she forgot about a date, even if it was to celebrate a promotion. Something had changed within him. Or, inside her. Had she become so wrapped up in being as good a DI as Kate that she'd transformed into somebody he didn't much like any more?

She returned to the sitting room, turned off the television and began clearing away the table. Dropping the rose petals into a cupped hand, she was overcome with sadness. This was on her. He'd obviously wanted to celebrate big time and she'd ruined the moment for him. She should have handled it differently. Their relationship was still so new and yet a crack had already appeared and was spreading.

The spare bedroom! She must have really upset him for him to be so callous. She would have to repair this damage before it got worse, and their relationship deteriorated beyond help.

Kate hugged the hedgerow as she edged towards the farm building. She pulled the hood of her waterproof coat over the woollen beanie hat she wore to afford her some protection against the driving rain that chilled her cheeks and lips. Ahead of her, a light burned brightly in the farmhouse where curtains hadn't been drawn. A figure passed in front of the window: Malcolm Hardcastle, arms waving as he spoke.

She slipped through the open gate and moved closer, a shadow in the darkness. Another person appeared by the window – a woman with white hair.

Kate waited until she had moved away before coming closer still. Sheltered slightly from the rain, she could hear the occasional bleating of sheep and raised voices: two men.

'The Hen . . .' – she couldn't catch the name – '. . . booked Digger months ago. We were lucky he was available to help us out over the last couple of nights. It's our own fault for not thinking ahead. He's moved on. We'll have to hire someone else to replace him.'

'And they'll rip us off!'

'Then we'll have to manage without any help.'

The voices died down. Kate peered in. Malcolm and his father were at opposite ends of the kitchen, both with mugs in their hands. There was no sign of the woman or Digger. She backed away and, guided by the outside lights, made her way to the barns. The rain began to fall harder, drops like tiny darts stinging her face. She sank into her shoulders, digging gloved hands deep into her pockets.

The mournful bleating intensified as she drew nearer and suddenly a barn door flew open. Light fell across the yard and a figure hastened towards the house. Within moments, both men were out of the house and sprinting back with the same white-haired woman. Before the door shut again, Kate could see into the barn, and the sheep in the pen about to give birth. There was nobody else there. It had been a fruitless journey.

She raced back to the Audi, took off her coat and threw it into the passenger footwell. Tendrils of soaked hair sprinkled water on to the seat as she got in and shut the door. Digger had disappeared again. She leant against the headrest and groaned.

'Tsk. Don't give up. You overheard their conversation. They were annoyed to have let him go and he's gone to another farm owned by somebody whose surname begins with Hen— You are still in with a shout.'

William's words hit home. Of course. That had to be it. Malcolm and his father had been left in the lurch. There was still hope. She stared into the darkness. Like it or not, she would have to ask the farmers where Digger had gone. Rain drummed on the roof.

'Chris,' she said. 'Is it all hopeless?'

The reply came not from Chris but William. Her husband still wasn't talking to her. Why? What had she done? '*Where's that self-belief that used to radiate from you?*'

'I'm tired, William. Tired and . . . I want this to be over.'

'*Then stop feeling sorry for yourself and find out where Digger is!*'

She threw open the door once more, grabbed her coat and held it over her head as she ran towards the farmhouse. This time, she banged on the barn door and pushed it open. A sheep was lying on its side, being tended to by Malcolm and the woman while his father watched on, arms folded.

'I thought I told you to clear off. You're trespassing,' he said.

Kate tried not to look at the distressed animal that was struggling to give birth.

'I'm sorry, but I need to know where Digger is.'

'I don't know.'

'I can do this the nice way or the hard way,' Kate said.

The noise in the barn intensified as the frightened sheep bleated repeatedly.

'Get out. Can't you see we're busy? I haven't time for you.'

Kate locked eyes with the man. 'I have to know where he's gone.'

'You can try the hard way, but I'll only tell you what I've already told you. I . . . don't . . . know. Now get lost before I throw you out.'

The woman looked up, her eyes flinty. 'Look, we've lost one lamb tonight and are in danger of losing another. Now, do as my husband asks, and leave us to get on. None of us have anything more to say to you.'

Kate backed away. She'd blown any chance of getting them to talk by barging in during such a challenging time. Once again, she'd made a bad call. Not for the first time, it occurred to her that she had lost her edge, and the realisation terrified her.

CHAPTER FOURTEEN

Emma couldn't sleep. Apart from the fact that the spare bed was narrow and nowhere near as comfortable as the king-size bed she shared with Morgan, she'd been unable to turn off the part of her brain that was determined to analyse every step they had taken so far on the investigation. She was still wide awake when she heard the pipes spluttering into life as Morgan took a shower before work. She was sorely tempted to speak to him before he left, apologise again and wish him luck, yet she couldn't seem to summon the resolve to leave the room. Maybe it would be better to let it blow over. By the time he got home tonight, he'd be in a different mood. He might even get a result from his interviews and be in high spirits.

Eventually, the floorboards on the landing creaked as they always did when someone walked on them. If she was going to do it, now would be the opportune moment. She only had to open the door and speak his name. Instead, she listened for the sound of the front door shutting quietly and his Jeep starting up. It could wait. She had more important things to concentrate on. She snuggled under the duvet, shut her eyes and drifted off to sleep.

◆ ◆ ◆

Kate was up and in her running gear an hour before her phone alarm went off. She'd had yet another restless night, mind flitting between the thought she had got it wrong about Harriet and finding Digger. She'd screwed up in so many ways. Whenever she thought she was in control, it transpired the syndicate was ahead of her by several miles. She wasn't as good as she believed.

She stretched her leg muscles in preparation for the run. Exercise usually helped her get things into perspective. Yet even before she began, she knew today wouldn't be one of those days.

She was in trouble. Deep, shitty, unwholesome trouble. Unless she could find Digger – so he could tell her who took the photographs at the reservoir – or unearth William's file containing the names of the syndicate members, she could find herself locked away. She spat a laugh at the irony: her in jail while Harriet walked free.

'I can't see how you're going to wring the information about Digger from the Hardcastles. They really don't like you, do they? Maybe you shouldn't have listened to William and instead waited until the morning rather than bulldoze your way into their lambing barn. It was obviously a distressing and difficult time for them. You did nothing to endear yourself to that family. Probably blew any chance of them telling you where Digger is.'

'Thank you, Dickson. I'd worked that out by myself.'

'Good to know you can still work out some things. Pity they aren't the same things you need to get an urgent handle on.'

She hated that he was right. She'd jumped in without really thinking through her actions and had effectively made the situation between them worse. They'd never give up Digger's location now.

With Dickson's reprimand ringing in her ears, she opened the front door, fully aware that she had to get a firmer grip on everything. All these stabs of conscience were dragging her down. Instead of driving to a park or heading to Blithfield Reservoir where, following the death of her husband, she'd run regularly, she decided to jog along the lanes and fields near her house. She took off at a gentle pace, gradually building up as she crossed a road on to a public right of way. The route would take her over fields to come back on itself in a huge circle. The going was difficult, the grass slippery from the heavy overnight rain, the wet blades slapping against her ankles. Her breathing became laboured, hampered by the icy air that seemed to cause her lungs to shrink, yet she ploughed on, eyes on the terrain, focus on maintaining a steady pace – anything to blot out the fears that constantly bombarded her.

◆ ◆ ◆

Emma felt surprisingly refreshed for a person who'd only had two hours' sleep. Which was more than she could say for her colleague, Scott, who looked like he had slept at his computer overnight.

'Here,' she said. 'Take my coffee. You look like you could do with the caffeine.'

'Cheers. I must admit, I've had better nights. I don't know how but Courtney caught chickenpox this weekend and was poorly all night. We're taking no chances and have kept all the kids off school.'

'I take it you've already had it.'

'Yes. I contracted it as a nipper, so I'm immune. Just to be on the safe side, though, I shall be hanging out here for as long as possible, and when I go home, I'll be staying out of the way of all the family. If my man shed was big enough, I'd move into it.' He gave a tired grin.

Emma started up her computer and immediately opened the email from the tech team. 'Brilliant! We've received video footage of Victoria on Saturday afternoon.'

Scott leapt to his feet and stood behind Emma as she downloaded the attached file and let the footage run. The camera, hidden on a private building, overlooked a narrow pedestrian street leading to Market Square.

Two figures came into view. The taller one, whose face was completely hidden by a hoodie, was supporting a woman in a coat and boots, who appeared to be weaving unsteadily.

'Fuck off! That looks like the same person who was with Leah,' said Scott. 'And she looks like she's drunk. Just like Leah.'

Emma downloaded a second attachment, a photo of Victoria at the Lloyds bank ATM on the same street. With eyes narrowed as if she couldn't see properly, she was withdrawing the maximum amount of money allowed in one transaction. The time, 5.45 p.m.

'These cases are definitely connected. Both women withdrawing money. Both in the company of a hooded person,' said Scott.

Emma nodded, her heartrate accelerating. She'd been right to trust her instinct. However, now she had to find this person before they targeted someone else.

Frankie bowled into the office with a box of doughnuts. 'Morning. Thought we could all do with a sugar fix. Freshly baked this morning and still warm. What? Has something happened?'

Emma filled her in on what they'd discovered. Frankie grinned. 'Then my news is going to totally make your morning. I spoke to a bartender last night who remembers seeing Leah with a man on three separate occasions, none of them the day she went missing. She didn't recognise the photograph of Zac, Leah's co-worker, but she hesitated when I showed her a picture of Russell. She wasn't sure but thought it could be him. She described him as about six feet, toned body and dark hair, which of course matches Russell's description.'

'And the description of the man who the barber saw,' said Scott.

'It's too vague,' said Emma with a sigh. 'There are lots of men who match that description. Did he have facial hair? Any distinguishing tattoos?'

Frankie pulled a face. 'Only Leah caught her attention because she looked glamorous and out of place in the bar, and always came in alone and waited at the same table in the furthest corner. The last time she came in, the bartender noticed they seemed to be having an argument. She thought it was getting heated and at one point, Leah walked off to the ladies, clearly upset. After she returned, they continued talking for a while before leaving together. She hasn't seen them since.'

'Any idea when this happened?'

'A couple of weeks before Christmas.'

'Do they have CCTV at the bar?'

'It was broken,' said Frankie with an apologetic shrug.

'Blast! Right then, it's going to have to be another job for the techies. Will you sweet-talk Rachid, Frankie? He likes you. Ask him to hunt through any CCTV in the area around that time. We must identify these suspects.'

As she picked up a photograph of Victoria to place on the whiteboard, she had another thought.

'We need to establish further connections between these women. They could have known each other. Both lived in this area and given Leah was in the hospitality industry, Victoria might have attended one of her events, or Leah might even have organised one for the estate agency. Scott, can you delve into that?'

Scott nodded.

'Let's get going. Lots to do, people. No time to waste.'

With that, she turned her attention back to her computer. It was going to be another very long day.

Kate sat in her office, considering facetiming her stepsister, Tilly. She craved some normality in her life. She needed somebody she could converse with who wasn't a voice in her head. Someone who would remind her that she was still in control.

Tilly knew much of what had transpired over the past few months: that Kate had been after Dickson and that she had accidentally killed him. As far as Kate knew, Tilly had kept everything secret. She was the only person who would understand the quandary that Kate was in.

The office phone rang just as she was about to press the FaceTime call button. A voice – weak, hesitant, as if the person didn't want to be overheard – spoke. 'Is that DCI Kate Young?'

'Yes, that's me.'

'It's Casey Clayton.'

'Hello, Casey. Thank you for ringing me back.'

'I only just picked up your message. You said it was urgent.'

'It's about Tommy. Have you seen him recently?'

The sigh at the other end of the line was audible. 'What's he done now?'

'He's not in any trouble. I do need to talk to him urgently though.'

'Why do you want to speak to him?'

'I'm not at liberty to tell you that. All I can say, Casey, is that I really must speak to him. Have you any idea where I might find him?'

'We split up three years ago. I was getting along perfectly well without him and then two of you ring me up, wanting to know if I've seen him. I'll tell you what I told the other officer. I haven't seen the bastard in bloody ages.'

'Another police officer called you?'

'Yes. Don't you lot talk to each other?'

'What was this officer's name?'

'Why does it matter?'

'Please, Casey, just answer my question.'

'Chase. He said he was called DCI Chase.'

Kate's mouth went dry. There was no way William had rung this woman. He couldn't have. He'd been dead for four months. She cleared her throat. 'Can you remember exactly when he phoned?'

'No, of course not. It was a few months ago.'

Her heart sank. William could have rung Casey before he was killed. That he hadn't mentioned it to Kate suggested he had deliberately kept it from her.

Kate racked her mind for reasons why William would be looking for Tommy, only to turn up negative answers – that he was working with the syndicate rather than against them, maybe even tracking Tommy down to silence him so he couldn't verify Harriet's alibi for why she'd been near the warehouse the day Kate was attacked.

She couldn't fathom it, and instead said, 'Can you find the number in your call log?'

'Sorry, no. I got an upgrade in November. DCI Chase spoke to me before I changed phones. I remember there was no caller ID when he rang, and I thought it was going to be some prick trying to sell me something.'

'Did you get the call at the beginning of November, then?'

'No, it was sometime in October.' There was a pause. 'Mid-October. I can't remember the exact date.'

William was buried on 2 October. If Casey was right, it couldn't have been him. A wave of relief washed over her, only to be followed quickly by more doubts. What if Casey was wrong?

'Okay. Can you remember what you told DCI Chase?'

'Same as I just told you. I hadn't seen Tommy in ages.'

'Did you give him any other information?'

There was a brief pause and then, 'I said he'd be better off trying Tommy's mate – Big Harry.'

Kate's heart skipped a couple of beats. She knew Big Harry. Memories stampeded through her mind of the snooker hall where she'd first encountered him while hunting for people traffickers who were moving young girls, one of them Stanka's little sister.

Harry had been instrumental in arranging a meeting between her and Stanka's pimp, Farai. He'd even steered her team in the right direction of a trio of human traffickers. It hadn't crossed her mind to ask him about Tommy. She knew where Harry hung out and was planning on what she'd say to him when reality slapped her in the face and she remembered that the person who had rung Casey, pretending to be William, also knew about Big Harry.

It had to have been someone from the syndicate. Somebody tying up loose ends to ensure that Tommy couldn't vouch for Harriet. If Big Harry had given up Tommy to that person, then the informant would certainly be dead.

'Are you still there?' asked Casey.

'Yes. Sorry, I lost signal for a second. Is there anybody else who might know Tommy's whereabouts?'

'I can't think of anyone.'

'Listen, if Tommy does contact you, would you please ring me straight away?'

'Okay. I doubt he will. Last time we spoke, I told him to fuck off out of my life. I was sick of him turning up when it suited him, begging for money we both knew he'd never repay. I don't need someone like him.'

'I appreciate your call, Casey.'

'Yeah, right. Good luck finding him. He can be a slippery bastard when it suits him.'

Kate stared at the screen long after the call had ended. Farai. The traffickers. Big Harry. Tommy. Harriet. The syndicate. The pieces were all there. If only she could make them fit.

Her next step was to talk to Harry. However, she would have to tread with extreme caution. Once the syndicate caught wind that she was trying to exonerate Harriet, she would be in danger and there was nobody left alive who could help her this time.

It took a couple of hours, but eventually Scott unearthed a connection between Leah and Victoria. Harlequin Events had organised a charity auction and dinner at the town hall in late October. Not only had Leah, Russell, Victoria and Craig all attended, but they had been seated at the same table for the evening.

'Who do we need to speak to?' she asked.

'Arabella Mordant,' said Scott. 'She's a chartered surveyor. She and her husband were on the same table as them. And before you ask, yes, I have arranged to speak to her.'

'The telepathy is working well, then.'

'Keep beaming those instructions across and I'll keep performing,' he replied. 'You want to come with me to interview Arabella?'

'I could do with getting out for a while.'

'And we could pick up some lunch while we're at it. Grab a sandwich or a burger. I really fancy a burger.'

The look he gave her reminded her of Morgan, who was ruled by his stomach, even mid-investigation. Scott was great to work with, but he wasn't Morgan. She really missed being in the thick of things with him. She suppressed the sadness that was bubbling up. Morgan was still in her life. Just in a different role. 'Drive-through it is.'

As they left, she spotted Morgan at the far end of the corridor, his head down, clearly on a mission. She stopped herself from calling out to him. He wouldn't appreciate the interruption and she had work to do.

There appeared to be even less white render on the exterior of Tony's Pool and Snooker Hall than Kate remembered, and the sign over the building had lost another two letters since she'd last visited. The entrance door, however, still required a shoulder heave to open it.

Inside, she took a moment to allow her eyes to adjust to the gloom and the dark stairwell that zigzagged to the main room. She heard rather than saw the man who coughed several times before hawking on to the stairs.

As soon as he spotted her, a stupid grin spread across his pinched features. 'You wanna have a drink with me, doll?'

'I'm here on business so move out of the way.'

His eyes narrowed. 'Fuck you, bitch.'

She ignored the obscenity and strode past, reaching the large room that housed seven tired-looking tables.

There were three lunchtime games in progress. None of the players paid her any attention, concentrating instead on potting the balls. She spotted quick movement behind the bar; somebody was shutting the door to the room marked *Private* – Big Harry's room. She strolled across and showed her ID to the surly-faced youth behind the bar. 'Please tell Big Harry that DCI Kate Young would like to speak to him about something extremely important.'

'He isn't here.'

'Listen, I've asked you nicely. You and I both know that he is here.' She pointed to the black door behind the man. 'Go through to the back and pass on my message.'

'Or what?'

'Or I'll have him arrested for perverting the course of justice.' She glared at the young man. He didn't flinch and Kate was about to force the issue further when the door opened. Harry filled the doorway.

'Let's get this over with. Come on in, DCI Young.'

The room contained several screens on a wall, each showing various areas of the snooker room. Facing it were two large chairs in a deep-brown velvet fabric. Between them sat a table containing a tray of glasses and a bottle of whisky. Harry reached for the bottle, unscrewed the cap and said, 'Fancy one?'

'It's too early for me.'

'Please yourself.' He poured a generous slug and returned the top to the bottle before sitting down in the chair furthest from the door. 'So, what's all this crap about perverting the course of justice? I helped you out a few months ago.'

'It isn't about what you did, more what you didn't do. You're friends with Tommy Clayton.'

'And?'

'And he's missing.'

'If you say so.'

'I do, and furthermore, I say you know that he is. Tommy is in a sticky situation. His life is in danger. If you have any idea at all where he might be, tell me.'

'I don't.'

'You see, that's where I have a problem. I think you do.'

'Then we'll have to agree to disagree.'

'No. I'm going to give you one last chance to tell me then I am going to arrest you not only for perverting the course of justice but for prostitution links and links to human trafficking. And that's just for starters. You'd be surprised what I could pin on you if I set my mind to it. I'll have this cesspit of a snooker hall closed down, and make sure a few villains currently under lock and key learn that you helped me put them there. I don't fancy your chances, Harry, so what will it be?'

He drained his glass in one. 'You win. Last I heard, he was hiding out in a mobile home near Rugeley.'

'Can you give me more? Is it on a site?'

He shook his head. 'Don't know any more than that, I swear.'

'Has Tommy contacted you?'

'Not heard from him since last October. He said he was going underground.'

'Did he say why?'

'No, and I didn't ask him. There are some things that even mates don't ask. There have been rumours about Tommy for a while, people saying that he was in a copper's pocket. You know what I mean. Now, I don't have a problem with that, but others do, and Tommy had a few enemies waiting to take him down. He's done the right thing to keep a low profile until the heat is off.'

Even though she knew the answer, she decided to test the waters. 'Who was he passing information to?'

'Haven't a clue. We never discussed it. Tommy came here for a few drinks and to get away from his problems, not to bring them to my door.'

'I heard you had somebody else asking about him.'

'That's right.'

'What did they look like?'

'I didn't set eyes on them. They rang me. Number withheld.'

'And who did they say they were?'

'Police. Like you. Gave the name DCI William Chase. I didn't believe them. Chase was your boss. The one who got wasted . . . by one of your own. Tsk. What a state the country is in when the police begin killing each other. As if we don't have enough criminals.'

Anger uncoiled in her stomach. She struggled to keep it reined in.

'Did you tell this person where Tommy was hiding?'

Harry barked a low laugh and reached for the bottle again. 'Do me a favour, I'm not that stupid.'

'I'm not convinced. You've spilled the beans to me. I'm sure somebody else could equally put pressure on you. What did they say to you, to make you talk? Did they threaten you like I did?'

His mood changed in an instant, his hand tightening around the bottle. Kate prepared to dodge, should he decide to launch at her with it. Instead, he bared yellow teeth. 'Fuck you. I don't care what you believe or don't. I've told you what you need to know, so piss off and stop bothering me. I don't have anything else to share with you.'

Kate didn't budge. 'You don't scare me. If I find out that Tommy is already dead, I'll come for you.'

He raised an empty glass to her. 'And I'll be ready for you, DCI Young.'

She spun on her heel and, with one hand on the door handle, said, 'Tommy is mixed up with some very dangerous people. If you had crossed them, they'd have done some truly horrendous things to you before killing you. I don't buy your act for one second. I'm going to look for Tommy and if you have any idea where he is, I suggest you get hold of him and tell him to find me before these people destroy you both, because they will. And even if they have got to Tommy, don't think for a second that will be the end of it for you. They will still come after you and they will silence you. They cover their tracks. They get rid of *all* the loose ends. I'm your only hope, Harry. You'd do well to remember that.'

With that, she marched into the snooker hall, past all the tables and down the stairs. Tommy's ex-wife had been right when she said he could be a slippery bastard. It would be the only way he could keep out of the syndicate's claws.

Scott turned off the engine. 'This has to be the place.' The building, once an old factory, sat in a sizeable plot, protected by railings and 'Keep Out' notices. Emma spotted a small group beside a pick-up truck, their backs to her, visible due to their yellow helmets and high-vis jackets. She got out of the car, an icy blast slapping her cheeks as she marched purposefully towards the protective railings and called out, 'Arabella Mordant!'

The people looked up and one of them waved.

'That's me. Won't be a minute,' she shouted.

Scott blew on his hands, rubbing them together vigorously. 'Good, cos it's bloody freezing out here.'

Emma agreed. The temperature had dropped several degrees and her coat wasn't keeping out the chill.

Arabella peeled away from the others and made for the fencing. At close quarters, she was plain-featured, with mousy hair in a stubby ponytail that stuck out from under her safety hat. Her face remained expressionless as she spoke. 'Hello, sorry we couldn't meet at the office. I can't even invite you on site for health and safety reasons.'

'That's okay,' said Emma. 'We understand. Thank you for taking time to talk to us.'

'Not a problem. What a shock to hear about Leah and Victoria,' she said. 'I only met them the once at the charity event but nevertheless . . . what a truly terrible thing to have happened.'

Although her face remained impassive, her words sounded sincere to Emma. 'We wanted to ask you about that evening.'

Arabella replied before Emma could ask her any specific questions.

'Similar to other charity functions I've attended. Everyone at tables with strangers, unless they've purchased a whole table for themselves, friends and families. I always find these types of events difficult. It's hard enough mingling but when you're stuck with the same people for two to three hours, it can be a drag. Fortunately, they were perfectly pleasant. We enjoyed a three-course dinner, participated in a charity auction, then there was dancing.'

'What can you tell us about the couples?'

'Not a great deal. I know what they did for jobs and a bit about their hobbies. I hardly spoke to the women, although I did chat to Leah in the cloakroom briefly. She won the bid for a lovely painting at the auction. I congratulated her. She confessed that Russell wasn't happy about her bidding so much for it and would give her a hard time over it later. My husband, Oliver, was sitting between Leah and Victoria so you might get a better idea from him. Although he's currently in New York until next Wednesday. I can only tell you that both Russell and Craig were very polite, although the conversation dried up quickly.'

'Could you explain the seating arrangement to us? How many others were there at the table?' asked Scott.

'The tables were set for ten, but the other four people who were supposed to be at ours pulled out at the last minute, leaving the six of us, so we spread out. Leah suggested we didn't sit next to our own partners but instead got to know each other. She sat between Oliver and Craig. I sat between Craig and Russell. Victoria sat between Russell and Oliver. Leah, Craig, then me, Russell, Victoria and Oliver,' she repeated, stabbing at imaginary place settings as she spoke.

'You said the conversation dried up fairly quickly,' said Scott. 'Was that the case with everyone?'

Arabella hesitated before replying. 'No. Although it wasn't unusual. I'm not very good in those sorts of social situations. I'm a workaholic and when I go out I don't have the sort of social chit-chat people enjoy. I went along at Oliver's insistence. He thinks it's important that we support events like that in the community. Ordinarily, I stick to Oliver's side, even at sit-down events. He's far more gregarious and at ease. I usually keep quiet unless I'm asked a question. Despite their efforts, I'm afraid Russell and Craig must have found me dreary. As it happened, their immediate neighbours were more outgoing. I was happy to sit back and let them get on with it. Leah and Craig hit it off immediately: lots of laughter, flirty conversation, that sort of thing. It got worse the more they drank. I think I even saw them slow dancing afterwards.'

'How did Russell react to that?' asked Scott.

'I haven't a clue. At the time, he was dancing with Victoria. By then, Oliver and I were ready to leave.'

'Did you talk about the event afterwards?'

'Only to say it was one of the worst we'd attended. Oliver said the conversation had been hard work and that Russell had been throwing Leah dirty looks throughout the night. He made a comment along the lines that he wouldn't be surprised if they didn't row once they got home.'

'Can you tell us anything about Victoria?'

'I don't want to sound mean – after all, people get noisier and more brash after a few drinks, don't they? I'm teetotal and Oliver doesn't drink much either, which means I pick up on people's behaviour, especially after they've consumed alcohol. I noticed they were all knocking back the wine. After the meal, Craig ordered shots for everyone. Victoria became . . . less inhibited. She might not have been as vocal or as pushy as Leah, but she was definitely sending out signals to Russell. That's about all I can tell you.'

'We'd really like to talk to Oliver.'

'I'll give you his phone number. He's in meetings most of the day, so it might be tricky to pin him down. If you prefer, I could message him your details and ask him to contact you.'

'Would you, please? As soon as possible would be great.'

Arabella paused again. 'There was one more thing. I can't be completely certain about this, but when I was heading back from the toilets, I saw Leah and Craig together in a small room off the corridor. And he appeared to have an arm around her. When I got back to the table, everyone but Oliver had gone. But given the music had started, they might have been on the dance floor.'

Emma thanked the woman, who left them to their deliberations. 'What do you think?' Emma asked Scott.

'We should talk to Craig again.'

'I agree.'

Frankie chose that moment to ring. 'I've spoken to Doctor Schmidt,' she said. 'Leah told her that her husband wasn't keen on having children and so she wanted to discuss termination, but after the consultation decided it wasn't an option. Leah fully intended having the baby.'

'What else could you glean?'

'A month later, she requested medication to help cope with anxiety. The combination of her workload and a strained relationship with the baby's father was causing her sleepless nights, along with fresh doubts about going through with the pregnancy. Doctor Schmidt advised her against taking tranquillisers and suggested she request fewer hours at work and/or look at alternative methods such as yoga to keep down stress levels. She also suggested Leah and her husband attend counselling to help work through their issues. Leah appeared to accept this advice but said an appointment with a counsellor wouldn't be necessary. That they'd sort things out.'

'Did Leah mention the possibility that Russell wasn't the baby's father?'

'It appears not. Doctor Schmidt assumed he was and didn't quiz her on the matter. During a follow-up appointment, Leah assured her that having taken up yoga classes she was feeling more relaxed, and that Russell had come around to the idea of being a father.'

'Jeez! Do we believe that Leah told Russell about the baby? And he was happy? Or that she was so stressed out about the situation that she asked for tranquillisers to help her cope? All these lies!'

'It seems to me as if she was frightened to face the truth. She must have been in quite a state,' said Frankie.

'I expect so. She was in a real pickle. Plus, she had the added pressure of Russell wanting her to quit her job and work with him. Anyway, thanks, Frankie. We're going to speak to Craig again before we head back.'

With the call over, Scott spoke up. 'I reckon Leah was out of her depth. She'd got herself into a sticky situation: a baby her husband didn't want and might not have fathered, a job she wanted to hang on to and all the while pressure to set up a new company. She was probably praying that things would work themselves out.'

Emma nodded. It was tricky enough managing a work/relationship balance. The addition of an unplanned child complicated career-minded couples even further. She couldn't help but think Russell might well have known about the situation. And if he did . . . well, what would he be capable of?

◆ ◆ ◆

Kate had taken a chance on heading to the only residential park she knew of that was not too far from Rugeley. Nevertheless, she wasn't very optimistic about her choice. It didn't seem to her the sort of place somebody would choose to hide. For one thing, it was a semi-retirement park for people aged over fifty; it was close to the busy main road that ran from Stafford to Lichfield, and it was opposite the Trent and Mersey Canal, where several narrowboats were moored. It wasn't a place where Tommy could easily blend in and vanish, even if he spent most of his time indoors. Somebody from the syndicate would easily have tracked him here and finished him off. This didn't seem like a clever move.

'Maybe that was exactly his thought process,' said William's voice. 'He could be hiding in plain sight. The syndicate might not even have considered this place. Like you, they'll have pegged it for a lousy hiding place. They would imagine Tommy to be shrewder, that if he is living *in a static home, then he'd have chosen one in a remote location, or at least somewhere very difficult to find. Check out this place and have a word with the publicans. There's every chance he'll have visited one or both nearby pubs. If he is or was here, there's no way he'd have sat inside day after day. He'd be feeling confident enough to get out and about. Try it at least. If I'm wrong, I'm wrong. It's surely worth investigating.'*

It was enough for her to pull off the road on to the tarmacadam that allowed her to drive around the site, getting a feel for which properties were occupied and which weren't. As she drove, it soon became obvious that this was an extensive plot, housing approximately one hundred and fifty static homes of all descriptions and sizes. Passing place after place, she got the feeling she was being observed by curtain twitchers. These residents were very curious. Maybe Tommy had chosen to come here after all.

The hardest decision was working out which door to bang on first. She could really do with her old team doing this legwork. It would take forever to get around all the houses and even then, she couldn't guarantee anyone would tell her anything useful.

'Got to start somewhere, Kate,' said William. *'Head to the far end and work your way back to the road in a clockwise direction. If I were hiding, I'd choose a home that had a good view of anyone approaching.'*

Once again, hearing his instructions gave her the motivation she needed. She pulled up in front of the shabbiest home and got out. The resident who answered the doorbell took one look at her and told her to shove off, telling her that cold callers weren't allowed on site.

'Policing is all about tenacity and footwork, Kate. I always taught you that. It can be laborious and often unrewarding. Still, it must be done. Try next door.'

With a sigh, Kate digested William's words. Without him, she would have given up, the task too onerous to contemplate.

'*Remember what is at stake here,*' he said. '*The syndicate might well have framed Harriet. You can't allow them to get away with it.*'

She opened the small gate and trudged up the path to the adjacent property. She was nothing if not tenacious. William had taught her well.

As she raised her hand to knock, doubts crept in, and the jeering tones of Dickson washed away William's voice. '*William isn't helping you – in fact, he's deliberately hindering you. He knows as well as I do that Tommy isn't here. The longer you spend chasing after shadows, the less time you will have to track down Digger and save your own skin. Still, you never listen to my voice, so go ahead, waste the rest of the day.*'

She hesitated, turned to go, then changed her mind. She was here now. Besides, she had no clue as to Digger's whereabouts.

'*Oh, you do,*' whispered William. '*Think back to your visit to the farm.*'

'*Yes, waste some more time,*' said Dickson.

She pressed her fingers against her ears. 'Stop it! Stop. Both of you.'

The door opened and an elderly woman gave her a curious look. 'You alright, dear?'

Taken aback, Kate regained her composure. 'Yes, thank you. A migraine. They come on quickly.'

The woman continued staring at her. 'If you say so. You should go home and lie down.'

'I'm looking for somebody who lives here. A man in his mid-forties, shaved head, medium build. He had a spider's web tattoo on his neck.'

The woman reached for the door. 'I haven't seen him.' The door shut before Kate could say any more.

'*Tick tock, Kate,*' said Dickson.

CHAPTER FIFTEEN

Craig Hannover's shoulders shook as he sobbed into his hands. It was proving impossible to speak to the man, who burst into tears at almost every mention of his wife. Emma could feel her nostrils flaring as she attempted for the fourth time to calm the man down and get some answers.

'Craig, I understand how difficult this must be for you—'

He lifted his blotchy face. 'Do you? Really? Have you ever lost anyone in such horrible circumstances?' he spluttered.

'Actually, I have,' Emma replied. 'My mother was murdered.'

The man's mouth opened. 'Oh!' was all he said.

'So, I do understand. I know you will be going through a range of emotions and that none of this is easy. Talking about Victoria only serves to highlight the fact that she has gone, which I know is painful to accept. All the same, you must accept it.'

He nodded; wiped away a snot bubble.

'We really need as much information as possible to help find her killer. We want justice for Victoria and for you and all her family.' Emma spoke as gently as possible. She never spoke about her mother's death. Only a handful of people knew what had transpired and she could feel Scott's eyes boring into her back. He'd had no idea until now.

'I just want to know a little about the charity event you attended. You sat on the same table as Russell and Leah Fairbrother and Arabella and Oliver Mordant. Arabella told us that you and Leah got on very well.'

He pushed his long fringe away from his eyes. 'Yes. She was fun.'

'I understand you were flirting.'

'Flirting? I suppose so. We all had a lot to drink. That sort of thing happens. She was very bubbly, and we enjoyed each other's company.'

'Is that all?'

'I don't know what you expect me to say. Nothing serious happened.'

'You were seen in another room in a situation that might be interpreted as more intimate.'

'What! I . . . Oh, wait. We did have a private moment. But that was nothing. Leah was upset about Russell. He was being an arse. He'd been making snide comments about her all evening. He'd taken her to one side and told her that she was showing him up. That was good coming from him. He'd been giving Victoria the full chat all evening. She said he was a right creep.' His eyes became glassy again. 'Sorry, but talking about Victoria is so painful.'

'Take your time,' said Emma. 'Victoria didn't like Russell?'

'He was a selfish prick who hogged her attention. Every time she started a conversation with Oliver, Russell interrupted them. She was too polite to tell him to butt out.'

This wasn't quite the same picture that Arabella had given them. They would need to speak to Oliver to get a better idea of what transpired.

Craig blew his nose, and his voice became thick with emotion again as he tried to speak. 'Russell tried it on with her later that evening. He cornered her when she went outside to get some fresh air. I was in the toilets and had no idea what was happening until I saw her in tears in the hall. She told me he'd tried to force himself on her. I went looking for him but both he and Leah had left.'

'Did you see either of them again?'

He shook his head.

'Did Victoria have any further contact with them?'

'No. It was one of those nights that you write off. Like I said. We'd all had too much to drink.'

Emma's phone rang and she excused herself, leaving Scott to continue interviewing Craig.

Ervin Saunders sounded very pleased with himself.

'Who's the daddy?' he said.

She couldn't help but smile. 'I assume it's you. Now please explain why you are so fantastic.'

'My dear, I am always fantastic. Today, however, I am magnificent. I called in a favour with a friend who works at the toxicology department, and they divulged that your latest victim had high levels of scopolamine in her system. I expect you'd like me to elucidate further.'

'Yes.'

Ervin cleared his throat before continuing. Emma could almost imagine him straightening one of the brightly coloured bow ties he usually wore to work before commencing.

'Scopolamine, also known as hyoscine or, more sinisterly, Devil's Breath, is formally used for treating motion sickness. Now, here's the part you will undoubtedly find interesting. It contains hallucinogenic properties, which means it is sought after as a drug of misuse. Moreover, it can also make someone subservient and obedient, along with impairing that person's ability to store facts and events.'

Emma's pulse quickened as he spoke. This could be the breakthrough she needed.

'How long does it last in the system?'

'Up to nine hours.'

'Damn! That means even if there had been some in Leah's system, it would be untraceable.'

'Aha! This is where my magnificence truly shines. I've been having a tête-à-tête with our friendly Canadian forensic anthropologist, who informs me that even though scopolamine leaves the body after nine hours, the sensitised effects in the vestibular nuclei centre can last for days to weeks.'

'Which means?'

'Which means he is going to re-examine those areas in Leah's brain, because one of the side-effects of an overdose of this drug is significant cerebral oedema.'

Emma could hardly breathe for excitement.

'Oh, wow!'

'I'd expected applause, but I'll take that as an expression of delight. I thought it sensible to ring you straight away.'

'I'm really grateful to you—'

'Uh-uh! No need for that. I did this because I like you and I want to see you crack this case so quickly they promote you from DI to DCI in a flash.'

His words gave her a warm fuzzy feeling. Ervin was one of a kind, generous and supportive. She wanted to reach out and hug him. 'Then at least let me take you out for a meal to say thanks.'

'You're on. Best wait until you've caught the perp first.'

'Okay, but we won't leave it too long.'

'I'm sure we won't need to.'

As soon as the call was ended, she punched the air. This was a huge step in their inquiries. She had method. Now she needed to uncover the motive and jealousy seemed as likely as anything else. What had really transpired at the charity event? Somebody wasn't telling the full story.

She made her way back up the path to Craig's house. Her gut told her that either he or Russell was lying. It was a matter of finding out which one.

◆ ◆ ◆

Kate had tried over half of the static caravans without success. Nobody had seen or heard of Tommy Clayton. She made for the nearest pub in the hope Tommy had visited it. If he had chosen this spot, it wasn't as bad a choice as she'd initially thought. There were rows and rows of mobile homes, many overlooking fields where a getaway on foot would be possible. Being next to a main road, he would be able to grab a lift or, if he had transport nearby, reach any number of destinations. In brief, it was a great place to hide out.

That she was here searching for Tommy, rather than hunting down Digger, was odd and she questioned why she had prioritised Harriet over herself.

'Because, Kate, it's your nature. That's why you are so good at your job. You always set aside your personal life and put others first,' said William.

Dickson scoffed. *'Even if you do catch Digger, the chances of him seeing anyone else that night are remote. It was pitch-black. He was hiding and his attention was on us fighting. You know in your heart of hearts he'll be unable to help.'*

As was now usual whenever she found herself alone, she spoke in each voice. She cast about in case anyone was around to hear her. There was nobody.

'He might,' she said to Dickson, even though she knew he had a point.

'That's right. Keep looking. You're not somebody to give up,' said William.

Nodding at that last statement, she made for the Plum Pudding Inn. With opening hours every day from noon until late, Italian and Spanish cuisine and live music of an evening, it was invariably busy – a good place for someone to blend in. The rear patio overlooked the canal where narrowboats would moor up, their crews stopping off at this spot. Peering through the lounge window, she had eyes on three such boats, two painted in traditional green and red colours and one, *Guinevere*, in blue, her hull embellished with intricate patterns of cream and yellow and folk artwork: a medieval castle on a hill. Even at this time of the year there were people keen to escape hectic lives and enjoy a slice of serendipity.

Kate's heels clacked across the wooden floor. A young couple with a baby asleep in a pushchair – the sole customers – seemed indifferent to her arrival, heads over steaming bowls of soup. Kate associated the decor with that of narrowboats: a grey wood-panelled bar with a gleaming dark wooden counter, oak cabinets stacked with plates and a coffee machine, half-wall panelling painted in dark green and paintings that contributed to a traditional, boating impression, along with a fire that burned brightly and added to the cosy feel.

There was no one behind the bar, so she rang the brass call bell. A stocky man with a broad beard soon appeared.

'What can I get you?'

'Just a bottled orange juice, please, and some information,' she said, placing her ID card on the counter.

He glanced at it and nodded. 'No problem.'

While he selected a bottle and uncapped it, she spoke. 'I'm looking for a man called Tommy Clayton.' She described him.

'Can't say that I've noticed anyone fitting that description, but it gets manic in here at times. You could try Suzie. She works evenings. She'll be here in about half an hour, if you're happy to wait.'

'I'll do that. Thanks.'

Having paid for her drink, she selected a table with a view of the door and waited.

'More time-wasting.'

She shut off Dickson's whispered voice in her head and turned her attention to her phone, flicking through emails to keep her distracted. Work was piling up. She ought to return to the office and answer her correspondence, yet having got this far, she was loath to give up hunting for Tommy just yet. One of the emails was from another DCI in Manchester, an officer going by the name of Henchard. The name triggered a sharp recollection of the conversation she had overheard at the Hardcastles' farm. They'd been talking about Digger going to work on another farm. Although she'd been unable to catch the farmer's name, she was sure it had started with 'Hen'.

She began searching names of local farmers, becoming so engrossed she didn't notice the arrival of a young woman with pink hair. It was only when the barman called her over to the bar that she realised Suzie had turned up for work.

'Suzie's seen your man,' he said in a hushed voice.

'When?' she asked.

'A few times. He drinks alone. Always in the main bar, even when the other rooms are quieter. He usually comes here on live music nights, and he only ever has the one drink – a pint of Boddingtons,' said Suzie.

'Has he ever chatted to you?'

'No. He's not the chatty sort.'

'When did you last see him?' asked Kate, sure she would say a couple of months ago. Her heart jumped when Suzie replied, 'He was here last Thursday.'

'Are you sure of that?'

'Definitely.'

'Has anyone else been asking about him?'

'Nobody.'

'No one has approached me either,' said the man.

Surely somebody from the syndicate would have done exactly the same as her – tried the mobile homes and this pub. It was puzzling that they hadn't. All the same, this was good news because if Suzie was right, it meant Tommy might still be alive.

'When he next comes in, I want you to ring me. Immediately. And don't tell him I'm looking for him. That part is extremely important.'

'Is he dangerous?' asked Suzie.

'No.'

The barman rubbed at his thick beard. 'Has he done something wrong?'

'All I can tell you is that it is vital I get in contact with him, so please, take these cards and call me as soon as you spot him.'

She placed the business cards in front of them. The door opened and a group of people entered. She thanked the bar staff and left. Tempting as it was to abandon her door-knocking, she couldn't leave the job half done. It wasn't in her nature. Only after she'd seen this through would she resume her hunt for Digger.

Back at the office, Emma had just come off the phone to Oliver Mordant. Convinced that Craig had played down events at the charity evening, she addressed her team.

'Oliver said Craig couldn't take his eyes off Leah, and there was little doubt that Russell was fuming about it. He believes Russell made advances to Victoria purely to get back at her flirtatious husband. Oliver is certain they were messing about under the table too: touching hands, playing footsie or *some such nonsense* as he described it.'

197

George fiddled with a propelling pencil, and cleared his throat before saying, 'Those are sweeping statements to make about people he didn't know.'

'I agree and saying, "some such nonsense"! That makes him sound a right fuddy-duddy,' said Harry.

'Yeah, he could be jealous cos Leah and Victoria didn't vibe with him?' suggested Frankie.

Emma couldn't agree. 'I didn't get the impression Oliver was interested in or bothered about what went on. He merely offered neutral observations. I hear you all, but I'm taking him at his word.'

Scott wrinkled his nose. 'Then I suppose we need to squeeze Craig and Russell harder. Neither of them has an alibi for the evenings that Victoria and Leah were attacked.'

'And lots of homicides are committed by spouses,' said Harry.

Frankie nodded earnestly. 'Maybe they got together and decided to bump off each other's partner like in that film . . . erm . . .'

The room went silent for a moment until Harry said, '*Throw Momma from the Train?*'

Frankie frowned. 'It's like that, but not funny. An old film.'

'*Strangers on a Train,*' said Scott. 'It was directed by Hitchcock. I think it was about . . . 1951. Yes, that feels about right.'

Frankie rolled her eyes. '1951! Sarge, how do you know stuff like that?'

'I'm a bit of a film buff in my spare time. Anyway, I doubt that's what happened. Sounds too fanciful.'

'But not impossible,' Frankie insisted. 'Shit happens all the time and some people get their criminal ideas from films. Or books.'

Emma wasn't up for debating nonsense. 'I appreciate that we shouldn't discount any theory, but let's stick to facts. We have nothing to suggest they met up to plan this.'

'Could have arranged it online,' muttered Frankie.

'Can we explore other possibilities first?' said Emma. She pointed at the board again. 'Craig and Russell have no obvious connection other than meeting at that charity event. We know Russell was annoyed with Leah for bidding on a painting, and for flirting with Craig. He might have taken her to task later. Added to what else we've uncovered, what we have is a picture of a marriage that's not very rosy. We still don't know if the baby was Russell's but we believe Leah might have been seeing somebody else, which opens up possibilities regarding the identity of the child's father. One of our priorities must be to identify the man she was spotted with, crossing over the bridge into Mill Bank.'

'You know,' said Frankie, who was now staring hard at the board. 'Russell, Craig, and that man all seem very similar. Looks like Leah had a type.'

It was a fact that hadn't escaped Emma's attention. 'I agree. Harry, would you prod the tech team for us? This description is too vague. I know we dumped a load of stuff on them, but we still need a photo of this mystery man. Maybe they could come up with a capture from CCTV. And now it's seven o'clock and I suggest we pack up.'

Frankie slid off the desk where she'd been sitting. 'I could give the bars another go.'

'Not tonight. You've been at it long enough today. Get some rest. We need to be on form again in the morning. Pack up. All of you. Tomorrow is a new day.'

No sooner had everyone left for the evening than Morgan strolled in, hands behind his back. For a moment, she was unable to react normally, aware that he might have come to continue their argument, or to tell her that everything was over between them. He'd been so angry the evening before, and she really didn't know what to expect from him.

'Hey!'

'Hey yourself,' he replied. 'Brings back memories, doesn't it? I miss this room.'

She weighed up his words. Did he miss 'this room' or the old times they'd spent here? She hoped it was the latter and said, 'It's not the same without you and Jamie.'

He pulled a face. 'And Jamie? You can have him back any day. He's still a nightmare to work with – bouncy, indefatigable and irritating.'

She kept up her end of the frivolous conversation. 'I've got Frankie now, who is equally animated and has more energy than a hyperactive toddler.'

'Maybe Jamie and Frankie are related,' said Morgan.

An awkward silence fell, the brief spell of light-heartedness over, and a serious look crossed his face. Her heart sank and she waited for him to come up with some bullshit excuse as to why he didn't want to continue being in a couple with her. Instead, he mumbled, 'Anyway, I came to bring you this.' He proffered a plain box, which she took from him.

'What is it?'

'A peace offering. Last night I was pissed, grumpy and kind of anxious about taking on the new role. I behaved like a shit and I'm truly sorry.'

She undid the ribbon, opened the box and laughed when she saw the contents – an extra-large Bourbon biscuit. 'Really?'

'You know that they're my absolute favourites . . . and I don't give away biscuits, especially giant ones, to just anybody. Only somebody special.'

Relief that he wasn't going to dump her, and that he'd acknowledged his bad behaviour with such a fun gesture, resulted in instant forgiveness.

'It would have been better if you'd talked things through with me, explained what was wrong instead of leaving me second-guessing what was going on in your head. Anyway, let's not dwell on it. It's forgotten. As long as you don't ever banish me to the spare room again.'

'I promise I won't. You have my word and my extra-special biscuit to prove it.'

'Tell you what, we'll share this later.'

'Sounds great, but I won't be home for another hour or so.'

'That's fine. I could do with a workout. I haven't been to the gym for ages. Want me to pick up any food on my way back?'

'Nah. I'll eat with the troops. We're ordering in.'

'I'll see you when I see you, then.'

'You bet.' He pulled her into an embrace, which he followed with another apology. 'I really am sorry. I behaved appallingly. Forgive me?'

His puppy-dog eyes won her over. 'Of course I do. I should have rung to let you know that I'd be late.'

'And I would do well to remember that this job can be all-consuming and none of us need extra pressure dumping on us from our loved ones. It was a one-off. Right, have a good workout and make sure you aren't too tired when you get in.' He winked.

'Same applies to you!'

'I'll choose whatever Jamie chooses. Something he eats keeps him going at full pelt. Hopefully it's pizza.'

After his heavy footsteps retreated into the distance, she packed away her paperwork, placing the gift at the top of her bag. Only Morgan would bring a biscuit as a peace offering. It was good they'd made up, so why did she still feel uneasy?

◆ ◆ ◆

By seven o'clock, Kate was weary of hammering on static caravan doors and getting nowhere. She'd noted homes where nobody had responded, intending to try them the following day. She opened her takeaway fish and chips box. Although she'd been tempted to head back into the Plum Pudding Inn to eat, she hadn't wanted the bar staff to feel uncomfortable by her presence, plus the chances of Tommy showing up this evening were slim. For one thing, there was no live music tonight.

'He isn't going to show his face in there again. One of the bar staff was lying. They'll have been paid off. Did you really believe for one second the syndicate would have tracked Tommy to the caravan park and not asked around the local pubs?' Dickson's voice droned on and on. She stabbed repeatedly at her chips, forced them down her drying throat until she could bear it no longer.

'I wish you'd fuck off.'

'Not going to happen. Not while you're doubting yourself every inch of the way and are terrified that any day now those photos are going to come to light. You are stuck with me and it's no good calling out to William. Even he thinks you are going around in circles.'

She shoved the half-empty box into the passenger footwell, started the engine and threw the car into gear. The car leapt forward like an angry bear. She throttled it again, foot to the floor, desperate to leave Dickson behind her, yet all the while knowing she couldn't shake him, not until her fears had been quelled. Realising she was driving too quickly, she lifted her foot slightly from the accelerator. All of this was too much for her: the voices; the job; her impossible quest to help Harriet and then find William's killer. It was suffocating her. Once again, she decided to ring Tilly, the one person she knew could calm her. The last time she'd thought about ringing her, Kate had been disturbed. So, this time, before something else could interrupt her, using her hands-free, she called her stepsister on WhatsApp.

'Hi, sis.'

Hot tears sprang to Kate's eyes. She blinked them away.

Mindful that it was six thirty in the morning in Australia, she said, 'Hi yourself. It's not too early for a quick chat, is it?'

'Nah. Never too early to talk to you. Besides, you knew I'd be up. This time of the year we're woken up at the crack of dawn by the bloody lorikeets chattering in the trees outside our bedroom window.'

Kate remembered the parrots with their bright blue, green, orange and yellow plumage, so colourful they looked like flying rainbows.

'So, how's the new job?'

'Good, thanks. Lots of desk work though.'

'Do I detect a note of regret? Missing the fieldwork, are you?'

'I suppose I am. There are a couple of important investigations I'd like to be handling, but I have enough to keep me busy.'

'Such as?' Tilly always loved to hear what Kate was up to. It was as if Kate's life was a television drama Tilly could tune into.

This was the opportunity to share her concerns. Tilly even knew about what had transpired at the reservoir, that Kate had killed Dickson and covered up the death. And she knew all about Harriet killing William. Maybe that wasn't fair on Tilly, but if she thought so, she hadn't told Kate. And right now, Kate was glad to be able to talk to someone real, who knew the truth.

'Things are going belly up, Tilly. It looks like Harriet didn't shoot William after all. She's asked me to help prove her innocence and although I haven't delved too deeply, it appears she could be right, which means she was set up.'

'Oh, fuckety fuck! By the syndicate?'

'Uh-huh.'

'I thought all this had blown over. That with Dickson dead, and Harriet in jail, they'd disband?'

'No such luck. It seems they're still active.'

'Then you're still in danger!'

'I don't know if I am. Nobody knows I'm looking into Harriet's claims. She's as anxious as me to keep it quiet. We both know what we're up against.'

'Listen to me, Kate. You can't believe a word that woman says. If she's one of the syndicate members, she'll still be working with them to make it look like it was a set-up.'

Headlights coming towards Kate made her squint. Her heart began hammering. If Tilly was right, she was walking into another trap. She kept her eyes on the road ahead, hands firmly on the wheel.

Tilly continued, 'You can't run that risk. If Harriet wants to prove her innocence, she should get her lawyer involved. Have you asked yourself why she turned to you, of all people?'

'I did. I thought . . . Oh, shit. I don't know what I thought. Listen, Felicity also suspects the footage we had of her committing the crime has been corrupted. She's getting it examined by a top expert.'

'Other *experts* checked it and found nothing to support that theory. Even if this person finds something, can you be sure that it hasn't been sabotaged after the event simply to support her claim of innocence?'

Tilly was sounding more like the detective and Kate the civilian. Tilly's reasoning was confusing the heck out of her. A car drew closer to her bumper, too close. She eased off the accelerator pedal, allowing the vehicle to slow, hoping the person behind would overtake her. Instead, they remained right behind her.

'Tilly, I'm going to have to pull over. Give me a second while I find a spot.'

There was a lay-by one hundred metres ahead and she made for it. The car stayed doggedly behind her. What if it was a syndicate member?

'Don't be silly. It's just a frustrated driver,' said William.

'Kate! Did I just hear a man's voice? Is there somebody with you?'

Startled, Kate said quickly, 'No. It's only the radio. Hang on.' She'd never told Tilly about the voices. She had no desire to confess she not only heard them in her mind, but also conversed with them when alone. She had just slipped up badly.

She pulled into the lay-by. The car followed suit, drawing up behind her. With a hammering heart she watched her rear-view mirror for any movement, ready to speed away if necessary.

'Kate?'

'One second, Tilly.'

The car flashed its lights several times then pulled away. Kate glimpsed the driver, a shadowy figure who wound down the window and extended a middle finger at her before driving off at speed.

'Okay. I'm back.'

'You had me worried there.'

'Some tailgater was giving me aggro. They're gone now.'

'I was saying, you can't help Harriet. Tell her to find somebody else.'

Her stepsister's words made sense, more than the unravelling logic in her turmoiled brain. Tilly's words gave Kate some much-needed clarity.

Harriet, in conjunction with the syndicate, could be playing a devious game. Kate had fought long and hard for her reputation. People would listen to her if she supported Harriet's claims. There was every chance she was being manipulated, which might also explain why the photos of her at the reservoir had not yet surfaced. The syndicate needed her.

While all these thoughts sloshed around her head, another surfaced. Kate couldn't ignore it.

'I hear you, Tilly. And part of me agrees. All the same, if I can prove Harriet *is* telling the truth, then I'll have an ally who'll help me unearth the syndicate members. I need to root them out, whatever that takes. Both Chris and William tried and failed. I must do this . . . for them.'

Tilly sighed loudly. 'Sis, you can't keep putting yourself under this ridiculous amount of strain. You promised me that with Dickson gone, and Harriet awaiting trial, this . . . quest of yours would be over; that I wouldn't have to fret about your safety or your sanity, for that matter. I can't go about my days, worrying as I do, wondering if you're still alive or have fallen victim to these awful people.'

'I'm sorry. I don't mean to cause you any anxiety. I'm in control, Tilly. I promise I always exercise the greatest caution. I know I should back off and yet . . . I think I believe Harriet. You haven't spoken to her face to face. Some people might be able to mask all sorts of emotions but that look in her eyes – a mixture of fear and anxiety – can't be put on. I'm going to take a chance on her. If I can find one shred of evidence, no matter how tiny, that supports her argument, I'll fight alongside her. If I can't, then I won't pursue it. I'll heed your advice and back off.'

'You know your trouble?'

'What's that?'

'You're a police officer, through and through. You always have to get to the truth.'

Kate gave a light laugh. 'I guess so.'

'All the same, what you're doing is risky. Think hard about what I've said. Sometimes, you are so dogmatic and determined that you can't see the danger in front of your nose.'

'You know you are the best sister in the world,' said Kate.

'And you are the most courageous.'

Kate felt the tears welling again. Hearing Tilly had been enough to ground her. With her coping mechanism restored, she chatted for a while longer about lighter subjects before making her way back to the station, this time with more focus.

◆　◆　◆

Clouds drift across the night sky of starlight and the waxing gibbous moon that up until then has been casting a straw-like glow on to the tarmac in front of Greg's martial arts academy and gym.

He can't understand why people find heavenly bodies so wondrous. He regards the moon with dispassion; after all, it's only a natural satellite that orbits the Earth. It's without much gravity, is not geologically active and can't support human life. Nothing more, nothing less. He knows the four lunar phases and is aware that some people believe in moon energy. Unlike those spiritual believers who think that a waxing moon signals redirection or adjustment, and that they should spring forward to finish whatever needs to be done, he has always followed his own trajectory. He makes his own decisions, none based on nonsense or beliefs, but on . . . whatever he feels like doing. And as for the starry dots above him, they are celestial bodies consisting mostly of hydrogen and helium and although visible to the human eye, many are already dead. And . . . they don't even twinkle.

He folds his arms and sinks further into his seat, eyes still on Emma's car. He has no idea how long he's been sitting here, nor does it matter. He can sit for hours if need be. Time is fluid. He's disrupted his usual schedule to concentrate on Emma. He can't express exactly how he feels about her. That is – according to his therapist and his mother – one of his problems. He simply doesn't know how to articulate his feelings or emotions. During one session, when asked if he loved his mother, he was unable to answer, thus reducing her to tears.

Once he hit thirteen, shot up in height and developed a temper, his mother, who treated him cruelly during his childhood, became wary of him. He can't remember exactly when she threw him out, screaming he was abnormal and the devil's spawn. That's on her though. She's the one who was off her tits on crack and alcohol at the time. Although maybe him slamming her head against the wall had something to do with it. Still, that's on her too. She shouldn't have been such a bitch.

Maybe he does believe a little in fate or karma. After all, his mother is now the imprisoned one, while he is free. He doesn't care one way or the other about her. For the time being, she has her uses, or at least her house does. He dropped off Victoria's designer handbag earlier, along with her rings. He prefers sparkling, shiny, expensive jewellery to stars. Come to think of it, Emma doesn't wear any. Never mind, this time it isn't about money.

He simply feels like killing her.

CHAPTER SIXTEEN

'I fancy a cooked breakfast,' said Morgan. 'Want to ride into work with me and stop off on the way for a coffee and bacon butty?' He bounded from the bed, causing the springs to groan.

'Jeez, Morgan. It's six o'clock and already you're thinking about food?' said Emma.

'I'm a growing lad,' he replied.

'I don't want to grow to be your size,' she replied, grabbing the duvet and covering her head with it. She felt the mattress give as he climbed back on to it, then giggled as he tickled her.

'Get off!' The words were half-hearted. They'd often behaved this way until recently.

She kicked off the covers and tried to wriggle away, only to be caught in his arms. He kissed her gently. 'Orange juice and a light pastry then?' he said.

'Pastries aren't light but go on. A croissant and juice would be great.'

He stood up again and made for the wardrobe to select a shirt for the day. Seizing her moment, Emma waited until his back was turned then raced to the bathroom, where she locked the door.

He banged on the door, rattled the doorknob. 'Emma Donaldson! You know the rules! I shower first then make coffee while you take forever to get ready.'

She laughed. 'Thought I'd shake things up a bit.'

'Open the door and we can both shake things up together.'

She didn't need to think for long. She unlocked the door and stepped away from it. When Morgan came in, she was already peeling off her nightshirt.

◆ ◆ ◆

An exhausted Kate had slept through the night. It was the first time for what felt like forever that she hadn't been haunted by nightmares. Even though she had still been unable to establish if there was a farmer whose surname began with 'Hen', she was feeling more like her old self – convinced her call with Tilly had worked its magic.

She'd eaten a quick breakfast of cereal and toast and forfeited her usual run to allow herself time to visit William's house. If a search could unearth the vital document, it would not only give her the proof she needed to bring down the syndicate but would go some way towards substantiating Harriet's claims. They would at least know the names of the enemies they were facing.

She unlocked William's front door, then stooped to collect the junk mail scattered on the mat, placing it on the console table in the hallway without looking at it. The place felt empty and hollow, as if the house missed its owner as much as Kate did. She paused to imagine what it had been like in times gone by, pictured the two creamy-white cats that had been William's companions, and then her mentor in his favourite gardening hat and wearing gardening gloves while he tended to his flowers. That was what was missing: the scent of freshly picked blooms. There had always been a jug of flowers on the hall table, and another in the kitchen.

Kate would soon have to decide what to do with the property. She couldn't live here. She already owned a house, the one she and Chris had purchased together, and her memories of her husband were there. She could put this place on the market, make use of the proceeds, maybe buy a new car and update her own kitchen. Nevertheless, to sell this place would be to part with William once and for all. A compromise would be to rent it out.

All this was speculation because until she located the document, she wasn't going to sell or let it. 'Where is it, William?'

The house mocked her with its silence, leaving her feeling crushed. She trudged into the utility room, where she cast about. She'd tried all the obvious hidey-holes, now it was time to pull the place apart.

She'd read that between almost every pair of upper cabinets, there was a half-inch gap, wide enough to accommodate a hanging manila envelope. She would start with those in this room and then move every piece of furniture, checking underneath, behind and inside it for false bottoms or panels. She reached for one of the screwdrivers she'd brought with her. It had to be here somewhere.

Rachid was waiting for Emma by the entrance to HQ, bouncing from foot to foot like a child. 'We found them – Leah and her mystery man. Come on. I have something to show you.'

He led her to the lab next door, swiping his pass on the keypad with expert ease and throwing open the door. 'I came in early this morning,' he said. 'I thought I'd been through every camera and piece of surveillance equipment in Stafford and then . . . I found footage from the NCP car park, only a short walk from Mill Bank. How we missed it the first time around, I don't know, and it was grainy – really grainy,' he added as he stalked past the tables laden with tech equipment. Emma spied Felicity in her glass office, phone pressed to her ear, and gave her a quick wave. She gave Emma a thumbs up. Rachid was almost scampering to Tech 1, one of the rooms used to go through surveillance camera footage, and flung the door open with so much gusto she expected it to come off its hinges.

The wall was covered in large screens but the largest, directly in front of several desks, was showing a black and white image of several cars.

Rachid slid on to a seat, patting the one next to him. 'Come and look. Not wishing to blow my own trumpet, but I've done an ace job and I'm happy with the results.' He pressed several buttons, murmuring, 'Come on, baby, work your magic.'

The time clock in the corner showed it was ten minutes past eight. The footage ran, the camera slowly scanning the car park, coming to rest on a white SUV for a few moments before returning to its initial position.

'Here we go,' said Rachid, reaching for a bag of gummy bears. 'Want one?'

'Bit early for me, but thanks.'

He grinned, popped a couple into his mouth and sat back with his arms folded.

Emma studied the screen. Sure enough, there was movement that made her pulse increase. Two people came into the picture: a man with his arm around a woman. It was difficult to identify either of them, especially as the camera swung away from them to retrace its arc back to the white SUV, but she was sure the woman was Leah.

'Hang on,' said Rachid. 'There's more.'

The camera rested a while before making the return journey. This time, the couple were kissing. Again, Emma couldn't see their faces. However, she noticed that the man was wearing a jacket. The camera moved off once more. Emma felt like groaning – this wasn't enough – then, catching sight of Rachid's grin, she realised the show wasn't over. As the camera settled again on the white SUV, a figure strode into the frame. It was the slim-built man in a jacket and shirt and dark trousers. He unlocked the SUV and drove away.

Rachid leant forward and worked the control panel until he had an enhanced still of the man, whose features were clearly visible. He fitted the barber's description perfectly.

'And wait a second,' said Rachid. He brought up a second still, taken from earlier in the footage. This time he had zoomed in and captured the woman's outfit. Judging by her hair and the cream ankle boots, there was little doubt that this was Leah.

'It's them! You *are* a genius!'

'I have one more trick.' His fingers flew over his keyboard and the screen changed once more. This time it showed the back view of the SUV as it left its parking spot. Emma gasped. The number plate was in full view.

'This is the name and address of the registered keeper of the SUV,' said Rachid, pushing over a sticky note. He pulled out another sweet, tossed it into the air and caught it in his open mouth. Emma applauded.

◆　◆　◆

Kate had pulled apart most of the furniture in the downstairs rooms and was on her way upstairs when Emma rang her. The call was a swift reminder that Kate had a job. All of this – hunting for Tommy, Digger and an elusive document – was keeping her from what was more important: a vocation she loved.

'And that is exactly what you are trying to protect,' argued William as she shoved her tools back into the bag that she'd brought along. *'You shouldn't feel any guilt. I didn't when I was trying to infiltrate the syndicate. Think about all the times I wasn't available for you. It wasn't because I was tied up on other investigations or bureaucratic issues. I was flying solo, working to clean out the rot from our force. You're in*

an ideal position. You can occasionally vanish without any questions being asked. Make the most of it.'

'I don't have any qualms about taking time out to pursue this. I can manage the workload that's waiting for me and everything else that is demanded of me as a DCI. Even so, I've not been keeping an eye on the time, and I ought to be more careful or somebody will call me out, ask where I've been, and start to become suspicious about my movements. We don't know how far up the line of command this decay extends. There are major investigations going on and I should be at my desk, demonstrating leadership and available should anyone come looking for me.'

'You've done a great job of training Emma and Morgan. They'll manage perfectly well without running to you every five minutes and you know it. You're just unwilling to let go. You still want to be part of their working lives; guide them. I understand. I felt the same way about you.'

'And you mentored me perfectly. I want them to learn from me what I learned from you. It's like passing on your legacy.'

With a lump in her throat, she swept up her bag and left for the station.

Both her protégés were working at a formidable pace. There was no doubt that she was proud of them, yet alongside the pride came a tinge of sorrow. She missed them . . . and her life as it had been before William was murdered.

As Kate drew into her parking spot, she spied Jamie at the far end of the car park, talking on his mobile. She had only spoken to him now and again since his promotion to sergeant and his move to Ali Rind's team. She still hadn't forgotten how uneasy he made her feel. Even now as he walked up and down, deep in conversation with somebody, she was sure he was up to something. Before Harriet had been charged with killing William, she had suspected him of being in cahoots with her and the syndicate. Now she wondered if he'd been part of the team that might have set Harriet up. He gave the impression of being super keen, and to an extent he was; all the same, sometimes his stories didn't quite add up. He had passed her information about the raid on the motel that went belly up. Watching him wave his arms around, clearly agitated about something, she questioned if Jamie could have been the person who blew that operation. DI Ali Rind had had issues with a mole. Kate had harboured a mole. Two and two . . .

As she got out of her car, Jamie's voice carried towards her, 'Fucking hell, mate. I can't take the risk. Not this time. You'll have to sort it out.'

She fiddled with her keys and bag, lingering beside the Audi in the hope of hearing more, but the conversation ended, and Jamie stormed towards the entrance, catching sight of her before he made it to the door.

'Oh! Hello, guv. I didn't see you there.'

He looked surprised, but Kate detected annoyance behind his eyes. Whether or not that was due to the conversation he'd been having, or realising she might have overheard it, she couldn't tell.

He flashed a smile that didn't reach his eyes. She'd had difficulties in trusting Jamie almost from the off, after Dickson first assigned him to her small unit. Initially, she'd put these worries down to her paranoia, but after he lied about his whereabouts one morning and she discovered he'd been working at the time for Dickson on his secret operation, she felt she had good reason to distrust this man. That feeling had returned and, once again, she couldn't pinpoint why, other than to think instinct was guiding her on this matter.

'Hello, Jamie. I've just pulled up. It's been a while since we chatted. How are things?'

'Bit rough at the moment. Baby Isla hardly ever sleeps, and the missus is struggling with permanent tiredness. Aren't we all? Still, it'll get better. I bet when Isla becomes a teenager, I'll be complaining that she's never awake.'

He seemed jumpy. She tried to keep him talking. Maybe he'd give something away. 'Sorry to hear it. It's tough to find a balance between home life and this demanding job.'

'Ack, it's okay. It's been rough, what with putting in all the extra hours on the operation, but as you know, we've made headway at last, so that's been a boost.' He shifted uncomfortably like a schoolboy in front of a teacher before saying, 'And having Morgan as lead on it is a bonus. He's really got a grip of the investigation and all the team get on well with him.'

It had taken a long while for Morgan and Jamie to get along. She wasn't completely convinced by the newfound admiration. Jamie was definitely on edge, eyes searching the car park. There was something he was hiding, that was for sure. It only served to heighten her wariness. Still, she wasn't going to let him get wind of that, so she threw him another smile.

'I'd better go. I have a stack of paperwork to deal with.'

'Yeah, things are a bit different now.'

His choice of words and the flat tone in which he delivered them furthered Kate's suspicions. She was sure he meant something other than the job situation. She could be reading too much into the conversation, and possibly something had shifted between them simply because their roles had changed, and she was now his DCI not DI. All the same, one thing was clear: Jamie was no longer at ease around her.

'Yes,' she said. 'It's very different.'

'Okay, well. I have another call to make. Have a good day.'

She headed towards the entrance, curious as to why he hadn't accompanied her inside. He'd been on his way into HQ when he'd bumped into her. The phone call was an excuse to remain outside until she had gone. The question was, why?

◆ ◆ ◆

Emma was pumped. Every nerve in her body was tingling. She clung to the grab handle as Scott urged the BMW past a line of traffic and on to the roundabout, his face grim. She was within moments of interviewing an important suspect, somebody who had clearly been intimate with Leah. He would have seen the news by now, learned of Leah's fate. That he hadn't come forward heaped suspicion on him. Her fear was that he had done a bunk.

Danny Greaves lived in Gnosall, a large village that lay half-way between Stafford and Newport. Emma hadn't visited it before today and was reliant on Scott, whose children attended the primary school there, for information about it.

'It's what I'd term a friendly village: plenty of parks, walks by the canal, family-friendly pubs.'

They turned on to the high street, lined with smart buildings – some red brick, others painted white, one a thatched cottage. Emma spotted the shops, a village noticeboard and a large white building – a pub.

'The Horns,' she said, reading the name under a gold stencil of a stag's head.

'Been in there. It's very nice,' said Scott. 'We sometimes come here on a weekend with the children and the dogs.'

'I didn't know you had dogs!'

'Two dachshunds: Rollo and Slinky. They're really the kids' pets,' he added. 'Although we do the majority of looking after them.'

'That's parenthood for you,' she said. There was no way she could imagine having children, or pets for that matter. It was hard enough dividing her time between work and Morgan.

That thought brought her up sharply. Morgan was her partner. She shouldn't be thinking of him in such a negative way. She enjoyed being with him and she wouldn't want to spend her free time with anyone else.

But she still worried: was Morgan having similar thoughts about juggling his career and time to be with her? This was her vocation, she reasoned, and she loved her job and Morgan equally. Surely he must feel the same way.

She cast off her concerns, determined to be fully focused like Kate. Emma's old boss had gone through hell, losing Chris and now William, yet she never allowed her private life to impact her work or lost focus. With that in mind, Emma gripped the grab handle more tightly and watched the houses flash past.

The street bled into the road where Danny lived, and Emma looked out for his property. A search on the police general database had only given scant details about the man, who had moved from Durham to Gnosall the year before and was a self-employed website tester. Emma had taken a chance on driving out here in the belief he would be working from home. Grand houses with high hedges gave way to semi-detached properties and smart frontages. Trees and pavements with green verges added to the feeling of rurality. Emma was used to concrete, hubbub and endless grey. Even on a miserable January day, here there were signs of nature and space.

They were soon upon a sharp turn into a narrow road. After passing a couple of properties, they spied a white SUV parked on a sloping drive. It stood in front of a detached sandstone house with what Emma considered to be a very large downstairs window, divided into a grid system of thirty-two small panes. The upstairs windows were a similar style, although slightly smaller with half the number of small panes. Attached to the property was a single garage, the shutter painted the same cherry red as the front door. Having checked on a map before coming, Emma knew that should Danny decide to do a runner, he would have no option other than to exit from this door.

Parking behind the SUV, they got out.

'Camera doorbell,' whispered Scott.

She strode towards it and pressed it firmly, holding her ID up to it so Danny could see exactly who he was dealing with. There was no means of escape for him and like it or not, he would have to face them. If he chose not to open the door, she would make sure they sat outside his home until he did.

As it happened, she didn't have to consider her options for long. The door opened and a tall man with neat facial hair, wearing jogging bottoms and a loose-fitting sweatshirt, beckoned them inside.

Emma found herself immediately inside a sitting room.

'Danny Greaves?' she asked.

'Yes. I knew it was only a matter of time before you came. I've been . . . in a state of confusion.'

'Then you know why we're here.'

'You've come about Leah.' He lowered himself on to one of two wide lounge chairs that resembled large mustard beanbags, both placed in front of a wall-mounted television screen. Glancing around the sparsely furnished room, Emma noticed a lack of personal items, no photographs or knick-knacks. The black shelves were stacked high with various games, controllers and box files. Behind him stood a contemporary writing desk in black wood, the top seemingly balanced on a metal arc. Her eye was drawn to a 24-inch iMac and the bubbles that appeared and disappeared across the screen.

'I'll cut to the chase. Why haven't you contacted us?'

He sank further into the chair. 'I . . . was afraid. Do you want to sit down? These chairs are more comfortable than they look, or I could get some from the kitchen.'

'I'll fetch them, sir,' said Scott.

'They're through the far door. You can't miss them.'

'I'll take a beanbag,' said Emma.

Once they were all settled, she continued. 'Why were you scared of coming forward?'

'Apart from the obvious reason: that you'd think I'd killed her?'

'We don't leap to conclusions. Surely you would have wanted to clear your name?'

'That's easier said than done though, isn't it? I don't come out looking good from this. I was probably the last person to see Leah alive that night. We had an argument in the pub. There were witnesses to it. I've been wrestling with my conscience ever since I knew her body had been found. I . . . hoped you'd find out who killed her way before you found out about me. Stupid, I guess.'

Emma didn't usually judge people; however, his poor excuses riled her. Had he not cared about Leah? 'Then tell me what happened the last time you saw her.'

'I'd better explain first that we'd been seeing each other for about five months, since mid-August. We'd been careful to keep our relationship a secret, mostly because Leah didn't want her husband finding out about us. It wasn't that serious, or at least that was the understanding we had. Leah was adamant we kept it light, which suited me because I didn't want any commitments. I left Durham because of an ex – Tara – who became a nightmare. I wasn't especially looking to jump into another relationship, but the night I met Leah, I was drinking alone at a bar, and she sat down on the stool next to me. She initiated the conversation by asking if I'd like another beer then ordered two bottles of the same, took one herself and raised it to mine and we toasted strangers who met at bars!

220

There was an instant vibe. After a few drinks, we arranged to meet again. Neither of us wanted anything more than a no-strings-at-tached, easy-going relationship. Leah wasn't looking to mess up her lifestyle or marriage. She just wanted some fun. We both did.'

He looked away for a moment and blinked a few times before speaking again. 'Anyway, you asked about the last time we met. We went to The Yard, the place that overlooks the river. We liked it there because it is usually busy and people are so occupied playing pool or watching live sport on one of the big HD screens, or per-forming karaoke, that you can have a quiet drink and chat without drawing attention to yourselves.

'I expected the evening to follow the usual format: a couple of drinks there, maybe a takeaway, then back to my place, but she was acting oddly from the get-go that night. After a second round of drinks, she dropped a bombshell: said she'd told Russell about us and was leaving him. Just like that! I was pissed off that she'd gone ahead without even discussing the matter with me and assumed I'd go along with whatever she decided. In actual fact, I wasn't ready to shack up with her, or anyone else for that matter. Especially after all the shit with Tara. That freaked me out big time.'

'What happened with your ex?' asked Scott.

'Hundreds of calls and text messages, every damn day, turning up at my house or work at all hours. She threatened me and torched my car. In the end, I got an injunction against her. She broke it – four times. Durham police have a case file on her. 'Anyway, that night, Leah and I argued . . .'

Emma's mind flashed back to the row that had led to her sleep-ing in the spare room. It had been over nothing as major as this, and yet had blown up rapidly and out of proportion.

Danny shut his eyes and fell silent. Emma was about to press him to continue when he shook his head, swallowed and said, 'It got a bit heated. People were starting to stare. At one stage, she marched off, so when she came back, I told her we needed to keep it down. We did, until she dropped another bomb. She said she was pregnant, and . . . I was the baby's father.'

The words caught in his throat. He stopped talking again.

Emma understood how the situation might have escalated. From what she could gather, Leah had blindsided him by announcing she was leaving her husband for him when the subject hadn't been discussed. Already shocked, Danny would have been knocked for six by her second revelation. It was easy to understand how he might have reacted.

She drew herself up sharply. Kate wouldn't speculate like this. It was unprofessional. Emma was projecting her own experiences on to him and empathising when she should remain neutral. After all, Danny could be lying.

'Would you like a glass of water?' asked Emma.

He shook his head, swallowed hard, then continued. 'At first, I didn't believe her. Then I decided that if there really was a baby, there was an equally good chance it was Russell's. She was angry that I didn't believe her and stalked off. I chased after her. This time, I heard her out. She insisted that they hadn't had sex in months, so Russell couldn't be the father. We talked it through while we walked to my car. I confess I still wasn't convinced. I . . . I told her I needed to see the results of a paternity test. That's a reasonable request, isn't it? After all, how could I be sure she was being honest about Russell? For all I knew, their marriage might have been more solid than Leah led me to believe. Or maybe she hadn't told Russell about our relationship and in fact he had found out about us, then thrown her out?'

Without waiting for a response, Danny carried on, 'I explained that to her. Nicely. I didn't raise my voice or anything. I simply told her I needed proof. After that, Leah refused to come home with me. She said she was disappointed by my reaction and suggested it might be better if we cooled things off for a while, and that she needed time to sort herself out. We left it at that.'

'You didn't consider the possibility the child was yours?'

Danny dragged a hand over his whiskered jaw. 'I put it out of my mind. When I didn't hear from her, I figured she'd been lying, to pressure me into letting her move in. If you had any idea what I'd been through with Tara, you'd understand where I was coming from. Tara was twisted. She lied all the time to manipulate me. I thought Leah was the same.'

Emma shifted position. The beanbag wasn't as comfortable as Danny had suggested and she wasn't sure she was buying his story. It seemed ostrich-like behaviour. Tara or no Tara, this man shouldn't have ghosted his lover. If Morgan behaved that way . . . She stopped those thoughts in their tracks. She and Morgan were different to Leah and Danny. A little voice in her head questioned that statement, reminding her that Morgan had changed. She pushed the thoughts away.

'When you didn't hear from Leah again, what did you do?' she asked.

He rubbed his face, held out his hands. 'I didn't do anything.'

'You didn't even message her?'

He shook his head. 'I thought *she* was ghosting *me*, that she'd decided to dump me, that she'd made up with Russell, or that she'd been lying to me all along and there was either no baby or it wasn't mine. I was . . . relieved the pressure was off.'

Emma couldn't believe what she was hearing. This man had been in an intimate relationship with Leah, and after learning that she was pregnant and was leaving her husband had basically shut her out of his life. How had his passion for her vanished so quickly? Was this what was happening to her and Morgan – his interest in her waning until a time she did or said something that would make him react in a similar way?

'Listen, this is hard for me to talk about. I'm being as open and honest as I possibly can be, because I need you to believe me,' Danny urged.

When Emma didn't respond, Scott spoke up. 'You must have known that she was missing!'

Danny looked him in the eye. 'I didn't have a clue. I don't usually pay a great deal of attention to the news, not unless I happen to hear it on the radio, which I didn't because I was working on a big project.'

Emma glanced at Scott, who, judging by his set expression, felt the same way she did. She tried hard not to express her surprise. 'You're telling us that you had no idea that Leah had gone missing?'

'I didn't. Honest.'

'You didn't read or hear anything about her disappearance or know the police had been asking for witnesses who had seen her the night she disappeared, yet you knew that her body was discovered a few days ago,' she said.

'The only reason I found out about the discovery was because I went into Stafford to visit a client and spotted the *Gazette* headlines.'

Emma couldn't prevent herself from saying, 'How convenient.'

'No . . . Listen . . . Please. Up until that day, I'd deliberately avoided town, I . . . I didn't want to bump into her. I swear that's the truth.'

Emma gave him a cold stare. He stabbed his finger in her direction, eyes narrowing.

'See, this is precisely why I didn't contact the police. I knew you wouldn't believe me. Leah and me . . . I shouldn't have let it go on for so long. It was . . . convenient. She was married and I didn't want any heavy commitments. I told her that at the outset!'

'Please don't point at me, sir.' Her icy tone had an immediate effect. He lowered his hand. His eyes, however, flashed in anger, giving Emma more reason to suspect him. This was a man whose temper could flare. She made a mental note to check out his story about his ex-girlfriend.

'I'd like to know your whereabouts for last Saturday evening,' she said.

He scrubbed his chin with his hand again, eyes darting from Emma to Scott. 'I don't understand.'

'We would like to know where you were on Saturday, the twenty-eighth of January,' said Scott.

'Here. At home.'

'Is there anybody who can confirm that?' asked Emma.

'Anybody? No. I was alone.'

'Did you order in any food? Maybe ring a friend?' suggested Scott.

'No. I watched television. Until about eleven. Then I went to bed.'

Emma weighed up his response. The alibi was something she could probe further if necessary. 'When did you move into this property?'

'Last year. May the fifth.'

'And which estate agency did you purchase it from?'

His brow creased. 'I can't remember. One of the local agents. I might still have the details.'

'Could it have been Property Plus?' Emma asked.

'That name sounds familiar. I think so.'

'You don't remember who showed you around the property, do you?'

'No. Why?'

'Can you describe them?'

He shook his head. 'I'm sorry, I can't remember what she looked like. It was seven months ago.'

Emma wasn't giving up. 'Was this the agent?' She pulled up the photograph of Victoria and passed across the phone. Danny shrugged.

'It might have been. Looks a bit like her. Can't be sure though. Why are you asking me this?'

'I'm afraid I'm not at liberty to say, but thank you for your time. We'll be in touch again, should we have any further questions.'

She got to her feet, glad to be out of the chair and keen to leave the house. It might be possible to find out who had shown Danny around his house before he purchased it. A warm tingling in her veins accompanied her thoughts. She was on the right lines. And if she were asked to lay a bet on this, she would say she was sure Victoria had been involved in the transaction.

Emma felt grimly satisfied. Now she had another connection and another person of interest. She was getting closer to the truth, and closer to stopping this man before he killed again.

CHAPTER SEVENTEEN

Emma and Scott were two minutes away from Russell's house when Frankie rang them back with the information they'd requested regarding Danny and his ex-girlfriend, Tara.

'We tumbled lucky again,' said Frankie. 'My oppo in Durham was involved in the case. He told me that Tara reported Danny to the police first, claiming he had attacked and raped her. It was followed up with Danny denying everything. Tara gave a convincing performance at the time, and it was only after one of Danny's friends became involved that she admitted she'd made up the whole thing, payback because she thought Danny was cheating on her. The team at Durham dropped the investigation. But a week later, they were called out to an altercation at his house. It transpired Tara had attacked Danny. He refused to press charges at the time. It was a further three weeks before he came forward to complain about Tara, who'd he'd thrown out of his house. There's a long list of complaints, including threatening behaviour and stalking.'

'Sounds like he was telling us the truth about Tara, then,' said Scott, after Frankie had hung up.

Emma was quick to respond. 'All the same, I still don't buy his story about Leah. Looking at that footage of them, it didn't seem to me as if they were having an intense conversation. He had his arm around her, and they looked like a normal, content couple.'

'The barber confirmed they were arguing beforehand as they crossed the bridge into Mill Bank.'

'And also said they made up and left hand in hand.'

'A lot can happen during a ten-minute walk,' said Scott.

Emma digested his words. How true. As she knew, a normal conversation could transform into a full-blown argument in less than ten minutes. Russell's house came into view, and before they pulled on to the drive she said, 'I think we should keep an open mind. I want to keep Danny in the frame, especially as he might have had contact with our other victim. I also wouldn't mind getting Tara's take on what happened between her and Danny, if needs be.'

◆ ◆ ◆

Russell answered the door, his dressing gown hanging open to reveal striped pyjamas. He stared at them through bloodshot eyes and shuffled aside to let them in without a word.

Once again, Emma found herself in the sitting room. This time, it was littered with large cardboard boxes.

'I've been sorting out her stuff. Going to donate it to charity,' said Russell, stifling a yawn. 'I was up until four thirty.'

'We'd like to ask you a few more questions, if that's alright,' said Emma.

Russell motioned towards the settee. 'Take a seat. You too,' he added to Scott. He turned a chair round to face them and, removing the cardboard box from it, sat down.

'We've spoken to Danny Greaves,' said Emma.

Russell rubbed at his eyes and yawned again. 'Who?'

Emma brushed aside the irritation that threatened to balloon. 'Do you understand what I'm saying, Russell?'

He rested his hands on his thighs and nodded.

'Danny Greaves was Leah's lover. Leah told you she was leaving you for him, didn't she?'

'No.'

'Danny says otherwise.'

'Danny doesn't know jack shit.'

'Then tell us your version of what happened the day she disappeared. You didn't argue about what she was wearing, did you?'

'Actually, we did.' He shrugged when he caught Emma's cold look. 'Okay. That was how it started. She'd been going out more frequently than usual, always supposedly with the girls, but I had an inkling she was seeing somebody. I confronted her that evening. In the end, she confessed she had been seeing some bloke, but she'd ended it with him.'

'Danny.'

'She wouldn't tell me his name. She said it had all been a mistake, that she'd never intended for it to happen or go on for as long as it had.'

'And you believed her?'

'Not at first. But she swore the relationship was over.'

'Surely you must still have suspected that she was going to see him that evening. Didn't you challenge her?' said Scott. 'I would have asked her to cancel her plans that evening to talk things through.'

'That wasn't how we went about things. We trusted each other—'

'She had just told you she'd been having an affair for five months. Why would you trust her?' Scott's voice remained quiet, his tone questioning yet reassuring.

'You didn't know her like I did,' Russell said. 'She handed me her phone. Told me to check it for messages, ring her friends if I didn't believe her, but I didn't. I had to demonstrate that I believed her. Without trust, there is no basis for a relationship.' He rubbed his eyes again, this time to wipe away the tears that fell.

'Why didn't you mention any of this when we last spoke?'

'Because I didn't know who she'd been sleeping with. I had no name to give you. Because I couldn't face telling you that she'd been unfaithful and because I . . . I don't know why. I loved her so much!'

Tears scattered over his cheeks as he shook his head. Snuffling heavily, he eventually managed to say, 'Why wouldn't she tell me about the baby? Why keep something as important as that from me? Was it . . . was it mine?'

Emma couldn't answer his questions. Leah had taken all her reasons and secrets to the grave with her.

◆ ◆ ◆

By late afternoon, Kate had made significant headway into her paperwork and was up to date with her calls.

'Why not spend five minutes searching for the farm where Digger might be working?' suggested William. *'If you don't act soon, he'll move off again.'*

Aware she couldn't use the police computer to check out information about civilians, she pulled out her iPad and began the laborious task of searching for the names of local farm owners. In the time she'd been hunting for Digger, she'd already come across many farmers and eliminated those whose surnames didn't begin 'Hen'. However, her current online searches were proving fruitless. She could do with some help.

Given how much she had already put on Felicity, she couldn't ask her for any more assistance, and tempting as it was to involve one of her officers, she didn't dare chance it. The more people involved, the greater the risk of somebody discovering what she was up to. Which meant, as daunting a prospect as it was, the hunt for

Digger would have to remain squarely on her shoulders. It was with reluctance she accepted this was going to require further fieldwork.

'*Don't bother. You're cornered,*' hissed Dickson. '*It won't be long before you're exposed.*'

Loath as she was to even listen to Dickson, she knew he had a point. Procrastination wasn't an option. Maybe if she narrowed down the search to East Staffordshire rather than the whole of the county, she would stand a better chance. Finding a number for Staffordshire County Council, she decided to bite the bullet and see if anyone there could help her.

◆ ◆ ◆

The trip to his mother's house is a necessary evil. He wants to double-check that his stash is safe. After he kills Emma, he intends going to London, where he'll take however much he's offered for the stolen goods. It's time to ditch the post box address and move on. Hasty Holdings has done its job. Besides, the police will be on to it by now. He'll move to Derbyshire or the West Midlands: start again with a new identity, pick out fresh victims and bamboozle another police force.

Letting himself into the house, he holds his breath and listens for any noise. Even though the helper's car isn't outside, he isn't taking any chances. If he's timed it right, his mother will be asleep in her wheelchair. She sleeps a lot these days.

He wrinkles his nose at the familiar stink of decay and age that clings to the furnishings and walls and stands stock still. Electronic noises and occasional applause indicate that she's watching a game show. His mother watches a great deal of television, although he's unsure of how much of what she sees now registers with her. It's difficult to know what she remembers or even can do. The stroke caused more than paralysis: her speech and brain are affected.

He checks the time. It's almost four o'clock. In theory he has an hour before somebody will bring his mother her evening meal. Apart from the health visitors and helpers, she sees nobody. Loneliness is exactly what she deserves. Karma. After all, she imprisoned him here in his youth. The house doesn't bring back bad memories or any emotions. It's nothing more than a place with a roof. He harbours no grudges towards it and certainly no affection. It's somewhere he once lived. Since then, he's dossed on floors, in empty buildings, in friends' houses and now has a place of his own: a rented flat in Highfields, which is basic but serves its purpose.

He creeps forward, catching sight of the old cow, her eyes closed. The snuffled snores confirm she's asleep. He'll be in and out within ten minutes and she'll be none the wiser. Moving swiftly up the stairs, he reflects that this is the perfect place to store his ill-gotten gains. Maybe he won't move too far from here. Not yet anyway, not until she finally passes away.

He eases open the bedroom door and makes for the hiding place. On second thoughts, it might be amusing to hang around after he kills Emma to watch the coppers racing about hunting for whoever killed one of their own. He retrieves the box and lifts its lid. The shiny objects inside it don't evoke any feelings: no elation, no guilt and no pleasure. They'll serve a purpose, much like this place. He picks up the shining engagement ring he pulled from Victoria's finger and wonders what it would be like to place it on Emma's. Forever his. That thought gives rise to what he acknowledges to be sexual desire, the same urge that had made him force himself on Leah.

Maybe Emma could help him feel something. It would be interesting to prolong the attack, test out his theory and see if he'll feel differently assaulting her than the other victims. After all, he knows Emma, can even count himself as one of her friends. He'd like to be more than a friend. Even if it is only for a few moments before she gasps her last breath. It's with that thought he slips the ring into his pocket. Emma is going to be in for a real treat.

◆ ◆ ◆

'I think we should bring both Danny and Russell in for further questioning,' said Scott to Emma.

'Not until we have reasonable grounds for doing so.'

'But one of them is lying.'

'For all we know, they might both be. Once we have more evidence, we can move forward,' said Emma. 'We're running around in circles and in danger of burning out. I'm calling it a day.'

'It's only five thirty,' said Frankie.

'We need to step back for a while and process what we know. We'll never make progress otherwise.'

Frankie unfolded her arms with a surly, 'You're the boss.'

Scott threw the young woman a look. 'Emma's right. We need a break to see the bigger picture more clearly. We aren't robots. Carry on like this and we'll become sleep deprived and unable to make good decisions. The temptation is to keep pushing on. We all want a result, but more importantly, we want the right result.'

'Yeah. I suppose so,' agreed Frankie. 'Sorry, Emma. I didn't mean to sound like a grumpy teenager.'

'I understand your frustration, especially when we have two potential persons of interest. I'd like nothing better than to quiz them all night, but any lawyer worth their salt would get their client off on the grounds we have insufficient evidence to hold them and inviting them to help with our inquiries will only lead to more lies or even a refusal to cooperate.'

Frankie reached for her coat and threw it over her arm. 'See you in the morning then.'

Scott hung back for a moment, taking his time to pack away. 'What are our plans for tomorrow?'

'I'm going to cross my fingers and hope we get a DNA result for the baby, then do what I've been doing since we were given this investigation – wing it!'

Scott laughed. 'I know that isn't true.'

'Seriously, I haven't fathomed that out yet. I'll take advantage of Morgan being busy to have a workout. A good session at the gym usually helps me think more clearly.'

'Really? It would send me straight to bed. Anyhow, see you tomorrow.'

She waved him off before messaging Morgan to let him know she'd get home around seven thirty, then left before she could change her mind. Before life with Morgan, whenever she'd needed to chew over an investigation or puzzle over a problem, she would have headed directly to her brother's gym.

A workout was exactly what she needed right now. With a second victim and two more potential suspects, this case was becoming increasingly complex. If she wanted to impress her superiors, she would need to pull something out of the bag and soon.

◆ ◆ ◆

Having left a message for somebody at Staffordshire County Council to come back to her regarding farms in the area, Kate had taken it upon herself to return to Geoff Unwin, the farmer who had directed her to the Hardcastles' farm.

Geoff came to the door, a half-eaten apple in his hand. 'Come back to tell me Digger has got his inheritance, have you?'

'No. I've come to ask for your help.'

He screwed up his face and took a bite from his apple, chewing it for the longest time before saying, 'I'm not going to be taken for a fool again. Malcolm Hardcastle told me about you. You're nothing to do with any inheritance. You're police, and you're hounding poor old Digger. Now, I helped you out of good faith and you lied to me, so this time you can clear off. I don't know where Digger is and if I did, I wouldn't tell you.'

Kate managed to jam her foot in the door before he could slam it shut. 'Mr Unwin, please hear me out. Okay, I didn't come clean about why I was looking for Digger the other day. I couldn't tell you because it was case sensitive. It is best if nobody knows. For Digger's sake. You see, he witnessed a serious crime. I know he won't come to the station to give a statement, and I know he hates towns and confined spaces and the police, which is why I've been asking around farms, trying to find him, trying not to spook him. I really must speak to him.' She hesitated before coming out with, 'I think his life could be in danger.'

'Pfft! That's another fib. How could he be in danger? He's just Digger. He doesn't do no harm to anyone.'

'He hasn't done anything wrong. I only need five minutes with him to speak to him about what he saw.'

'And how will you protect him?'

'I'll work on the information he gives me . . . please.'

She noticed the pressure on the door eased. 'I don't know where he is,' said Geoff.

'Do you know any farmers whose surnames start with "Hen"?'

'Hen?'

'Like Henchard, Henshaw, or Henley,' she offered.

He studied his half-eaten apple. 'Nothing springs to mind.'

'Could you give it some serious thought for me?'

'I'll ask my wife. She remembers names better than me.'

'Can you ask her now?'

'She's visiting her sister.'

'Have you any idea when she'll be back?'

He shrugged. 'Some time tonight.'

'Here's my card. Ring me if she knows anyone. It's important.'

He took it reluctantly.

'Thank you. And if you hear where Digger might be, again, ring me.'

'Is his life really in danger?'

'I believe so.'

'That was a major error on your part.' Dickson's voice was weak but audible. She crossed the yard back to her car, willing it to stop. It didn't. *If Geoff tells Digger about you, Digger will run for the hills. Or he'll spread the word that he saw you shoot me. You're making this very easy for the syndicate. At this rate, they might not need those photographs. Digger will do our work for us.'*

'I had no other choice,' she replied. 'You forced my hand.'

Dickson chuckled. *'I did, didn't I? And you fell into my trap. More haste and less speed.'* She dug her nails into her palms until his voice had faded completely. She hadn't considered the implications of this visit to Geoff Unwin. She'd expected him to be as obliging as he had been the first time around. With hindsight, she ought to have waited for a call back from the council. She had screwed up. Again. This wasn't like her. She had to be more rational, or she really would be in the mire. She retreated into the Audi's warm interior and glanced back at the farm, where she was sure she saw a curtain at the bottom window move. She turned up the heater to ease the shivering that had begun.

'Get a grip, Kate,' she said. This time, it was only her own voice that she heard.

◆ ◆ ◆

Emma rubbed the towel over her face. An hour in the company of like-minded people who took martial arts seriously, and worked hard to keep up their skill levels, had refreshed rather than tired her. Her thoughts were less jumbled, and she'd formed a plan of action for the following morning.

As she headed for the changing rooms she passed Fergus, one of her brother's old schoolfriends, who was with Andy Sullivan, the man she'd recently bumped into at the coffee shop. They were just leaving the ring, where they'd clearly been working on Andy's fighting skills. His eyes burned into her and stripped to the waist, with sweat glistening on his muscular torso, he appeared more animated than usual.

'Morgan finally let you out then?' said Fergus. 'Or did you escape from the bedroom and shimmy down the drainpipe?'

She laughed. 'You know me better than that. I don't shimmy anywhere.'

'That's a fact. So what, then? Did you practise a few taekwondo moves on him until he gave in and let you join us this evening?' His eyes sparkled with mischief. Fergus had been a troublemaker in his youth until he'd started hanging out with Greg and taken up martial arts. When her brother had opened the martial arts academy and gym, he'd employed Fergus as one of his trainers. Fergus, in turn, had encouraged and helped Emma to gain her black belt in taekwondo. He'd been a tough taskmaster, yet she had risen to every challenge.

Back then, she'd had a crush on him, working extra hard to impress. The crush had worn off after Fergus seemed to ignore her flirting, apparently only interested in making her work harder. So she had started dating other guys, relegating Fergus to simply being her trainer and friend.

'We were beginning to think you'd given up coming here, weren't we, Andy?' he said, straight-faced.

Andy took up the baton. 'Yeah, we thought you'd taken up knitting and baking as hobbies instead.'

'No chance. I love this place. Nobody and nothing could stop me from coming here. Besides, I wouldn't want to miss out on all this intellectual conversation.'

Fergus grinned, exposing a large gap in his front teeth that Emma had always found attractive.

'According to Greg,' Fergus said, a slight southern Irish lilt in his voice, 'you've gone all housewifey.'

'And he told us that you even watch *Bake Off* to pick up the latest recipes,' said Andy.

'Greg had better watch out, because if he persists in spreading rumours like that, I'll force-feed him some of my homemade scones. And you pair too, if you keep this up.'

Fergus nudged Andy in the ribs. 'Tetchy, see? We've hit a sore spot. Although I'd take her threat seriously. I've had the misfortune of trying out her cakes in the past. Her sponge cake was so heavy we added it to the weight stack for training purposes.'

Andy grinned. 'No way!'

'He's not joking,' said Emma, recalling the occasion when she'd arrived with a surprise birthday cake for her brother. Greg had made a big show of weightlifting it. She hadn't minded, especially when he'd hugged her in front of everyone and told them all she was the best sister a man could have. The teasing had all been in good humour and she couldn't deny that the cake had been a disaster.

'I'd have loved to have seen that,' said Andy. 'Anyway, on the grounds I want to keep all my teeth, I'll pass up the opportunity to sample your scones, Emma. Consider my piss-taking ended.'

The look he gave her produced tiny flutters in her stomach. She dragged her eyes away from him.

'Coward!' said Fergus. 'Hey, Emma, can we expect to see you again tomorrow or have you got to clean the house and make sure Morgan's uniform is ironed to perfection?'

'Fergus, you wouldn't know what an iron was even if you were hit in the face with one,' she replied. Andy burst out laughing.

Slinging the towel over her shoulder, she made for the changing room.

Fergus called out, 'There's a few of us heading into town for a curry. You fancy joining us? Me . . . Andy and a couple of the others.'

She stopped and turned back.

'Greg's meeting us there too.'

'Yeah, come on, Emma,' said Andy, a hopeful look on his face.

She'd enjoyed many a night out before she'd moved in with Morgan. But this evening, as tempting as the offer was, she couldn't go. In the past, she wouldn't have thought twice about a curry and a few drinks after a session, but with things the way they'd been between them, she owed Morgan a night in, and a quiet dinner for two. Besides, she didn't want to give Morgan an excuse to go off on one.

'Not tonight. I've got a lot on,' she said. Her eyes rested for a moment on Andy, his sculpted torso on display. He was definitely her type. Then again, so was Morgan.

'Hmm. Do you mean work or Morgan?' said Fergus with a wink.

'That's enough. You know what I mean. *Work*,' she added. 'Thanks for the invite, but no thanks. Another time.' She set off again.

'Better get a move on, Emma. Morgan will be expecting his usual three-course meal,' called Fergus.

She raised her middle finger, making the men laugh. Banter was the norm here and not only had she missed the regular exercise and seeing familiar faces, but she'd also missed the ribbing. The guys at the gym knew her well enough to realise work and training came before anything else, including relationships. She couldn't let this part of her life change. She caught sight of her face in the mirror, hair slick with sweat and cheeks pink through exertion. Her body was exercised and her mind relaxed. After a good night's sleep, she'd be able to tackle the next day with enthusiasm and a clear mind.

◆　◆　◆

Still feeling the benefits of her workout, Emma opened the front door and called out a cheery, 'Hi, there!'

When there was no forthcoming response, she made for the sitting room. It was empty. After checking the kitchen and bedrooms, she realised Morgan wasn't at home. Checking her phone, she found a message from him, saying he would be late back. She stomped around the kitchen, opening cupboards, searching for something simple and quick to cook, annoyed that she'd turned down a post-workout meal and drink with her friends.

She hadn't been joking when she'd admitted to being a lousy cook. She wasn't so much bad at it as messy, and soon the kitchen was filled with the smell of fried food while work surfaces were littered with an array of herb pots, sauce bottles and vegetable peelings. With her stomach rumbling, her priority was to eat rather than tidy up, so pouring the stir-fry into a soup bowl, she munched greedily. It was a good thing the exercise had given her an appetite because no matter how much soya sauce she poured over the food, it still tasted bland. She would have to up her game in this department if she was going to start sharing the household responsibilities. Morgan wouldn't put up forever with her meagre offerings or takeaways when it was her turn to cook. Nor could they keep relying on Morgan's superior culinary skills, especially as, like her, he now had an even more demanding job. The thought of one of his signature dishes – baked penne pasta with roasted vegetables – made her own efforts even less appetising.

At that very moment, she heard the key in the front door. Morgan was back earlier than anticipated.

She leapt to her feet and began clearing away the debris, but no sooner had she put away half of the herb pots than Morgan appeared. The smile on his face disappeared instantly.

'Fucking hell, Emma. Have you been having a food fight in here?'

'Ha ha! I was going to clean up as soon as I finished eating.' The moment she spoke, she realised he wasn't in a jovial mood and her heart lurched in her chest.

He strode to the hob and, peering at it, frowned. 'There's something glued to it.'

'It'll clean off,' she said brightly, hoping to change his demeanour.

'It's a ceramic hob.'

'I know,' she said, gritting her teeth.

'Is this . . .' He picked up a bottle. 'Hoisin sauce?'

'Yes, sorry. I sort of missed the pan,' she replied. 'Stop making a fuss. I'll clean it up.'

'Fuss! This sort of sticky goo takes ages to clean off a ceramic cooker once it's dried on.'

'Okay, I'm sorry. I'll sort it.'

'No. I'll do it.'

'There's no need, I can—'

'I said I'll do it. You need to be careful how you clean it, or it'll scratch.'

'It's only a spill on a cooker,' she said, her heart suddenly racing. What was the matter with him? She hadn't smashed it to bits with a sledgehammer.

He gave her a cold look. '*My* cooker. It cost me an arm and a leg.'

It was all the answer she required. The tension that had been mounting inside bubbled and erupted before she could contain it. She hated these petty disagreements that blew up for no good reason. Could he not see how badly he was behaving? *His* cooker. *His* house. None of it was *theirs* and that made her feel unwelcome.

More to the point, she didn't need this shit. 'Then you shouldn't have bought such a fancy cooker. Ordinary gas hobs can be wiped clean easily enough.'

He made for the sink, where he ran the hot tap. She started to clear away the peelings.

'And those. Leave them too. I'll sort it all,' he said wearily.

'Don't make this a big deal, Morgan.'

He reached for the washing-up liquid. 'I'm not. I'm tired. I don't want to argue. Just leave me to it.'

'Fine. You do just that and you can wear that martyred expression while you do it!'

She stormed out of the room, every muscle once again taut. In less than five minutes, he had ruined her mood. Sod him! She marched up the stairs and made for the spare room again, where she lay on the bed, waiting for him to come and apologise. After an hour, she realised he wasn't going to. This couldn't continue. If they were going to keep falling out over little things, they wouldn't survive as a couple.

CHAPTER EIGHTEEN

Although she could hear the bleeping of her mobile alarm, Emma's eyelids remained stuck fast. She'd returned to the main bedroom at around eleven to find Morgan fast asleep. She'd eased between the cold sheets, trying not to disturb him, even though part of her wanted him to rouse from his slumber so she could apologise for her short fuse that had resulted in the rift between them. She'd lost her rag and instead of giving Morgan the space he needed, she'd tried to rile him.

A grunt beside her indicated Morgan was also having difficulty in waking up. He mumbled, 'Turn it off, Em.'

She forced herself on to one side and stopped the repeater, falling immediately back on to the pillow where, ignoring the warmth and comfort, she forced herself to remain conscious.

The mattress gave as Morgan shifted and she wondered if she should apologise. When he snaked his arm around her, an enormous relief flooded her entire body. The spat had been forgotten.

Remembering it was February the first, she said, 'Pinch, punch.'

Morgan groaned. 'No pinches. Please. And none of your punches. You could lay a man out for a fortnight with one of those.'

She rolled over to face him and kissed him. 'I was a bitch last night.'

'I don't remember. And even if you were, I was too tired to care.'

'Can we forget it then?'

'Forget what?'

'Good.' She kissed him again then pulled away. 'Come on, big man. Time to rise and shine.'

He groaned again.

She swung her legs out of the bed. 'I thought you'd be mad keen to get to work. Haven't you got the info you were after and are ready to swoop on the guys at the top?'

'Fuckers have clammed up. We had them. They were willing to spill the beans, then suddenly, once the lawyers arrived, that was it. We've been stuck in the "no comment" arena ever since.'

Emma reached into the drawer for clean underwear, pulling on a pair of knickers as she spoke. 'Has somebody got to them?'

'If they did, I haven't a clue how. Nobody has been allowed to have any contact with them, apart from their lawyers.'

'Then I'd guess the lawyers advised them to stay schtum.'

'I disagree. I reckon there's more to it. This stays between us, right?'

She sat back on the bed and nodded. 'Sure.'

'There's a mole on the team. I figured it was DI Rind, especially when he left so suddenly after we caught these traffickers.'

'DI Rind?'

'No. I was wrong about him. Rumour has it he left cos he couldn't persuade the chief constable to wade in and get his informant a visa. The mole is still on the team and got to the traffickers.'

'Really? Aren't you being paranoid? Someone from outside could have got a message to these men, threatened them, probably via the lawyers.'

'Okay, that's possible. But I have a gut feeling it came from inside. The same person who caused that sting operation at the motel to go belly up.'

'Jamie told us about it,' she said, eyebrows lifting.

Morgan laughed. 'No chance it's him. He might be irritating but at least he's dependable. Besides, he wasn't part of Operation Moonbeam until he got promoted.'

'What about Toady Trev? He passed that info to Jamie.'

'Nah, he was out on surveillance with other officers for most of the day.'

'Any one of your team could have had messages slipped to the traffickers. Have you spoken to Kate about this?'

'Yes, and she was going to come up with a plan to trap them, but so far she hasn't come good. Too busy, I guess.'

'But this is important. See her again.'

'Okay.'

'In the meantime, suspect everyone.'

'Even Jamie?'

She cocked her head. 'Well, maybe everyone except Jamie. Then again, you shouldn't eliminate anyone, should you?'

'How about me?'

She smiled. 'My money would be on it not being you.' She leant forward and kissed him on the lips before easing herself away. 'Now, look lively. Kate's usually in early. You can grab a couple of minutes with her if you get going.'

'Yes, boss. By the way, how are you getting on with your case?'

'So-so. But I intend to make progress today.'

'Positivity,' he said. 'That's one thing I miss about you when we're at work. You were always so upbeat about everything. I wish you were on Operation Moonbeam with me.'

She threw him a smile. 'Coffee?'

'That'd be good, but for heaven's sake, don't mess up the kitchen making it.'

◆   ◆   ◆

Kate stared at the photograph of William and her father. Overnight, she had become so anxious about having spoken to Geoff Unwin she'd got palpitations that had forced her to walk the house until they calmed. The voices had plagued her, first Dickson then William, one after another giving conflicting commentary on her actions until she had sat down with her head in her hands and wept.

'William, you promised to guide me,' she whispered.

The knock at the door made her jump. Sitting upright, she called, 'Yes, come in.'

'Morning, Kate,' said Morgan.

Immediately, she knew what he wanted. She'd forgotten about helping him to track down the leak. How could she have let that slip her mind?

'I haven't forgotten about your problem,' she said, before he could speak. 'I just haven't come up with the best way to handle the situation.'

'That is why I'm here, but not because I wanted to hassle you. The traffickers we brought in – Hasan Demir and Yusuf Osman – we had them at breaking point. They were going to tell us everything they knew about the organisation and those at the very top. Both were ready to spill everything. Then at the interviews, they suddenly refused to speak. Kate, I think somebody got to them.'

'Neither of them is speaking?'

'Not a word. They've shut down. Since their arrest, they've been kept in separate cells, and they've had no contact with anyone other than officers on duty and those of us who interviewed them.'

'Who was present at the interviews?'

'Only Jamie and myself. And the suspects' lawyers.'

'Well, surely the lawyers would have told them to keep silent.'

'No. They were going along with it. They were hoping to get reduced sentences for their clients. They seemed as surprised as me when the two suddenly clammed up.'

'Jamie,' she repeated, the thudding of blood threatening to drown out the sound of her own voice. 'Did you leave him alone with the suspects?'

'No. Besides, it's unlikely to be him. There were leaks way before Jamie joined the operation. He wouldn't jeopardise it. He wants it to succeed, if only so he can take credit for his part in it. I know him and he's all about the job. We both know him well.'

She resisted saying that they'd all worked under Dickson, oblivious to *his* exploits until he was exposed. Morgan believed he was a good judge of character and as far as he was concerned, Jamie was not the mole. Not wishing to alienate her protégé by continuing to force the issue, she said, 'Could be that somebody up the chain got word to them. Threatened them,' she said.

'True.'

'I'm not saying that is what happened, but we should keep an open mind. All the same, it might be an idea to feed false information to Jamie and see if it gets back to the traffickers.' It was a ploy she had used on Harriet. It had, at the time, seemingly worked and had sent Harriet scurrying to warn the traffickers. Although now, that appeared not to have been the case.

'That's worth a try.'

'And keep me informed.'

He gave a sharp nod before striding from the office.

Jamie . . . again. Her mind sprang back to the phone conversation she'd partly overheard at the car park, one during which Jamie told somebody to sort out a problem that he could no longer help with. It added up.

◆ ◆ ◆

Emma had positioned photographs of the two victims on the evidence boards, together with pictures of the persons of interest, times of attacks and any other relevant information she felt would help them create a clearer picture of how to proceed.

George had established that Victoria had been the estate agent who showed Danny his house, so now Russell, Craig and Danny were all connected to both victims. None of them had firm alibis for the evening Leah disappeared or the night Victoria was attacked. All had lied at some stage during their inquiries. Was she looking in the right direction, or had she become so fixated on these three she was overlooking other potential suspects?

Harry was poised over a notebook, a pencil in his hand. 'Do we speak to the husbands again?'

Emma felt her forehead tighten into a frown. 'Until we find further evidence to implicate them, I doubt we could squeeze anything more from them.'

'There's been no joy regarding the post box held by Hasty Holdings,' said Frankie. 'Nothing's been delivered there recently.'

Emma gave a tight-lipped nod. The post box was proving to be a dead end. Especially as Harry had discovered there were no surveillance cameras in or near the building where the boxes were housed.

George echoed her own thoughts. 'If I was the killer, I wouldn't use that post box address again.'

'There's been no comeback on the list of women's possessions and jewellery yet,' said Harry. 'I've tried all the local pawnbrokers and jewellers.'

'Probably sold them in some backstreet pub, or online,' muttered Scott. 'Clever bastard won't have risked selling them locally either.'

'Had to be checked out though, sarge,' said Harry.

Scott finished unpeeling a satsuma and tossed the rind into the bin. 'I know. I've been thinking, whoever is behind this must need the cash for some reason.' He pointed at the photos on the board. 'We've run financial checks on those potential suspects and none of them are exactly short of money.'

'That could be a smokescreen though,' said Frankie. 'Maybe they intended all along to make it look like a robbery gone wrong.'

Scott tugged a segment free, then said, 'They drugged the victims with Devil's Breath. It mostly causes disorientation, not death.' He dropped the piece into his mouth and looked at Emma. 'Boss?'

'That's a valid point. Maybe we're looking too close to home. The person who assaulted these women might only have intended to rob them, which also suggests there might be other victims before Leah and Victoria who survived an attack. I think we should follow up on that. Scott, put out a request to all police stations in Staffordshire for any details of robberies where the victim has been too disorientated to recall what transpired. Especially those who discovered they'd withdrawn large amounts of money from cashpoints, lost belongings: phones, credit cards, jewellery. If it's happened before, somebody will have reported it.'

'On it,' he said.

'I'm still not done with these three. Talk to Danny's ex-girlfriend, Tara. Find out what she has to say about him. Speak to Danny's friend, whoever it was who spoke up for him about not raping Tara. We need to conduct a more in-depth check on each of them. I want to know everything about these men.'

She quickly settled back to work. The investigation was progressing once more, and she was again confident and in control. If only they could keep up this momentum.

◆ ◆ ◆

Following her conversation with Morgan, Kate was about to ask William for his advice again when her phone rang, and a low voice asked if she was speaking to DCI Kate Young.

'You are. I'm DCI Young.'

'I'm Geoff Unwin's wife. He told me you were asking about farmers whose names begin with Hen.'

'That's right.'

'I can only think of one – Paul Hennessey. He lives near Tutbury – Castle Farm.'

'Thank you, I appreciate—'

The caller had rung off.

Armed with this fresh information, Kate leapt to her feet. If luck was on her side, she would be able to speak to Digger before the morning was out.

◆ ◆ ◆

Emma was beginning to flag. They'd worked the last four hours without a break and with her thoughts almost as jumbled as they had been the day before, she knew she had to take time out from the cramped atmosphere of the office.

She made for the nearby café where she intended buying doughnuts and coffee for her team and was surprised to find Morgan and Jamie there.

'Hey!' She caught sight of the doughnut on Morgan's plate and grinned. 'Aha! Caught you out.'

'In his defence, he was suffering from a sugar dip, Emma,' said Jamie. 'And getting extremely grumpy. It was my idea to come here.'

'It *was* his suggestion. Really.' Morgan shoved the last piece of the sweet pastry into his mouth and, with hamster-like cheeks, chomped.

'I bet you didn't take much persuasion,' said Emma. 'Anyway, how's the investigation going?'

Jamie rolled his eyes in an exaggerated fashion. 'Could be better.'

'Did you do what I suggested?' she said to Morgan, who swallowed his mouthful and nodded.

'In hand,' he replied.

'Good. Right. I'd better get some food for my lot.'

'And we'd better cut and run,' said Morgan. 'See you later.'

The doorbell tinkled as they bustled out of the place and on to the street. Morgan turned back and gave her a wink before disappearing.

It felt odd, seeing her ex-colleagues together, the emptiness in the pit of her stomach suggesting she felt left out. She approached the counter and placed her order, reminding herself that she had another team to work with who had their own quirks and strengths, that she couldn't stay in a bubble, working with the same people for ever and a day. That wasn't progress. All the same, the void remained and even after paying and making her way back to the station, she couldn't shake off the slight sadness that dulled her mood. This investigation would have been so much better if it had been handled by her, Morgan and Jamie, with Kate at the helm.

This is the closest café to police HQ, so it's no surprise to see Emma walk in, especially as her boyfriend was already here with another copper. The pair were deep in conversation until she arrived, then pulled away like they'd been caught with their pants down. He's observed enough people to know when they are behaving suspiciously. He knows when they are up to no good.

After talking to them, Emma collects an order and heads straight back out without glancing in his direction. If she had . . . well, that was something he'd been prepared for.

He likes the way she carries herself: her posture no doubt down to her training sessions. He also takes great care of his body, ensuring it's in peak condition. His speed, strength and stealth have served him well over the years. Emma stands out from the crowd, and in her work clothes – a crisp white shirt, smart boot-cut trousers over shining Doc Martens and a long black coat – she reminds him of Trinity from *The Matrix*. She is her own woman and doesn't need Morgan Meredith in her life.

He watches her stride down the road and knows that Emma is the perfect choice. His final victim in this area.

He puts away his phone. He'll steer clear of this café for the foreseeable and most definitely not return after Emma has been dealt with. The surveillance camera will have picked him up. Not that he'll worry about today's visit. It's been a test to see if he could sit undetected or noticed in a café full of police officers who haven't a clue as to what he has done. It hasn't given him the thrill he hoped for; nevertheless, it's been worthwhile. He waits for a woman and her partner to leave, getting swiftly to his feet and following them out of the door before slipping away.

Kate found herself travelling along yet another country lane, driving through muddy debris deposited by tractors and clinging to stick-like hedgerows every time a large vehicle approached from the opposite direction. Dense nimbostratus clouds were building on the horizon; the damp roads, flanked by skeletal trees, glistened like black rivers. Days like this sucked Kate's energy, leaving her empty and low. With little to boost her morale, it wasn't long before Dickson's voice whispered throughout the car, tormenting her, reminding her she was out of her depth.

'You've been hunting for that drifter for weeks. These people are going to be no more accommodating than all the others you spoke to. By now, word has got out that a half-crazed police officer is after Digger, and he will have told them that you want to silence him. This community is tight knit. They look out for each other. Don't fool yourself that your badge will open doors.'

She flinched and squeezed the steering wheel more tightly, quietly chanting 'William . . . William . . . William', urging his voice to replace Dickson's.

Dickson laughed – a menacing sound that made her look up and catch sight of her face in the mirror, eyes narrowed to slits and lips twisted. The sight shocked her. This was another unwelcome development. It was one thing to talk in his voice, quite another to take on his persona. *What the . . . !*

A van sped around the bend towards her, the vehicle rapidly filling her windscreen. She slammed on her brakes, yanked on the steering wheel and manoeuvred the car out of harm's way. The driver raised his hand by way of thanks, barely glancing in her direction. She caught her breath, slowed her heartrate. She'd overreacted. There'd been sufficient room for the two vehicles to pass each other if only she had been concentrating on the road rather than on the voices. These conversations were a dangerous distraction. For a moment, she considered therapy, then immediately dropped the idea. She knew what was wrong with her and why. She'd killed Dickson and this was her way of serving penance. As for William, she needed him, just like she had needed Chris – for guidance. They were entwined and part of her. As stupid as it sounded, they were stopping her from tipping over the edge.

Kate thought instead about her father and when he had taken her to visit Tutbury Castle, little more than a ruin but still of historic importance. It was, he had explained, where Mary, Queen of Scots had been held prisoner on four occasions and where she had become involved in a plot that ultimately led to her execution. Her father had been fascinated by history, a passion Kate had not shared.

Thoughts of her father inevitably led to those of his best friend, William. She didn't regret lying to William when she had denied killing Dickson. He had kept secrets from her, after all. But even now, she couldn't be certain that he had told the truth about infiltrating the syndicate to expose them. Once again, she dwelled on the possibility that she couldn't find the document because it didn't exist.

'Search your soul. At that point, when you called me out, I came clean. The only reason I kept you in the dark was to protect you. Answer me this: who told your captors at the warehouse to release you unharmed?' said William.

'You did.'

'Exactly, and I have always protected you: from the syndicate and Dickson. You should have complete faith in me. I've never let you down. I've given you little reason to doubt me. Once you've found Digger and cleared up this mess, search for the document again. It's there.'

She wanted to believe William so badly, tears sprang to her eyes. She blinked them away. As she did so, her navigation system alerted her to the fact she'd arrived at her destination.

A sign swinging on thick chains attached to a solid wooden post indicated she was at the muddy entrance to a dairy farm, home to a herd of Friesian cows, belonging to Paul Hennessey. She could see the place perched halfway up a hill, a large Victorian building with a decorative brick frontage surrounded by enormous outbuildings. The high-pitched sound of a back-up beeper, accompanied by a volley of barking, suggested she wouldn't be able to investigate this place without being spotted.

The Audi growled along the uneven track – more suited to off-road vehicles – periodically throwing her against the door as it bounced over thick ruts. Now she had eyes on two tractors transporting hay bales from one outbuilding to another. A grubby old Land Rover, complete with trailer, appeared from around the back of one of the sheds and started towards her, stopping when the driver saw the Audi making its steady, slow progress. She had no option other than to come to a halt, wind down the window and speak to the occupants – two men in their late sixties.

'I'm looking for Paul Hennessey,' she said.

The passenger jerked a thumb behind him. 'He's around the back. You might want to leave your car in front of the house though.'

The Land Rover set off, exhaust fumes puffing in its wake. Following their advice, she parked beside a pick-up truck and set off on foot only to stop once again, this time because of a sheepdog that appeared out of nowhere and began circling her, growling all the while.

She stood stock still, assuming the dog wasn't dangerous, more likely only protecting its territory. 'Good dog,' she said with as much confidence as she could muster. The loud, sharp whistle almost made her jump.

'Misty. Here!'

The dog was gone in a flash, flanking the side of its master, a man in a dark jacket, jeans and wellington boots who strode towards her. At close range, she established he was fresh-faced, possibly in his thirties or forties and slim built. She decided to be upfront.

'Mr Hennessey?'

'Yes, and you are?'

'DCI Kate Young. I'm after your help.'

'Misty, sit.' The dog obeyed instantly, although it didn't take its eyes off Kate. 'What sort of help?'

'I've been told that a farm labourer called Digger has been or still is working for you.' The lie didn't faze her. She was determined to give this man no opportunity to deny it. As it was, he didn't seem to be obstructive.

'That's right, but you just missed him. He finished work an hour ago.'

'Is he returning tomorrow?'

'No. He's done what he came to do.'

'When you need him, how do you contact him? He doesn't have a phone.'

'Word of mouth.'

'And how does that work?'

'I ask around or I let my fellow farmers know I've work for him.'

'I've been asking around and not getting anywhere.'

'You're asking in the wrong places. You should try the pubs.'

'I thought he hated enclosed spaces.'

'He does, but he likes pub gardens. If I were you, I'd try the local pubs. He's just been paid, and I bet he'll spend some on a warm meal and a pint of beer around these parts.'

'You've been most helpful.'

'You're welcome. Can I ask why you want him? In case I see him.'

She thought for a moment. Anything that might be passed on to Digger would frighten him away. 'I'm sorry but I can't tell you. It's very sensitive. All I can say is that he isn't in any trouble with the police. We want to help him. If you should come across him or know where he is, give me a call. This is my number.'

The dog watched her as she pulled out a card from her pocket and handed it to the man.

'Seems a bit irregular,' he said.

'I can assure you it isn't. It's important we reach Digger without worrying him or scaring him off.'

She thanked him again and, walking away, felt his eyes boring into her back. There was no denying that it did sound irregular, no matter how sincerely she put across her request. For now, though, she had another avenue to pursue – she might find out more from local publicans.

CHAPTER NINETEEN

Emma let out a small yelp then called out, 'Listen up. I think I've found something.'

The room fell silent, all eyes on her.

Emma cleared her throat and read out the information she'd just come across. 'At 10.27 p.m. on November the twenty-fifth, 2022, thirty-eight-year-old Ava Mason, a manageress of a clothes store, was discovered slumped in the doorway of Marks & Spencer in the Riverside Shopping Centre, confused and agitated.

'Ava reported that while crossing the Asda car park to catch her usual bus, a man approached her and blew white powder into her face. She had no further recollections of the evening.'

Harry piped up, 'Devil's Breath is a powder, right?'

'Uh-huh, I think so,' said Scott. 'There have been recorded incidents of it being used in Colombia in this fashion, but I haven't come across anything like that in this country.'

'Then the perp could have drugged Ava by blowing that shit right in her face. Wow!'

Emma waited until Harry had fallen silent again before continuing. 'Ava's phone, purse, watch, three rings and a silver chain containing a large silver cross were missing. It was established that at 6.14 p.m. that evening, Ava withdrew one hundred pounds from Barclays ATM in Queensway, and . . .' Emma paused for effect.

'Her credit card was used that same day to purchase an iPad and a GoPro.'

'Let me guess,' said Frankie, 'they were sent to a post box address in the name of Hasty Holdings.'

Emma shook her head. 'To one called Safeguard Holdings. And it wasn't used again afterwards. I want to interview her as soon as possible. There may be other victims, people left zombified without any memory.'

George cleared his throat. 'Shouldn't we also see if there are any connections between Ava and the other victims? I mean, apart from the fact they were all attacked in the centre of Stafford.'

'They are all managers too, aren't they?' said Frankie. 'I mean, this victim is . . . and Victoria Hannover was manager of Property Plus, right? Leah Fairbrother was a sort of a manager in as much as she was Jackson's right-hand person, and about to be made partner. Do you think our perpetrator is targeting that sort of woman – a highflier, middle-management sort of person?'

It was a valid question, and one Emma couldn't answer with certainty. 'I think they're targeting women who appear to have some financial substance: nice clothes, jewellery, which sometimes comes with a decent income. Their positions might not be relevant, although I think you're right to point it out.'

'Also, if we are considering this possibility, it could mean we've been barking up the wrong tree or even trees, in our pursuit of Danny and Russell,' said Scott.

'Oh shit, yeah.' Frankie folded her arms and stared at the evidence board. 'We can't have wasted our time. How about we check to see if Ava was at that same charity event? Emma?'

'I agree. Okay, people, let's line up an interview with her. There's also something else we should consider: Ava didn't die.'

'That might have been because she didn't inhale as much powder as Victoria and Leah,' said Frankie.

'True, or maybe, since November, our killer has increased the dosage of powder, changed supplier—'

George interrupted Harry with, 'Or they deliberately increased it because they intended killing their victims.'

Emma hadn't considered that possibility, but now it had been voiced she wasn't completely set against the theory. 'Could be, George. Let's keep searching for other potential cases. I have an inkling that this person is evolving. Maybe Ava wasn't his first victim.'

◆ ◆ ◆

Kate climbed back into her car with the sound of Dickson's laughter echoing in her head. It had been the same story in each of the five pubs she had tried: either nobody had heard of Digger, or they knew him, just had not seen him since late summer. With every failed attempt to find him, Dickson's mocking laugh had increased in volume, causing her to clench her teeth so tightly, her jaw now ached. Thinking about it as she followed her sat nav to the next pub, it seemed unlikely that anyone, not even Digger, would sit outside on a damp bench on a freezing January afternoon to enjoy a beer and a meal. Paul Hennessey might have sent her on a wild goose chase. She sighed. She had no other choice but to see this through. There weren't too many places to check out – after all, if Digger had left Castle Farm an hour before she got there, he couldn't have travelled far on foot.

He could have got a long way if he'd been hiding in the trailer that the Land Rover was towing. There's every chance he saw you coming and high-tailed it out of there, leaving Paul Hennessey to cover for him, said Dickson.

She thumped the steering wheel hard. Damn Dickson! What made hearing his voice even worse was the fact he could be right.

For all his mocking, he was stating the obvious, so that the Kate who had accepted promotion to DCI, confident she would bring down the syndicate, was now full of self-doubt and racing about the countryside like a headless chicken, unable to even find a farm labourer, let alone an incriminating document planted in an empty house.

'Kate, calm down,' said William. 'You've always approached things methodically. Stick to your tried and tested methods. Check out more pubs in this vicinity. Assume Digger got a lift to one of them. He is a private person. Look for one that isn't in a village or town, somewhere rural where he'd feel safe. Breathe deeply. Remember who you are. You are doing this so you can continue the fight against those individuals who are corrupt and tarnishing the good name of our force. Keep clinging to that belief and you won't flounder.'

She checked the sat nav again, searching for nearby pub icons. She might well be better off visiting those on the edge of town. There were a couple in Hatton, at either end of the village; however, another one sounded more promising – The Spread Eagle in the nearby village of Rolleston-on-Dove, a country public house with a tranquil garden. She turned off the road and made for it.

One of the oldest buildings in the village, parts of The Spread Eagle dated back to the sixteenth century. It had in its lifetime been a schoolhouse and a venue for local courts as well as an alehouse. Kate hadn't journeyed far into the village before she came across the white L-shaped building next to the main bridge. She followed the car parking sign to the rear of the pub, taking in the empty picnic tables that overlooked Alder Brook to her left. With no sign of anyone outside, she considered abandoning this place and trying another, before deciding that now she was here, she may as well go inside and ask if anyone knew Digger.

The interior appeared to be open plan, with several linked rooms around a central bar. The mixture of high and low ceilings, some with beams, combined with slate, quarry tile, wooden and carpeted floors, along with dim lighting and a crackling fire in the grate, helped create an old-fashioned charm that Kate rather liked. This was the sort of place William would have loved. She could imagine him seated in front of the fire, a book in one hand, a pint in the other. The thought caused a physical pain in her chest, making her flinch.

'You alright?' asked the barman.

'Yes. Thanks. I've got a migraine coming.'

'If you want to take a seat by the fire, I can bring a drink or menu over to you,' he said.

'That's really kind of you, but I'm on duty. I came in to ask if you know Digger?'

'Yes. I know him.'

'Have you seen him recently?'

'Funny you should ask. He came in for a meal earlier.'

'When did he leave?'

'Only about ten minutes ago.'

'I don't suppose you have any idea where he's gone, do you?'

'He mentioned he was going to the Coles' place to work the night shift, lamb checking. I didn't get the impression that was today though. He said something about staying the night in Hatton. The Coles live near Repton, which isn't far away. I'm guessing that he'll probably be there tomorrow. You a friend?'

'Sort of. I'm trying to help him with something, but I never seem to catch up with him.'

The barman laughed. 'That's Digger all over. He turns up out of the blue, then he vanishes for weeks on end. He's been coming here on and off for as long as I can remember. He usually waits by the door until somebody notices him, orders his food then sits outside, no matter what the weather. Try the Coles at Bracken Farm.'

'You've been very helpful. Thank you.'

She hastened back to her car. William had been right about being methodical. It yielded results. With Digger not starting work at the Coles' farm until at least tomorrow, there was nothing to be gained by heading up there yet. She would have to stake the place out the following day and hope Digger reappeared.

◆ ◆ ◆

Emma and Scott found Ava Mason assisting a customer. She was pulling out garment after garment, suggesting which might suit the customer best. She looked up when the shop doorbell tinkled, and smiled at the two detectives.

'Won't be a moment,' she said.

Emma acknowledged her with a smile and, leaving Scott standing beside the window display, she meandered around the boutique, unlike any of the clothes shops she frequented. Careful consideration had been given to the design and layout to give the impression of space: patterned black and white tiles spiralled from a black central desk on which stood a magnificent white floral display broken only by green foliage and gold grasses. There were four distinct areas, each with a changing room where thick red curtains had been swept to one side and held in place by twisted gold and red braid. Each zone contained colour-coordinated clothing on several rails: black, grey and white in one section, blue and green in another, orange, red and pink in a third and cream, beige and yellow in the last. Pausing beside the nearest rail, Emma casually eyed the stylish items hanging there and, until she saw the eye-watering price tags, considered returning here to upgrade her wardrobe.

Once the customer had gone, Emma showed Ava her identity card.

'I had a feeling you were police officers,' said Ava.

'I know you've probably answered many questions about it before, but we'd appreciate it if you'd go through what happened to you in November,' said Emma.

'It's still a blur, like it never happened. At times, I even wonder if I made it up. I was going home, via the car park like I usually do to get to my bus. It was getting dark, and I was changing a playlist on my phone. I don't know why but I looked up and a man was walking towards me. I didn't have time to think. Sometimes, when I really try to remember, I imagine he was looking at me, which was how I knew something wasn't right. He had his fist clenched. Maybe I thought he was going to thump me.' A deep line formed between her brows as she spoke. 'I stopped walking, so we didn't collide, and he brought his hand right up to my face, uncurled it and blew. I remember white powder like flour then . . . nothing. The next thing, I was in an ambulance. I was groggy and hadn't a clue what had happened. When the police spoke to me, I couldn't even tell them as much as I just told you. It took a while to piece together what had happened. I was robbed . . . somehow, he'd managed to convince me to withdraw money from the ATM.'

She shook her head and pressed her lips together. Her eyes became glassy, and Emma placed a gentle hand on her shoulder. 'It's okay. We don't want to upset you. Would you like to sit down for a moment?'

'It's . . . okay. I still get . . . nightmares. I can't travel by bus any more, I get an Uber. I . . .'

'Listen, I understand. It was a traumatic experience.'

Ava nodded dumbly.

'Come and sit down,' said Emma, shepherding the woman towards a stool behind the cash desk.

Ava obeyed without protest.

'I know this is hard for you, but we want to find the person who assaulted you. You said you remember him looking at you. Can you describe him at all?' Emma asked.

Ava wetted her lips. 'I only remember a blur of movement. He was in dark clothing. I can't remember what he looked like. I think he was wearing a hoodie or a beanie or something that hid his hair. I can't recall any other details other than his eyes. They were dark-coloured. He was staring at me . . . no . . . through me. Like I wasn't there.'

'What about his eyebrows? Heavy, thick?'

She shook her head.

'Lips?'

'I can't remember. It happened so fast. I glanced up. He was there, then the powder and then . . . I rubbed my face and . . . then . . . that's it. Nothing more.'

'Before this happened, did you have any male customers who came in looking for presents for girlfriends, wives, mothers?'

Ava screwed up her face again. 'There was someone. He was studying the window display for quite a while. I half expected him to come in. I was dealing with another customer at the time, so I didn't pay him much attention. When I next looked, he had gone. Apart from him, there have been no unaccompanied men in the shop . . . apart from delivery drivers.'

Emma glanced at Scott, who had been quietly listening. Ava's words had set her thinking. Could the culprit be somebody who delivered goods? Scott gave a slight nod, obviously picking up on the same thoughts.

'Ava, DS Hart is going to show you some photographs. Could you tell us if you recognise any of the men in them?'

Scott placed a photo of Russell on the desk in front of Ava. She leant forward and shook her head. He replaced it with one of Craig and again received a negative response. He put the photo of

Danny on top of it. Ava studied it, looked at Scott, then back at the picture. Emma held her breath. Ava eventually looked directly at her and in a small voice said, 'I'm fairly certain that's the man who was staring at the window display.'

◆ ◆ ◆

Matching Emma stride for stride, Scott said, 'Looks like we've found our perpetrator.'

Emma was struggling to temper the bubbling euphoria with common sense. She knew better than to jump too quickly – after all, Ava had only seen somebody who looked like Danny through a shop window. That didn't make him the perpetrator. 'We can't afford to be too hasty.'

'Come on, Emma! Ava identified him. And he is the right height and weight to be the hooded figure we've seen with the other victims. You must be giving this some credence.'

'Some, yes. We must be certain of our facts. Ava can't have seen him for more than a few fleeting moments – she was attending to a customer at the time. I'm not saying she was mistaken, but we can't rush off and arrest the man for being outside a shop.'

'I know that. It's just it's quite a coincidence, isn't it? Bloke happens to have bought his house from the estate agency where Victoria worked, was Leah's boyfriend, and was spotted outside Ava's shop.'

'I grant you, it is something we need to look into.' Their footsteps rang out in unison along the pavement and Scott fell silent. Deep down, Emma wanted their perpetrator to be Danny, who had ghosted his pregnant girlfriend. There was something about the supposed arguments that didn't sit right with her. She would love nothing more than to arrest him, extract a confession, congratulate her team and claim the praise; however, working with Kate had taught her that mistakes occurred when assumptions were made. Kate had been meticulous in gathering evidence to support her hunches and actions. Emma was going to follow in her footsteps. First off, she'd ascertain Danny's whereabouts on the evening Ava was attacked.

'I think—'

Scott's words were cut off by the ringing of Emma's mobile.

'It's Frankie,' she said, putting on speakerphone so Scott could hear.

'Harry came across another similar attack that took place in May. Again, in Stafford. The victim was Beth Meadows. Do you want one of us to interview her?' said Frankie.

'We were on our way to talk to Danny Greaves again, but I'd rather speak to Beth before we do that. Ava has identified Danny as somebody who was watching her prior to her attack. It would be very helpful if Beth could also identify him.'

'Okay, Harry is sending contact details to your phone as we speak.'

'How similar was this attack?'

'Very. Beth had been out with friends and was headed back to her car when a man appeared from nowhere, pushed her against a wall and blew white dust into her face, before knocking her to the ground, where he ripped off the gold chain from her neck. She tried to fight back but had no energy or coordination. Then she lost consciousness. She described her attacker as tall, probably six foot or over, slim built, muscular and wearing dark clothing and a hooded top.'

'Did she not describe any features?'

'She was unclear as to the assailant's looks and thought he might have had a beard or was wearing some sort of dark face covering.'

'Did the perpetrator steal anything other than the chain?'

267

'A new mobile phone and wallet, although he didn't use Beth's credit card.'

'Did he take her to an ATM?'

'It appears not.'

'Okay, thanks, everyone. We'll follow that up.' She ended the call and got into the car.

'That happened eight months ago. No ATM visit and the perp didn't buy anything using the vic's credit card.'

'This could be one of his first victims. Maybe he didn't use sufficient Devil's Breath to control Beth.'

Scott started up the car. 'I reckon he's getting cocky and bolder. Worse still, he doesn't care what happens to his victims as long as he steals money and valuables from them. He's a twisted individual.'

Emma mumbled an agreement, her attention taken up by the message Harry had sent. 'Beth's a twenty-six-year-old editor for an online magazine. She's single and works from home. Owns a three-storey detached house on Burleyfields.'

'Must be a job that pays well then. That's one of those luxury home estates. I think you called it earlier at the meeting. Our perpetrator is targeting people who look like they're well-off.'

Emma agreed. 'We'll show her the photo of Danny. This could be the clincher.'

Given it was now almost five thirty, she typed a text for Morgan to let him know she would be late home. If things went well, she would be extremely late, because she would have hauled Danny in for questioning.

◆　◆　◆

He beats a steady rhythm against the steering wheel. He's been waiting for over an hour and Emma still hasn't shown up. Instead of trailing her and running the risk of being spotted, he cruised past her house at six o'clock, where he only saw Morgan's Jeep. Her car wasn't in the police station car park either, so he drove to Greg's gym where he was now waiting in his car, expecting her to show.

He's waited too long. There's no sign of Emma and he doesn't know where she is.

Without warning, he senses a change. His fingers grip the wheel and the monster that usually remains coiled in the pit of his stomach unfurls slowly. He has no control over these moments. When they occur, he reacts rather than feels.

If Emma Donaldson were here at this very moment, he would constrict her windpipe until it ruptured and her eyeballs popped.

CHAPTER TWENTY

Beth Meadows' striking white-rendered house, with vertical strips of grey timber cladding, stood out from its popular red-brick neighbours.

Emma bounded up the few steps to the front door and rang the bell, heart thudding. If Beth identified Danny Greaves as her assailant, or her team established a connection between this victim and Danny, she would drag the latter's sorry arse to the station so quickly he wouldn't have time to put on his shoes.

She stabbed the doorbell again. Scott peered through one of the front windows.

'The blinds are drawn,' he said.

'Maybe she can't hear us.'

Emma had already tried Beth's phone, only to discover it was switched off with no messaging service available. She should have taken that as a sign Beth might be out.

'We could try around the back,' she said, making for the adjacent wall, which was about a foot taller than her.

'I'll go,' said Scott.

He was about to haul himself over when one of the doors opposite opened and a man emerged.

'Oi! You!' he shouted, breaking into a run towards them.

'It's okay. We're police,' Emma called, holding up her ID.

The man slowed but continued making his way across the road. As he drew nearer, she noticed he was well-built, tattooed hands curled and ready to strike a blow if necessary. She waited until he was in front of them, then said, 'We're looking for Beth Meadows. I'm Acting DI Emma Donaldson, and this is my colleague, DS Scott Hart.'

The man studied her pass. 'Sorry I shouted. We're all a bit wary of strangers, especially after the attack on her.'

'What do you know about that?'

'Only the same details she probably gave to the police. She's been understandably nervous about going out alone ever since. You caught the bastard yet?'

'I can't discuss an ongoing investigation with you, but we would like to talk to Beth.'

'Beth's not at home. She's gone camping with a group of friends.'

'Camping? In January?'

'At Rocky Bay Caravan Park on the south coast of KwaZulu-Natal in South Africa.'

'Oh, okay. Have you any idea when she'll be back?'

'Not until next Wednesday. She asked me to keep an eye on her house, which is why I got a bit shouty.'

'That's understandable. It's good that she has somebody to watch over it. We tried to contact Beth earlier but couldn't get hold of her. Do you have another number for her?'

'No. You won't be able to reach her or her friends. They're on a digital detox holiday. They've gone to probably one of a handful of places on this planet where there's no phone signal or internet.'

'Then she can't be reached at all?'

'No. That's why she was glad I offered to look after her place while she's away. She can't check the camera apps as she would normally. She's off-grid.'

Emma thanked the man. For the time being, they were unable to gather any new information from this victim. That wasn't, however, going to prevent her from quizzing Danny.

◆ ◆ ◆

Danny Greaves folded his arms and glared at Emma. 'I haven't been anywhere near the clothes shop you mentioned. Not alone. Not with *anyone*. I've never even bought clothes for women!'

'You were identified,' said Emma.

'I don't see how when I've never been there! Who is this person who thinks they've seen me?'

'We can't—'

Danny lifted his palm to stop Scott from continuing. 'Save it. You won't reveal their identity. You're worried that I'll go looking for them and smack them one. Well, I wouldn't because I'm not a violent person. Take me to the station, get this witness to look me in the eyes and say they recognise me! Go on. I haven't got anything to hide.'

'Mr Greaves, there's no need—'

This time, Danny silenced Scott with a look. 'I've been as truthful and as helpful as I can be. I understand how it looks with regards to me and Leah, but I swear that I didn't kill her. On the night she disappeared, I said goodbye to her at the car park, got into my car and drove away, and that is the gospel truth. Now you're asking about some boutique in town that I can say, hand on heart, I've never even noticed, let alone visited. It's beginning to feel like you're harassing me.'

'We're trying to get to the bottom of Leah's murder. If our questions are inconvenient or make you feel uncomfortable, then I apologise. However, I would have thought you would want to give us all the help possible. You do want Leah's killer to be brought to justice, don't you?' said Emma.

Her sharp words struck a nerve. His shoulders slumped. 'Sorry that I'm coming across as prickly. It's just that I know you're going to have doubts about me. All of this is . . . I don't want to be falsely accused. I swear that everything I've told you so far is the truth. As for this shop . . . I know nothing about it.'

Emma was forced to concede. She couldn't prove he was outside the boutique in town. Until they could speak to Beth and get a description of the attacker from her, they were thwarted.

◆ ◆ ◆

The following morning, Emma woke up feeling disorientated.

'Hey, you awake?' asked Morgan.

Opening one eye, she spotted him towelling his body dry.

'Hi,' she mumbled.

'Shower's free.'

'Mmm.'

'Go on. It'll help wake you up.'

She tried and failed to move the duvet. Morgan grinned. 'Come on, sleepyhead.' He leant across and dragged the duvet off her.

'No! Give it back.'

'Nope. It's quarter to eight.'

Her eyes opened properly this time. 'What?'

'Uh-huh, so if I were you, I'd get a shift on.'

The combination of his words and the cool air against her bare legs galvanised her into action. 'Are you going into work immediately, or do you want breakfast?' she said.

'Yes and no thanks. I'll get a coffee there. I'm working on a plan to expose the mole in my team.'

'Did Kate not suggest anything?' she asked.

'It was her suggestion.'

'What do you intend doing?'

'Trip the bastard up. I'm gradually feeding false information through those people I suspect the most. If I'm right, the mole will pass it on.'

'I hope that works,' she said, as she hunted in the drawer for clean clothes. Morgan had buttoned his shirt and was tucking it into his waistband.

'So do I,' he said. 'If not, then I'm stumped, and I don't want to end up like DI Ali Rind – being removed from the operation.'

'I guess I'm lucky having a small team. It's easier to keep an eye on what they're up to. I envy you yours though. Must feel good having so many officers in your control.' She looked over her shoulder as she spoke.

Morgan wasn't listening. His eyes had taken on a faraway look.

'Morgan?'

'Hmm?'

'Never mind. I'll see you later.'

'You bet. Have a good one. I might even see you at the station.'

He picked up his belt and left the room. Emma felt strangely empty. Work really was interfering with their relationship. By the time she'd got in from interviewing Danny the previous night, she was so exhausted that she'd conked out almost as soon as her head touched the pillow, and this morning Morgan was so distracted by his problems he hadn't even kissed her goodbye. She hoped work was the only reason and not that he was keeping something from her.

◆ ◆ ◆

Even after four months, it still felt strange just walking into William's house. Every time she opened the door, she expected to hear him shout hello or for one of his cats to appear. With no heating on, the air felt chilly, and she kept her coat on while she collected junk mail from the mat.

She'd allowed herself an hour to hunt for the document before she went into work. Overnight, she'd had an idea that it could be hidden inside a large can and recalling there were several paint tins in William's garage, she'd decided to check them, along with any other tins she found.

She ran a finger along the dusty kitchen top and, ashamed of herself for letting the place get so dirty, she considered using the time to run the vacuum cleaner over the carpets and wipe the surfaces, before reminding herself she simply didn't have the time for housework. She turned her attention to the task in hand and, searching through her box of tools, chose a screwdriver to lever open the tins. The first was over half full of white ceiling paint, the second almost full of an apricot emulsion, a colour that Kate had never seen on any of his walls. It was the same story with the other eight tins she opened, leaving her once again frustrated.

'Where is it?' she muttered. 'It's here somewhere. Where the hell is it?'

Her eyes alighted on a box marked 'Memories' – one she had overlooked in previous searches. Opening it, she pulled out several large photograph albums, turning each page carefully in case the document fell out. When nothing dropped, she examined it again to ensure William had not stuck paperwork behind photographs, her attention gradually being diverted as she pieced together his life: pictures of William as a schoolboy, on holiday by the seaside with two people who she assumed to be his parents. It seemed odd to think of him as a child. He had never spoken about his childhood, but according to her father, William had been through several foster homes before he spent time with a couple who ran a smallholding.

There were pictures of him during his early days on the force, when he'd been a skinny young man with an unlined face and thick dark hair, but the same broad smile that she would always associate with him.

She picked up another album, this one filled with photos of him with his wife, Tanya, who had died during childbirth, along with the baby. William had never really got over the loss and to Kate's knowledge never had a serious relationship again. He'd been out on dates, but nobody had been good enough to replace his beloved Tanya and, by then, William only had one love – the police force. It was this belief that kept her searching for the document she knew was hidden in this house. William's whole life had been given over to the job and only somebody with that much love for it would want to infiltrate a corrupt syndicate, put themselves in jeopardy and try to clean it up.

She was like William in many ways: upholding the old values and morals he and her father had upheld.

Dickson scoffed, *'Listen to yourself! William and your father were ordinary coppers. They weren't superheroes.'*

'They were both worth a hundred of you.'

'Say that when you find this alleged document,' he said. *'Because, for all your rose-tinted-glasses, nostalgic memories of William, you have fuck-all proof that he was trying to bring down the syndicate. His word was meaningless. As you will find out when you finally accept that there is nothing here to back up what he told you.'*

She shut the album and replaced it in the box then stomped out of the garage, leaving Dickson there. She would prove him wrong. Patience would win out. With that in mind, she made for the utility room, where she'd spotted large tubs of cat litter. William might have poured out the contents, placed the document in the bottom of the tub, then refilled it. If it wasn't there, then there were still other hiding places she hadn't thought of. William might even have a false tread on the stairs. She would check them out next.

She was halfway through tipping out the second container of cat litter when her phone rang. Seeing it was Morgan, she answered the call.

'Morning, Kate,' he said. 'Could you spare me five minutes? I think I might have identified the leak in my team.'

'Can you meet me in my office in twenty minutes?'

'Sure.'

'Who is it?' she asked.

'I'd rather speak to you face to face,' he replied. 'It's complicated.'

'Okay. I'll see you in a while.'

She poured out the remainder of the contents. There was nothing stuck to the bottom of the plastic bin; however, she wasn't disillusioned, and her interest had been piqued by the call. If Morgan had caught the mole, that person might be able to lead them to the other syndicate members. She tidied up the mess she'd made before leaving. As she locked the door once again, she whispered, 'I'm on to the syndicate, Dickson. Patience will win out.'

◆　◆　◆

Forensic anthropologist Terry Wiggins swivelled in Ervin's chair, a drink in his hand. From her own seat, opposite him, Emma was able to read the slogan on the white china mug, one of Ervin's – *I am trained in Forensics so yes, I can murder you and get away with it.*

Scott, next to her, had his eyes fixed on Ervin, who – propped against the wall with his arms folded – was wearing a black polo-neck shirt and black trousers, teamed with a single-breasted cadmium-yellow velvet blazer. Ervin's outfits were often the subject of conversation at the station; today, however, Emma was more interested in what he had to say.

'Not only can scopolamine make someone subservient and obedient, but it can also impair a person's declarative memory, which is the ability to store facts and events. In brief, it causes amnesia, which is why Ava, and indeed Beth, were unable to recollect anything.'

'How much of this drug was in their system?' asked Emma.

'A high toxic concentration of fourteen nanograms per millilitre was detected in Victoria's blood and 263 nanograms per millilitre in her urine. Terry was unable to determine exact levels in Leah because over time scopolamine degrades.'

'Still found traces though,' said Terry. 'The cause of death can't be put down to the amount of scopolamine that would have been in her system, but we can be fairly certain an overdose of it caused her death.'

'What would be a lethal dose?' asked Emma.

'The actual lethal dose of scopolamine is unknown, although one study I came across revealed the lowest ingested dose that produced life-threatening symptoms was between two and four milligrams,' said Ervin.

'And what about Ava and Beth? Were they just lucky?'

'Their toxicology reports revealed they had much lower doses in their systems than Victoria.'

'Then our perpetrator most likely used higher dosages on his later victims,' said Emma.

'That's the conclusion I would reach,' said Ervin. 'I would also consider the possibility that the attacker might have changed their modus operandi, because scopolamine can be administered into drinks as well as blown into the face of victims. Ergo, you may find even more victims prior to Ava and Beth, people whose drink was spiked. If so, it would be safe to assume that this perpetrator could be evolving, becoming bolder and more cavalier in their attitude towards their victims, possibly unconcerned whether they live or die. That said, I would also consider other factors: for example, Victoria had been drinking wine prior to her attack. Neither Ava nor Beth had been drinking alcohol. Alcohol consumption would exacerbate the effect of scopolamine.'

Scott piped up with, 'What about Leah, though? She was expecting a baby and from what we can gather, she only drank soft drinks the night she was attacked.'

Ervin looked at Terry, who put down his mug. 'The results of her hair samples came back an hour ago. Leah had been taking diazepam for a couple of months.'

'But that's a tranquilliser,' said Scott. 'Why would she take drugs if she was pregnant?'

'It's safe in small doses. Combined with the scopolamine . . . well . . . it might have contributed to her death. Without an idea of how much scopolamine was in her system at the time of death, I can only speculate,' said Terry.

Emma rubbed at the frown that was tugging her skin. 'Russell didn't mention her taking diazepam.'

'Maybe he didn't know she was doing so,' Ervin suggested.

Scott spoke again. 'Her doctor said she refused to prescribe any drugs for Leah.'

Emma caught Ervin's patient expression. He and Terry were trying to help them out, not throw curveballs, and she was grateful to them. 'Then Leah must have gone elsewhere for them,' she said.

Terry joined in with, 'We all know that you can purchase anything on the internet if you look hard enough. I'd wager she got them online.'

Scott shook his head slowly. 'No. Her search history was checked on her laptop, home computer and phone. Nothing was flagged.'

Ervin gave a light shrug. 'If it were me, I'd erase my browsing history. And I would use the dark web. Try Felicity. Her team are best placed to unearth any evidence. However, don't forget that there's also a chance Leah got the drugs from someone she knew.'

'I'll follow up on this. After all, it might lead us to our killer,' said Emma.

'Which would be the perfect result,' said Ervin.

A glow filled Emma's chest. She was lucky to have such great support from this man. She was sure he wouldn't have given up his time for other DIs. 'Thank you. Both of you. Come on, Scott, we'd better shift.'

'Any time, Emma,' said Ervin. 'Oh, and for what it's worth, I'd question that husband of hers again. I can't understand why he not only didn't know she was pregnant but failed to mention how stressed she was.'

As Emma headed back out into the laboratory, she digested his comment and wondered what sort of marriage Leah and Russell had. Leah kept secrets; Russell appeared to be oblivious to his wife's desires and needs. The more Emma dug into their marriage, the more she realised the relationship was as fragile as a butterfly's wings.

◆ ◆ ◆

Kate hadn't been back in her office for more than two minutes when Morgan knocked at the door.

'Thanks for seeing me,' he began.

She beckoned to the chair opposite. 'Sit down.'

He sat on the edge of the seat, eyebrows knitted together. 'I'll get straight to the point. Just after the morning briefing, a prison guard informed me that one of our arrested traffickers, Hasan Demir, wanted to talk to me in private. I visited him alone in the holding cell, where he explained that he was willing to trade the name of somebody high up in the organisation in exchange for protection for himself and his family. He's jittery as hell, Kate. Because somebody on Operation Moonbeam is keeping an eye on Hasan Demir and Yusuf Osman to make sure they keep schtum. They've been threatening them.'

'Go on.'

'Hasan will only divulge this valuable information after we've provided protection and got rid of this mole, but here's my dilemma: Hasan is too scared to reveal who that person is. It has to be somebody who visited the cells this morning. Here's the thing. Jamie was late for the briefing and when I asked Trevor Wray if he knew where Jamie was, he mentioned that he'd last seen him heading in the direction of the cells. Also, Jamie was in on the interviews and accompanied the men back to their cells afterwards. I don't want to believe Jamie is involved, but if he is and we challenge him, he'll deny everything. Worse still, he might have Hasan silenced, then we'll lose any chance of finding out who is behind this huge trafficking ring. I don't know about you, but I don't want to throw away an opportunity like this. So, what do you suggest we do?'

Morgan was edgy, eyes sparkling.

Jamie! Maybe her gut feeling about him had been right all along. This was an opportunity to expose him and yet Morgan was right. They badly needed the info Hasan was willing to provide.

'We fabricate something,' said Kate. 'I'll transfer Jamie, along with another officer of your choice, to a different team, with the excuse that Operation Moonbeam is stalling again, and we can't afford the manpower to keep supporting it. DI Oliver Turner is currently investigating a drugs ring in Stoke and could do with some extra bodies. I'll tell Jamie that once Operation Moonbeam starts making progress again, he can return. If it comes from me, he shouldn't suspect anything, especially if you give up another one of your team to join him. You are sure nobody at all knows that Hasan intends helping you?'

'Nobody. But what if Jamie becomes suspicious?'

'Then we must keep this as quiet as possible. Only you and I can know about this. Lie. You can't confide in anyone other than me.'

'But—'

'Nobody. Not even Emma.'

The frown deepened. She realised that he wasn't as experienced as her in the art of deception. He would have to learn that there were times when everyone had to keep secrets.

'Morgan, if you play this right, you could be in for a very high recommendation, not to mention the kudos your team will get for tracking down these people. Don't stuff it up. Who else would you not mind losing from your team?'

He thought for a moment. 'Detective Constable Daniel Newman.'

'Jamie and Daniel it is then. Let me speak to DI Turner first and set this up. I'll ring you on the office phone and ask to speak to them once I've arranged it. That shouldn't be an issue, especially as he asked me for extra officers only a couple of days ago.'

Morgan took his leave. Kate picked up the phone, ready to put her plan into action. Jamie. She should have got on to him sooner than this. Dialling DI Turner's office, she became aware of an uncomfortable sensation, like hundreds of tiny ants were crawling over her scalp. She hoped Jamie fell for this subterfuge and, more importantly, that he was involved with the syndicate. If not, this ploy would go belly up.

◆ ◆ ◆

Scott pulled on to Russell's driveway. Emma was out of the car like a shot and ringing the doorbell before Scott had joined her. All the way across town, her irritation had been mounting and, convinced

Russell was hiding information from her, she was ready to charge him with perverting the course of justice and question him at the station.

This time, Russell answered the door without a word. There was no ignoring his dishevelled state, dirty hair and unkempt beard.

'I won't beat about the bush, Russell. We need access to Leah's laptop and phone and your computer.'

'They were taken away and examined after I reported her missing. What are you hoping to find on them?'

'Something to indicate she was on medication.'

'Medi— I don't understand what you're implying.'

'We know Leah was taking tranquillisers – diazepam, to be exact.'

'No. She wasn't on anything, other than the odd aspirin.'

'You're saying you had no idea she was taking tranquillisers?'

'Fuck no! I didn't know she intended staying at Harlequin Events or that she didn't want to go ahead with our joint venture, or that she'd been seeing somebody behind my back. I didn't even know she was expecting a baby! Turns out I knew fuck-all about my wife!' His voice rose and his hands began to shake. Tears fell. 'I didn't . . . know her . . . at all.'

He slumped against the wall and sank to the floor, sobbing. Scott stepped inside and, with gentle words, helped Russell back on to his feet before escorting him into the sitting room, where he guided him to a chair. Russell continued crying, head now in his hands. Emma took in the mess on the floor, the photographs of the couple that were scattered over the carpet, the empty vodka bottle next to a half-full glass, and understood that Russell was truly on the edge. Leah might have felt pressured by Russell, but he had loved his wife, and her death – and, moreover, the secrets she had taken with her – had turned his world upside down.

◆ ◆ ◆

Kate was drained. She'd spent a long time with Jamie and Daniel, explaining the false reasons as to why she was moving them to DI Oliver Turner's team . . .

'I don't get it. We've been at this for frigging months, and when we finally start to get somewhere, you decide progress isn't being made and we're off the team,' said Jamie. Two red spots had appeared on his cheeks.

Kate had never seen him so riled, causing her to wonder if his protests were because he needed to maintain his position on the operation to continue to leak information and to continue to lean on the traffickers who had been willing to spill the beans.

'It's simply a case of repositioning resources. Operation Moonbeam is stalling again because the traffickers who were brought in refuse to cooperate. We have far too many officers assigned, and DI Turner is in need of assistance. It makes sense to redeploy you both for the time being.'

'I'm not being funny, but I really would rather work with Acting DI Meredith than DI Turner. I'm far more familiar with his way of doing things.'

'I'm sure you would, but it isn't customary for any officer to pick and choose who their team leader is going to be.'

Jamie sighed. 'And I've only just started to prove myself as a sergeant. This trafficking investigation will be huge for me when we pull it off. You can't deny me my part in it.'

'Jamie, I fully understand your concerns, but this isn't a permanent move. It's only until we get more momentum with Operation Moonbeam. You weren't selected because you're not valuable team members. You both are,' she said, nodding in the direction of Daniel, who

stood, lips together, head bowed. He had taken the news far better than Jamie, who was off again.

'Why us then?' he demanded.

'You were chosen at random. It was nothing more than that.' She'd been prepared for the question and pointed to the two unfolded slips of paper on her desk, next to a box of folded ones. 'Whoever was chosen was bound to feel a little aggrieved.' She kept her voice level, her eyes on Jamie, watching for any tells.

'Look, can't you choose again?' he asked.

Daniel finally piped up, 'Ma'am, I'm happy to be reassigned but DS Webster is passionate about this operation, and you'd be losing a good team player.'

'Cheers, mate,' said Jamie, who then looked intently at her. This was all she needed: both of them trying to twist her arm.

'This isn't up for debate, and moreover a move to DI Turner's team will give you both exposure to another challenge and the opportunity to shine. You'll be brought back on board here as soon as progress is made. For now, you will have to accept that resources are stretched, and the team needs slimming down.'

'You know I'm a loyal soldier,' said Jamie, glowering as he spoke. 'You and I have spoken about it before. I can be of greater value to you and to Operation Moonbeam than moving across to the drugs team. I'm up to speed with this investigation. I've poured myself into it, given up hours of free time. I was instrumental in tracking down those traffickers who are in custody. It's not my fault that they won't talk. I should be allowed to continue to prove myself.'

For a second, she was reminded of the conversation she'd had with him when they'd been alone, waiting to pounce on the bolt gun killer. After the events of that evening, she'd decided she was wrong about him being in Dickson's pocket and believed he would support her. Was she wrong to still suspect him?

Other thoughts replaced these: of meetings with DI Harriet Khatri when Kate thought Harriet and Jamie were in cahoots and both working for the syndicate. She had been wrong about Harriet. It was possible she was wrong again, and yet she still couldn't be sure about him.

Jamie stood his ground, his jaw jutting. She took in the clenched fists and knew she'd probably ruined what trust had been built between them. If he was guilty then that wouldn't matter, but if she was mistaken, it would probably never be repaired. She had to carry on regardless. She'd always followed her gut and would do so on this occasion.

'Jamie, Daniel, I'm sorry you feel that way, but rest assured I see this as an opportunity for you both to shine. There's no more to be said. Please report to DI Turner.'

Despite his protests, she was certain Jamie had bought her act. Once he and Daniel were gone, she had spoken to Superintendent Bree O'Sullivan and requested Hasan Demir's family be given the protection they required. Three hours later, she was still waiting for assurances that this would happen. All the while, her stomach tied itself into knots as she imagined what Jamie might do –the many ways he could get to Hasan and stop him from revealing this vital information.

She was about to ask William for his advice when Felicity's number flashed up on her mobile.

'Hi, Felicity.'

'Are you free for a chat?'

'I can be.'

'Same place as last time. I'm already there,' said Felicity.

Kate bounded from her chair. Felicity clearly had news she didn't want to discuss at work, which meant it had to be regarding the video footage. Striding towards the entrance, she noticed Jamie talking to Trevor. Neither of them spotted her. For a second, she wondered if they were discussing Hasan and feared Trevor might also be involved in the syndicate, until Trevor placed a hand on Jamie's shoulder and shook his head sadly. He was only consoling his friend who'd been taken off the team. She couldn't suspect everyone at HQ of being corrupt.

◆ ◆ ◆

Felicity was waiting at the same table where they'd met previously. She nodded towards the plump, half-eaten toasted sandwich on her plate and wiped a crumb from her lips. 'I can highly recommend these. You want one?'

'I'm good, thanks. I ate earlier.'

'Bev made smoothies for breakfast, bless her. She thinks she's helping me to stay healthy. She probably is. Nevertheless, I hate them. Especially detox smoothies.' She counted each item off on her fingers. 'Kale, avocado, lime, pineapple and cashews. Yuck!'

Kate sat down, allowing time for Felicity to sip her black coffee. No sooner had she replaced the cup on the saucer than she said, 'I was right.'

Kate's heart jumped against her ribcage. 'The footage was tampered with?'

Felicity nodded. 'It was a very professional job and they almost got away with it, if it hadn't been for this.'

She slid her phone across to Kate, who once again watched the footage even though she'd seen it so many times she knew every second off by heart. Harriet, hood up and back to the pet camera, was clearly arguing with William. She glanced at Felicity, who urged her to keep watching.

'Wait a moment,' said Felicity. 'And now, pause it!'

Kate stopped the recording. It was a millisecond before Harriet raised the gun and shot William.

'Look hard.'

'I can't see anything.'

'Go back an instant and pause it.'

Kate did as bid.

'Now run it and pause again. Can you spot the difference?'

Kate performed the act several times. 'What am I looking for?'

'Look at the mantelpiece behind William.'

Kate ran it back. She could barely make out the photographs sitting on it.

'Now . . . stop.'

This time, Kate saw what Felicity meant. There was a slight beam of light on one of the picture frames.

'That's moonlight,' said Felicity. 'As you watch the rest of the footage, you'll notice where it falls on various objects in the room.'

'Okay.' Kate looked keenly at her, waiting for the punchline.

'Moonrise was at 11.59 p.m. the night William was killed. We spoke to the Met Office and established that it was overcast until 2 a.m. There would have been no visible moonlight during the whole time Harriet visited William. My friend believes this is the point where the footage was altered, before the figure lifts the gun and shoots. After this, using computer-generated imagery, Harriet's face and body were superimposed or used to replace the person who really shot William. As I said, it's very professional.'

'How could they possibly have known about the pet camera app?'

'We talked about that. Either William's phone was hacked, and the pet cam footage altered remotely, or there was a spy device in William's house, watching what was going on. There would have been sufficient time after Harriet left for the real killer to shoot William and for that version to be fabricated.'

'But to alter an app?'

'You'd be amazed at what some of these tech wizards can do. Honestly, Kate, you are dealing with somebody who knows their stuff and with people corrupt enough to carry out this audacious plan, simply to frame Harriet. It's bloody scary.'

'How much do you trust your friend?'

'Implicitly. He works on top secret projects for various governments. Apart from that, he and I go way back.'

'Would he testify in court?'

'I can convince him to, but it would help our argument if you could find a spy device. If it's there, it will be hidden somewhere in the lounge. Be warned, there might be others placed throughout the house too.'

Kate felt her jaw tighten. The fuckers could have been watching her every move. They would know she'd been hunting for the document. Worse still, they probably knew where William had hidden it and it was in their hands.

'What am I looking for?'

'I really don't know. It could be something tiny and sophisticated. You will need this to help you locate it.' She pushed across a small plastic bag. Kate opened it and peered at a small circular ring with six LED lights and a colour filter at its centre.

'It's a mini hidden camera detector that uses LED infrared laser scanning technology to uncover spy cams. It's highly sensitive and comes with a built-in earphone jack so you can use it covertly. There are instructions with it and it's easy to use,' said Felicity. 'It plugs into your mobile's charging point.'

'Shit, Felicity, what am I up against here?'

'I don't know, but it scares me. You must take great care. If you need to talk to me, make sure we keep our meetings away from work.'

'So you can't give me any idea of what I should be looking for?'

'Spy devices come in so many forms nowadays. It could be hidden anywhere. Would you prefer me to send a couple of the tech team across to the house to do a sweep?'

'If you do that and these people are still watching, they'll know we're on to them. I'll have to do it surreptitiously, pretend I'm clearing out William's stuff, something along those lines . . . Oh, goodness, Felicity . . . I don't really know what to do for the best.'

'If you could find the surveillance device, it would lend weight to our argument.'

'And you're sure of your findings?'

Felicity placed a hand on top of Kate's, the warmth from it instantly comforting to Kate, whose erratic heartrate was getting worse. 'There is little doubt that Harriet has been set up. It's going to be down to us to make sure she is liberated. You'll find the surveillance camera.'

'But William didn't twig it was there.'

'I don't know why he didn't. All I can say is that somebody was watching him. They could even be watching your house.'

'And what should I tell Harriet?'

'It might be better to wait until you've located the spy device before you say anything to her. I suspect once these people know we're on to them, they could become desperate – and as we know, those sorts of people can be extremely dangerous.'

CHAPTER
TWENTY-ONE

It was late afternoon when Emma finally established that Leah had purchased her anti-anxiety medication from an online pharmacy based in India.

Frankie examined her well-chewed apple core before launching the remains into the nearby bin. Her action reminded Emma of Morgan, who had been a dab hand at throwing rubbish into the same bin when they worked together.

She found her thoughts drifting back to Morgan, whose mood swings were of increasing concern. Whether he was withdrawing because he wanted out of their relationship or because there was something else that he wasn't sharing with her, she couldn't tell. All she knew was that things between them were suddenly different, and she felt more and more frequently that she was walking on eggshells with him.

Frankie's face wore a slight frown. 'I wonder if Leah would still be alive if she hadn't taken tranquillisers?'

Scott looked up from his computer screen and said, 'For all we know, the killer might have administered a sufficiently high dosage of scopolamine to kill her, and the tranquillisers didn't play any part in her death.'

'I can't get my head around the fact she bought them online. I mean, who buys stuff like that off the internet? Don't they know that a lot of these so-called pills aren't genuine? At best, many are simply placebos and at worst . . .' She screwed up her face. 'It was a stupid thing to do. Especially as she was expecting a baby.'

'Frankie, give it a rest,' said Scott. 'The woman is dead. It's not for us to judge her.'

'Yeah, I know. I just get . . . exasperated. If she hadn't been under such duress, she might never have taken the drugs and might have walked away from the attack, admittedly shaken and upset but at least alive. There are other ways of dealing with stress. She could have talked to somebody: a professional or a mate. She didn't tell her friends, family, work colleagues or husband. I mean . . . who behaves like that? I tell my mum and sister everything, especially when I'm pissed off about something. Sarge, you surely talk to your wife when you are feeling down, don't you?'

'Yes.'

'Then you understand what I mean. It's weird that she discussed nothing with her husband, Russell, or her boyfriend, Danny.'

'We get it,' snapped Emma, exasperated by her concerns over Morgan and unable to concentrate with Frankie wittering on. 'Leah kept everything bottled up. It has no bearing on her death.'

Frankie, oblivious to Emma's cold tone, continued, 'I feel sorry for her. To an outsider, she had everything: great job, fancy car, designer clothes, posh house, and yet her life was completely screwed up. After all, what would have happened once the truth about her baby got out: career, relationship . . .' She made a diving motion with one hand.

Emma, who hadn't eaten lunch, was becoming increasingly irked not only by the lack of progress but also by Frankie's unhelpful monologue.

Every twist and turn of this investigation sent them running about like headless chickens. They had very little concrete evidence and no proper suspects. At the start, she'd been optimistic that she'd wrap the case up quickly. Now, with Morgan making strides in a much bigger investigation, she was beginning to wonder if she'd handled this incorrectly and messed up. Nothing added up and, overriding everything, she had the feeling that almost everyone she'd spoken to – Leah's boss, husband, lover, and even Victoria's husband, Craig – had been holding back, maybe even lying.

'That'll do, Frankie. Why or how she bought tranquillisers isn't relevant.'

'It is if she bought them from the person who killed her,' Frankie fired back. 'We haven't considered that option, have we? Or even examined the possibility that Victoria, Ava and Beth also all purchased drugs.'

'You're letting your imagination run away with you,' said Emma. 'I understand you're trying hard to cover every base, but if we go that route, we'll be busy fools for ever and a day. What we really need to establish is who drugged these people. It's clearly one and the same person – a man. Until we speak to Beth, we're unable to get any further information, so keep digging and see if there are any other victims, who, like Ava and Beth, were attacked in this same manner.'

Having finished, Emma immediately turned her attention back to her screen, hoping that Frankie would stop pontificating and get on with something useful. Given the sluggish progress they were making, there was every chance the killer, undoubtedly growing in confidence by the day, could strike again.

◆ ◆ ◆

Opening William's front door, Kate's senses were on alert as she considered the possibility that somebody from the syndicate might be watching her every move. Even the opening of the door could have alerted them to the fact she was on the premises.

She had read through the camera detector instruction booklet and attached the device to her phone. The device weighed only eight grams and was so small it wouldn't be noticed; however, if she drew attention to her actions and the syndicate guessed what she was up to, they'd also know that she was on to them.

There was also a possibility that this exercise would prove futile if the pet cam app had been hacked remotely. Before arriving here, she had researched all the possible places where she might find such a device. Given some were tiny, it could be hidden almost anywhere. She'd have to make it seem as if she were still searching for the damn document rather than a device and then she might be able to pull this off.

She began by lifting all of William's books from a bookcase, a task she'd already performed. Muttering to herself, she hoped that should anyone be observing, they would assume she was getting to the end of her tether in her quest. To support that, she tossed the odd book on to the carpet and grumbled aloud that she wouldn't be surprised if there was no bloody document and William had made it up.

Throughout the performance, she ran the device over the book-case and books, waiting for the LED lights to flash to show it had picked up a hidden camera's radio frequency emissions. Felicity had warned her that such a camera was likely to be minuscule, maybe even two and a half to five centimetres in diameter, and that in order to function 24/7 it would require an electronic source. She'd advised Kate to scan telephones, televisions, sockets; anywhere that would give the camera a reliable source of power. If she found nothing, she was then to check out any keyholes, small holes or unusual objects that could conceal a camera lens.

In Kate's opinion, it would make sense for a camera to be hidden somewhere near the ceiling, affording it a bird's-eye view of the room while its height would make it physically inaccessible. She stood up again and meandered across the room, running a hand through her hair as if frustrated, until she reached a heavy dark-oak sideboard on which stood a deep peat-brown glass cigar ashtray, alongside a matching decanter, an ice bucket and three whisky tumblers. At the far end stood a walnut and oak tray containing three untouched bottles of whisky: a Balvenie DoubleWood twelve-year-old single malt, a Bunnahabhain Islay single malt and a Glenlivet Founder's Reserve. A vision of William raising a glass to her and toasting one of her successes sprang to mind, along with a lump in her throat. His death had been like losing her father all over again. He had been part of her family for as long as she could remember and a regular visitor to her own home when her husband, Chris, had been alive. All the men in her life were now gone and the holes they had left would never heal.

She shook off the sadness and memories and stole a glance at the matt black and copper pendant lamp that hung over a dining table. With her back to it, and pretending to read the label on a bottle, she aimed the RF towards the light. The LED didn't light up. Replacing the bottle and again mumbling to herself, she made for the other end of the lounge, where she hunched over the television cabinet. Making out that she was going through the drawer that housed William's DVDs, she tried again. Still nothing. The only other object that was positioned high up was a smoke detector at the far end of the room. It was logical to assume any camera inside it would be facing forwards. With that in mind, she paced up and down a few times, then when she was close enough and hopefully out of sight of the camera lens, she lifted the RF. Nothing happened. Her heart sank. She'd been sure that if anywhere, a spy device would be here.

Her grip on her phone tightened. Damn! This was all pointless. The fuckers had more than likely accessed the pet cam app remotely. All she was doing was wasting more of her precious time.

She was about to give up when a gentle bleep halted her in her tracks and the LED display lit up.

◆ ◆ ◆

Emma's mood had not lifted. By the end of the day, they were no further forward than they'd been that morning. She'd sent her team home and stopped by Morgan's office to let him know she was going training to rid herself of the frustration before heading home.

The door was ajar, so she wandered into the brightly lit open-plan office. Without knocking. It was far grander than her own, with several desks back to back, covering the length of the room and, at the far end, Morgan's office, the door shut.

One of the junior officers, sitting at the first desk, barely acknowledged Emma as she walked in.

'I'm looking for DI Meredith,' said Emma.

The girl dragged her eyes from the computer screen. 'He went out an hour ago.' As an afterthought, she added, 'Ma'am.'

'Have you any idea where he was going?'

'No, ma'am.'

'Or if he is coming back?'

'No, ma'am. Would you like to leave a message for him?'

'No, it's okay. I'll catch up with him.'

The girl's attitude needled her, not that Emma wanted officers to jump to their feet and salute her wherever she went. She would, however, like to be treated with the same respect she had afforded her superiors over the years. She would never have spoken to Kate in such a bored tone.

She spied Trevor at his desk and wandered across.

'Hi, you don't know where Morgan is, do you?' she asked.

'Hi, Emma. He went out earlier but didn't say where he was going. Soz. Is it important?'

'It'll wait.'

'I'll tell him you came by. How's the investigation going?'

'You know how it is: one step forward . . .'

He laughed. 'Oh, I know only too well. This team is the expert in that. Sometimes I think we're further back than when we started. Still, Morgan has a grip on things. So, fingers crossed and all that.'

'You'll get there.'

'We're banking on Mighty Morgan Meredith for a result.'

'Mighty Morgan Meredith!'

Trevor gave a light shrug. 'You didn't know?'

'No, but I do now.'

'Don't tell him.'

'It's not the worst nickname I've heard.'

'I know, but we don't want his head to swell.' He grinned at her, lightening her mood.

'Thanks, Trevor.'

'Any time, ma'am.'

In the corridor she tried ringing Morgan, only to have the call go direct to answerphone. She left a message to let him know where she was going and made for the changing rooms, where she hauled her gym bag from her locker before slamming the door to it hard.

'Bad day?'

She spotted another female officer – Hazel – who was also part of Morgan's team on Operation Moonbeam.

'I've had better.'

'Yeah, same here. Two of our team were transferred today. It means the rest of us are having to work harder. By work, I mean charge about in ever decreasing circles. Remind me again why we do this job?' said Hazel.

'I wish I could, but all I can think about is smashing my fists into a punchbag.'

'I've got to collect my two youngest from a childminder and the eldest from football practice, and then cook them all dinner, get them ready for bed and prepare all their kit for school again tomorrow, in between stopping them from wrecking the house. I'll happily swap.'

Emma managed a smile. 'I'm good, thanks. Besides, I'd probably poison them with my cooking.'

'Have fun,' said Hazel, reaching for an anorak and putting it on. 'My offer stands any time you feel like taking it up.'

Emma left the station in a brighter mood. Hazel had put things back into perspective. They were all trying to do the best they could and got equally frustrated when they couldn't make progress. At least she didn't have to go back to a family who were probably even more demanding than the job. She hoisted her kit bag on to her shoulder and marched towards her car. An hour at Greg's would sort her out, then she could relax with Morgan.

After much consideration, Kate left William's house without removing the hidden camera. She had, however, tested every inch of his house in case there were any more, or any recording devices. It was now close to seven o'clock and she was heading home, her mind a complete whirl of confusion and indecision.

To add to her concerns, she was now anxious that her actions had been observed. If the syndicate members suspected for one moment that Kate was looking for a hidden camera rather than the document, it might encourage them to bring forward their plans to expose her by making public the photographs of her and Dickson at the reservoir.

'*Calm down,*' said William. '*Think about this logically. The syndicate is unlikely to be watching the house twenty-four hours a day. They can't have enough manpower for that. There's every chance you weren't seen. You should remove the device and store it somewhere safe. Not only will it help prove Harriet's innocence but should the syndicate suspect you know about the camera, somebody will be sent to remove it. You can't allow that to happen.*'

'If I say anything about it, or touch it, a prosecutor could say I planted it.'

'*I reckon the device will be identifiable. You'll be able to trace the manufacturer. The best course of action is to update Harriet. She could work with you on this and give you advice on how best to treat the situation. Visit her first.*'

Kate pulled over to consider her options further, then decided visiting Harriet would be the only way forward. It would have to be done immediately, in case the syndicate were already considering removing the camera.

She was about to ring Harriet to let her know she was coming to see her when William's voice piped up again. '*Don't! The syndicate might have bugged her place or planted a camera there too. Turn up at her house unannounced and lure her outside, where neither of you can be overheard. You mustn't forget who you are dealing with. If the syndicate becomes aware that you've uncovered evidence proving Harriet to be innocent, they could clear up their mess before the truth gets out. They might resort to disposing of her, or for that matter, you, just like they did with Chris, Cooper and many others. These are desperate individuals who are so embroiled in this that they'll think nothing of taking either of you out.*'

Heeding his advice, she changed direction and headed to Harriet's place. There was no doubt they could both be in danger, yet neither of them had any choice in the matter. If they were to ensnare these people and get to the truth, there were risks; and where there were such perils, there would be consequences. She could handle those. No matter what they were. If the last thing she ever did was expose the bastards who had caused so much grief, then she would die happy.

◆ ◆ ◆

The session in the gym left Emma feeling pleasantly exhausted and after a quick but icy-cold shower, she was back on form. Her shoes squeaked along the floorboards towards the octagonal contest area, where a taekwondo bout was in progress. The air was thick with sweat and the smell of ointment. She felt completely at home here. It was where she had always sought refuge and where she had friends who understood her need to train and her passion for the sport. Had she not chosen to become a police officer, she would have followed her desire to become a professional taekwondo fighter. Greg and Fergus had both encouraged her to go that route, but she'd chosen the police force. It offered a more stable career path and allowed her to pursue her hobby whenever she had time. She had the best of both worlds.

Andy Sullivan was confident, light-footed and a deadly accurate fighter. He'd taken on a fellow brown belt in a friendly practice match, and it was difficult to choose between them. She observed Andy's movements, executed to perfection as he spun smoothly on his heel and planted a textbook kick to his opponent's head. The man went down. She caught Andy's eye for a moment, was going to say something encouraging, but realised he was in the zone, unaware of anyone other than the man he was fighting. Greg, her brother, was watching from afar, leaning against the wall with Fergus. She joined them.

'The lad's come on in a ridiculously short time, hasn't he?' said Fergus.

'Impressive,' she said.

Greg didn't take his eyes off the duo. 'He's ready to progress to black belt. Is he interested in the competition we talked about, Fergus?'

'I think so.'

'He should enter,' said Greg, then, turning to Emma, said, 'So, little sis. I saw you working out earlier. What the fuck is eating you?'

'What do you mean?'

'You nearly punched a hole in the bag. Somebody got your goat?'

'I needed to let off some steam, that's all.'

Fergus nudged Greg. 'Man trouble.'

'Fuck off. It isn't. I had a tough day at work. That's all,' she replied.

The training bout came to an end and Andy joined them.

'What do you think?' he asked Emma.

He smelled of sweat, mixed with something else – a manly scent – and she tried hard not to stare at his washboard abdominals.

'You were good. Really good.'

'Thanks.'

For a moment she was flustered, aware she was attracted to him, then Fergus broke the spell.

'I agree with Emma. We'll talk in the changing rooms about the competition. Come on. Oh, Emma, do you fancy joining us for a drink later or are you playing Mr and Mrs again?'

She stuck out her tongue, which only served to make him guffaw. Andy gave her another long look, causing a stirring in the pit of her stomach – desire.

Greg waited until the men were out of earshot. 'Everything is okay between you and Morgan, isn't it?'

Her face muscles tightened. Had she given away a sign that she was attracted to Andy? 'Sure. Why the sudden concern?'

'Not so much concern, more that I know you, Emma, and you like your independence far too much to anchor yourself down. Besides, I couldn't help but notice you were having a lot of eye contact with Andy.'

'Pfft! You're reading too much into it.'

'Am I?' he said with a grin. 'He's your type. And he likes you. He told me so.'

'Fuck off!'

'I sense that you're being a little defensive, sis.'

'In case you've forgotten, I'm in a couple.'

'I hadn't forgotten. Fergus and I have a bet running on how long it will last.'

'What! You two are incorrigible.'

'Yes, we are. And you love us both for it.'

'Okay. How long have you given it?'

'Fergus reckons it'll be over by March. I think you'll get to May.'

'Why May?'

'Because none of your previous relationships have lasted longer than eight months. Besides, domesticity doesn't suit you. You are a free spirit. You will break poor Morgan's heart. I know you will,' he said, ruffling her hair.

She stepped back smartly. 'Don't do that. I'm not five years old.'

'You're still my little sister and I'm your favourite big brother . . . who you listen to, so you know I am right.'

'Not this time. I'm very . . . fond of Morgan.'

'Fond? I'm fond of chocolate and pizza.'

'Stop it, Greg. I know what I'm doing. I've never felt this way about anyone else before. It's still all fresh and I'm feeling my way around while holding down a demanding job. Don't tease me about this, because it matters to me. Morgan matters.'

His face became serious. 'You know I'm only kidding. It's what we do. I tease you and you retaliate. We've always been the same. Tell you what, why don't you join me and Fergus for dinner when he comes back. It's fish and chips night at Sparkles. I haven't had a chance to chat to you properly since you got promoted and you look like you could do with a couple of hours off the clock and a proper laugh.'

Emma wanted to say yes. Before Morgan, she would have leapt at the chance to spend time with her brother and Fergus. They would make her laugh so hard her belly hurt and she'd always enjoyed their company.

'I'd love to, but Morgan's expecting me home.'

He gave her the longest look then said, 'He's a great lad and all that, but don't let him clip your wings, sis.'

'I won't. I know my own mind.'

'That's what worries me. Does Morgan know what he's let himself in for?' He reached out to ruffle her hair again, but she caught his hand in a tight grip.

'Nice reflexes,' he said.

'Had a good tutor.' She let him go. 'We'll go out soon.'

'If you change your mind, you know where to find us and those chips are the best! Way better than anything you'll manage to cook.'

She lurched towards him as if to hit him but planted a kiss on his cheek instead.

'Laters!' he called as she strolled away. Her lips pulled into an automatic smile. It was a huge shame she'd messaged Morgan. A night out with Greg and Fergus would have been the perfect tonic after a shit day.

◆ ◆ ◆

Kate had travelled the distance to Harriet's house and sat in her car on the street for a full five minutes. A car she recognised as belonging to Harriet's husband was outside. Another was parked alongside. Harriet had visitors, which meant it probably wasn't a good time to visit.

With some reluctance, she started up the engine again. Her next step should be to head to the Coles' farm near Repton, in search of Digger.

'How interesting that you've chosen to save your reputation rather than return to William's house and hunt for the document. Are you beginning to doubt its existence?'

Even though she shouldn't encourage it, she couldn't help herself and replied with, 'I'm simply being cautious. Until I decide what to do about that camera, I'm not going back to be observed by one of your lot.'

Outside, trees bent and bowed in the wind and small twigs tumbled against her car, making noises like small, clawed mammals scurrying across the metal roof.

She turned the volume up on the Weeknd's 'Dawn FM', hopeful that the music would drown out Dickson. All the same, she could hear his muttering.

'That's bullshit and you know it. There's only one camera and you've found it. You could hunt elsewhere in the house without attracting any attention. Besides, we've already found the document, so we don't care what you're up to.'

Ahead of her, a ghostlike figure rose from the road and hastened towards her vehicle. She pumped the brake pedal yet still it rushed forward, blanketing the windscreen. With her vision impaired and no car behind her, she ground the pedal hard. The car came to a halt and the screen cleared as the plastic bag deflated and slid away. Her pulse beat so loudly in her ears she couldn't hear the music. The fact that this could have resulted in an accident reminded her that talking to the voices in her head could have devastating consequences. Ordinarily, she wouldn't be unnerved by a plastic bag being carried by the wind.

'You're jittery because you know we are on to you—'

'Stop,' she whispered, this time to herself. Determined not to allow anything else to distract her, she kept her lips tightly pressed together. It required all her self-control to refrain from conversing with either William or Dickson, a habit she'd fallen into with more ease than she was comfortable with.

She eventually drew up on the road next to the Coles' farm, a plain brick three-storey house that stood behind a low brick wall. A line of outbuildings backed on to the road and were reached by a driveway to the left and rear of the property. If Digger was inside one of the buildings, she wouldn't be able to surprise him. She would have to bowl up and try to stop him from bolting.

She opened the car door, clinging to it as an invisible hand attempted to tug it from her grasp. The sound of bleating, if there was any, was drowned out by the creaking of trees as they were pummelled by the strengthening wind. She drew her coat collar up to her neck and, with her head lowered, followed the drive.

No dogs barked and nobody emerged from the house to see who was prowling, and once around the back she discovered a series of brick buildings illuminated by soft lighting. She chose the closest and approached it. Pressing her ear against the door, she listened for sounds inside. Hearing nothing, she moved to the next and repeated the action. This time, despite the noise outside, she made out a voice.

She knocked on the door and heard a soft, 'Yes?'

The warmth from a heat lamp and the fresh and slightly sweet smell of straw was welcoming. Her eyes were drawn to a pen where a man was feeding a newborn lamb from a bottle, his attention monopolised by the animal. When she made no attempt to approach, he looked up. His jaw dropped.

'You!' said Digger.

She held up both her palms. 'Don't run. I won't hurt you. I promise.'

His eyes widened.

'Digger, I swear. I've come to ask for help.'

'Help you? No. You're a . . . you're a murderer.'

'Please. I know what you think you saw at the reservoir, but it wasn't what you imagine.'

'I know what I saw. I might prefer to live a nomadic life but that doesn't mean I'm ignorant of what goes on around me. The person you killed was a superintendent, *the* superintendent who the newspapers said went missing. I told DCI Chase I'd seen you and now he's dead too. You're here to shut me up.'

'No! I'm not. DCI Chase was my father's best friend. He was my friend too. I . . . loved him, like my father. No! I want to find whoever is responsible for his death and that person is linked to a group of officers who are dangerous and corrupt. The superintendent was one of the members. Digger, I'm not the one you should be afraid of. Without your help, neither of us is safe.'

The lamb, which had unlocked from the teat, butted against Digger, demanding his attention. Digger took his eyes off Kate, who remained stock still while he continued to feed the creature.

'It wasn't my gun, Digger. It belonged to the superintendent, who was trying to kill me because I was on to him. It went off accidentally during the struggle. You must have seen that. I didn't point it at him and fire in cold blood. You saw that, didn't you?'

The lamb sucked greedily, its tail wagging. Digger kept his head lowered.

'It was an accident,' she said. 'What happened afterwards was necessary. I had to cover up his death. I needed to expose criminals and I could only do that if they believed he was alive.'

Digger still wouldn't look at her.

'These people are dangerous. They're after me and they're after you.'

'I don't believe you,' he said. 'Why are they after me?'

'You were a witness not only to what happened. Somebody else was at the reservoir that night, weren't they? They were taking photographs, and . . . I believe you saw that person.'

Digger gently prised the now empty bottle from the lamb and stroked the creature.

'Digger, if you help me, I'll keep you safe.'

'I move about. Nobody ever knows where I am.'

'And yet I found you. If I can, they will too.'

'How can I trust you?'

'Because I haven't hurt you. There's been plenty of opportunity for me to do so here, while you've been feeding the lamb. I want to protect you from these people. I want them to face justice.'

'And you? Will you face justice too? I saw what you did!'

She hesitated. William's voice whispered in her mind. '*You've lied before. Lie to him.*' This time she didn't listen to him. It was time for the lies to stop.

'That case is closed. They believe the superintendent's killer is dead. There was a solid witness who testified that somebody else killed him. I was never a suspect.'

'And if I tell the police the truth?'

'They won't believe a drifter with no evidence to support their claim. How could you prove any of it? They'd think you were a crank. I know what I did was wrong, but I killed him in self-defence. The only way I'll find justice for the death of my friend, DCI William Chase, is to unearth these individuals and ensure they pay for all their crimes. Digger, I have lost two people I loved because of this gang: my friend William was undercover, investigating these people, as was my husband, who was a journalist. He was murdered on a train from London by a hitman hired by this group.'

'You're that man's wife! I remember the story in the paper. He saved people on the train by attacking the gunman.' His eyes narrowed as he examined her. 'You don't look the same as in the picture I saw. You look different, thinner . . . older.'

'I'm not the same,' she said. 'Losing Chris changed me forever. The only thing that has kept me going has been my quest to bring this syndicate down. Chris was a brave man. Ever since his murder, I've been on the trail of the people responsible for it.'

He looked at her afresh, his mouth agape. She continued, 'You can help by describing the person at the reservoir. They will be part of the gang. I'm begging you, Digger. Help me.'

The lamb wobbled on its spindly legs before dropping on to the straw. Digger patted its head. 'This one's mother died,' he said. 'Needs feeding throughout the night. It's strong though. It'll be okay. I'll make sure it is. I like looking after animals. I prefer them to humans.'

She gave a small smile. 'I can see you're kind-hearted. All creatures need caring for. I want to make sure nobody else gets hurt or loses their families because of these evil people. I want to make sure you are safe.'

Digger stroked the lamb gently, then, when it had closed its eyes, shuffled to his feet.

'Did you see somebody else at the reservoir that night?' she asked.

'I don't want any trouble. I just want to be left alone. None of this is my business. I didn't even want to talk to your friend. William, or whatever his name was. He coaxed it out of me.'

'William had that way about him. He loved his job, but he was due to retire. Had he not been asked to stay on to investigate the superintendent's death, he would be alive. It's complicated and I can't explain everything to you. I can only say that every action has a consequence. William should be at home now, with his cats and his bees. In a way, my actions resulted in his murder, so, Digger, I owe it to him to expose these corrupt individuals. You saw somebody, didn't you?'

At last, he nodded.

'Can you describe them at all?'

Another nod.

'Digger?'

'It was another police officer. I didn't know it was at the time, only afterwards when I saw a photo in the newspaper of your team who caught the murderer who'd been shooting folk with a bolt gun.'

Her mouth went dry. *Could it have been Jamie?* 'It was one of my officers?'

He nodded.

She fumbled in her pocket for her phone and with trembling fingers searched for a picture she had taken of the three of them: Morgan, Emma and Jamie at a bowling alley, when they had gone out to celebrate Emma's birthday. She leant over the pen and showed the photo to him.

'Which one was it, Digger?'

He pointed directly at the person.

Her pulse drummed in her ears. 'Are you sure?'

'One hundred per cent.'

A buzzing began in her head. She had been sure it would be Jamie. Digger had identified the last person she imagined would betray her or be corrupt in any way – Morgan Meredith.

'Digger, I know you want to look after the lamb, but you need to get away and hide somewhere where nobody will find you.'

'There's a place in the woods. I go there when I have no work. Nobody knows about it.'

'I will need to check on you and make sure you're safe. You don't have a phone. How can I contact you?'

'Leave a message with Eric at the Dog & Partridge in Marchington. He's in every evening from six until seven.'

'Can he be trusted?'

'Eric is my cousin. He won't drop me in it.'

'Okay. But if I leave a message, I'll expect you to get back to me.'

'I shall.' He looked back at the lamb. 'It'll need feeding in another couple of hours. I'll get my head down for a bit.'

'I think you should leave soon. I can't even be sure I haven't been followed here.'

He shook his head. 'I'll be fine. If you can sort this out, I'll have nothing to worry about, will I?'

She wanted to assure him everything would be okay but the cacophony in her head prevented her. She ran from the warm building and, reaching her car, bent over and retched. How had she been so blind!

CHAPTER
TWENTY-TWO

Kate drove along the lanes, unaware of much other than the road and the confusion in her head. Morgan had been the one who took those photographs of her and Dickson!

'*Digger's lying,*' said William.

Dickson was quick to answer, '*Why would he? He pointed to Morgan without hesitation. He knew who he saw at the reservoir.*'

William tried again. '*Okay, if not lying, then mistaken. In the dark, he might easily have been mistaken and saw somebody who vaguely resembled Morgan. Come on, Kate, think about it. He couldn't possibly have seen Morgan's face close up.*'

She clung to that thought. Although Digger had been positive about who he'd seen, he might still have been mistaken. Witnesses sometimes were.

'*Morgan is instantly recognisable. You could identify him purely by his physique,*' said Dickson. '*And Digger is no fool. He's quick-witted and observant. He had plenty of time while he was there to study Morgan. He saw everything else that happened that night, didn't he? And he identified Kate.*'

Kate's head began to throb. This was all too much to take in. She could have handled anyone else taking those photos, anyone other than a close friend and ally.

'Morgan's a good lad. He wouldn't be involved in anything nefarious,' said William.

Dickson laughed. 'He's definitely good. Good at subterfuge. Jamie was never the plant in your team, Morgan was all along, and you didn't suspect a thing.'

'Please, just stop,' Kate murmured. 'I can't do this. It can't be Morgan. It just can't.'

'Why not?' said Dickson.

'Because he's—'

'Loyal? Your friend? A good officer? You trust him?' said Dickson.

'Shut . . . the fuck . . . up!'

She pressed her lips together, yet the voices persisted in her head.

Dickson laughed again. 'You haven't grasped the enormity of this situation yet. If Morgan was at the reservoir, you have to ask yourself why? Did somebody send him? Or was he following you?'

This fresh thought startled her, causing her to lose concentration, and she veered towards the far hedge. She righted the car in time, focused on the grey ribbon of road ahead while the voices continued to battle it out.

'Kate would have noticed somebody following her. She left her car hidden in a side road and cycled to the reservoir. She saw your car pass her, she didn't see anybody else on the road,' said William.

'But did she see inside my car? Morgan was with me and exited at the reservoir, before hiding in the bushes to observe what transpired. Kate invited me there to talk, to tender her resignation, and I knew all along it was a ploy, so I took Morgan for insurance, a back-up plan,' said Dickson.

Her blood ran cold. That was the most plausible explanation of all.

'No. Morgan wouldn't have done that. He respects Kate.'

Dickson's voice dropped to a conspiratorial whisper. 'How do you think he affords to live in that rather nice house of his? Think about it. His salary wouldn't stretch to mortgage payments on that property *plus living expenses. And you, William, you knew he was part of it, so don't play the innocent.'*

She now drove past properties rather than hedgerows and was almost at William's house. She didn't want to believe Digger, yet she did. For all her suspicions, she had never fully realised the extent of the corruption she was facing. The poison ran far deeper than she had imagined and now with concerns over Morgan, she couldn't help but think William might have been part of it all too.

She threw open the door and marched down the hallway to the kitchen, throwing her bag on to the table while she made for the sink, where she ran the cold tap, filled a mug, and drank the water greedily.

The fluid cooled her hot throat but not her head, where thoughts ebbed and flowed but didn't anchor themselves long enough for her to grasp them or form a plan of action.

She left the mug in the sink and turned around, eyes scanning the cupboards and drawers she had checked for the elusive document.

The fact was, there was no such document. William had been as embroiled in this as all the others – officers she would, only two years ago, have trusted with her life. She'd been duped. Fooled by both him and Morgan. How many more of them were there, right under her nose, laughing at her ignorance and waiting to pounce and change her world? Hadn't they already messed it up enough? She'd lost Chris, William and her sanity chasing after these people. They were toying with her, playing a sick game of cat and mouse, waiting for her to crack. The thought sickened her.

'Why, William?' she said.

'What does anyone do when their back is against the wall, Kate? They lie, they perjure themselves, they kill.' William's voice was feeble and difficult to hear.

'But you?'

It wasn't William who replied but Dickson. *'Grow up! He was human like the rest of us. Mankind is driven by two forces: greed and fear. You will never change that, Kate Young.'*

The leaden weight in her chest sank to her stomach. She couldn't continue this quest. She crossed the room, pausing beside yet another photograph of her father with William, arms around each other's shoulders, smiles on their young faces. The tears began, hot and furious, leaving molten trails down her cheeks. Sobs accompanied them, and she staggered from the room to get out of the house that contained too many painful memories, colliding as she did with an upright vacuum cleaner that stood in an alcove by the door. The cleaner toppled forward on to the tiles, the plastic front falling off. She wiped away the tears and stooped to pick it up. As she righted it, she gasped. In the cavity where a dust bag should be hung was a large, transparent Ziploc bag, inside which was a brown envelope. With shaking hands, she unzipped the bag, extracted the envelope and pulled out an A4 document from it.

She scanned the pages: names of corrupt officers, details of their dealings, payments made by human traffickers to the said officers. Once again, tears sprang to her eyes. This time for the man who had always had her back. William had been telling the truth after all. He *had* infiltrated the syndicate to prepare information to bring them down.

'I promised we would bring them down together. Now we can,' said William.

She read through the names and code names. William had been wrong or lied about the code names being assigned to members according to the order of their surnames. The list confirmed that code names had been assigned willy-nilly, maybe depending on when members were recruited. Why he had told her otherwise was a mystery, unless he had not wanted her to believe he really had been second in command.

314

'Ha!' said Dickson. '*You wanted so badly to believe William infiltrated the group with the sole purpose of exposing us, when in truth he was one of us!*'

'*No,*' said William. '*Kate, listen to me. The only way I could convince Dickson of my loyalty was to prove myself. I had to step up, do things I didn't want to do but only for the endgame. I admit I was second in command, which was why Gamma rang me after you were captured at the warehouse. It was to get permission to have you silenced. I couldn't allow it. I was all about protecting you.*'

'*Yadda, yadda, yadda. The fact is, after my death, William became top dog. He was corrupt.*'

'That's enough!' she growled, her attention drawn to the footnote at the bottom of the list. William had handwritten his own name under the others. Attached were bank account details showing payments made from the syndicate, dating back a few years. Looking at the balance, it was obvious that he hadn't touched a penny of it. William had intended coming clean.

William had done what had been necessary to gather this information. She understood that. She'd been forced to cross the line too in her attempts to get to the truth. They were two of a kind. That he had kept secret from her the fact he was high up the chain of command was no worse than her own lie to him – that she had not killed Dickson.

She scanned the list for Morgan's name. It wasn't there. However, the identities of Gamma and Iota had evaded William. Her mind cleared, and one thing became obvious: that either Gamma or Iota, or both of them, had killed William to protect themselves.

She returned the document to the envelope.

'We will bring them down, William. We will.'

Another voice replied in her head, one she hadn't heard in a long time – Chris. '*I always believed in you, Kate. You stuck it out. You've weathered adversity, you've pushed ahead during impossible situations, and you have at last found the answers. I'm proud of you.*'

Her heart soared at her husband's voice. They were almost at the end of the crusade that had started with his murder. 'I love you,' she whispered. 'So much.'

◆ ◆ ◆

Emma stood by the door unobserved by Morgan, who had his head lowered over his phone, fingers tapping out a message. She was going to shout *boo!* for a laugh and to make him jump, but instead breezed into the sitting room with a cheerful, 'Hey!'

Morgan hastily shoved the mobile into his trouser pocket. 'Hey, yourself! Sorry I missed you earlier. You know how it is.'

Something about the way he'd thrust the phone so quickly out of sight, as if he'd been caught doing something he shouldn't, made her suspicious. She was about to ask him who he'd been texting when he crossed the room and kissed her.

'Bloody work,' he mumbled into her hair. 'Never seem to get a moment to ourselves.'

'We need time off – a week or two – to just hang together.'

'I second that. Have you eaten?'

'Nah, I went to the gym. Greg invited me for a meal with him and a couple of the others, but I bailed. Told him I was going home to spend the evening with you because I've been neglecting you recently.'

There must have been something in her tone because Morgan pulled away from her.

'What's up?' she said.

'Nothing.'

'Come on. I know you well enough to know you've suddenly got the ick.'

'Don't be stupid. I haven't.'

'Morgan!'

'It's just that I have to go out. I was about to leave when you came in.'

'Oh! Work again?' The question wasn't intended to be confrontational. She understood that their jobs came first. All the same, Morgan couldn't meet her gaze and when he replied, she felt he was deflecting.

'I didn't expect you back so early.'

'Are you following up on a lead?'

His lips parted and he stared at her, then shook his head. 'I have to go out and that's the end of it, alright?'

'I don't know. Is it?'

'Don't make this into something it isn't,' he said.

She studied his face, saw sadness in his eyes. She was being unreasonable. After all, she wasn't likely to tell him all the ins and outs of her investigation and if she needed to go out at the drop of a hat, then she would, even if it meant letting Morgan down.

'It doesn't matter in the least,' she said. 'I'll make myself something to eat and chill out.'

He kept his eyes on her. 'This is hard, isn't it? Either you're bogged down or I am. I want us to be like we were before, Emma.'

'So do I. It's not like we've gone into this blindfolded.'

'We didn't both expect to get promoted though, did we?'

'No, but we can find a work/life balance if we really want to.'

'Do you, though? I get the impression, work, your life . . . it comes before us. I know how much your career matters. It matters to me too, as does mine, but *us* . . . that matters more to me.'

His sincerity surprised her. She'd been drifting along wondering if they would make it, not fully aware of how much their relationship meant to Morgan.

'I need to know, Em.'

Thoughts tumbled in her mind: her anxieties about their future, her desire to forward her career, her independence. As they churned, she looked at the man studying her. They were more than lovers or work colleagues. They'd been best friends for what felt like forever and there was nobody she trusted more than Morgan. They could make this work and while she loved him as much as she clearly did, she would do everything to ensure they were happy. His face was a mask of concern, eyebrows drawn together. The light drew attention to the circles under his eyes, and she noticed he was looking thinner faced. She'd been too wrapped up in her own concerns to notice tell-tale signs that he was under pressure.

'Morgan, you have no need to worry. We'll work through any issues. We will be absolutely fine. As long as we're open with each other.'

He didn't smile but instead took both her hands in his. 'You have no idea how much you mean to me. Promise you will never let resentment build up between us and that you'll always tell me if you have any worries about us.'

'Promise.'

He pulled her into an embrace and when they parted, he planted a kiss on her forehead. 'I love you, Emma Donaldson.'

'Love you back, Morgan Meredith.'

He made for the hall to put on his coat and boots. She followed him through.

'You know, you should head out to meet Greg. It would save you cooking,' he said, snatching his phone and keys from the table.

'True, it's fish and chips night at Sparkles. I might go along.'

'If you do go, say hi to Greg for me. See you later.'

After his Jeep had rattled away, her stomach rumbled loudly, and on the spur of the moment she decided she could murder a plate of thick-cut vinegar-soaked chips and would join Greg after all. She headed into the lounge to switch off the light and spotted a mobile, lying on the carpet. Picking it up, her mind flashed to the hallway a few moments earlier when Morgan's iPhone had been next to his car keys. He'd been talking, distracting her, yet she now recalled seeing him grab it along with his keys before leaving. He hadn't been on that phone when she walked into the room, surprising him. He'd been using this phone, an old Nokia, which explained why he'd stuffed it into his back pocket so quickly.

Why Morgan would have such a phone was a mystery, unless . . . all the talk about how much he loved her. The fact he'd not given her a straight answer about where he was going. Her stomach somersaulted. She'd been here before: men lying, playing her along. Surely Morgan wasn't like that?

She thought it over logically. In recent weeks, Morgan had behaved differently, something she'd put down to work, and yet . . . could he have met somebody else, someone on his team? Maybe the junior DC who was so dismissive when she'd gone to the office? Then there was the fact he'd been tetchy, and the stupid rows over nothing. While she had been blaming herself for not giving him enough of her time, his reactions could have been down to guilt. He'd been secretive too. Out at all hours, supposedly on the job, but no openness or explanation to confirm that. He might simply have been cheating on her. In fact, he could be with this other person right now. She breathed heavily, trying to still the avalanche of thoughts that cascaded. She was tired, irritable because of work. She was fabricating nonsense. Morgan loved her.

She switched the phone on, tried the code she knew Morgan used for his other phone and found it wouldn't unlock. Reason was washed away by anger. The fucker! If he was cheating on her, she was going to have it out with him when he got back! She'd keep the phone as proof. She shoved the Nokia, still switched on, into an inside pocket, which she zipped up, then stormed out of the house, completely oblivious to the car parked opposite that started up as she drove off and followed her down the road.

Emma parked up, still fuming about Morgan, upset about the possibility he was deceiving her. The whole short journey into town, she'd replayed recent events: Morgan getting angry over petty things, the pair of them bickering, him not being in his office and nobody knowing where he was. Everything pointed at the same conclusion. Tempted as she was to ring him, this was one argument she would have with him face to face, with the phone as evidence.

Locking the car, she marched across the car park in the direction of the pub where she would find her brother. She needed to ask Greg for his advice because as much as it grieved her, she loved Morgan and hoped she was wrong about all of this. Maybe the phone belonged to a colleague, and he'd picked it up by accident . . . or had found it . . . or . . . She ran out of possibilities.

She exited the car park and walked along the dimly lit street. The pub was only a minute's walk away and her heels clopped briskly as she hastened towards the place where she would find warmth and camaraderie. A keen breeze carried the aroma of fish and chips towards her and whetted her waning appetite. A chat with Greg, some food and maybe even a beer would put things into perspective.

A hefty shove from the side caused all thoughts to explode as she was pushed into an alleyway, where she collapsed against a wall, winded. It took a few seconds to work out what was happening. A figure in dark clothing, wearing a hoodie, stood in front of her. His face was distorted, teeth bared, and a crazed look in his eyes. It took a further moment for her to realise she knew him. This was Andy Sullivan, who she'd seen only a short while ago at Greg's gym, where he'd been fighting a friendly bout in the contest area. This was somebody she knew and liked. He was one of Greg's protégés. One of Fergus's lads.

She had opened her mouth to ask what he was doing when it dawned on her. Andy was the person she and her team had been hunting for.

Words lodged firmly in her gullet, releasing only a pathetic caw, the sound of a dying crow. Andy's face loomed towards hers and he raised a curled fist in front of her eyes. His movements seemed to be conducted in slow motion, each finger unfurling bit by bit to reveal a mound of white powder. She couldn't react. Every muscle was frozen solid. Even though her mind screamed for her to blow the powder into his face before he could carry out the act himself, she remained transfixed, all the while realising she had screwed up.

Then he blew hard.

◆ ◆ ◆

Kate sat in her car outside William's house in a stupor. The evidence she had been searching for finally lay on the car seat beside her, yet there was no euphoria. If anything, she had become numb. Tonight had produced too many revelations. When her phone rang and she saw the caller ID, she guessed there would be another.

Felicity was succinct. 'I'm sorry, I wasn't checking as regularly as I should, but I've noticed that one of those burner phones, belonging to Iota, was activated half an hour ago and is still transmitting. I've pinpointed its signal near a bar in Stafford called Sparkles.'

'Sparkles?'

'That's it.'

'I know the place. I'm only half a mile away,' said Kate, immediately turning on the engine. 'And, Felicity, I need to talk to you later. About that other matter.'

'Come to the house. I'll wait up.'

'Will do.'

She tore down the street. This would be yet another breakthrough. With Iota captured and the document listing the other members of the syndicate, there was sufficient evidence to submit to Superintendent Bree O'Sullivan and Chief Constable Atwell.

None of the syndicate members would be able to wriggle out of this.

In the distance she saw blue lights. What the heck had happened? As she got closer, she made out a small group of people. One of them was Morgan.

The car screeched to a halt and she bounded out. 'Morgan!'

'Kate. It's Emma. She's been attacked.'

His face was pulled into a picture of dismay, mouth turned down, eyes damp. Kate spun around, saw the figure on a stretcher and rushed to the ambulance, where a paramedic was closing the doors. 'Is she okay? I'm her colleague. DCI Young.'

Through the gap she could see Emma flat on her back, an oxygen mask covering her face and another paramedic hunched over her.

'Sorry, we can't hang around. It's touch and go,' he replied.

The door slammed shut and he raced to the front. The ambulance sped away, siren ringing out into the night.

She returned to Morgan, who stood next to a young man she recognised as Emma's brother, Greg.

'What the fuck happened?' she asked.

'It's . . . complicated. I was . . . Emma found . . . No. She . . .' He paused, took a breath and started again. 'Emma picked up my phone by mistake. She'd told me that she might be at Sparkles with Greg, so I came here to find her and collect it. I spotted her walking along the road, a guy behind her. Suddenly he pushed her into the alley. By the time I reached them, she was unconscious. I chased after the bastard who attacked her. He's cuffed and in my car with another officer who attended the scene, but Emma . . . I don't know. She was out for the count when I went back to her.'

He shook his head again, eyes filling.

'I rang an ambulance first, and then I called Greg. Turns out he knows the fucker.'

'Greg?' she said, turning to him.

'Yeah. It's one of the lads who goes to my gym. Name of Andy Sullivan. I thought he was sound. I had no idea what he was capable of.'

'He had a bag of white powder on him,' said Morgan. 'I thought it might be cocaine.'

'I think you'll find it's scopolamine. He's been using it to turn his victims into zombies who do whatever he tells them.' Kate didn't add that two people they knew of had died of associated effects.

Morgan wiped his eyes. 'I'll take the fucker back to the station.'

'I'll follow you. Greg, I take it you'll be going to the hospital?' she said.

'Damn right.'

'We've got to deal with Andy first, then we'll follow on. Let us know if . . .' She couldn't say the words.

Greg nodded. 'I'll keep you updated. Thanks, mate,' he said to Morgan. 'If you hadn't come along when you did, I hate to think what might have happened to her.'

Morgan blinked back tears. 'I wish it had been two minutes earlier.'

Greg placed a hand on his shoulder. 'She'll make it. She's a fighter.'

He raced off, leaving Morgan and Kate standing in the street. 'Take Andy in, Morgan. I'll be right behind you.'

She headed back to the Audi, watched Morgan get into his Jeep and turn his head. He was clearly yelling at the man cuffed behind him. She beeped her horn to remind him that she had an eye on him. She wouldn't put it past him to hammer seven bells out of the man. Emma meant the world to him and to her. If she didn't make it, Andy would have more than Morgan's wrath to deal with.

CHAPTER
TWENTY-THREE

With Andy Sullivan in the cells, she invited Morgan to her office. All the usual fight appeared to have been drained from him, leaving his face ashen. He sat with his head in his hands.

'If only I'd got there sooner,' he said.

'Morgan, you got there, and she was alive when she was taken to hospital. That's the most important thing. Greg's right when he said she's a fighter. She'll pull through.' The words sounded hollow to her ears.

'We need to have a chat. It's cards on the table time. Tell me again why you went to Sparkles,' she said.

'To find Emma and get my phone from her.'

'Your work phone?'

'Yes.'

'The phone you used to ring for an ambulance and then call Greg?'

A muscle flexed in Morgan's jaw.

Kate steepled her fingers together. Her calm outward appearance was at odds with the pounding in her chest. 'Where did you find it? You thought Emma was dying and yet you patted her down and rummaged through her handbag to see if she had your phone on her person. No, Morgan. I don't buy your story. You used the phone that was on your person to ring 999, and then Greg. Emma picked up your other phone.'

She wanted to scream at him, ask him how he could possibly betray her and how he could deceive the people he cared about, especially dear Emma, who was in a critical state. She'd cared so much about the pair of them. They were family, dammit! The headache that had started on her way to William's house had worsened, the throbbing making her feel nauseous, or maybe the latter was down to disappointment and sorrow at her protégé's actions.

Morgan broke eye contact. 'You know.'

She nodded, sadness now flooding through her. 'Weren't you surprised that I turned up outside Sparkles when I did?'

He shrugged.

'I've been tracking phones belonging to various members of a corrupt syndicate, led by Superintendent Dickson. I was notified that the burner belonging to somebody known as Iota was switched on and was transmitting near Sparkles. What do you have to say?'

His voice was flat, resignation in every word. 'Nothing.'

'The phone was either in your possession or Emma's. One of you is a member of this syndicate.' Logic dictated Morgan was Iota, especially as he took the photos at the reservoir and was involved with the syndicate. However, if Emma was involved as well, Kate didn't think she would cope with another heartbreak.

'Emma! She would never, ever, be so stupid as to get involved in something like that. Her career is everything. She's the best fucking officer we have at HQ. How could you even entertain that idea?'

She swallowed down a clawing in her throat, struggling to keep her voice even. 'Then, Morgan, it is you.'

'Oh, what's the point in denying it? Yes, it's my fucking phone. Emma almost caught me using it. I shoved it in my trouser pocket before she asked any awkward questions, but I could tell she'd clocked it. I only realised it was missing after I'd driven off. I stopped and searched the car, figured it had fallen out of my pocket at home and went back immediately. By then, Emma had gone out and the phone wasn't on the floor in the hallway or lounge, and I couldn't see it anywhere, so I guessed she'd found it. I didn't know if she'd hidden it to challenge me later or had taken it, but all the same, because she'd found it, and would be jumping to all sorts of conclusions about it, I had to see her face to face and cough up an explanation. I was planning some cock-and-bull story about it being a burner to contact a snitch. I'm not sure what I'll tell her now. If she recovers.'

He studied his hands for a moment, leaving Kate lost for words. Regardless of this confession, she had not only trusted Morgan and Emma but loved them, like they were her children or siblings. First William and now Morgan. She had cared so deeply for them and yet both had lied to her. Morgan looked up. Her head throbbed so badly it felt like it might explode. Her heart along with it.

'The phone's probably on her. I didn't check. I was too concerned about what had happened to her. For the record, I am Iota. And I wish with all my heart that I wasn't.'

Even though it was expected, his confession speared her own heart. 'Oh, Morgan, of all people. I never thought you would have got involved in this . . . this shitshow. How did you ever get mixed up with these people?'

He shrugged. 'Same way everyone does, I suppose.'

Even now she still wanted to protect him, extract him from this situation. 'Tell me. I'd like to know.'

'I needed extra cash. I don't know how I came to their attention, probably because I moaned so much about the poor salary that it reached the syndicate's ears. Anyhow, one day I discovered a mobile in my drawer, along with a message asking me to call the number on it if I wanted some lucrative work. I thought about reporting it, then . . . well, curiosity took over. It was two weeks before I rang that number. It turned out to belong to somebody calling themselves Alpha, who offered me good money for delivering a package.' Morgan paused, ran a hand across his brow. 'It was supposed to be just the one job, then I got another call and one job turned into two, then several more. Each time, I was paid handsomely. After I settled all my debts, and was back on course, I stupidly thought I could give it up. I rang Alpha, explained I didn't want to do any more jobs. I wanted out. He laughed and explained there was no get-out. He called the shots, not me. Furthermore, if I didn't play along, I could expect people I cared about to suffer "accidents". I was down a hole.'

'He threatened you?'

Morgan nodded. 'I had little choice but to do as I was told. I continued with the deliveries.'

'What was inside the packages that you delivered?'

'I never looked, but it was most likely drugs and weapons. Before you ask, I never dealt with people, only drop zones, so I've no idea who left the parcels for me to collect or who picked them up.'

'You should have confided in me.'

'And you would have made me face the consequences. You always did everything by the book.'

'I would have heard you out,' she said.

'No, you wouldn't. Not once you knew I wasn't on the level. I couldn't go to anyone else, because I didn't know who to trust.'

She had let him down. He'd been unable to confide in her and that was heartbreaking in itself. She could have prevented this happening if only she hadn't been so fixated on following the right path. And now look at her, in the same position as him, her moral compass shattered. 'I'm . . . so sorry.'

'I've been over this hundreds of times, trying to work out what best to do: come clean and accept my punishment, speak to Alpha again and persuade him to let me go. Believe me. I really didn't want to continue. I was trapped.'

Kate shook her head slowly. This was one mess she couldn't clean up.

Morgan cleared his throat. 'Then, just after we caught the bolt gun killer, Superintendent Dickson stopped me in the corridor and instructed me to scope out Blithfield Reservoir ahead of an urgent meeting he'd agreed to, in case it was a trap. I was intrigued as to why he'd think it was a set-up so instead of leaving after I'd checked it out, I remained behind, hidden from view in some undergrowth.'

His voice lowered. 'I heard everything you said and accused him of. I heard his replies. I saw what transpired.'

'Morgan—'

He lifted a finger to stop her. 'Afterwards, after the shock and confusion, I wondered if Superintendent Dickson was the person I knew as Alpha. It added up: the corruption, his anger towards you and attempt to silence you. When I didn't hear from him again, I knew I'd guessed right. You see, I'm not the only person carrying dark secrets, Kate. We both have heavy shit that we don't want to get out.'

'I know that you took the photographs. I found out earlier today.'

'You did?'

'It appears there was somebody else at the reservoir that night. They saw us all, and you.'

'Ah,' was all he said.

'Are you blackmailing me?'

He sighed heavily. 'No, Kate. That was never my intention.'

'What was it then? To scare me?'

'I don't know what I was thinking. Kate, I was in a state after what I witnessed. And scared. For you. If the syndicate had the slightest idea of what you'd done—' He paused, tears in his eyes. 'I had this half-arsed idea that if you saw the photos, you'd watch your back.'

Kate stared open-mouthed. 'A warning? No. That's crazy. You could have told me all this instead.'

'I realise . . . but at the time, I was afraid to break cover. I might only have been a gofer, but I know there are others who get their hands dirty, and have done far worse than simply deliver some packages, no questions asked. They're capable of anything. I had to think about Emma. And you.'

Kate was struck dumb. Morgan had known exactly what had transpired at the reservoir and had carried on as normal, even going along with the investigation into Dickson's disappearance as if he had no idea of what had happened. He'd completely fooled her. She shouldn't trust him.

'You've shown the photos to somebody else, too, haven't you? They're going to be used against me.'

'No!' His response was effusive. 'No. Ask yourself why those photos haven't come to light since the day I left them on your desk. If I'd wanted to expose you, I'd have done so, wouldn't I? Kate, I haven't told a soul about them. Not a soul. I . . . couldn't. I can't.'

'Why not?'

'The honest truth is I don't want you to be killed!'

'And what's happened since Dickson's disappearance? Any more *jobs*?'

'No. Nothing. It's gone quiet.'

'Who else is involved in the syndicate?'

'Hand on heart, I haven't a clue. There are only two numbers on my burner. You can check if you want. One belongs to Alpha, one to Gamma. Gamma is the syndicate's fixer. He gives me instructions about where to pick up and deliver goods. I don't know how many other members know about me and have my number on their phones.'

'You could have deleted the other members' numbers,' she said.

Morgan ran a hand over his brow again. 'Please, Kate, I'm levelling with you. Get the fucking thing checked out if you don't believe me. The tech team will be able to tell if I've deleted anything. Hand on heart, I'm telling you the truth. I have nothing left to lose. You know that I go by the code name Iota. You know what I've done. There's nothing to be gained by bullshitting you. Besides, you know about the members. You're tracking their phones. You'll be able to see exactly who I've contacted and who has contacted me.'

She conceded that he sounded sincere. 'Have you spoken to Gamma since that night at the reservoir?'

'Only once. Gamma rang to tell me to keep my head down until I heard from Alpha or Gamma again.'

'Male voice or female voice?'

'Couldn't tell. It was disguised.'

'You honestly don't know any other members of the syndicate?'

'I swear that I don't know who any of them are.'

She still couldn't be sure. The man had proven himself a tremendous performer and had hoodwinked her completely up until today.

'You knew Dickson was dead and yet you played along with the whole investigation into his disappearance!'

He lifted his head and looked her straight in the eye. 'We both did. Probably for the same reason. To protect ourselves. So, what now?'

'I hand you over. You hand me over. I don't know. What do you suggest?'

'Stalemate. We have to trust each other. Surely, by keeping quiet about that night at the reservoir, I've earned yours.'

'What about the photographs?'

'Yours were the only copies. I deleted the pictures from my phone. Look.' He handed it out to her. She checked, looking through endless selfies of Morgan with Emma, many more photos of Emma on various trips out, petting alpacas, eating a large croissant with a satisfied expression on her face, leaping from waves, huddled on the sofa looking at an iPad. There were no pictures taken at Blithfield Reservoir.

She handed it back. 'You could have transferred them to a hard disk.'

'Believe me, if I had, I'd use them to prevent you from marching me in front of the chief constable and exposing me as a member of the syndicate. Kate, you have the power to ruin my career and life. I have nothing to prove what happened at the reservoir.'

She put her head in her hands. This was all too much. She wanted to believe him, yet the months since Chris's murder had proved only one thing – nobody could be trusted. She almost didn't hear his urgent words.

'I . . . want to be the person Emma believes me to be. I know that sounds soppy and unbelievable, but now I've got the promotion I worked hard for, and corny as it sounds, I have the woman of my dreams, I really must break free from the syndicate. Last night, when Emma caught me with the burner, I was trying to get hold of Gamma to say that because I believed Alpha to be dead, I was out once and for all.'

She took in his earnest face. She wanted to believe him. Badly.

'If they'd refused or threatened me again, I intended handing in my resignation with immediate effect and leaving Staffordshire.'

'What! Just like that? And leave Emma?'

'I'd have to if I want her to be safe. Kate, I have no other choice. I can't go on, knowing they own me and wondering when I'll next get a call from them.'

She couldn't process the information fast enough. Morgan was going to throw away his entire career over this. There had to be another way.

'I'm not a bad guy, only somebody who made a mistake and then couldn't get out of a very sticky situation. But I'm also aware that I have to own this. Emma doesn't deserve to be mixed up with somebody who is corrupt. Either I get out of the syndicate, or I walk away from everything I care about.'

331

Kate wanted to believe him. If she didn't, there was no way out for either of them.

'I owe Emma. I've been horrible to live with recently, what with the promotion and being on an investigation that was going nowhere and worrying about the bloody syndicate. I've been bottling it up and taking things out on her. I must make things right for her . . . for us. I don't know what else to say. You've known me for a long time. I've always looked up to you, Kate. You've been more than my boss. You've been my friend. Trust your instinct and do what you must.'

She rubbed her throbbing head. This was so messed up. Then Chris's quiet voice offered a suggestion and the pain diminished slightly. 'There might be another way,' she said.

'There is?'

'I reckon so. I can't explain though. You'll have to trust me on this. First you'll have to help me to entrap this Gamma.'

'Whatever it takes. I want a second chance, Kate. I need to make this work. For me and for Emma.'

Her mind worked at full pelt. To lure Gamma, she would need to place her faith in Morgan – somebody who had admitted to being part of a corrupt group, who had committed crimes that would see him stripped not only of his promotion but his job and sent down. The same criteria applied to her. They were as guilty as each other and yet both wanted to make amends.

'Use your burner to arrange a face-to-face meeting, then let me know the details of when and where.'

'We never have face-to-face meetings.'

'They'll agree when you tell them the reason for it is me. You tell Gamma that I've unearthed proof of the identities of the syndicate and that you know where it is.'

'Is that true?'

'Does it matter? What's important is that you get Gamma to agree to a meeting in person. Do we have a deal?'

'Yes. I won't let you down,' he said.

'No. You won't.'

◆ ◆ ◆

Emma had never felt so ill. She had the mother of all headaches, as if her brain was pushing against her skull in an attempt to escape. Wave after wave of shooting pains fired into her head, face, neck and eyeballs, rendering movement impossible. Thoughts were jumbled. Nothing made sense.

At first, she thought she was suffering from a hangover, but as she tried to turn over to curl back into a ball, she was vaguely aware of being tethered by the wrist, to a wire. She was a puppet. Somebody had transformed her into a puppet and added strings to the back of her hand. The haze thickened in her head, and she lost what little consciousness she had regained.

When she next fought through the ever-thickening fog, she ascertained that she wasn't in her bed. The mattress felt firmer, bedsheets tucked so tightly she couldn't move, unfamiliar pillow that propped her head up rather than the usual soft one she cuddled most nights. A persistent beeping forced her to open her eyelids, pain shooting arrows through them. At last, she had some vision: a dimly lit room, a door. That was all before, once again, her world went black.

◆ ◆ ◆

She had no idea what time it was when she was disturbed by the lemony scent that seemed to come from someone standing next to her, close to the infernal beeping. A soft voice said something about 'promising signs', and another that sounded strangely like her brother's whispered close to her ear, 'Come on, Emma. Fight.'

Her mind scrabbled for leverage. She must be at the gym or have been knocked out in a friendly bout of taekwondo. She'd been to the gym to train and then . . . a fight in the contest area . . . a high kick to her head and down she went. No. That wasn't her. Was it?

Pain washed away all sense and she struggled in a sea of confusion, drifting away for the longest time until she felt a warm hand on top of hers.

'Emma, it's Morgan. I don't know what to say, but when people are in comas, they can still hear things, so I hope you can hear me. I know this is going to be confusing for you, but we're all looking out for you. One of us will be here all the time. Greg has just left and I'm going to stay with you for a while now until he comes back. Kate's on her way too. You're attached to a saline drip. There's some shit in your system that needs to work its way out and you're being monitored on a machine in case . . .'

His voice faded. Had she been in an accident? Morgan sounded concerned. She struggled as darts of pain fired into her skull; then, using every ounce of willpower, she forced her eyes open. Morgan wasn't there. The noise of a small door opening caused her to search, her gaze bouncing over an empty chair, somebody on their knees holding a jacket. They unzipped a pocket and pulled out a phone then bundled the jacket back into a locker. The vision became blurry and the pain too intense. Her eyelids drooped and closed. Maybe she was simply dreaming. That was it. This was some crazy mixed-up nightmare.

Morgan had stopped talking. Maybe he had never been there at all, and this was nothing more than a weird, bad dream. She'd had some horrific nightmares before now. None as mixed up as this though. What would happen next in this hallucinogenic wonderland? Would she see all her estranged brothers gathered around the bed, or maybe her mother?

Her heart stuttered.

Her mother.

Was this going to turn into one of those horrendous recollection dreams?

Her heart jumped again.

Would it be a twisted rerun of the memory that had plagued her for several years: one she had worked so hard to dispel. Would she be propelled back to that dreadful day she found her mother dead in her bedroom, her cowering husband naked and bawling on the floor? Naked. Cuffs. Bruises. On her knees screaming, 'Mum! Mum!'

Her heart leapt in her chest, beating erratically and so loudly it drowned out the sound of the bleeping machine. She couldn't catch her breath. Her heart was clattering, bashing against her ribs. She couldn't face that memory. It was buried deep. A kerfuffle around her drew her attention away from her darkest thoughts. The lemon scent was back, along with other people and strange voices. She distinguished Morgan's in the distance, calling to her, yelling that she had to hang on. Somebody shouted that she was going into cardiac arrest.

All the while, her mother's vacant eyes stared at her.

Then . . . blackness.

'You had us all worried there for a while,' said Kate. 'But you're not somebody who gives in easily. I knew that from the off. I could see a bit of me in you when you joined my team – the same grit and determination. I'm so proud of everything you've achieved, Emma. You are going to go far. Believe me. You won't stop at DI. You might not remember what happened, but we caught Leah and

Victoria's killer thanks to you. I'll save that story for when you are back on your feet. For now, you must rest. Doctors say you still have a way to go. All the team are rooting for you. So, come on, Emma. Don't disappoint us.'

Emma wanted to tell Kate not to worry. That she was only having a dream, and when she woke up everything would be fine.

Then Kate's voice grew thick. 'I . . . I don't really know what you'd think of me if you knew how bad an officer I truly am. I've always followed a strict moral code and expected the same from my officers. I led by example, but recently I've been a terrible example. I've concealed so much from you and been forced to make decisions that are far from honourable.'

Emma wanted to reach out and comfort Kate, who had begun to sob gently, yet she could do no more than listen and wait for the snuffles to cease.

'I . . . I did something dreadful – I met Dickson at Blithfield Reservoir, where I planned on forcing him to confess to his part in Chris's murder and admit that he was corrupt. All those things you read about him in the newspaper were true. I gave that information to the *Gazette*. When he found out I'd recorded his admission of guilt, he turned a gun on me, and we fought. The gun went off and shot him by accident. I tried to save him, but it was too late, and then, Emma, I did the unthinkable and arranged for his body to be disposed of at the pig farm. I've been living with the guilt and lying to you all. I did it so that I could continue to hunt down and unmask the other members of this corrupt circle. All the same, it doesn't justify in any shape or way what I have done.

'You are going to be a far better officer than me. I know you will shine. Stick to your principles, Emma. Never stray. Don't be weak, like me, and always be that courageous and determined officer I know and care about.'

Emma's mind willed her lips to move but her brain couldn't send the command. She wanted to tell Kate that she understood her reasons, that Emma would forgive her because Kate was one of the best people she knew. The effort proved too great for Emma and millions of shooting stars burst in front of her closed eyelids, falling like sparks from exploding fireworks. As they fizzled out, one by one, Emma found herself drifting back into darkness.

◆ ◆ ◆

'Hi, Emma! It's Frankie. Scott is here with me. We're not allowed to stay long but we wanted to see you. I've brought you some nice shampoo and shower gel. The hospital stuff smells like antiseptic. When you are up and about, you can use them and smell of roses instead.' Frankie wasn't her usual bubbly self. Her voice was muffled as if she was wearing a mask, or she'd been crying, or maybe Emma's ears were blocked, probably by her brain, which was mushrooming and expanding at such a rate it was filling her skull, her nose, her mouth.

This had to be one of those nightmares based on a horror film she had watched. In a moment, her head would explode, and Frankie would turn out to be a zombie who would feast on the contents of her skull . . .

Her heart jackhammered again and as she plunged into a black pit, she heard Frankie screaming, 'Emma! Emma! Nurse!'

◆ ◆ ◆

'For crying out loud, Emma! You're going to have to stop scaring us like this. Or I'll end up in the bed next to you.'

Emma pushed through the darkness towards her brother's voice. Even though the pain was still intense, she urged on. This

337

couldn't be a dream. It was lasting too long, and it made no sense. The lemony smell had gone, to be replaced by a combination of disinfectant and something she couldn't identify – an artificial fragrance, like the one in air fresheners.

The beeping continued and now she was more aware of a throbbing in the top of her left hand. She managed to unglue her eyes. A cannula stuck out, the drip feeding into a bag by her bedside. Greg was lying against her covers, head cradled in his arms, his shoulders shaking as he sobbed. She tried to move her hand, to reach him and tell him she was okay, but a shaft of pain drilled through her skull, knocking her senseless again; and when she next came to, he had gone.

In his place sat Morgan, face grey and drawn, eyes on his mobile, staring, waiting. She tried again to speak, willing her lips to move and her voice box to cooperate. She closed her eyes to concentrate her efforts. The pain intensified but she didn't give up. She had to let him know that she was fine. *'I'm okay. I'm okay. I'm okay.'*

The words didn't reach her mouth and as she made one final valiant effort, she heard him say, 'This is Iota. You took your fucking time. I've been waiting all bloody day for you to ring. We need to meet. It's urgent. No. In person. What I have to tell you can't be said over the phone. What's it about? Kate Young has found something that exposes us all. I know where she's keeping it. That's all I'm willing to say over the phone.' There was a pause. Then, 'Okay. Top floor of the station multistorey car park, 6 p.m.'

Emma fought the confusion. What was she hearing? Was this a dream or was Morgan by her side? She was sure he was. Yes, he was looking at his phone. What had he been talking about? A meeting. Kate exposing them? Iota. Was Morgan in trouble? Was that why he'd been so moody? By the time he had finished speaking, Emma's energy was depleted, and she sank back into a dreamless sleep.

♦ ♦ ♦

Kate, who had hardly slept all night, splashed water over her face and geared herself up to return to the interview room. Andy Sullivan had been 'no commenting' even though they'd found incriminating evidence, a diamond ring belonging to Leah, that linked him to more than the attack on Emma. Officers searching his apartment had uncovered more scopolamine hidden in a washing powder box, but nothing else so far; however, Kate was optimistic that they would amass enough on him to have him put safely away. She assigned extra officers to the case and two of them, who had been interviewing Andy's mother, had just provided her with some information that might help her crack the man.

Her phone buzzed with an unknown number.

'Hey, how's Emma?' said Felicity.

Kate was relieved to hear her friend's voice rather than bad news from the hospital. 'Still touch and go. We nearly lost her twice overnight. We've been taking it in turns to sit with her. I'm going back in later. To be honest, I'm worried. She ingested a high dose of scopolamine, and we don't have a clue if or when she'll recover or what after-effects there might be.'

'It was definitely scopolamine, then?'

'Uh-huh. As soon as Ervin found out what happened, he headed straight for the lab to test the powder Morgan seized from her attacker. That fucker still won't confess, but we will have enough evidence to nail him. We've got hold of some of his past victims to identify him.'

'He's going to rue the day he attacked Emma,' said Felicity. 'Especially if . . . No, I'm not going to say it because Emma's a trooper. She'll pull through.'

Kate swallowed hard. They'd all voiced the same positive affirmations to each other, yet none of them knew for certain what the drug was doing to Emma's organs. She couldn't bear to consider the possibilities.

'Yes, Emma has no idea how many people are currently concerned for her well-being and who will want a piece of Andy Sullivan if the worst happens.'

'Don't even think that way.'

'Tricky not to when you've already seen her crash. I honestly thought that she was a goner. They tried three times before the defibrillator got her heart working again.'

'You must stay positive, Kate. We all must.'

'I know, and I am trying.'

There was a hiatus, during which Kate was sure Felicity was wondering if she should continue the conversation, until she heard, 'Anyway, I haven't only rung to ask about our Emma. And just for the record, we can talk freely – I'm sitting in the park, calling from a pay-as-you-go phone to tell you that my hacker friend has made an incredible breakthrough.'

'Breakthrough? Have you seen the footage?'

'Not yet. He's dropping off a USB in the next hour. I thought you and I could examine the contents together in the café where we usually meet.'

Kate rubbed her forehead, torn between finally uncovering the true identity of William's murderer, and thus proving Harriet Khatri's innocence, or shaking a confession out of Andy Sullivan to ensure Emma and all of Andy's other victims got the justice they deserved. She paced the floor. What would William do? It wasn't William's voice that she heard in her mind, it was Chris's. *Harriet will understand. In many ways, she's like you. She believes in the system and fighting for justice. She'll wait a little while longer.*

'I really want to see it, but I can't, not until I've finished with Andy. I'll give you a ring as soon as I'm free.'

Kate glanced at the time. It was almost two in the afternoon. At six, she had her rendezvous with Gamma. She might be able to fit in a meeting with Felicity in between times but it would be tight. She sighed. 'If I can't find time—'

Felicity jumped in. 'I know what you're going to suggest, and I would happily watch it, and relay what I see. But I think you should look at it yourself. It means a great deal to you, Kate. You and William were very close, father and daughter close. You owe it to yourself to see it. Apart from anything else, you must, for closure. Ring me whenever you can. I'll make sure the USB is safe.'

'Thank you. And take great care. I don't know what the syndicate might do if they find out.'

'Not to blow my own trumpet, but I think I'm better at covering my tracks than they might imagine. I have technology on my side.'

'I wouldn't put anything past these people.'

'I'll watch my back. Go nail that son of a bitch, Andy, and tell Emma we love her.'

The phone went dead. Kate stared at her reflection. She no longer felt exhausted. By the end of the day, she ought to have two pieces of shit locked up, Andy and Gamma. She tidied a strand of hair that had got loose, tucked in her blouse and straightened her shoulders.

She ought to be firing on all cylinders, adrenaline pumping through every cell, not feel as flat as she did. She put it down to the combination of mental fatigue and disappointment in Morgan. She had had such high hopes for him.

'Give the lad a break. He'll prove himself. He isn't rotten, not like the others. He got a bit . . . lost. I'm sure if you get the entire story from him, it will prove he was manipulated into joining the syndicate. You know how devious Dickson was,' said William.

'I guess we all deserve second chances.'

'*You know it's the right thing to do. He'll come up trumps with Gamma and you'll be able to put this all to bed.*'

'And then what?'

'*What do you mean?*'

'You know exactly what I mean. I'm done. Once I identify Gamma and hand over everything about the syndicate to Bree, I've accomplished everything I set out to do. I don't have the passion I once had to continue as a police officer. I don't especially enjoy being a DCI. I took the promotion to ensure I was in a good position to bring down the syndicate. I'm exhausted, William. And I'm sick . . . mentally. We both know that. I haven't been right ever since Chris died. Once this is over, I won't need to talk to you for advice, or have Dickson whispering insults or doubts. Even Chris will leave me again, and this time for good. I'll be alone and I'll hate every second. I won't be able to cope, will I?'

She stared at her reflection in the bathroom mirror. She didn't reply in any of the voices. All of this . . . the voices . . . would end, and so would she.

◆ ◆ ◆

Andy Sullivan didn't move a muscle when she re-entered the room, although his lawyer acknowledged her presence with a quiet 'Hello'. Morgan, who was stony-faced, had been waiting for her to continue the interview. At first, she'd been loath to allow him to conduct the interview, concerned that his emotions would get in the way of his questioning, before concluding she would rather he was with her during the hours before she met with Gamma. At least this way she could keep an eye on him, while also making sure he followed procedure. She got into position, hands relaxed, face composed. She wasn't going to allow Andy or his lawyer to pick up on any animosity.

'DCI Kate Young has re-entered the room,' said Morgan, for the recording.

Kate shuffled her papers, looked up and smiled at Andy. 'I'd like to ask you again about the ring we found in your pocket at the scene of the crime. How did you come by it?'

'No comment.'

'It's been identified as belonging to Leah Fairbrother, who was attacked in a very similar way to Acting DI Emma Donaldson. It was her engagement ring. How did it come into your possession?'

'No comment.'

She gave another smile. 'Leah was also attacked using a substance known as Devil's Breath, the same substance you used on Emma. We have found a large quantity of the substance at your apartment.'

Andy cracked his head, this way and that, glared at Kate and said, 'No comment.'

'Did you attack Leah Fairbrother?'

'No comment.'

'Why did you attack Emma?'

'No comment.'

'Her brother told us that you and Emma were friendly. That you got along well. Why, then, would you try to harm her? Had there been a falling-out? Had she rebuffed your advances? Belittled you in any way?'

Kate sensed Morgan bristling beside her every time she spoke Emma's name. But he was doing well to keep a lid on his temper. She'd told him about the information from the officers who'd been interviewing Andy's mother, so he – like Kate – was holding it together, waiting to pounce.

She nodded. 'Okay. I understand. You're going to keep this up for as long as possible. Let me tell you that it won't be for much longer, because all the while you've been sitting there, dragging this out, my officers have been working hard.'

He gave a half-hearted shrug.

'Lorraine Galloway,' she said. Andy flinched. 'Does that name mean anything to you?'

The lawyer looked quickly at Andy.

'No comment,' Andy replied.

'Oh, come on, we know she's your mother.'

'No comment,' he said more quickly. This time he shifted in his chair, folded his arms tightly. A muscle near his eye twitched.

'In fact, we know a lot more than that. You see, my officers have already visited her. They had a nice chat to Lorraine and the woman who looks after her.'

Andy shifted again, rubbed his lips together. She'd hit a nerve. At the mention of his mother, he'd begun to unravel.

'She's a daft old cow. She hates me.'

'I disagree. She isn't daft at all. In fact, she came across as quite astute. Admittedly, she had difficulty with her speech, what with having had a stroke and all, but there doesn't seem to be much wrong with her eyes or her hearing and she had a lot to tell us.'

'Whatever she told you is a pack of lies. She really does hate me. She always has,' he said. 'You know, she used to bully me when I was a kid, torture me. She'd lock me in a cupboard for hours on end. The bitch!' His face contorted. 'You've no idea what it was like living with her. She's a fucking control freak who should never have given birth. Anyway, you can't trust a word that comes out of her mouth.'

'I'm not here to discuss what you went through when you were a child. I'm here to establish what you've been up to, and according to your mother, you've been paying her random visits. Although when I say paying visits, I mean going to her house, then disappearing upstairs for a while before leaving. She told us that you don't bother with her at all. In fact, she said she was scared of you and would often pretend to be asleep when you were there.'

He shook his head. 'What the fuck? Her scared of me?! Not a chance. She's lying. She's bloody lying.'

Kate observed his sudden jerkiness, the way he looked from Morgan to his lawyer, to her. This mention of his mother had transformed him, made him vulnerable. Now Kate could twist the knife.

'Andy, it might be a good time for you to open up to your lawyer,' said Kate. 'Your mother gave us permission to search upstairs. What do you think we might find there?'

Andy's face crumpled. Even though what she had told him was true, they hadn't yet uncovered anything significant. Andy's reaction told her everything she needed to know. He had hidden evidence in his mother's house. Andy dropped his head in his hands and moaned. Maybe Lorraine had bullied and tortured him, done something to screw him up as an individual. Whatever had transpired had helped create this monster who preyed on successful women. She wasn't interested in what made him tick, only in ensuring he paid for his crimes.

She glanced at Morgan, who acknowledged her with a small nod. They had Andy on the ropes. He would be held accountable for the attacks and deaths they knew about and maybe some they hadn't yet uncovered. Once they'd tidied up here, got a full confession and charged Andy, she would send Morgan back to the hospital to be with Emma. She doubted she'd have time to see Felicity before she had to arrange to be at the car park to meet Gamma. As keen as she was to uncover the identity of the person who had killed William, it was more important to expose the person who'd been the syndicate's fixer. This had always been her quest, and William's. Glancing for a second time at Morgan, she hoped with all her heart that he wasn't going to let her down again. She wasn't sure she could cope if he did.

◆ ◆ ◆

Emma was trapped in a thick fog that wouldn't clear. Although she picked up on voices and knew people were nearby, she couldn't reach them.

The lemony smell came and went. Emma drifted in and out of consciousness. Every time she attempted to open her eyes or move, she was attacked by thousands of tiny electric thunderbolts that pummelled her head and immobilised her. This time, she lay still and listened.

'How's she doing?' asked Greg.

The second voice was Morgan's. 'No change. I . . . I don't know what I'll do if I lose her. Shit, Greg. She's my fucking world and she doesn't even know it.'

'Hey, it's okay. Let it out.'

She had never heard Morgan cry before, and it pained her, especially as she was the reason he was in tears. She needed to escape this foggy confusion. If only the pain would ease in her head. She pushed past it, let the arrows puncture her eyeballs and forced her eyes to open.

'Shit! Morgan! Emma's eyes opened. She can hear us.'

'What?'

'She's coming round. Emma, can you hear me? It's Greg! Come on, my girl. Open your fucking eyes and give us a smile.'

Morgan joined him. 'Emma, we need you to do this. You must open your eyes. It's your two favourite men in the whole world. Do it for us.'

Dark clouds were gathering in her head, and every effort to stay in the moment, or even move, was monumental.

'Fight, Emma. Fight like you always do. You can kick the shit out of whatever is holding you back.'

'Emma Donaldson, if you don't open those beautiful eyes, I won't be able to ask you what I've been dying to ask you for weeks.'

The voices became clearer and although she desperately wanted to go back to sleep, she felt a magnetic pull. She fought the clouds, pushed through the arrows of pain and managed to force her lids fully open. Both Greg and Morgan were holding her hands and leaning over the bed, staring at her, stubble on their faces, dark bruises under their eyes, which were glassy with tears.

The sight jolted her to find the strength to stay in the zone, not retreat into the darkness.

Greg grabbed Morgan's arm, hanging on to him as he said, 'She's awake. She's awake!'

Emma entered a world of confusion: her throat was raw, constricted by an object, her tongue trapped, and attempts to swallow spiralled her into panic. Morgan's face loomed over her, his hand on her cheek calming her as he spoke.

'Don't try to talk. There's a tube in your trachea to help you breathe. You've had us all scared witless but you're back now and you're going to be just fine. I'm going to make sure of that.' Two silvery tracks ran over his stubbled cheeks.

He moved his hand to rest it on hers. Warmth spread through it, easing her panic. Morgan was with her. He cared about her. She'd heard him say so, hadn't she? But she'd heard him say other things too that made little sense. Snippets of conversation drifted back, mentions of Iota, meetings, Kate exposing Morgan and other urgent whispers. Her mind was too fuzzy for her to work it out. She had to concentrate on staying in the here and now. The rest she would deal with when she felt better.

CHAPTER
TWENTY-FOUR

It was almost six o'clock and Kate, along with two plain-clothes officers, was lying in wait on the top floor of the station car park. She'd insisted Morgan remain at Emma's beside. It was imperative that Gamma didn't suspect Morgan of setting them up; therefore she had chosen officers from an undercover unit to accompany her.

Despite everything, she couldn't shake off concerns that Morgan would somehow turn the tables, alert Gamma and produce the photographic evidence he claimed to have deleted. The minutes had ticked by slowly, each one bringing fresh doubts.

She chastised herself. Morgan wouldn't let her down, would he?

She replayed the conversation they'd had. Every gesture he'd made, conscious and unconscious. Everything, including his body language, indicated he was being honest and open with her. Yet he was far better at duplicity than she could ever have imagined.

Had he fooled her yet again? After all, she'd been off her game recently. Had she missed something when questioning him, a miniscule tell she hadn't picked up on because she was racked with pain and anguish at the thought of him deceiving her?

She considered the moment when he'd looked her in the eye and assured her that he wanted out of the syndicate. When he'd revealed his vulnerability and love for Emma. She believed that, didn't she? The truth of the matter was that although he was no longer the man she thought he was, she had no other choice.

Pushing aside her worries, she thought about Gamma. Having been potentially outed as the person who'd leaked information from Operation Moonbeam and persuaded the traffickers to stay schtum, she wondered if Jamie Webster was the fixer. William's list now proved the code names had no bearing on individuals' surnames. It no longer followed that somebody whose surname came alphabetically ahead of Morgan's would be Gamma.

It struck her that although she didn't have strong evidence to support her suspicions, Jamie had, at times, given her cause for concern. Thoughts churned and tumbled like washing in a dryer; her latest theory was regarding Harriet Khatri, who had been set up. On reflection, it seemed that Jamie had sown seeds of doubt about Harriet Khatri in Kate's mind. She recalled the times she had seen him talking to Harriet, at a pub when he should have been at home, in the corridor where he claimed to be chatting about his son.

Had it been a con, designed to make Kate believe Harriet was a member of the syndicate? It was plausible that the syndicate had misled Kate so she came to distrust Harriet so much she would believe unequivocally that Harriet had murdered William. It wouldn't be the first time she'd been set up in such a manner. Following the murder of her husband, she'd been brought off sick leave to run the investigation into the murder of Dickson's friend, Alex Corby, because Dickson believed she wouldn't be up to the task and would make mistakes that would allow him to escape scrutiny.

She should have had it out with Jamie ages ago, when he first lied about his whereabouts on the morning of a call out. Instead of dropping off his son, as he claimed, he had been working undercover for Dickson at Stoke station. The people he had been watching were now both dead, casualties of Dickson's attempts to cover his trail. She wondered if Jamie knew they were dead or indeed had played any part in their demise. The shock of learning Morgan had betrayed her allowed her imagination to run riot. She couldn't trust any of her officers, and certainly not Jamie.

That Jamie's phone number had appeared in Dickson's contact list had thrown her off the scent. Dickson had contacted him using the burner during the clandestine operation into underage sex workers. It hadn't crossed her mind that he might appear twice: once with his usual phone number and secondly under the code name Gamma.

Her heartrate increased. This now made perfect sense to her. She needed him bang to rights, unable to contact anyone. As the syndicate's fixer, he might have information about William's killer. She could use this information, along with the cleaned footage, to ensure there was a watertight case against the scumbag who had murdered her friend.

Morgan's burner phone lay on the console. The officer beside her had instructions to answer it when it rang. Meanwhile, Kate waited and watched, every sense on alert.

Six o'clock came and went. It worried her that Gamma was late, had maybe, having scoped out the car park and surrounding area, cried off. Even so, it was unlikely that anyone would suspect the seven-year-old white Transit van that Kate had procured for this purpose. It wasn't a registered police vehicle and its tinted windows ensured nobody could see inside.

They'd been in situ for forty minutes, during which time three cars had come and eleven cars had departed, leaving the floor almost empty. Their vehicle, however, didn't stand out any more than the unmarked cars on lower levels, each with officers inside them, waiting for the command to block, chase or capture their suspect should he attempt to flee.

She'd demanded radio silence. Whoever it was, and she was sure it was Jamie, was one of their own and might be tuned in to their radio frequency.

Her thoughts were interrupted by the arrival of a vehicle she recognised immediately – an unmarked squad car. Even with the tinted windows, she hunkered down, ensuring she was not visible. It was driven into a space in the far corner and the engine switched off. From her position, she couldn't make out the driver's face.

Five minutes passed. It wouldn't be much longer before Gamma decided either to depart or call Morgan's phone. Twenty heartbeats later, the burner rang. The officer covered the speaker with a handkerchief and answered, 'This is Iota.'

Kate slipped from the van and sped across to the car, heart thumping. The driver didn't see her coming. His head was lowered, phone to his ear. Behind her, other officers were advancing. She'd ensured every entry and exit point was covered. She reached the car before the others, fury aimed at this officer who had caused so much heartache and suffering, who had manipulated them, all in the name of greed. She wanted this son of a bitch to pay, along with all the other bastards who made up the syndicate. All the pain and misery she had endured since Chris's death came to a head. She hammered on the window, pulled on the door handle and yelled, 'Open up!'

Gamma lifted his face, eyes wide, mouth open. Time stood still. It wasn't Jamie Webster. She felt her own jaw drop.

Had Morgan and Jamie orchestrated this? Had they found a patsy to play the role of Gamma?

The officer in the car was quiet, mild-mannered DS Trevor Wray. Surprised, shocked and confused, she momentarily stepped back.

Trevor took advantage of the moment to shove the door hard, knocking her backwards. He bolted from the car and zigzagged his way towards the exit before being tackled by one of the officers. Kate rubbed her smarting shin. Had she just fucked up? William's voice spoke clearly in her head.

'Think about this logically. The perfect fixer would be somebody who keeps their head down and doesn't draw attention to themselves. Check out Trevor's bank accounts, see if he has been receiving money. Do your due diligence. You know Morgan wouldn't let you down. In fact, he's proved his loyalty by protecting you and going along with your investigation into Dickson's disappearance. He knew you killed Dickson but didn't challenge Stanka's story that her pimp Farai had murdered him. He could have produced those photos back then and changed the course of events, but he didn't. You might not like the fact that you were wrong about Jamie, but this is your man. Gather the proof and you will have all the evidence you need.'

She made her way towards Trevor, who stared at her, his eyes wild. 'I haven't done anything wrong.'

'Then why did you try to escape?'

'I didn't know it was you, ma'am. I thought somebody was going to rob me. I panicked. That's all.'

'Bollocks! Give me that phone.'

He held it out.

She immediately passed it to another officer with instructions to have it processed and sent to Forensics.

Trevor shook his head. 'I don't know what this is all about. I haven't done anything wrong, and that isn't my phone. It belongs to someone else.'

'Who?'

'DS Jamie Webster, ma'am. I was following up on a lead that he received. He couldn't do it himself because you moved him to a different team, and he wasn't involved in Operation Moonbeam any longer. He passed on the info to me. I was supposed to meet with an informant. Jamie said the guy was ultra-cautious and only used stupid code names to ensure he was talking to the right person. He was Iota, and I was to say I was Gamma.'

'And if I ask Jamie, he'll verify that?'

He pulled a face. 'Given what is happening, I'm not so sure. He might deny it. It looks like he's set me up for something. What is it? A drugs deal? I thought I was here to listen to what this Iota person had to say, that it was to do with Operation Moonbeam.'

Trevor was gaining in confidence now, putting layers into his story to make it sound more credible. Kate nipped it in the bud before she lost her rag completely and smashed him in the face.

'We'll discuss this back at the station.'

Trevor stared hard at her and for the first time she noticed how soulless his eyes were, black irises merging with black pupils. 'What's this all about, ma'am?'

'I believe you to be involved in a corrupt syndicate operating within our force and intend questioning you further at HQ.'

'What?' he spluttered. 'No! You can't take me in for that.'

'Oh, but I can, and I am. Officers, would you please escort DS Wray back to the station and place him in an interview room under watch until I arrive to speak to him in person. He is to have no contact with anyone or access to a phone.'

Wide-eyed, he pleaded with her, 'Ma'am, this is a mistake.'

'We'll talk about it in a while.'

She watched him being led away and returned to the van, where, alone for the moment, she caught her breath. Had she not seen the look of contempt on his face, she might have believed Trevor's denials. As it was, she was sure that this time they had the right man. But hadn't she, up until she saw Trevor's face, believed Jamie to be Gamma?

Of course, she might be wrong again, like she had been about Harriet and Jamie. She would find out in due course if she'd stuffed up. First, she had other important business to attend to. She rang Felicity's number. 'I'm ready. Can we meet in the usual place?'

'When?' asked Felicity.

'Half an hour.'

'I'll be there.'

She pocketed the phone. Trevor would wait. Finding out who had killed William couldn't.

◆ ◆ ◆

Felicity was staring at her laptop when Kate arrived at the almost empty café. A steaming cup of coffee was waiting for her.

'You look done for,' said Felicity.

'The last twenty-four hours have been hellish.'

'I'm sure. Morgan rang me to say Emma has come round.'

'He rang me too. Thank goodness she has. I hope there aren't any lasting effects from the drugs that bastard put in her system.'

'She'll be fine,' said Felicity. 'She's like you – determined and courageous.'

Kate gave a small smile. She inhaled the aroma of the coffee then sipped it. The sweet taste, which vaguely resembled caramel, was exactly what she needed.

'Okay, let's do this,' she said.

Felicity moved into position next to Kate, inserted a memory stick into the side of her laptop, tapped a few keys and sat back.

This time it wasn't Harriet who entered William's lounge. Although a similar height, this person was dressed in dark clothing and wearing trainers. After the shot was fired, the figure turned towards the camera. It was none other than DS Trevor Wray. She locked eyes with Felicity.

'This is the original footage?'

'Without doubt.'

'There can be no quibble over this?'

'None whatsoever. My friend can unequivocally confirm that the other recording was tampered with, using deepfake graphics.'

Kate studied the frozen image on the screen. It seemed, at last, they had identified William's real murderer.

◆ ◆ ◆

Kate entered the interview room where Trevor Wray sat quietly.

'Ma'am, I'm sorry for the way I reacted,' he said, even before she'd got into position. 'You startled me in the car park. I didn't know what was going on.'

She nodded. 'For your information, this interview is being video recorded and observed by Superintendent Bree O'Sullivan in the adjacent room. Beside me is DS Scott Hart. Also present in the room is DC Francesca Porter. DS Wray, please remind me why you were making a phone call from a burner phone to a person, code name Iota, while at the station car park this evening.'

'DS Jamie Webster was contacted by an informant who wanted to meet and pass on info about traffickers. DS Webster was unable to make the meet himself, so he asked me to do it.'

'Why didn't he pass on this information to Acting DI Morgan Meredith, who is leading the operation?'

Trevor shrugged. 'I guess he couldn't find him.'

'Or tell me?'

'I don't know what goes on in his head, ma'am. He and I are mates, so I guess he thought he would ask me.'

'What if I told you that the phone belongs to a member of a corrupt syndicate that was run by Superintendent Dickson?'

His jaw dropped and his eyes opened wide. 'Wow! Then Jamie really has conned me good and proper. That throws a different light on everything. He must have known you'd be waiting for him and—' He paused, as if assimilating the information. 'He's shoved me under the bus, hasn't he, the bastard!'

'If you know nothing about the syndicate then you'll be surprised to know that DCI William Chase infiltrated it to blow the whistle on the other members. He left behind a document containing the names of the members and details of what they'd been up to. There is a lot of information about a fixer known as Gamma, the person who owns that phone.'

Trevor shook his head slowly from side to side. 'That can only mean Jamie is Gamma. Then *that's* why he told me to use the code name. It all makes sense. And, on reflection, he was acting a bit weird at the time. I thought he was stressed, what with being moved off Operation Moonbeam and all. Ma'am, please, you need to question him. I honestly know nothing about any of this.'

She ignored his pleas and continued quietly, 'Furthermore, DCI William Chase was murdered by one of the members of the syndicate.'

'No way! Then DI Harriet Khatri was part of this too! I can't believe what you're telling me.'

'DI Khatri isn't involved. She also didn't shoot DCI William Chase.'

She sat back, allowing a weighty silence to fall.

His eyes opened even wider. 'I don't understand, ma'am. I thought there was hard evidence to prove she had killed him. And this phone. I haven't any idea why Jamie would do this to me. We're friends. He must be covering his back. You believe me, don't you, ma'am? I've never given you cause to distrust me. I do my duty and I love my job.'

His performance was convincing, the amount of concern in his voice and actions she would associate with somebody who had been hoodwinked. She'd expect no less from the syndicate's fixer. She'd almost be convinced if it weren't for the fact that Trevor Wray had murdered her friend and mentor.

Trevor would stop at nothing to save his own skin. He had dropped Jamie in it before when he'd told Morgan that he'd seen his friend heading to the cells where they were holding the traffickers. Once again, he was trying to pass the blame on to Jamie. She began to clap, slowly. 'Good performance,' she said.

Trevor's jaw dropped, his eyebrows raised, and he looked affronted. 'What do you mean? I've told you the truth. You can't pin anything on me. Jamie's set me up. Fooled you all.'

'It's only a matter of time before we compile sufficient evidence to prove you are Gamma. I already have a team looking into your finances. I'm confident we'll be able to trace payments that have been made to you.'

For a split second his lips curled in annoyance, then he recovered. 'But, ma'am, Jamie—'

'That's enough of this farce. I'm sick of listening to your lies. DS Trevor Wray, I am placing you under arrest for the murder of DCI William Chase. You do not have to say anything. But it may harm your defence if you do not mention when questioned something which you later rely on in court.'

'That's mental. Harriet Khatri shot him.' He pushed back his chair and jumped to his feet. Frankie, who'd been standing by the door, stepped forward to arrest him.

Kate blinked away the images of Trevor kicking William to ensure he was dead, then planting the gun in her friend's left hand.

'Hands behind your back,' said Frankie.

'I didn't kill him!' Trevor yelled and pushed Frankie away.

Scott was on his feet in a flash. He grabbed Trevor's hands and yanked them behind his back, where Frankie cuffed them. Scott then placed a firm hand on Trevor's shoulder to guide him to the cells.

'I didn't do it! You've got the wrong person.'

She ignored his performance. Looking directly at Scott and Frankie, she said, 'Get him out of my sight.'

Once the room was empty, she rested her head between her hands. There would be months to wait before Trevor and his syndicate friends were dealt with, but one thing she was sure of: he wouldn't get off. He would pay the full penance for murdering William.

Her mission was at an end. Wasn't it? Trevor had planted a seed of doubt about Jamie's part in this. Had Trevor, like Morgan, simply been somebody the syndicate used for certain jobs? And if so, was Jamie the real fixer?

A weight lay heavily in her chest. She'd been surrounded by deceit for too long. She was at the point when she couldn't work out who was trustworthy and who not. The syndicate members were cunning and slippery. She couldn't be sure that she had them all. That Trevor was Gamma was likely; however, at this stage she couldn't even be completely certain of that fact. The only thing she was sure about was that William's list would help destroy the syndicate and that Trevor had unequivocally murdered William.

CHAPTER
TWENTY-FIVE

Morgan held on to Emma's arm and pushed the door open with his foot before guiding her through. 'Easy does it. Here we are. Home sweet home.'

Emma brushed his hand away. 'I appreciate the fuss, but I'm not an invalid.'

'You heard what the doctors said. You've got to take it easy.'

'Taking it easy didn't mean demanding a wheelchair to take me out of hospital!' she said with a smile.

'There were lots of long corridors. I didn't want you keeling over on me . . . again. Now, let me help you take your coat off.'

She unzipped the jacket and, wriggling it from her shoulders, let him hang it up. 'Are you going to be like this all the time?'

'Yes. So, get used to it. Now, sit down in the lounge and I'll make you a cup of tea.'

'Morgan! I'll make the tea. If you want to be helpful, you can fetch in my stuff from the car.'

'I'll do that in a minute, but not until you go into the lounge,' he said, again guiding her to the door.

'I'm not sure I like being bossed about.'

'Not being bossy, just making sure that you follow doctor's orders for the next few days until you are feeling A1. The swelling in your brain might have gone but you've been left with some memory loss, and as well as being unable to remember anything after going to the gym, you've clearly forgotten that you promised you'd do anything I told you to.'

She laughed. 'As if!'

'Seriously, Emma. You must take care, at least for a short while. You can get back to normal soon enough. So, come on, humour me.'

'I'll behave. But don't mollycoddle me.'

'Wouldn't dream of it.'

She turned the handle and walked into the lounge, coming to a rapid halt. Her mouth opened in surprise. The carpet was festooned with rose petals, their perfume filling the room. Red heart-shaped helium-filled balloons floated from a silver box; a huge floral display of roses took centre stage on the dining table, along with an ice bucket containing a bottle of champagne.

'What on earth—'

She turned towards him, then covered her mouth with both hands as he dropped on one knee.

'I don't know if you remember in hospital when I told you to open your eyes so I could ask you a question. For all the years we've known each other, you've made me feel more complete, and have shown me the true meaning of happiness. Before I say it, there's something I have to confess that's been eating me up inside. I think it's what's been making me behave poorly, especially the last few weeks. Emma, I'm not the person you think I am. But I truly want to be, and can be with you by my side, but first I need to come clean.'

Emma held his gaze, even though icy tentacles gripped her heart. What was it that had made his face turn pale? She recalled the weird telephone conversation he'd had when she was semi-conscious, the name Iota, Kate exposing him and something about a meeting. Was it to do with that? Another memory floated to the surface, something to do with Kate and another confession. What was it? Morgan's voice chased away all thoughts.

'Emma, I've been involved in some shady inside dealings, working for members of a corrupt syndicate. They wouldn't let me leave, but I have now. I was involved in entrapping one of the members – a fixer – and so I've righted some of the wrongs. Up until then, I couldn't get away, believe me when I say I tried. I truly tried. I wanted nothing more than to be a good officer, like you. So now that you know, will you forgive me and stay by my side? Please stay next to me forever. Marry me, Emma.'

It had been two weeks since Trevor's arrest. Kate sat on a cold, wet bench outside the pub. Digger, beside her, didn't seem to mind the inclement weather. He raised his pint glass to admire the liquid inside it.

'So, you caught the bad guys then?' he said.

'Yes. And I wanted to tell you that nobody will come after you. You're safe.'

'I suppose I should thank you then.'

'Don't. You didn't deserve to get caught up in all of this . . . business.'

He took a lengthy sip of his drink and then looked her in the eye. 'What about you? Will you go to jail too?'

'I don't think so. I didn't deliberately kill anyone. You saw that what happened at the reservoir was an accident.'

'But afterwards wasn't an accident. You took his body away somewhere.'

'I know. It had to be done that way. If I hadn't, I wouldn't have been able to capture all the bad guys, as you call them.'

'What is your punishment going to be then?' he asked.

'Living with what I did,' she said. 'I'll never be able to defend my actions to myself.'

'Seems you got off lightly.'

'You have no idea how wrong you are,' she replied.

Back in the office, Kate rubbed her hands over the aged leather chair arms and stared out of her office window.

'It's over, William. Your document is in safe hands and the syndicate members are being investigated thoroughly by the corruption squad. Trevor wasn't as clever as he imagined, and we've discovered an offshore bank account where he was squirrelling away money. You did a great job, William. And just as you promised, we've exposed them. I still don't understand why you lied about the code names being given out in alphabetical order, according to members' surnames. I suspect you didn't want me to know you were so high up the chain of command. We've all done things we've not been proud of to expose this syndicate, so I understand if that was the reason. One thing I'm glad about is that you couldn't identify Morgan as Iota. As far as anyone is concerned, that identity will remain a secret forever. He got his second chance. Or did you know all along, and simply kept schtum?'

'Sorry, Kate, but you'll never truly know,' said William. *'I always liked Morgan though. He will make a good superintendent himself, one day.'*

She smiled at the thought of William keeping Morgan out of this. It was the sort of thing he would have done.

'Things have changed here, what with Morgan and Emma both running their own teams, and I think I've proved I'm not really DCI material. I prefer to lead a team from the front, not manage people from my desk.

'My memories, along with my drive and motivation, are consigned to the past. They lie in the embers of what was: you at the helm, me in charge of one of the best teams at HQ. More than all of that, after what I've done – the lies I've told and the crimes I've committed – I can't possibly continue to work here. A police officer should uphold the law and while I can justify my actions because they were for the greater good, they were still wrong, William. They went against every fibre of my being and none of what I have done to get this result sits well with me. How can I possibly continue in my role, or in any official capacity now? I prided myself on always doing the right thing, playing by the rules and being honest. This quest has forced me to turn my back on values I upheld.

'I've given this a great deal of thought: it's time to start a new life. I'm going to tender my resignation and visit Tilly in Australia. I don't know if I'll stay over there or return. Either way, for now I need time away from the madness of this pursuit that has consumed my existence ever since Chris was murdered. More importantly, I need to be with people who love me. I wish with all my heart that you and Chris were still alive, but neither of you are. And even though I've finished what you both started, I've become an empty vessel.'

She sighed, the sound coming from a place deep inside her and lasting an age, even if it failed to relieve the heavy ache in her heart. She caressed the leathery chair arms again, imagining William doing the same.

'It's time to say goodbye, William. Thank you for all your guidance and belief in me. Most of all, thank you for caring about me.'

She thought she heard a faint *'Goodbye, Kate'*, but she shut it out. All this talking to herself and listening to voices in her head was over for good.

A knock at the door stopped her from bursting into tears. 'Come in.'

Although thinner, Harriet Khatri was looking smart in a pristine white blouse and black skirt and jacket combination, hair in a neat bun and her make-up on point.

With fresh video evidence and a new suspect for William's murder, Harriet's bail conditions had been immediately dropped and, after long talks with Chief Constable Atwell, her position restored.

'Good to see you back,' said Kate.

'I wanted to drop in to thank you again. I wouldn't be here if it weren't for you—'

Kate stopped her with a smile. 'We've had that conversation. You should never have been put in that position.'

'And I should congratulate you on your outstanding achievement of breaking up the corrupt ring.'

'William has to take credit for most of that.'

'Have you outed everyone in the syndicate?'

'Truth be told, I can't be sure. However, I think most of them have been dealt with.'

Harriet looked down at her feet and hesitated before lifting her chin. 'I find this sort of thing difficult. I mean, speaking about my feelings. You and I . . . well, let's say I never fully appreciated why everyone talked about you in such exalted tones. When I took over your team after you took sick leave, all I ever heard was *Kate this* and *Kate that*. It was hard work to get them to even listen to me, let alone treat me like their DI. That coloured my opinion of you. I knew I could never fill your boots, so I chose to be your opponent. With hindsight, I realise I should have considered you a role model.'

'No, please—'

'No, I have to say this. Please let me finish. Nobody else could have gone through the traumas you've experienced and performed the way you have. Your success rate is second to none. What you did for me went beyond any call of duty, and what you must have been enduring while you single-handedly went against this highly corrupt group beggars belief. In brief, I admire you. You are exemplary, an inspiration, and you can count on me to follow in your footsteps, ensure we rid this station of the stigma of corruption and serve the people who live in this county.'

Harriet cleared her throat. 'I hope that wasn't too much. I felt it had to be said.'

Not only had the app footage been faked but Harriet's confidential informant, Tommy Clayton, had – with Harriet's encouragement – finally come forward to support her claim that she had been set up at the warehouse. Had Kate not listened to William's voice, Harriet would be behind bars, her life ruined. It struck Kate that so much depended on judgement and getting it right. On this occasion, she almost hadn't.

'Thank you. I can say, hand on heart, I don't feel I'm any better than anyone else here. We all do our best and I have the highest regard for you. Had you not been falsely accused of a crime you didn't commit, you'd be sitting at this desk. You deserved the promotion as much as I did. So, in that respect, we are equals and I'll always consider you as one.'

A tight smile tugged at the corners of Harriet's mouth.

'So, enough of all this fangirling. I'm not very good at expressing my feelings either, but if you're free later, I'll toast your return with you at Fred's bar,' said Kate.

'I'd like that.'

'See you at seven o'clock.'

Once the door had shut, Kate stood up and stared out of the window again. Below her, Jamie was scurrying back to the main entrance, a takeaway bag in his hand. He stopped to chat to a fellow officer, high-fiving him before they parted. Checks on Jamie and subsequent interviews with him had determined he was not complicit in framing Trevor Wray. Along with the financial trail indicating Trevor had been receiving substantial deposits of money, Forensics recovered Trevor's fingerprints, and his alone, from the burner phone. The tech team had produced a list of times and places when the mobile had been used, all proving to be in locations where Trevor Wray, rather than Jamie, had been at the time of use.

That she had mistaken Jamie's actions for those of somebody who was working for the syndicate troubled her. She wasn't often wrong about people and had badly misjudged him. For that she felt heart heavy. However, she was sure about Harriet, who would be more than capable of taking on the mantle of DCI and, together with Bree O'Sullivan, would eradicate any negative impressions the public had of HQ and its officers. If Kate walked away now, this place and the people it served were in the very best hands.

It was time to leave.

CHAPTER
TWENTY-SIX

The boarding gate was bustling with anticipation, squeals of excitement from children who raced after each other between the rows of seats, people checking cases and bags for reading material and electronic devices they would require for the long flight. The room was too warm for Kate, who was still wearing a winter jacket. Studying her fellow travellers, some clad in shorts, many in light baggy trousers and loose-fitting tops, she realised she would have been wiser to have worn more comfortable clothes for travelling. At least she'd only brought hand luggage, having decided she would purchase whatever she required once she arrived down under. Tilly loved shopping. She'd delight in spending time choosing new clothes for her stepsister.

She clutched the bag containing the toy purchased at one of the airport shops, a surprise for her dinosaur-mad nephew, Daniel – a LEGO Jurassic World set that she had already decided she would construct with him.

She hadn't told anyone at HQ of her intentions, merely – in an old-fashioned gesture and a nod to the memories of her father and William, who had preferred the old-school way of doing things – left a resignation letter on Chief Constable Atwell's desk. It felt more personal than an email and, for all her courage, she couldn't face explaining her decision to leave or risk him persuading her to stay.

She didn't deserve to serve on the police force. It would be unethical, given the lie she was living. Whatever success they credited her with would be false praise because in her attempt to get to the truth, she had sacrificed the thing that was most important – her moral compass. She was as guilty as those names on William's list. Although she might not have profited financially, or deliberately harmed anyone, she had trodden on toes, been deceitful, and no matter how hard she tried to defend her actions, she felt dirty. The end didn't justify the means and she'd sold her soul to bring down corrupt individuals when she was no better than them.

A navy-suited woman with a pink and red scarf tied at her throat approached the desk to invite passengers sitting in the first twenty rows to come forward. The room came alive with the rustling of bags as people jostled forward to join a quickly forming queue. Kate, whose seat was to the rear of the plane, remained sitting down.

Ignoring everyone, her mind drifted back to her thoughts. Digger had asked her what her punishment would be. The fact was that neither she nor Morgan were going to atone for their crimes. It didn't sit right that it should be so easy for them. She'd spent her life ensuring that the bad guys, as Digger had called them, were put away for their crimes.

She had done wrong. But so had Morgan, who had willingly become involved with the syndicate. Moreover, he had pulled the wool successfully over both Kate and Emma's eyes. That she and Morgan weren't going to pay for their misdemeanours made a mockery of everything she had stood for.

She hugged the box of toy bricks to her chest. They shouldn't get off scot-free. It was immoral.

The queue dwindled to only three passengers, who were currently having passports and tickets checked.

A man also in navy, with a white shirt and a pink and red tie that matched the woman's scarf, spoke into the tannoy. 'Thank you for waiting. We would now like to invite all passengers seated in rows twenty-one to thirty-five to come forward with your tickets ready and passports open at your photograph page.'

Her mind jumped back to the trade-off with Morgan, and the promise that she would keep his secret if he kept hers. Everything had happened because of people hiding dark secrets. It rankled that even at the end of this journey, she was still concealing truths. This wasn't how she used to act. She believed in honesty and integrity, not deceit.

A voice whispered in her head, making her start. *'Kate, you were the best, bravest, and most honest person I knew.'*

Tears sprang to her eyes at Chris's voice. He had spoken those very words to her on many an occasion. He had frequently voiced how proud he was of her and reminded her that her father would also have been proud of everything she had achieved. Chris had loved her for being that person – that Kate.

'Thank you for your patience. We now invite passengers seated in rows thirty-six to forty-five to come forward with . . .'

The voice was obliterated by the commotion in her head. She lurched to her feet, still clutching the bag containing her nephew's present, and bent to retrieve her hand luggage. She attached herself to the end of the queue. Could she live with herself, knowing all this? Was it punishment enough? There was still a chance she could return and fix this, be the Kate that Chris knew and loved.

At the desk, the two beaming ground staff continued checking tickets and passports, bidding everyone a good flight.

The person behind her urged her forward.

'You go ahead,' she said, standing aside for them and three more people behind her to pass.

Like she told Harriet, she couldn't be sure that she had unearthed every member of the syndicate. Had she been right in bargaining with Morgan, who might still be working for them?

If she left now, there was a chance he and any remaining members could and would continue unimpeded, build the syndicate back up again with new members. He had turned once. He could turn again.

More importantly, if she got on that flight, she was accepting the new, morally weak Kate.

The last traveller passed through the desk.

'Madam?' said the neatly dressed man. 'Are you ready to board?'

The gift slipped in her clammy hands. She caught it before it fell to the floor. Her heart shuddered and jolted like an unwilling car engine on a freezing cold morning.

Was she ready?

'Follow your heart,' said Chris. *'I know you will do the right thing.'*

'Madam? We're waiting for you to board.'

She hardly heard the man.

What would the real Kate Young do?

In a flash, her mind was made up. She picked up her case.

She knew the right course of action.

ACKNOWLEDGEMENTS

I'd like to start with thanking you, my readers, for not only purchasing *A Soul for a Soul* but for being with Kate every inch of the way on her turbulent journey. I have appreciated all your messages, comments and emails, telling me how much you have enjoyed the series and all wanting Kate to succeed. For those of you who expressed concern about William's cats, I can assure you that they are in the very best of hands and want for nothing.

A warm thank you to beekeeper Ann Gore, who advised me on all aspects of apiculture. Although I am fond of bees, I have yet to take up beekeeping.

As always, there are many people to thank for bringing *A Soul for a Soul* to publication and I would like especially to mention my developmental editor, Russel McLean, who is himself an excellent writer (check him out!). Russel has worked with me on the entire series, and it is so much the better for his invaluable input.

Heartfelt thanks to Kasim Mohammed, whose praise and enthusiasm for this book kept me motivated throughout, and to all the superb editors at Thomas & Mercer. I couldn't ask for a better team.

Once again, thanks to my agent, Amy Tannenbaum, who had first eyes on the manuscript and ensured it was in the best possible shape before it was submitted.

And finally, to the person who has offered me quiet support throughout the writing of this book and the twenty-nine before it. Thank you Mr Grumpy for looking after everything while I hid away for weeks on end and for believing in me. I couldn't have done it without you.

ABOUT THE AUTHOR

Carol Wyer is a *USA Today* bestselling author and winner of the People's Book Prize Award. Her crime novels have sold over one million copies and have been translated into nine languages.

A move from humour to the 'dark side' in 2017, with the introduction of popular DI Robyn Carter in *Little Girl Lost*, proved that Carol had found her true niche.

February 2021 saw the release of the first in the much-anticipated new series featuring DI Kate Young. *An Eye for an Eye* was chosen as a Kindle First Reads and became the #1 bestselling book on Amazon UK and Amazon Australia.

Her first standalone psychological thriller, *Behind Closed Doors*, was an Amazon Editor's Pick and selected as one of the Best Books of December 2022.

Carol has had articles published in national magazines such as *Woman's Weekly*, and has been featured in *Take a Break*, *Choice*,

Yours and *Woman's Own* and in *HuffPost*. She's also been inter-viewed on numerous radio shows, and on Sky and *BBC Breakfast* television.

She currently lives on a windy hill in rural Staffordshire with her husband, Mr Grumpy . . . who is very, very grumpy.

To learn more, go to https://carolwyer.com, subscribe to her YouTube channel, or follow her on Twitter: https://twitter.com/carolewyer.

Follow the Author on Amazon

If you enjoyed this book, follow Carol Wyer on Amazon to be notified when the author releases a new book!

To do this, please follow these instructions:

Desktop:

1) Search for the author's name on Amazon or in the Amazon App.
2) Click on the author's name to arrive on their Amazon page.
3) Click the 'Follow' button.

Mobile and Tablet:

1) Search for the author's name on Amazon or in the Amazon App.
2) Click on one of the author's books.
3) Click on the author's name to arrive on their Amazon page.
4) Click the 'Follow' button.

Kindle eReader and Kindle App:

If you enjoyed this book on a Kindle eReader or in the Kindle App, you will find the author 'Follow' button after the last page.